Praise for
Paula E. Downing's
earlier novels:

Rinn's Star

"I'd call *Rinn's Star* a 'one gulper'—because you want to finish it in the first go. Paula Downing is off to a great start."

—ANNE MCCAFFREY

Flare Star— a *Locus* Best Science Fiction Novel of 1992

"A gripping and convincing story of disaster and the conflicting human emotions that arise in its aftermath."

—*Science Fiction Chronicle*

"Paula Downing's *Flare Star* is an energetic space disaster tale, with a compelling cast of characters, nifty hard science, and lots of danger to put them all to the test."

—JOHN E. STITH, author of
Redshift Rendezvous and *Manhattan Transfer*

"Excellent SF with interesting characters and lots of drama . . . Highly recommended for any collection."

—*Kliatt*

Fallway

"An exciting, imaginative tale of conflict between species, cultures and individuals."

—POUL ANDERSON

"A well-realized alien world."

—C.J. CHERRYH

By Paula E. Downing
Published by Ballantine Books

A WHISPER OF TIME

Paula E. Downing

A Del Rey Book
BALLANTINE BOOKS • NEW YORK

A Del Rey Book
Published by Ballantine Books

Copyright © 1994 Paula E. Downing

Library of Congress Catalog Card Number: 93-90707

ISBN 0-345-38195-5

Manufactured in the United States of America

First Edition: April 1994

10 9 8 7 6 5 4 3 2 1

To Tom.

The Hand of God
Stirs the hushed and drifting void
Scatters the suns
Begins time . . .

Be still and listen
for Her whisper comes
and the whisper tells you
Who you are
Where you go
Why it is

In the silence
A thousand shades breathe their story
A thousand empires build their monuments
A thousand children are born to sorrow
Listen . . .

Listen for the whisper
Of time.

Prologue _____

The city lay barren, emptied of movement and life, with a subtle dust sifting over sculptured stone and slowly crumbling walls. Above, a few stars gleamed dimly in a sky rapidly darkening to deepest purple and black. In a street near an ancient plaza, near the Stones of the Conquered, near the Temple of the Resurgent, a childish figure stumbled wearily over the pavestones, her steps hesitant. She no longer thought of a destination, but wandered blindly in a waking dream, numbed by loss and confusion. Though still a child, she sensed that stopping would mean the end, an end she only dimly understood but instinctively feared.

The cool air of the evening sighed against her sensitive skin, bringing its messages from this strange place. Her alien vision lay deep into the infrared, her heritage from a distant world of deep shadows: in this place, the buildings still glowed with the warmth of the faded day, with sounds preternaturally loud in the echoing spaces of the city. The first day, after she had lost everyone, she had listened fearfully to every echo, caught motionless for a heart-stopping instant, then propelled to run, her heart thumping frantically. She had run often during that first day and night, run from the service robots that prowled mindlessly through the city, run from a fall of stone, from the wind keening through corroded metal in a narrow alley. But she had grown used to the sounds and now plodded onward, her small boots scuffing on the street-stones.

1

She lifted her head dully as she heard a faint noise from a shadowed alcove and slowed, then watched until the service robot trundled into the street ahead. The machine creaked along its well-worn path, oblivious to her as it inspected for debris, fallen stone, cracked paving. She stopped as it passed in front of her: a small machine with faded panels and winking lights. She gestured greeting; it ignored her. She took a step toward it, but it did not slow nor speed its steady clanking. It could not see her, as nothing saw her in this empty city. Defeated, she watched it move off.

I could sit down, the child thought, her mind suffused with hopeless grief. If I wanted to. She watched as the robot turned into a low doorway across the street; its sound faded into silence, like all the other sounds of this place.

Three mornings before, she had seen a shimmering multiwinged insect on the edge of the Ship clearing and had impulsively chased it into a nearby street, leaving the game that occupied the other children. The adults had not seen her leave, still occupied with adult things in nearby buildings that little interested her. As she chased the shiny creature, she had laughed and shouted, inviting it to play. When it spun away out of sight over a tall building, she made her own game of bobbing and spinning, entranced by the room to run and leap in this wide place, so different than the narrow corridors of the black-hulled Ship, her home. The sunlight was intoxicating, warm and all-surrounding; the breeze had teased her relentlessly, blowing in cool and salt-scented from the distant beach beyond the city, tossing her feathery hair into her eyes as she jumped and ran.

Each street led to another street and then into a wide plaza larger than any she had seen, a hundred times longer than the Ship, a hundred times wider: never had she seen such space in one place and with all the sky above. She had played in the plaza for hours, running up and down stairs, racing around the stone bases of massive statues that towered over her head, bathed by the warmth of the air and bright sunlight. Then, tired to happy satiety, she had slept in the shadows of a tall serpentine statue that watched vigilantly over the plaza with the others, its stone fronds stretched out protectively, its fangs bared in threat against anyone who would disturb its charge's sleep.

Later, as reddish shadows spread into every street and the first stars emerged, she had found her way back to the Ship clearing—only the Ship was gone. She saw the charred ground where it had stood, found the depressions from its metal feet, but it was gone. Frantically she looked in other streets, widening her circle far into the night, but she could not find the Ship anywhere.

She had looked and looked for it since, wandering aimlessly through the deserted city, numb with the shock of her loss. Now she was weakening, her legs shaking so hard she could barely stand, and a terror of that weakness had begun in her mind and spread steadily, darkening memory, ending need. She wiped her eyes with her sleeve, then pushed her fine hair back from her dusty face. If I wanted to sit down, I could, she thought. Her eyes roamed over the reds of the evening, searching. If I wanted to.

It was then, as she stood still in the deep evening, that she heard the music, a delicate chiming aloft on the breeze, a beckoning sound, a different sound than those that had pursued her from every dark corner and turn of stone. The sound jangled her senses, an odd jangling, and she waited, holding her breath for it to stop like all the other sounds had stopped. But the singing continued, calling to her. She took a step forward and swayed off balance in her weakness, then took another step.

Where?

She stumbled down the street and paused at the intersection, her head turning from side to side as she sought the direction of the sound. To the left, she thought: through a carved gate at the end of the long street, shadowed by the deepening night. She stumbled forward down the street and rushed into the garden, crushing the first flowers in her haste, then took greater care, moving deep into the frost-flower glade and its shimmering light.

The frostflowers glittered in fantastic colonnades, a faerie's city touched by the breeze, swaying in intricate, shimmering patterns. And they sang, their ethereal melody bending and dipping in improbable arpeggios at the very edges of her hearing. She tipped her head to listen, a smile on her face, forgetting her terror, forgetting the loss, as they sang to her in glad welcome. She walked from flower to flower, talking back to them in a lisping melodic speech, touching each new crystalline blossom to hear its answer. Her grief eased still more in their fascination: their spell grew, binding her round and round in memories not her own, but memories that did not hurt, did not remind her of her loss . . . and replaced. She smiled, then laughed aloud, and the melody swelled in response.

I am Medoret, she told them all. What is your name? And they sang to her of a distant world, a home remembered and lost, but ever remembered.

She sighed and walked onward, brushing her palms against the glowing blooms. Deep in the glade, surrounded by a thousand singing flowers, she tripped on a clod of soil and sat down with a thump, chorting to herself with a child's amusement. The frostflowers nodded gravely and entwined her with their chiming and shimmering light, lulling her to sleep with their whispers. Dream, child. . . . dream of us. . . .

It was there in the alien garden that the humans found her, asleep in the ancient city of the Targethi, and took her home with them into captivity.

Chapter One _____

Medoret leaned her arm on the ledge of her open apartment window and looked out over the city and the glittering expanse of dark ice beyond the city dome. She sniffed at the warm overcirculated air that sighed gently against her face. The humans had built their small domed city on a wide shelf of volcanic rock overlooking the great southern ice plain of Epsilon Eridani III, a planet they had named Ariadan after a Sumerian word meaning "river"—though Ariadan had no flowing rivers, only ice. But the old name had pleased the chief archaeologists, as all their naming of things pleased them—as if naming captured a thing and made it human-owned. Humans liked owning things. She felt especially owned today; it was not a feeling that pleased her.

The air brought a murmur of traffic from the street ten stories below and an array of alien scents that had become long familiar—a clinging dust, the acidic smell of human flesh, a pleasant touch of roses and columbine from the gardens several blocks away, the faint metallic burning odor from the humans' mobile machines and the deep-buried ventilators that had sustained the city's enclosed environment. During her ten years among the humans, she had lived on Ariadan in the care of her keepers, safe in the control of the Targethi Project, far away from the crowded cities of Earth and the possible terrorists who might seek political or religious catharsis by killing Earth's only alien child.

There are worse forms of captivity, she told herself, knowing she had limited options even if the humans allowed her to choose, which they had not.

Her sensitive pupils expanded as she looked away from the brightness of the street below. Beyond the roofs of the other residential buildings, Ariadan's dark ice plains glittered under a blue-black sky, faintly obscured by the fabric of the dome. The ice plain reminded her of something she could not quite remember, a problem that she knew from recent experience would not resolve with hard thought. The memory teased at her mind, refusing to move beyond a vague *knowing*. She had been too young when the humans had taken her, and had lost something that was important.

Lost what? she wondered. I don't even know what the right questions are. How can I find the answers?

She sighed and looked at her pale hand resting on the windowsill, its nails more slender talons than fingernails, its fingers more jointed and slender than human fingers, mobile and graceful with a language of their own she no longer remembered. A human male might find her face beautiful, and overlook the differences in digits and length of her limbs, the odd fineness of her feathery hair, even overlook her lack of breasts—though other applicable literature implied that could be a potential problem. What lay beneath her pale skin, organs and structures and fluids, differed even more markedly from the human norm, a difference that extended deep into the biochemistry of her cells.

Recently Dr. Sieyes, her psychiatrist, had traded pointed articles with an Earth academic about Medoret's obvious failure to achieve puberty, reacting scornfully to his rival's theories of an undiagnosed dietary insufficiency, tri-sex drones as a sexual alien variant, even psychological repression. She looked down at her flat chest and scowled. Tri-sex drone? she thought irritably. Where had *that* come from?

Label: female. Am I? In the beginning, the Project had decided she was female from their anatomical studies, with explicit pictures of her sexual physical structures in early articles she had read once and now avoided. She had an apparent womb, genitals that vaguely resembled human female genitals in structure and apparent function, apparent nipples displaced several inches downward from human positioning, which had caused frowns but . . . a girl, they decided. And likely she *was* female: she had dreamed of her mother and felt a definite link of gender, but how gender arranged itself among her people, how children were engendered and born—she had been a child, uninterested in adult things.

She could name the two proteins that Earth biochemistry did not share with her body, could even sketch a reliable diagram of their structure. During those first few weeks, as the Earth survey ship raced frantically back to Ariadan and its sophisticated labs, she had nearly died of starvation and fever, then had attempted a deliberate death as her young mind retreated into months of catatonia. The humans had overcome that death, too, wanting both mind and body of the child, not one without the other.

She could recite the formula of the enzyme that had cured the cyclic fevers that later had recurred and nearly killed her twice, though not even the clever biochemists were quite sure why their miracle drug had worked. The humans were clever with their chemicals, clever with many things. Now her dietary supplements ruled her life, a fact she tried to not remember. If the humans withdrew the supplements, she would die. Sometimes she wondered if she cared.

Stop this, she told herself.

She had nearly escaped, in the early months, fleeing from her terror into her own dream world, safe from terror

and lostness and pain she pushed away, but they had cajoled and pressured, touched and wheedled, punished, re-
warded, medicated, caressed, embraced, stripping her of the
safe blackness and its comforting images, imposing their
version of reality. A cause for gratitude, she supposed: as
much as she rued it, her survival had depended on accepting their world eventually—though a child could not understand such things. Her psychological growth since that time
was fully documented in the literature, the ups and downs,
the rebellions, the depressions, the appearance of joy, the
increasing social behavior—all matched against human children, the only analogue they knew. She supposed she
should be grateful.

But they still watched for the madness, while so oblivious to their own kinds of insanity, the mind chemists as
vigilant to heal as the biochemists who had worked feverishly in those first few weeks to save her.

And what if I don't wish to be *healed*? she asked irritably. What if I don't want their reality?

She turned from the window and let her eyes roam over
the familiar sights of her bedroom: a narrow bed with its
bright covering, the study desk with its viewer, the wall
decorations patterned after Targethi glyphs. As a child
raised among scientists preoccupied by the Targethi ruins at
70 Ophiuchi and Cebalrai, she had adopted their fascination
with the long-dead Ophiuchi aliens, hunting for some sense
of connection in the survey material sent back to Ariadan
for study. Project scholars had speculated in weighty academic papers about her connection to the Targethi, but she
had decided there was none. Her people had come from
Outside, from the other edge of Targethi space: her recent
dreams hinted at that and she believed it, but she had not
told the humans what she knew. She hid many things the
humans did not suspect; it was the only form of rebellion
left to her.

The computer screen on her desk blinked steadily for attention, prompting her to return to the study of Targethi glyphs she had started yesterday, but the thought bored her. Beside the monitor lay the Project's weekly report form that required her to document her daily physical functions in intrusive detail—a rating scale of her moods, her self-affirmatory thoughts, her day-to-day well-being, all dressed up in Dr. Sieyes's psychojargon and behaviorist measures. She was a marvel: a test animal who could write her own data reports. She hadn't bothered with the form last week; this week's form remained as empty. Let them write a report about that, she thought. She turned back to the window.

To a few of the humans, the fact that Medoret could do anything sentient was a wonder, much like the marvel of a chimpanzee manipulating sign buttons to his handler's pleased satisfaction. Sometimes she felt exactly like a jackanapes performing in a circus; sometimes she despaired of ever finding a true connection with anything. She suspected that Dr. Sieyes encouraged that feeling; it increased his control, and thus the security of his Project prestige. Conrad Sieyes had built a lustrous career from Medoret's existence, and he guarded its perks assiduously. She looked longingly at the dark ice plain, glittering beneath the stars, the old memory teasing at her mind.

Where? From where do I know you?

Recently she had begun to dream more often, after years of frequent oblivion in the night. Dreaming of a dark plain like this one beneath brilliant stars, of an entrancing garden of pallid flowers that changed to sudden and paralyzing terror, of long adventures with the Vision Serpent and the other Maya friends she had created for her daytime fantasy; and of other faces and forms and potent images that were not human—she felt sure of that, and fumbled as best she could in the understanding.

In her dreams, a white-skinned goddess, naked and pale and unbreasted like herself, knelt gracefully by a pool and poured a stream of stars into the Void, her arms graceful and strong, her body perfect. A cloud of drifting dark hair encircled her pale face and shoulders, merging into the dark sky behind her; her half-closed eyes watched a cascade of stars tumbling from her jar, the dark feathered lashes shading a luminous darkness. She smiled slightly, lips curving with such grace that Medoret ached for the luminous eyes to lift, to see the child who watched from a distance.

The image haunted her, somehow replacing emptiness and loss in a dark room of her mind with warmth and peace, a *knowing* of profound significance that eluded her waking mind. The Goddess was important, but why? Once during a dream, greatly daring, she had asked the Vision Serpent about the Star Goddess, but the Serpent had grown angry and refused to answer, finally withdrawing completely for nights on end. When she returned, the Serpent played at word games, pretending mystery and flipping her fronds irritably as Medoret persisted, then ending the questions with a savage chase through forest and glade that had terrified Medoret into better prudence. Sadly, though the thought seemed incomprehensible, Medoret suspected the Serpent did not know, either.

Strange that her dream friends should be Maya, she thought, but then perhaps not strange at all. It was the Maya gods who had enticed her from the void she had created for herself, her foster father's lucky choosing. During her first year with Ian Douglas in this human outpost dominated by archaeologists, she had been surrounded by his tapes and drawings of Mayan and Targethi iconography, so oddly similar, and had felt drawn to the images that both ancient peoples, one human, one alien, had carved in stone. Pleased, Ian had encouraged her interest, happily relieved that he had found something concrete he could give her after so many months of her listless attention. He had sought out illustrated book-tapes, bought her prints of the Maya glyphs for her nursery walls, and sat with her often in those early months, telling her stories about the pictures she loved.

In his telling, the Jaguar Sun seemed vividly alive, a crafty king caught in the Otherworld drama of the Heroic Twins, those demigods of the Maya who had stolen the visible world from the Underworld and had given it to Maya kings to rule. Lady Rainbow, the Moon Goddess, danced with her followers up a long stone stair beneath the spreading branches of the World Tree, laughing at the Celestial Bird who scolded her from the Tree's highest branches. In the temple plaza beneath them, Maya king-priests slashed themselves with obsidian knives in horrible ceremony, evoking the Vision Serpent and her ecstasy, then warred fiercely on other Maya cities, celebrating their victories in intricately carved panels that boasted of captives and sacrifice and the kingship of the Morning Star, brother to the Jaguar Sun.

The Maya had lived on the doorstep to Xibalba, the Otherworld, Ian told her solemnly in his pedantic way; perhaps the Targethi had, too, and so he had made up stories about the Targethi gods, too, telling of the Cricket God and his beetlelike devotees that chanted solemnly as they stalked through jungle trails, celebrating the Hunt. He had showed her holograms of the six great Targethi gods that stood in the Great Plaza of Tikal, the Targethi city at Cebalrai where the humans had found her, naming them one by one and asking her to recite their names afterward, then coining unlikely stories of their great exploits borrowed freely from half a dozen human cultures: Sumer's heroic Gilgamesh, Maelduin of the Celtic seas, Valkyrie and Odin's Doom, the Dream myths of ancient Australia.

She realized later, that he must have spent hours reading about myths, copying them out carefully and stolidly practicing in secret for that night's story, when he sat by her bed and waved his arms dramatically, his hoarse voice rising and falling, invoking the magic of Xibalba and worlds beyond as she lay wide-eyed, watching him. He had tried so hard, fumbling to find some way to bring her out of the lethargy that still gripped her in her deep depression. And he had succeeded, to the Project's dubious amazement. Later, when she was older, Ian had abruptly given up the nightly stories, making vague excuses and encouraging her to more sober studies. She suspected that Dr. Sieyes, then newly arrived on Ariadan, had intervened: the psychiatrist did not approve of fantasy.

And so she had found her comfort afterward in her own solitary play, re-creating Ian's heroic play-creatures to escape the intrusive attention of the humans who studied her, denying the fact of her captivity and her aloneness in endless imagined adventures, where the Jaguar Sun became a fierce and protective lover, growling and crafty, where the Nine Lords were implacable enemies to challenge and outwit, where the Vision Serpent and the Cricket God, the Star Goddess and Lady Rainbow, all joined in the high drama, while the Mayan kings 18-Rabbit, Ah-Cacaw, and Shield-Jaguar shook their lances and warred on each other in jungle clearings. She knew them all, as intimately as she knew the real humans in Ariadan's real world—and usually preferred them more, despite their fierceness.

Fantasy—but perhaps fantasy that had saved her sanity in those early years without defenses. And fantasy that comforted still. She smiled.

I am the Vision Serpent, she thought, coiling her hands over her head gracefully and fluttering her fingers. I am the Cricket God, she thought next, turning her palms inward into insectoid prayer. She got up from her seat and paced in a circle, crouched low in menace. I am the Jaguar Sun, God of Destiny, the Heroic Twin who saves the World. Beware, Nine Lords of Xibalba! I am coming to make your doom. She paced once more in her short circle, gnashing her teeth ferociously as the dread Gods of the Underworld trembled and shook in terror, as was fitting, and then sat calmly down, Medoret again, pale and thin and strange among humans, who hadn't got her breasts yet and maybe couldn't. Who owns reality? The Maya had given her many labels that pleased her better. She fluttered her fingers again, invoking the Vision Serpent.

Beware, she warned Dr. Sieyes. When I am loosed into your world, you'll be first for the dining.

She started guiltily as she heard the hiss of the outer door in the room beyond, then relaxed as she recognized the muffled footsteps. Bootheels rang twice on the tile of the hallway, paused as Ian sorted through the fax-mail in the bin, then resumed their measured clatter toward her room. His scent preceded him: the familiar tang of his cologne, the smell of his flesh, the mints he liked to chew, a whiff of coffee mist in his hair and eyebrows. *His* smells, though others owned them, too, but still his. She turned from the window to face the door, her lips turned upward in welcome.

Ian filled the doorframe, his eyes bent on the mail in his square hands, a middle-aged human with too many pounds of extra flesh and growing wrinkles in his face. His dark hair had begun to gray in recent years, but his gestures had remained firm, his confidence unalloyed—except in questions about his alien foster-daughter. A respected scientist in his own archaeological specialty, linguistic analysis, Ian Douglas deferred too much to Dr. Sieyes on that constant other issue, quietly convinced he lacked an essential as a father just as he blamed himself for an early failed marriage he rarely discussed. Though she sometimes felt a lack of connection with Ian, as she always felt in all situations in this human place, she sometimes wished she could persuade him of a few things. He finished riffling through the mail, then looked up, his blue eyes lighting. "I never catch you looking out that window," he pretended to grumble. "You always know I'm here."

"Of course."

He padded forward into the room. "You've noticed I stopped my experiments of trying to sneak in."

"Months ago."

"Right," he agreed absently, dismissing the topic, and handed her one of the messages. "Dr. McGill wants us to come to her ship party."

Medoret wrinkled her nose. "I'd rather not."

He snorted in exasperation. "My dear girl, how can you finish your adolescent socialization if you don't go to social affairs?"

"Is that the goal? Socialized?" she asked, more sharply than she intended. "Or has Dr. Sieyes started worrying about my social index again?" She turned her shoulder to him and looked back out the window.

"I thought you liked Ruth McGill," he said, sounding confused. "You can talk glyphs with her. She's interested in your ideas." Medoret said nothing, not looking at him, and Ian shuffled his feet. "And Dr. Sieyes means well, Medoret." He paused, then cleared his throat. "I think you should go."

She hunched her shoulders, knowing he would not give it up easily. Ian loved her in his own way, but sometimes it seemed an absentminded love, like a reflexive habit: he cared equally—or more—about other things, and his choice to be her parental figure had been made by Medoret and others, not sought by himself. For ten years Ian had postponed his own ship assignments on Ophiuchus survey, contenting himself with the videos and artifacts brought back by others, consulting frequently with Dr. Sieyes about how to parent an alien child. He took his duty seriously.

"You should go."

"Ian. . . ."

She had never called him "Father," for all Dr. Sieyes's oily encouragement, stubborn in that also. Ian had not seemed to mind, had not even inquired why.

He leaned over her and took the flimsy from her hand.

"I'll send our acceptance," he said with a note of finality, and turned to leave.

"I *like* Dr. Ruth," she declared, not looking at him. "I *don't* like Dr. Sieyes."

Ian sighed feelingly and left the room. Medoret thumped her fist on the windowsill, then stared at the dark plain beyond the dome, hoping the fixed attention might bring it into her dreams. Ian's scents lingered in the room for several minutes, distracting her, then blew to vague fragments on the city breeze. She stared at the plain until her vision sparkled with jagged spots, then blinked tiredly. She buried her face in her arms.

When she was younger, she could pretend she belonged in this place. Confused, she could pretend Ian was her real father, others a kind uncle or cousin, all the adults the warmth of welcoming arms she remembered from the before-time. But maturity now brought insistent dreams that denied that reality, that disjointed her and filled her with an aching loss. Her people could not tolerate outsiders well, she believed, and tried to ignore Dr. Sieyes's insistence that her recent obstinacy was a failing, a reproof, an ingratitude. She chose to be obstinate. She had tried denial, acceptance, cooperation, endurance. But nothing had filled the void inside her for long. Wasn't flexibility a sign of intelligence? Why not obstinacy?

He had such clever words, did Dr. Sieyes, and Ian trusted him. If she confided in Dr. Sieyes, she knew from experience, the psychologist would only cluck his disapproval and offer a dozen other reasons to confuse her, then mark his charts and pull at his chin in ostentatious thought, unaware that she knew how much he detested her alienness, a primal fear of the Other he probably denied even in his secret thoughts. The Vision Serpent had told her that about Dr. Sieyes; she believed it. Yet he did not wish her to be human, for all his cajoling; he had too much of a vested stake in her difference, Earth's one alien child, a foundation for an alienist's career, much better than mysterious crumbling stone and centuries-dead civilization. A living trophy could perform, could be truly owned.

Stop this, she told herself. Stop thinking about it.

The warm air riffled her hair, tickling her cheek, and surrounded her with the scents of Ariadan, teasing at her. From the distance she heard a metallic chiming she could not identify; it reminded her of the frostflowers, the last memory untainted by the humans. Her dreams sometimes began in that garden at Cebalrai, surrounded by carved stone and a silent city: she focused on the memory, allowing it to calm her.

I wish I could sleep, she thought. I wish I could sleep forever in that garden, waiting for the Black Ship. And my mother would walk toward me through the blooms, her face alight, all sternness and despair erased in her joy, and she would gather me close to her, glad in the welcoming. The others would crowd around us, happy with her, and together we would go to the Black Ship, our home. I so wish . . .

It was a familiar wish. She raised her head and stared for several more moments at the dark plain beyond the dome, then got up to dress for Dr. McGill's party.

"Good evening, Medoret," Dr. Ruth McGill said as she took Medoret's hand, squeezing it warmly. A tiny dark-haired woman in her early forties, Ruth McGill had a high social index that Medoret envied, one that easily included aliens at any party. She sniffed at Dr. Ruth's flowery perfume, a bit overwhelmed by the heady scent, and caught fainter undersmells of bath powder and scotch. Dr. Ruth's scents, she thought, her answering smile unforced. In another five years, Ian had told her, he expected Dr. McGill would leave her post as head of Glyphs at Cebalrai and become the Ophiuchi Project's overall director. Medoret hoped so.

"That's a pretty outfit," Dr. Ruth said. "Red becomes you."

"Thank you."

"Hello, Ian. You look your usual self. Smart of you to let Medoret outshine you."

"What?" Ian asked absently, and then looked sharply at Dr. Ruth down his long nose.

Dr. McGill laughed and pressed Ian's hand, then led them into the apartment foyer. A babble of voices issued from the room beyond as glasses clinked and Dr. McGill's guests talked a combination of gossip and shop. On Ariadan, with a population of scientists obsessed with the mystery of the Targethi ruins, one could go anywhere and overhear voices in affable argument about glyphs, technic structure, and xenobiology. Medoret recognized representatives of all the major Cebalrai teams in the room: Metals, Urban Map, BioSurvey, and Glyphs. She had met a few of Dr. Ruth's guests now and then, seen fax-photos of several others in article bios.

For fifteen years, first at the smaller Targethi mining outpost at 70 Ophiuchi, the first ruins discovered by the Ariadan probes, and then at the larger ruins at Cebalrai, the scientists of Earth had plunged into the exploration of an alien culture, the first and only alien culture—save Medoret herself, of course, in all her different mysteries. Though the Earth legislature debated the expense every year, sometimes in rancorous dispute with the other colony governments who had their own agendas, every year the Project got what it asked for in ships and support and money, with a suitable smaller largesse for an archaeological subproject named Medoret Douglas. She and Ian lived well, as did Dr. Sieyes. She glimpsed Dr. Sieyes's portly figure in the far corner of the next room. He was laughing jovially with a group of admiring friends, gesturing with the drink in his hand as he told his story. She winced and looked back longingly at the door.

"Come along, Medoret," Ian said.

"Yes, Ian."

I hate parties, she thought rebelliously.

In the large inner room, several groups of people gathered in different parts of the room talking, several voices already too loud from alcohol. To Medoret's sensitive hearing, the noise rose to a painful level, but she tried to ignore the clamor as she reluctantly followed in Ian's and Dr. McGill's wake. As always, Medoret's presence attracted immediate covert glances: though she looked nearly human, her overly pale complexion and different bone structure, the odd greenish shade of her eyes, the sheen of her feather-fine hair, even the way she moved, Ian had told her once, were enough to catch attention. Many of the adults in the room had known her for several years and the others from video and a wide academic literature, but they still looked, usually askance and then quickly away. She tried to ignore that, too, practicing the vague social smile that made her look dim-witted. Sometimes when she looked stupid enough, nearly everyone left her alone; she wished to be left alone tonight.

I don't *want* to be socialized, she thought, gritting her teeth. Maybe I could tell that to Dr. Sieyes and give him grist for another paper. *Alien child alienated!* Right. *Learned doctor makes new discovery, he announced today. . . .*

Dr. Sieyes noticed her and turned to smile unpleasantly, then said something to his group with a vague wave in her direction. Two in the group swiveled to look at her; she ignored them and him.

Dr. McGill took her elbow and guided her to a couch by the wall, but her choice of social companion for Medoret showed too many years away at Cebalrai. The redheaded boy on the couch looked up warily.

"Here's Jimmy Sieyes, Medoret," Dr. McGill said pleasantly. "Why don't you two get some punch from the table and have a good time?" She patted Medoret on the shoulder and then turned as the door chime sounded faintly, announcing another guest. "Ian, there's Dr. Mueller waving at you, wanting to argue. Why don't you oblige him?"

As Dr. Ruth and Ian moved off in different directions, Jimmy stared up at Medoret for a long moment, then put on his familiar mocking half smile. Slowly relishing the moment, he mouthed his favorite taunt.

Freak. His grin widened.

"Mushbrain," Medoret retorted, glaring back at him. "Why don't you stuff your head in an air compressor? It might improve your intelligence."

"Tut, tut," Jimmy said, tipping his head to the side, one of his father's common gestures. "Is that a nice thing for an alien freak to say?"

"You should know, being one. Is your father here?"

"Naturally. *You* are. Wherever you are, he is."

"If you've got jealousy problems," she said brutally, "solve them yourself. Don't expect me to help."

"Oh, *tut* at that," Jimmy cried. "I'll tell Father about *that* comment. He's sure to drop your social index way down." Jimmy stood up and moved closer to her, stopping only when his face was inches away. "Tut."

She felt herself flush despite herself. Jimmy Sieyes had led the group of children who chose to taunt her in school, ignoring every lecture from the teachers in his systematic campaign to make her life a torment. Finally Ian had taken her out of school for private tutoring, and even Dr. Sieyes had admitted defeat in getting the colony children to accept her. But somehow that, too, had become more Medoret's failing than the children's.

Jimmy fluttered his eyelashes, mocking her, then opened his eyes wide to stare ostentatiously at her alien face. Jimmy knew all about her dislike for stares, had known it from the beginning with a bully's infalliable instincts. She studied his thin freckled face, her anger rising within her like a cold flame.

"Bug off, Jimmy." She looked away.

"Freak."

She turned back to face him and narrowed her eyes angrily. At this distance, Jimmy's scent filled her nostrils, an acrid pool of odor in the odor-laden warm air of the room. The noise of the party rose around them, assaulting her ears and starting the slow dull throb of a headache.

"Freak," Jimmy whispered, drawing out the word in a long hiss, taunting her.

Medoret smiled and hit Jimmy squarely in the face, putting strength into her fist. The blow caught Jimmy totally off guard and lifted him clean off his feet, then bounced him neatly on and off the couch. Jimmy yelped as he landed hard on the floor, sprawling, and every conversation in the room stopped as all eyes swiveled in their direction. Medoret stood still, smiling down at Jimmy, as Ian and Dr. Sieyes arrowed in from different directions.

"She hit me!" Jimmy declared to his father, his outrage maybe half real. He fingered his nose gingerly and winced, then looked up at Medoret in genuine astonishment. Medoret's smile widened with intense satisfaction.

"Is this true, Medoret?" Dr. Sieyes rumbled.

"Is this true, Medoret?" Ian said at almost the same time. She turned to Ian and smiled up at him, batting her eyelashes.

"Can I go home now?" she asked brightly.

Chapter Two _____

After the predictable uproar and a hasty exit from Dr. Ruth's ship party, Medoret lay in her bed and listened to the conversation in the outer room. Dr. Sieyes had officiously accompanied Ian and Medoret home, to "confer" with Ian—making sure everyone at the party knew of his intention. In some ways, Dr. Sieyes had his own predictability, and he guarded his role as Medoret's handler with vigilance. Medoret relaxed into the mattress comfortably, then put her hands behind her head and watched the shadows on the ceiling.

I am the Jaguar Sun, she thought fiercely. She bared her teeth in a toothy Jaguar smile. Beware.

"She's never been violent before," Dr. Sieyes said in hushed concern. Medoret quirked her mouth irritably.

"Jimmy started it," Ian retorted. "He's always ragged her."

"Who knows who starts such conflicts?" Dr. Sieyes rumbled.

"I do; in this instance, so do you." She heard a clank as Ian put his glass down too hard on the divan table. "She's an adult, Conrad, by our terms and probably by hers, too. It's time that she took up an adult life, not this cosseted cottony existence that goes nowhere. I put in my request three months ago; it's time you made your recommendation and got on with it."

"We cannot risk injury to—"

"Medoret would be useful. Ruth McGill's been asking for her in every Glyphs report for the past year. She wants to let Medoret look at the glyphs on-site at Cebalrai, tell us what she sees."

Cebalrai? Medoret sat up and looked at the half-open door, her heart pounding.

Dr. Sieyes snorted skeptically. "It's doubtful that Medoret knows anything more than we do about Targethi iconography. How can she understand the Cebalrai glyphs?"

"She came from Cebalrai."

"She did not 'come from Cebalrai.' We only *found* her there—and traces of a ship setdown two miles away. Dalgren's proven conclusively that Medoret is not Targethi. How can she offer anything about their glyphs?"

"Theory, pure theory."

"Are you that eager to get back to the field, Douglas?" Sieyes's voice was snide. "She's tied you down, hasn't she? Tired of being foster father?"

"Don't accuse me of that. Ruth wants Medoret on this next survey trip; I agree. So put in your report and let the subproject committee decide."

"This unexpected violence. . . . I don't know." She could almost see that doleful shaking of the head, the tugging on the long chin, the tap of a slender index finger—she knew it all so well. Medoret curled her fingers into her palms, pressing her nails hard in the flesh.

"Bullshit," Ian snorted. "Jimmy asked for it."

Sieyes shifted tactics, knowing a losing point even when it involved defending his son. For a moment, Medoret almost felt sorry for Jimmy—almost. "What if she comes down with her fever again?" Sieyes asked, still a-murmur with concern.

"Medoret hasn't had a serious bout of fever for four years—and Survey has excellent medical support." She heard a rustle on fabric as Ian stood up, then the muffled footsteps as he paced. "Listen, I haven't been much of a father to her. How would I know that she'd accept only me as parent, just because I happened to find her in that garden? I don't know how to parent even a human child—and *your* ideas haven't helped me much."

"Basic imprinting. . . ."

Ian snorted. "Imprinting belongs to ducks, Conrad, not people. You don't know why she wouldn't accept a woman as parent, so don't pretend to me you do. But now she's not accepting me, either. I can see it in her face, like I'm part of the enemy—and it's getting worse. Does she ever confide in you about anything? She used to talk to me. I come home now and she's staring out the window, hour after hour, and she's *polite* to me." Ian's voice cracked.

"Hmmm . . . I didn't know about the staring. . . ."

"Like I said, bullshit. Get out of your neo-Freudian mind-set and think of her as a person. Let her go with Dr. Ruth to Cebalrai—let her out of jail." His voice rose angrily. "And if we don't get your concurrence by tomorrow, Ruth and I and a few others will petition the committee for your replacement. You just squeaked by with the troubles at her school—a predictable problem of group dynamics and you go in fumble-fingered; then you nearly killed her with your antidepressant drug therapy last year. You can't cover up everything with bullshit reports, Conrad. The committee sometimes has a brain—so don't think we don't."

There was a pause.

"You're bluffing," Sieyes said in a wary tone.

"Want to find out? It's easy."

Medoret held her breath for several moments, straining for Sieyes's answer. "I'll take it under advisement."

"Tomorrow, Conrad, so we can pack before *Narenjo* lifts off. Want that drink refreshed?"

"No, thanks." The voice was a snarl.

"Anytime. Oh, you're leaving?"

"You think you've won, Douglas? Just wait and see."

"Since when is Medoret's happiness a contest?" Sieyes

did not answer, and a minute later, Medoret heard the muffled sound of the door closing. Ian's footsteps paced back across the room and stopped near the window. Medoret slipped from underneath the covers and padded into the hall. As she stepped into the narrow living room beyond, Ian half turned toward her.

"Um, you heard."

"You know I did. You didn't have to leave the bedroom door ajar." She waved toward the open living-room window. "I would have heard through there. Good acoustics tonight."

"With your good ears, a shoo-in, I admit. Conrad consistently forgets those ears of yours. But just making sure, chick." He smiled tentatively. "I do stand up for you sometimes."

Medoret nodded. "Thanks for trying."

Ian shrugged, pretending nonchalance with a jaunty smile that became him well. "You're welcome. Of course, if Sieyes lets you go, he'll insist on coming along. I'm not omnipotent, however much I try."

"That *is* too bad," she said lightly, and joined him at the window. Together they leaned on the broad sill and faced into the warm breeze blowing over the city, a companionable silence between them. Ian pointed at one of the brilliant stars near the horizon.

"Cebalrai."

"I know." They watched the star in a comfortable silence.

"Why did you choose me?" he asked in a muffled voice, not looking at her. She turned toward him and leaned on her elbow, craning her head to see his face until he had to oblige her by looking at her, his lined face shadowed by the night and the bright light behind them.

"You were the one I wanted." She touched his sleeve. "Since I couldn't have the other, I chose an honest face. I remember my mother best, Ian; you don't replace someone like that, not her. I think that's why." She paused, thinking about it. "I really don't remember why—I was so young—but I dream sometimes about my mother. She was severe but fierce in her love: she never gave up on anything. If I had let someone else in, I would have lost her. I couldn't have borne that." She shrugged, a human gesture she had adopted for herself, and looked back outward over the city. "I remember a dark plain like that, too; I don't know quite where it was—but it's associated with my Ship. I dream about many things."

"A ship? You've never mentioned remembering the ship."

"I didn't dream for a long time, and later I decided not to tell." She shrugged again. "Dr. Sieyes would think my dreams *amusing*, Ian. He shows me a different face than he shows you; you saw a part of that face tonight because you caught him by surprise. Next time he won't allow himself to be surprised. And he is very good at convincing committees." She grimaced. "When you have one precious thing left, you don't let others ruin it. Especially him." She met his eyes. "You've tried so hard to understand me; maybe it's not possible?"

Ian snorted and straightened from his stoop. "Nonsense. I know everything about you. I would think that's obvious." He smiled down at her, the lines in his face easing. "You have no mysteries."

"No more ship parties, Ian."

"Okay." He looked outward at the gleaming sparkle of light that was Cebalrai.

"You've been a good father, Ian," she said softly, offering.

But that embarrassed him all over again; he harrumphed and turned away to clink glasses at the bar to mix a new drink, then stalked around the living room, talking about boring colony gossip. She watched him pace, bemused by his behavior, and wondered wistfully if Ian Douglas would ever give up believing he had failed her in a dozen ways, taking all the blame on himself, as was his way.

The phone chimed and saved him with Dr. McGill's call. As he talked, Medoret turned back to the dark plain beyond their window and its vista of stars and black rock and the glitter of shadowed ice, the rise and fall of Ian's voice behind her a comforting sound that soothed her frayed senses. The scents of Ariadan washed over her on the warm breeze; she absently cataloged the components, as she always did, her attention on Cebalrai.

What will you find there, if you go? she asked herself, watching the star glitter among a dozen companion stars, a deep yellow-orange jewel among other brilliant gemstones. What will you find? The Jaguar's Xibalba? Or a reality she didn't want? The fine hairs on her nape lifted apprehensively.

She sniffed at the warm air of Ariadan's human city, enveloped in the sensations of scent and touch. In the past few months, her dreams had changed in timbre and content, leaving behind childish randomness and moving toward the True Knowledge, the gestalt of purpose and meaning so valued by her people. Yet . . . the understanding still eluded her, never quite coalescing into answers to the questions that haunted her. Who am I? *Why* did they leave me? That the answers lay within her half-remembered turns of sleep she did not doubt; her people believed in dreams for reasons she could not remember, but she remembered that dreams were important. She looked at the black plain glittering beneath the stars, the old memory teasing again at her mind.

Where was it? Will I find them again? And, when I do, will I still have a place among them?

That she might not terrified her, and had made each slow year among the humans a further anxiety as human ways and human insistences steadily eroded the alien within her, making her a stranger to her own kind. Beyond a certain point there might be no returning, but she didn't know where that division lay and feared she had already passed it. And so she had resisted the humans' wishes to make her more human, clinging to her dreams and alien senses, the two alien parts of her they could not change. Where was it, that plain? On what world? And when? She sighed and rubbed her face tiredly. No use, not tonight.

Easier to play with fantasy friends in a jungle glade. Easier to be stubborn about stupid things because it pleased her to confound. Easier to lash out at a bully, choosing violence. She had not expected this, that the humans would risk letting her go—and wondered what guards they would fashion to hold her.

She deliberately turned away from the window before she wished it and walked over to Ian to perch on his chairarm. He winked at her and she smiled in response, then watched his face as he waved his hands about, aloft in the political scheming he loved so well.

In her daydreams, she remembered fondly, Ian was always the Cricket God, diffident and wise, the magic-spinner of legends, and the source of the Jaguar Sun's best schemes against the Nine Lords—though the Jaguar and the Vision Serpent argued afterward for the credit, conveniently forgetting who had suggested the plan. The Cricket God never seemed to mind, content to stand placidly by, chewing slowly on a succulent reed, his large dark eyes deep and knowing as he thought about secret things.

Medoret curled her hand around Ian's collar and leaned her forehead against his brushy hair. Ian rarely touched her—he was not a tactile man, as some humans were not—but she felt his hand slip around her waist. And when he looked up into her face, his eyes lighted with shy pleasure.

"You are the Cricket God," she whispered in his ear, and made him chortle until Dr. Ruth demanded quite irritably to know the joke.

* * *

The next night she dreamed of a black plain beneath a jeweled array of stars, and stood on the dark cracked rock, looking upward at the star-strewn darkness. The icy wind whipped into her eyes, chilling her naked body. She shivered, and looked uncertainly around her at the empty plain, a quick darting glance, then lifted her eyes again to the sky.

What is this place? she wondered fearfully, and lifted her hand to will another, wishing the comfort of her Mayan dream world, as she had willed it before. Above her the darkness of sky and plain coiled and fragmented, arranging itself into a canopy of shadowed leaves and the dark webbing of branches, becoming warm and shadowed green. A scudding of dark rainclouds swept overhead, quickly gone, then stars sparkled through the high canopy of leaves, touching each leaf-edge with an opalescent gleam.

She found herself on a jungle path she knew from other dreams, her flesh cool white in the dim starlight, surrounded above and to either side by the hushed whisper of moving leaves. The night breeze brought a hundred tantalizing scents and moved over her body with a silky touch, teasing at her. She breathed deeply and touched the nearby fronds with her fingers, caressing their fine-haired softness, then felt their answering caress as she walked easily down the path, the underbrush on each side whispering against her thighs, each footstep firm on the crumbling rich soil. In the distance a jaguar screamed and she smiled in response, then hurried forward. At a turning in the path, she emerged into a narrow clearing and faced the tall pyramid of a Maya temple, cool silver in the starlight.

The temple's sides ascended smoothly in staircased stone, narrow tier upon tier, pale gray in the shadowed night. On its crest, four graceful pillars supported a wide block of stone, framing open space that looked into infinity. There in that space stood a door to the Otherworld, caught by a king's deft magic and his right to rule, sealed by his own blood in war and ceremony. In that space, knives flashed through human flesh to summon the Vision Serpent and her knowledge of the deepest mysteries, renewing the connection between the worlds, seen and unseen. The Maya had understood that magic; so, perhaps, had the Targethi, who also built in stone to celebrate their gods.

Her eyes on the Doorway, Medoret stepped forward, every sense alert to the unseen power that filled this place, throbbing upon the air. A step, then two, and she found herself suddenly blocked by an invisible wall of air. She struggled against the barrier, angered, then retreated in bafflement.

"Let me by," she cried.

The air before her took coherent shape as a smoky mist, coiling visibly on itself, gathering substance, becoming real. She stepped backward hastily as the Vision Serpent appeared from the mist before her, floating gracefully on the air. Beneath glittering eyes and a long-jawed head, the Serpent fluttered her graceful fronds from her upper limbs, half shielding a slim body encased in glittering scales; her long tail flashed and coiled beneath the long body, moving restlessly. The Serpent drifted forward. Her depthless eyes regarded Medoret coolly.

In a voice that chimed like edged crystal, like the dark sharpness of obsidian, she asked, "Child, what do you seek?"

"Answers," Medoret said, trembling. "Myself."

The Serpent turned and moved gracefully past her, no play-companion here but the terrible truth of the Mayan Vision Serpent, served by self-inflicted pain and death. As Medoret turned to follow the Serpent, the sky stretched oddly and re-coiled, and she stood again on the black plain beneath the stars, the Serpent hovering before her. The wind blew coldly, whipping against her body. She shivered.

"What is this place?" she asked. "Do you know?"

The Serpent turned her head to regard her, her scales gleaming in the starlight, her fringed arms and tail moving lazily in a complicated pattern. Her jaws opened, showing long white teeth and a slivered tongue.

"Name yourself," she commanded in her voice of slashing flint.

"I am Medoret," she answered timidly.

"Who is Medoret?" the Serpent mocked.

"I don't know," she said, ashamed. "Can you tell me, Serpent?"

The Vision Serpent raised a hand and gestured a spiral with long taloned fingers, invoking her Serpent's magic. A coil of smoke entwined around her body, concealing her behind a wall of mist. Medoret strained forward anxiously.

"Do you know?" she demanded urgently, fearing the Serpent would slip back into the Otherworld, refusing her.

The mist swirled upward, making no answer, then swept downward over Medoret, taking her into its concealment. She stood still, feeling the silky touch of smoke slip uneasily over her body; she coughed shallowly as the acrid scent of burning japalya, the sacred herb, struck at her breath. Then, softly, at first so softly she barely heard, the mist echoed with a sound of bootheels, the sigh of air currents confined by metal, the scrape of a chair.

I still dispute, a deep voice rumbled. Medoret gasped: she knew that voice.

Their gods failed them, another voice said clearly. Medoret gasped again with recognition, as if a vise had suddenly seized her body, twisting it.

"Mother!" she cried aloud in shock.

And they never knew why, her mother continued, oblivious. *A fitting fate for such a people. Unlike them, we know why our gods failed us, though the knowledge brings little comfort. In the end, all answers come to a single imperative.*

Philosophy proves nothing, Saryen, the other voice grumbled.

"Mother!" Medoret cried again, and stumbled forward, beating against the mist with her arms. "Where are you?"

We shall go on, Bael, her mother said firmly. *We cannot go home; that is lost to us. But for the children's sake, we will continue. Raise ship.*

There's no hope in it. She heard strain in Bael's voice, the exhaustion and stubborness of an argument carried too long.

I claim the Dream-Knowledge: we will go on. Is that understood?

There was a silence. *Yes, Captain.* The assent was grudging.

"Mother!"

Medoret, what are you doing? her mother said suddenly, sounding startled. Medoret heard her own child's high-pitched laughter, muffled beneath the table, then a series of thumps and a squeak of surprise.

I've got her, Bael said. Another thump and a squeal of protest, then more muffled giggles. *Well, I had her. She's as elusive as you are, Saryen. Hmmm. I see the cup is empty. What did she do with the water?*

Poured it down my boot, her mother said irritably. Soft laughter echoed around the table from the others. *See, Bael? I'll never be as arrogant as you think I am—my daughter will see to that.*

"Mother!"

Before her, the Serpent re-formed from her mists, coiling upon herself. She fluttered her fronds gracefully and drifted closer in subtle menace. "I am the Dream-Knowledge," she intoned. "I am the Answer. Seek Me and all will be known."

Medoret took a step toward the Serpent, her talons flexing. "Bring her back!"

The Serpent raised her jaw, her tongue flickering quickly over her gums, polishing obsidian teeth. "But dreams are not real," she mocked in Dr. Sieyes's voice. "You delude yourself."

"Bring her back!"

"But *I* am not real, either." And she laughed cruelly in Medoret's own voice, her dark serpent eyes glinting. Smoke swirled upward around her glittering body, and the Serpent vanished into the cold wind, blown to wisps and fragments.

"Mother . . ." Mother whispered in despair, bereft.

Medoret . . . her mother's voice answered quietly from the distant hills, its sound shuddering on the cold wind.

"Where are you?" Medoret called, lifting her arms. "Where are you?" But there was no further answer. She was alone again on the black plain, the stars watching from above without pity.

Medoret opened her eyes, finding herself in bed among the warm shadows of her own room, a familiar place of other awakenings. The air currents of the dome city sighed through the open window, tickling the hair on her damp face, bringing the city's odors and sounds, the teasing touch of air on her skin. In the street below, the city rumbled with activity as it awoke to the new morning: she heard distant voices, a shout, the rattling of machines on the pavement. Her alarm clock chimed a moment later and she stretched out an arm quickly to silence it.

Wrapping her bedcover around her, she went to the window and looked out on the black plain. Twice she and Ian had changed apartments in the years they had been together, but the view of the vast plain changed little from a different vantage of a few streets. She shivered in the coolness of the air on her body, sweat-dampened by her sleep, and pulled the coverlet more closely around her.

Most humans did not believe in dreams, she knew, not really. To their psychologists, dreams had no true meaning beyond the sleeping mind's schizophrenic reworking of the day's experiences, a mental counter recoiling back to zero, a way the mind kept its sanity through the madness of disordered thought. To some others, however, dreams had esoteric links to the cosmic order, to proof of astral travel and the inner light, to the demigod of the human ego-consciousness. The terminology varied as all speculated, scientists and pseudoscientists, skeptics and fervent believers, none agreeing on the essentials. Medoret had read vainly through the literature when her dreams returned to trouble her, unsure if human dreams had any relevance to her own.

A few of the articles hinted that some humans could direct their dreams, as she did night after night with her Maya images, and sometimes human dreams had a persistent clarity upon wakening, as did hers, as if a part of her still walked in that other place for a time after waking. But when fantasies truly walked in one's waking world, the analysis grew wary, distrusting a madman's ravings. Am I mad? she wondered. She shivered slightly, feeling the slight touch of the black plain's icy wind on her skin. Imagination? Or memory? How can a dream be real? She scowled, trying to understand. The Dream-Knowledge: her mother had claimed it and Bael had conceded in the face of that claim, as if such a speaking settled a mattter essential. Knowledge of what? Destiny? She shivered again.

I was there once, she thought, staring out at the black plain. There with the Ship, with my mother Saryen on the Black Ship. Not this plain, but another—somewhere else. She looked up at the stars, a thousand points of light scattered across the blackness. But where? And where are they now? She thumped her fist slowly on the window-ledge, frustrated with her own blockages. A jungle clearing and the Vision Serpent, the black plain and a tantalizing distant murmur of her mother's voice: one a doorway to the other? Is *that* the answer?

Ian tapped at her bedroom door. "Are you up, Medoret?" he asked, his voice muffled by the closed panel.

"Yes, Ian," she called.

"Don't dawdle now." Ian always fussed at her when he had an agenda for the day, and would continue to fuss until she complied with The Plan. She shrugged at the closed door and fluttered her fingers at him.

"I won't."

"The ship leaves in four hours," he warned.

"I won't dawdle."

He grunted and padded away down the hall.

I am the Vision Serpent, she intoned silently, and fluttered her fingers over her head again. *I am the Jaguar Sun.* . . .

"Medoret!" Ian bellowed.

"I'm moving!"

She sighed, and padded dutifully into the shower cubicle, stripping off her nightdress and rubbing its soft folds over her body, then opened her bathroom cabinet. She swallowed her supplement pills, held her hand briefly to the thermometer plate to check for fever, then studied her face in the mirror for several minutes. *This* is reality, she told herself sternly, not taunting Serpents and black plains and voices in the mist. And you're dawdling, she told herself further. And you promised.

Twenty minutes later, showered, powdered, and dutifully dressed, she packed several spare sets of clothing in a wide carryall—though *Narenjo* kept ship suits in its stores, she reminded herself. The Project had *everything* in stores, for that matter, and as a Team member she'd have the chits to draw anything within reason. Her eyes narrowed as she looked at the framed prints and bas-reliefs on her walls, then at the several heavy carvings on her shelf. She tossed out half the clothes in a heap on her bed.

Ian stomped by outside in the hall, moving fast. "Take your data disks for that glyphs project!" he commanded. "Dr. Ruth asked specifically."

"Ian! I need your help!"

His footsteps stomped back and the bedroom door opened. "With what?" he asked, scowling at her. She waved her hand helplessly at the wall and shelves. "Oh. I see. Hmmm." He moved into the room and glowered at the carvings and prints. "Holos won't do?"

"Ian. . . ."

He grunted and made a Solomon's decision. He pointed imperiously. "Two Maya, two Targethi. Take a Jaguar and a Serpent for the Maya—that Palenque relief with Lady Xoc is especially good for the Serpent. Hmmm." He looked at the Targethi carvings and hesitated. "You can see the Targethi stuff there, Medoret," he hedged, "and the real thing—not repros."

"Can I cart the walls I like back to my room?" she demanded.

He grinned. "A point." He picked up the small statue of the Cricket God and cradled it in his hands. "This one," he said gruffly. She took it from him, smiling. "How about only three?" he suggested, eyeing the others on the shelf.

"You said four."

"So I did. I lied." He frowned at her. "It's only for ten weeks, after all. I'll have the rest shipped if we stay longer than that. Okay?"

"Okay . . . I guess."

"The problem isn't weight, it's bulk."

"I know." She looked at him solemnly.

He eyed her back. "I could maybe make room in my carryall for a small carving—a very small one, mind you."

"You'll ship the others if I take only three?"

He grunted. "I love negotiating with you, Medoret. We can wheedle forwards and backwards for hours while *Narenjo* takes off and leaves us behind. It'll be fun."

"I'll take three."

"Good." He snorted. "I'm glad that's over." As he started to stomp out of the room, she picked up her bed pillow and threw it at him, hitting him neatly between the shoulders. He turned and wagged his finger at her.

"*That* cost you three points on your social index, m'girl."

"Stuff the index."

"A solid academic comment, Doctor M.," he said loftily. "Don't forget the glyph tapes."

"I won't." She sighed dramatically.

But he was gone, back on his agenda. Smiling to herself, Medoret shifted the Cricket God statue safely inside her carryall, packing clothing around it to protect it, then retrieved the glyph tapes from her desk.

Today is the day, she thought, allowing herself to feel excited at last. No last countermand by the Project, no last maneuver by Dr. Sieyes. Today is the day. She zipped the bag closed and hefted it onto her shoulder, then took a quick last glance around her room, her mind filled with too many things. The air sighed through the open window, bringing a touch of columbine and a faint metallic chiming, the dusty rumble of street traffic far below. She stood still a moment, feeling the air move on her face, gathering the scents in a last farewell. On the black plain beyond her window-ledge, an icy wind blew unseen, scattering a Serpent's mist into fragments.

"Medoret!" Ian bellowed from the outer room.

"Coming!"

Chapter Three _____

The ship field lay at the edge of the ice plain a kilometer downslope from the city, next to a busy Ship Support complex of warehouses, repair facilities, and the central passenger dock with its small bubble dome. Medoret set down her carryall by the outer wall facing the ship field and looked around at the crowd of people gathered on the dock, then peered outward through the dome wall at the shadowed shape of *Narenjo*. The Survey ship stood firmly on its tall jacks, its slim hull towering fifty meters high, gleaming under the bright lights of the field. In the tubeway connecting the ship's passenger lock to the dome, she could see shadowed movement as people passed to and fro. Ground vehicles whizzed back and forth from a nearby warehouse, loading supplies and equipment into the smaller cargo bay. She watched as a powered forklift maneuvered a huge box into the main cargo lock, wondering what was inside. A space-suited figure ran out on the field and waved his arms frantically at the forklift driver inside his cab and then, totally ignored by the other, jumped up and down emphatically. The driver calmly deposited the box within the ship, then stood up in his cab seat and gestured rudely to the man on the ground.

They waved at each other for a while, trading semantics; finally the other man stamped off, saluted by a defiant final flip of the forklift arms. Medoret smiled. Ian said Ship Support took no guff off anyone, and had the priorities to back

up the arrogance. Though technically subordinate to the
other four Project teams, Ship Support made the teams'
work possible and saw little reason to grovel, even for
show. She watched the forklift whisk neatly back across the
field toward a distant warehouse and vanish, then watched
vainly for more ship-field activity before turning back to
the crowd in the dome.

In a far corner of the dome, Dr. Ruth was the center of
an admiring crowd, gathering adherents like lint on a felt
jacket. Medoret watched the group for a few moments,
wondering what they laughed about so uproariously, a smile
tugging at her own mouth. Then she noticed a dark-skinned
young man looking at her intently from across the room.
His proud carriage, straight black hair, and bronzed skin reminded her of the tall Maya chieftains from Yucatan, a look
as exotic as her own. As he saw her looking, he took a step
in her direction. She quickly bent down to her carryall, pretending to adjust the straps. When she looked up again, he
had turned away.

She kicked at her carryall in disgust. Your social index is
the pits today, she thought. You have to meet these people,
endure the looks. Everything changes today. So go talk to
him.

Her feet stayed put, rooted to the floor like a jungle tree.
Medoret, she told herself, you are the most spineless, idi-
otic, fainting excuse I've ever—

"There you are, Medoret." Ian pushed past another group
of people chatting nearby and walked up to her, accompanied by a tall blond man in the olive-green uniform of Ship
Support. "This is Captain Stein. Joseph, my daughter,
Medoret."

Stein stretched his lips into a slight smile and clicked his
heels as he bowed. "I've long wanted to meet our alien
guest. You've grown since the last videos."

Medoret nodded, trying to think of a suitable answer and

coming up with nothing. She smiled awkwardly. She usually didn't meet ship's crew.

"So you're to be our alien expert," Stein drawled. Medoret saw Ian's flicking glance at the captain and tensed: in some of the subtler human reactions, Ian was an infallible guide. She tried to keep her expression pleasant.

"In whatever way I can, sir. Dr. Ruth says she's interested in my—"

"Well, good. Just stay out of the way when you can, too." The thin lips turned down. "I'm not pleased about this, Dr. Douglas. I've got enough responsibility to not have the care of the Project's famous ward."

"Not in front of Medoret," Ian protested.

"Why not? Let her know from the start." The captain's look this time lacked the vague friendliness he had pretended earlier.

"I am an inconvenience to everyone," Medoret acknowledged in a pleasant tone, keeping a slight smile on her face. "By my mere existence, I annoy, bother, inflict, remove, end. I have learned this all my life from every person possible. Thank you again for the lesson, Captain."

She saw him blink in surprise, then turned on her heel and stalked off toward the tube tunnel to the ship. She would find her own way to whatever quarters Stein had assigned her. *I am not an animal for study,* she told herself through clenched teeth, trembling with her anger. *I am not a burden for overworked bureaucrats. I am not what you want me to be, weak and dependent and owned! I am not!*

"Medoret! Wait!" Ian called after her.

She slowed in automatic response to his voice and nearly turned, then shook her head violently and walked into the tubeway. Her boots reverberated hollowly as she stepped onto the temporary ramp, filling the enclosed space with echoes half-baffled by the people passing to and fro into the ship. She stayed near one wall, making her way patiently through the buffeting, trying to ignore the startled looks as some looked at her. It might be easier if I didn't look so human she realized. Outright alien might be easier to accept, but I'm too close—I surprise them too late when they look. Unfortunately, it's not a problem I can fix.

At the end of the tunnel, she reached the squared rim of the ship's airlock and stepped across the threshold. The air seemed closer here, tinged with environmental chemicals and a musty smell, palpably warmer than the ship lounge. A curving metal wall defined the small entryhold, pierced by three stairwells leading upward, one to the left, two to the right. At a podium just inside the door stood a young woman in a neatly tailored uniform, her dark hair pulled tightly into a severe style, her dark eyes alert. Medoret repressed a sigh as the young woman, like the others, blinked in startlement a second too late.

"Can you tell me where my room is?" she asked. "I am—"

"You're Medoret."

"Yes."

To Medoret's surprise, the young woman smiled, her face lighting with genuine pleasure. "You're more beautiful than your videos, Medoret—grown up now, aren't you?" She looked Medoret up and down for another moment, then extended her hand. "I've read so much about you," she added in a clipped British accent. "I'm Hillary Dalton, one of the grad students. BioSurvey."

"Hello, Hillary," Medoret said cautiously, returning the handshake. "Glyphs."

"We *do* get defined that way, don't we?" Hillary laughed attractively and waved her hand airily at the podium and the small entryhold. "In my peon role, I'm also a watch officer, which means I handle room assignments today. Isn't the bustle awesome? This is my first season out on Survey; I've been *dying* to see Cebalrai. I mean, studying pollen grains in paleolithic Afghanistan is one thing, but everybody already *knows* what the plants are. Out here everything is new. Is Dr. Douglas coming with you?"

"Yes, he is. You said you're with BioSurvey?"

"Plants," Hillary said firmly. "Flowers, shrubs, trees, anything jungle." She waved her hand, and the attractive grin flashed again. "I've had my sights on Cebalrai ever since I was in first-year Honors at Oxford—you wouldn't believe the chores I did to impress the Oxford bigshots and get their recommendation to EuroSurvey. Why would *anybody* be interested in algae?" She shuddered dramatically. "But that's academics, right? I'm going to help Dr. Falk in completing the Cebalrai biosurvey this season. I've always wanted to meet you—I *never* agreed with their attitude that you should be hidden away—but now you're here at last. Welcome aboard!"

Medoret blinked, then scrambled together her manners. "Thank you." Several people had piled up behind her in the tubeway as they talked, and a tall lean man stamped restlessly behind her. He scowled over Medoret's shoulder at Hillary.

"Do I get to come aboard, too?" he asked pointedly over Medoret's shoulder.

"Right away, Dr. Seidel." Hillary tugged peremptorily at Medoret's sleeve and hauled her behind her to the other side of the podium. "Hang around a minute, Medoret, will you? Dr. Seidel? You're on B deck."

Hillary handed the man a small oblong rod, a key-plate dangling from the end. She half turned to point up one of the right stairwells. "Go up there and turn left, then right. Number twenty-eight."

"I know where it is, Ms. Dalton." Seidel stamped past them and disappeared up the stairwell.

Hillary smiled at Medoret over her shoulder as the next in line stepped up to the podium. "Will you be coming to the ship-launch dinner, Medoret?"

"I suppose . . . I hadn't heard about that."

"Well, do!" Hillary smiled again. "The grad students have their own table, suitably mean and at the back, but who cares? Hello, Mrs. Temsor. You're on B deck, too." The gray-haired woman, dressed in a trim shipsuit and a sour expression, swept Medoret with a cool glance of distaste and took her key, then stalked off after Dr. Seidel. Hillary saw the look and turned to wrinkle her nose at Medoret, her dark eyes sparkling. "If God ever asked for an assistant, she'd volunteer, believe me. She's Dr. Mueller's subchief on Metals—infosystems, mostly—and a total bitch. Just stay out of her way and life's fine—and George Seidel is a treasure when he's not being so grim. He's Urban Map subchief this season. Not to worry, Medoret. Hi, John; you're in A16. There's three of us this trip—and now you're the fourth, aren't you?"

Medoret blinked again, a bit dazzled by Hillary's chatter. "Four what?"

"Grad students, of course. You've finished your first degree, haven't you?"

"No, not exactly," Medoret admitted. "Why I'm going to Cebalrai hasn't been quite defined."

"Well, any degree-in-progress except postdoc makes you a grad student—take my word for it." Hillary bent over the podium to look down the tubeway. "Oh, drat, it's a horde coming. Listen, look for our table, will you? I want so much to talk with you—when I let you talk, that is. Sorry. Isn't this all exciting?" She grinned and shook Medoret's hand firmly, then handed her a key-plate. "C deck. Go up the left stairs two flights and turn right. See you later!"

"I will."

"Bye!"

Medoret moved on as more people crowded through the tubeway entrance. She followed Hillary's directions to the safety of her cabin, a little dazed by the young woman's open friendliness. I get too used to feeling odd, she thought;

it would be nice to fit in ... She quirked her lips, feeling both out and in today.

She turned the corner and counted down the doors to her own, then touched the key to the doorlock. The automatic door opened and she stepped into the dark room, the reddish glow of its warmth radiating from every surface. It was a small place, a quarter the size of her bedroom at home, but roomy enough. She sat down on the bunk, her carryall at her feet, and stared at the opposite wall.

"Hillary."

She said the name aloud, liking the sound. Occasionally a new person liked to meet Medoret, but she had learned to be wary: sometimes the reasons behind the friendly smiles were not good. But she thought about Hillary anyway, a slow flush of pleasure blurring the memory of Captain Stein's abruptness. An interesting baptism to ship life, those two. And quite enough for today.

She was often confused by such encounters with strangers, kept away too much from ordinary human society, always different enough in her alienness to pull people out of their normal patterns. She presumed humans had some order of rules in how they reacted to each other, but she couldn't precisely factor how those rules changed when they reacted to herself; even the persons she thought she had deciphered could change, turning cool, warm, indifferent, distracted, angry.

She watched sometimes when the humans talked to each other, studying the cues, trying to figure out what they meant to each other. What she had learned about humankind and tried to copy for herself lay as a thin veneer over deeper instincts she sensed in herself—though what *they* were sometimes eluded her, too. She knew that her tempers of the past few days would get her in trouble, and maybe Ian, too. In her current frame of mind, she didn't mind the trouble for herself, but Ian didn't deserve it.

She heard a hiss, then a crackle of static, from the intercom disk on the opposite wall. "Last boarding call," a calm male voice announced. "All passengers and crew to their staterooms, please."

She lay down on the bunk and maneuvered her arms into the straps fastened to the edges of the bed, then worked her boots into the pockets at its base, then got up to store her carryall by tying it firmly to the base of the small cabinet of drawers, then lay down again. A few minutes later, she was up once more to find some water to ease her dry throat. The small bathroom had a cup and a tap. She was settling herself for the third time when Ian opened the door.

"Ready?" he asked.

"Yes, Ian."

"Boost only lasts a few minutes. Don't worry now."

She closed her eyes. "I won't worry."

"I'm in the room next door if you need anyone."

"Thank you, Ian."

He hesitated, then left hurriedly as a measured hooting began over the intercom, signaling imminent liftoff. Medoret tightened her hands on the bed straps and stared hard at the ceiling. I lived through this before, she told herself; I was born to the Ship, I've known what it's like. Her heart pounded a frantic rhythm, making her ears ring with their pounding. She tried to still that excitement, knowing that Sieyes would sedate her if he had monitor leads in the straps, a camera to watch, stealing it from her, that first step back to Cebalrai. She closed her eyes again, listening to her heartbeat and measuring it against a longer rhythm; slowly it came under her control, dropping its frantic leaping in her chest, its surging through her blood. Quiet, she soothed. You were born to the Ship; this belongs to you.

It began with the rumbling, a steady vibration she sensed through the mattress, then a slow pressure forcing her downward into its softness. She matched her heartbeat to a long beat in that steady vibration, counting the cycles with the ship, lifting with it, her mind swept suddenly with a

keen exaltation as the vibration reached its peak: *We rise!*
They had shouted on every liftoff, with each launch affirm-
ing what they were, what they sought, knowing the right-
ness of it. I remember, Mother: I remember.

Her body sank deeper into the mattress, pressed down by
a heavy invisible hand, her heart pounding in her chest. She
surrendered fully to that frantic rhythm, casting herself
madly into the void with the ship. I rise, I rise! Exaltation
swept through her again like a sheet of hot flame, awakening every nerve, every pore. She had a sudden vision of
herself naked against the sky, straining her arms upward,
propelled by the thunder at her feet, defying the limits of
any world that thought it could bind her or any of her kind.
We are the People! she shouted with the others. We rise!
Oh, we rise!

In the distant blackness, a Goddess poured a stream of
stars into a dark pool of the unending void, then raised her
luminous eyes and saw Medoret rising exultant before her,
the flames roaring at her feet. Those exquisite lips curved.

My child, welcome . . .

Mother!

Gradually the heavy acceleration receded, taking part of
the wild exaltation of the launch with it, like a tide sweeping outward. Medoret waited impatiently for the artificial
gravity to engage, her senses still thrumming oddly. When
she felt the shift in gravity, she unhooked her belts and
lunged to her feet, impelled to some motion, anything.
Then abruptly she gasped for air and dizzily reached for
support as the strange emotion left her fully, forcing her to
lean heavily on the mattress.

She shook her head to clear it, a bad mistake she realized
as the room promptly tipped and moved sideways. She sat
down and leaned forward as the room began spinning inward to a single black point. Don't faint, she told herself
weakly. Lie down. She collapsed backward on the mattress,

dragging up one leg. The other could hang where it was, she decided when she could think again.

Some Star Child, she thought ruefully. First rule about We Rise, Medoret: don't stand up right away.

After a time, she sat up gingerly and watched for the room to tip—thankfully, it didn't—then waited a little longer before she tried her feet again. They worked, better than she expected. She paced the cabin slowly, aware of the chemical scents on the air, the muffled thumps of activity nearby, her pupils expanding in the gloom of the cabin as she deliberately reconnected herself to her senses. She had not turned on the ceiling light, she realized; a human would, but she did not need the glaring light. Shadows surrounded her, reddish with warmth, bathing her body. She reached out to touch her alien senses, encompassing them all, remembering how they patterned together into a different life, stretching for the memory. I choose . . .

A hand rapped at her cabin door. She sighed.

"Enter," she said.

The door hissed open and she stopped to face the bulking figure in the doorway, tensing automatically as she recognized him.

"And how did you weather launch, my girl?" Dr. Sieyes rumbled, his broad face stretched into a self-satisfied smile. How well she knew that smile. Without invitation, he stepped in and switched on the light, throwing glances right and left to inspect the room. Games. Medoret clasped her hands in front of her belt and stood still, watching him warily. "Well?" he prompted.

"For your report, Doctor?"

She saw the flash of irritation in Dr. Sieyes's dark eyes. "I opposed this."

"I know." They glared at each other, the antagonism finally out in the open. For three days Dr. Sieyes had made his comments, trying to undermine her acceptance of Ian's offer, warning of this, questioning that, suggesting Medoret remain at Ariadan. She had ignored it all, putting on a cheerful face, blithefully denying all his suggestions. "Let's say I'm tired of being your pet, Doctor."

"*You're* tired of—since when do you have any say?" He wandered over to the bureau and picked up her carryall, then casually rummaged through it. He pulled out her statue of the Cricket God and juggled it idly from hand to hand, frowning for effect. "This was unnecessary weight," he remarked, and put it into his shipsuit pocket.

"Put that back," she challenged him.

"Let's understand where the line still remains, my girl."

"Or I'll report you for theft," she said flatly.

He flushed and retrieved the carving from his pocket, then clunked it on the top of the bureau.

"You aren't Targethi," he said, waving at the carved god.

"Neither are you." She turned away from him. "What is this, Doctor? Another test of my emotional matrix? A dominance scoring? Or is it just spleen because Ian outmaneuvered you? I'm interested. I'm always interested in you."

He said nothing and she turned to face him defiantly. His expression had turned cool and wary, his thoughts hidden, as he regarded her. Then he smiled, showing his teeth.

"Obviously you're emotionally disturbed by the liftoff, a not-unexpected development after your protected existence—as *pet*, as you say. All this is *so* new." He tapped his jaw, pretended to think deeply, then raised a finger in delighted self-revelation. "Of course! You must remain in this cabin until you've recovered your equilibrium, I'd say at least twenty-four hours—then we'll reassess." The threat lay on the air for a moment. "I worry about overstressing you with too much stimulation. Might bring on another of those nervous attacks of yours—and we can't have that."

She took a step toward him, her fists clenched. "You can't keep me here. I'm invited to the liftoff dinner."

"Oh? I thought you didn't like parties." He smiled and

keyed open the door. "Later we'll talk about delusions and *pets*."

"I'll tell Ian," she said tightly. "I'll tell him everything you've said—and what's behind it, too."

"Captain Stein listens to *me*, Medoret; I'm the alienist, after all. Academics—and the captain is one, too, you know—respect specialty lines. Go ahead: try it and see." He waved his hand airily as he turned. "Rest well, my dear."

The door hissed shut. Medoret clenched and reclenched her fists as she stared at the closed door, a hot rage blurring her vision. Careful, careful, she warned herself. He'll use it—he'll use it to keep you locked up all the way there and back. She bowed her head and took a step backward, then another, making a patterned ceremony of the retreat. She should have known Dr. Sieyes would not lose so easily; she should have known. Never had he shown his malice so plainly—but, then, never had his ownership been at risk, not even from Ian's protests.

I'm his career, she thought. I'm his fame and the source of his adulation, his renowned treatises, his video appearances, his authority on board this ship. He'll never let me go.

She felt a wail build inside her throat and forced herself to sit down on her bed, denying it, then lay back and closed her eyes, her fists still clenching.

I would like to kill him, she thought, and the violence within herself frightened her. She stretched out her talons into raking claws, imagining their use, ripping flesh, blinding, tearing away life . . . Stop, stop. She covered her eyes, refusing the impulse that might fling her out of the room and into the corridor in pursuit of Sieyes, ending all chances more neatly than even he could ever manage.

If I were the Jaguar, I could kill—but I am not the Jaguar. Am I? What is the reality?

* * *

While *Narenjo* completed its jump to 70 Oph and descended into the star system, Medoret spent the interlude confined to her stateroom. She had appealed twice to Ian, who had gone to the captain each time, but Sieyes's prediction had proven accurate: Captain Stein's own wishes obviously paralleled his expert's advice. Ian had fretted, but said he hoped to get the ban lifted before they left 70 Oph.

"You *hope*?" she had asked incredulously. "I'm not jump-shocked—I'm fine! Why does Stein let him win? It's not fair!"

Ian looked pained. "Stein's in command of the ship, Medoret, and Ship Support outrules everybody when we're in transit. Dr. Ruth has asked, so have I, but the captain still says no. But maybe later. . . ."

He tried to smile at her encouragingly, and she knew how this decision tore at him; blaming himself, as always. She ground her teeth furiously, feeling trapped from all directions. She turned away from him, trying to get her anger under control for his sake, and stared at the Palenque carving she had hung on her wall. In the bas-relief, Lady Xoc pulled a thorned vine through her pierced tongue, invoking the Vision Serpent with self-inflicted agony. Medoret winced in sympathy.

"Besides," Ian said into the silence, putting on a false cheer, "the stop at 70 Oph will be short, just enough time to pick up some additional personnel and offload supplies. The real excitement is at Cebalrai."

She turned her head and glared. "Are you wheedling me?" she asked.

"No." He scowled unpleasantly, his own anger starting to rise. "I'm just suggesting you choose ground you can win, and right now you can't win, not until Stein relents. I'm sorry, but that's the way it is."

"Great," she muttered, looking down at her boots. "Thanks a lot."

He waved his hand at her desk. "You have your viewer and your glyphs project: work on that."

"I don't want to."

"Then sit and sulk like a child." Ian stamped out, and Medoret kicked the base of her bunk hard enough to sting.

"I haven't done anything wrong!" she shouted at the closing door, then threw herself down on her bed. Not fair, not fair! she fumed. But glaring at the ceiling lost its charm after a while, so she got up and sat down resentfully at her viewer. I win if I do what Sieyes wants: sure. She punched up her glyphs program.

She used the next several hours to tap into the ship's computer library, advancing her research into the Targethi glyphs. In her life among humans, she had often needed to occupy herself during long hours of solitude—Ian was often away at academic meetings and she had accepted a student's preoccupation with intricate study. It helped to divert her from frustrations that only gave Sieyes greater advantage—Ian was right on that, she conceded ungraciously—especially now when she had a goal to win through self-control.

To her satisfaction, when Sieyes oiled in and out of her stateroom that afternoon to check up, she saw his disappointment in her calmness: sometimes the psychiatrist read as clearly as tempered glass. She decorated the small triumph by burbling enthusiastically about her glyphs program, burying the psychiatrist in technical glyph-talk until he retreated in angry confusion—Dr. Sieyes hated other people knowing things he didn't. The petty victory didn't spring her from her confinement, but it soothed her mood.

After Dr. Sieyes stomped out, she admired her plaque of Lady Xoc and the Vision Serpent, then leaned back and interlaced her fingers behind her head, imagining herself in a forest glade of the Serpent's world, when the heat of the high day shimmered through the jungle, lying heavy on the lowlands. She had climbed upward from the valley that morning, she reminded herself, seeking the Jaguar, but he was elusive. On the hillside above the valley, she walked over high grass, breathing deep of the cool mountain air, then smiled as the Jaguar turned and looked at her.

My greetings, Jaguar Sun, Medoret said, bowing gracefully in her shimmering robes of the Moon Goddess, Ixchel.

Lady Rainbow. The Jaguar bowed low, his teeth flashing white in the bright light of the jungle glade. *You are well?*

The birds are flying up the mountain, flashing bright color. Medoret turned and watched a flight of jungle parrots racing upward across dark green. She stretched her hands toward them in blessing. *Yes, I feel well.*

They fly to cheer you, Lady Rainbow. I have missed you.

You? she teased. *When have you ever needed anyone but yourself, O Terrible One?* The Jaguar stepped closer and looked down into her face, his eyes fiercely tender.

We of the Otherworld are one essence, Lady. He raised her hand to his lips. *And you and I are legend.*

And he danced her away with him across the grass, laughing with her at the brightness of the day. They danced and danced, bearing her away from all memories, redesigning the world as they willed.

She let the daydream fade and sighed, then stretched her talons languorously, thinking Jaguar thoughts about Sieyes. Confine me, will you? I know doorways you cannot imagine. And you won't win.

Chapter Four _____

She sat at her desk again the next morning, calmly working on her continuing research, refusing to be distracted by the fascinating bumps and noises following the ship's setdown at 70 Oph. She focused on the screen, drawing from the habit of long hours to keep calm, to focus. Restlessly, she flipped through her tape of 70 Oph, tantalized by the beautiful carvings, a depth of beauty she would be proud to call her people's own, if it were.

The torrid tropical setting and the monumental stone of 70 Oph's small third world had reminded the Project scientists of the ancient Maya jungles of Yucatan, and the convenience of the nomenclature had stuck. A distinctive row of glyphs, transliterated into Maya syllables, had named the Targethi as a race; the 70 Oph site itself the Project had named Caracol, after a minor but bellicose Maya city, yet unaware that even greater ruins were yet to be discovered at Cebalrai, first great Tikal itself, and then its seven homegrounds, each outlying site another magnificent study in carved stone and a stepped temple rising above the treetops, outrivaled only by Tikal's vaster size and complexity. With such wonders elsewhere, the 70 Oph glyphs had become a minor study, a token nod beside the fantastic and intricate carvings of Cebalrai's larger site.

Had the humans erred in their excited Maya naming, she wondered, finding connections where none truly existed? But the artwork did seem curiously reminiscent, enough to prompt a few speculative papers about early Targethi contact with Earth, a theory Medoret herself doubted. It was a human thing to look for connections to help understanding, as she did herself with her own Maya preoccupations, and so the Project scientists had found goddesses and quetzals, danzantes and Lady Rainbow among the strange glyphed shapes carved on every Targethi wall. A carved mouth around a portal became a Witz Monster, ancient guardian of the Maya underworld. A vaguely feline figure became the Jaguar Sun, bravest of the Heroic Twins who had founded the Maya nation in the long struggle against the Nine Lords of the Underworld. One circular glyph, intricately carved in broad rings around a central sun, became the Calendar of the Long Count, though none really believed it a calendar and the naming had sparked dissenting papers.

To name is to own, she reminded herself, and so they believed.

She stopped at a favorite glyph, the Celestial Bird, a jeweled and fantastic creature with sweeping plumes and a fierce eagle's head. Stalking on its delicate fringed legs, the beautiful bird led a procession of five carapaced squat creatures, suspected to be Targethi themselves, each named after an ancient Mayan king. "Great-Jaguar-Paw, Stormy-Sky, 18-Rabbit, Ah-Cacaw, Lord Water," she whispered, tapping each with her finger.

She leaned her chin upon her hand and smiled at the procession, wondering about each of the Targethi depicted there—who they were, what they had known, what age they had lived in, what stars they had seen. If they were Targethi at all. In the fierce tropical climate of either Targethi world, little survived the biotic corrosion of the jungle; of the Targethi, no certain biological traces had been found, not even bones in graves. Yet she agreed that these beetlelike figures, dancing gracefully behind the Celestial Bird, were Targethi. Perhaps her mother had once pointed out the glyph-figure and named it so; perhaps she merely guessed

like the humans and found certainty in her own willing—
her dreams weren't clear enough to be sure of a chance
memory.

She scrolled through to the glyphs that dominated the
smaller site at 70 Oph, a complex dedicated to the Vision
Serpent and a Crocodile God. Perhaps the symbols were the
Targethi name of the place, a single-temple complex near
an exposed mine-face. The Targethi had sought silver and
several other technological metals here, and some of the
components of Tikal machines had been traced by metallurgical analysis back to this site. There was a clear connection in that link, proven by objective fact beyond beloved
assumptions: perhaps 70 Oph was an outpost like the outlying homegrounds on Tikal's peninsula, not a separate colony but part of the Tikal complex as a whole. A few Urban
Map writers had thought so.

She touched the pebbly skin of the Crocodile who danced
along smaller beetled figures, his snout held impossibly high,
his clawed hands beseeching the Serpent who twined its
coils around the scene. It was a beautiful carving, intricately
repeating upon itself, meaning upon meaning. Like her
dreams, she thought, and about as impenetrable. Vainly she
wished for someone who would listen about her dreams,
who would understand the apartness they brought to her,
would care about the needs of a person cast apart from all
that meant anything.

Why can't Dr. Sieyes just let me be? she wondered and
rubbed her face tiredly, letting her sensitive fingertips ease
the muscles. Her back cramped suddenly, stiff from her
hours of bending over the desk viewer, and she got up to
pace back and forth for a few minutes, stretching from side
to side in slow bends, bathed by the warm reddish glow of
the darkened room. The viewer screen shed its pale light in
a dim cone into the reddish shadows, illuminating small
specks of dust. She dipped in and out of the light, watching
the glow move on her skin. One bend led to a turn on a

foot, a half crouch as she completed the turn, her arms rising in smooth arcs to shoulder height; she brought in her arms and turned again on the other foot, keeping her balance easily in the slow dance.

Smiling slightly, she paced through the rest of the exercise she was inventing, inspired by a vague memory of the Black Ship. She bent forward, brushing the floor with her fingertips, then pirouetted slowly as she reached upward, stretching the long muscles, realigning her bones, calming her space. I am a stalk-spider, she thought. I weave my web like this and that . . .

She stopped her dance abruptly, almost remembering that spider-form—but the image darted away into the mists, as usual. A pet? A food animal? She couldn't remember. She sighed and sat down at her desk, then stared at the screen blankly.

More footsteps tramped by her closed door, more of the muffled thumps and voices of the ship landing she had not been permitted to see. She ground her teeth, then bent forward again to her viewer, blocking away the anger. He wins if you are angry, she told herself. Still, she was too aware of her metal prison, of the city that lay all about the ship, a city she had seen only in videotape, photos, the few artifacts Ian had collected for his shelves. Not the right city, not the one she awaited, but a Targethi city.

It's not fair. She leaned her forehead on the cabinet of her viewer and wished she could break something—freely, without punishment, just for the satisfying smash. She wished she could run away forever into her daydreams, to dance with Jaguar, to trade fierce posturing with the Vision Serpent, to sit comfortably within the circle of the Cricket's arms. My friends, she thought, why can't you be real and this reality the dream world? She wished . . . for too many things she couldn't have. Where is the answer?

Lady Rainbow, the Jaguar growled, enticing her, *will you come dance with me?* He posed proudly in his jungle glade, his tail flashing. Behind him, the Cricket God turned and beckoned to her, then invoked the mist and the Serpent within, not the Maya terror that had frightened her in dreams, but the friend who knew her as no one else did, not even the Jaguar Sun. *Beloved,* the Jaguar called, *leave this place and live forever with me, in the Xibalba . . .*

Beloved, she answered wistfully, could it be forever, truly forever?

You need only wish it, Lady Rainbow . . .

She heard new footsteps outside in the hallway and tried to ignore them, seeing the Jaguar in her mind, vibrant and real, a god of destiny. She reached out her hands, as if she could touch him from this world, as if the doorway had truly opened and all she need do is step through it . . . A moment later, to her startlement, her cabin door shushed open behind her.

"Quiet!" a voice whispered urgently. "Samta, get off my foot, you clod."

Medoret turned her chair quickly and saw three human shapes crowding in the doorway, the bright light of the hallway vivid against the darkness of their shapes, blinding her.

"Is she here?" another voice whispered. "Hit the light switch, will you?"

Medoret stood. The ceiling light flashed on and she blinked dazedly against the sudden brilliant light. The visitors quickly shut the door behind them.

"I don't have much tape to run in front of the camera," a third voice said irritably. "Make this quick."

Medoret blinked again against the dazzlement of the lights, then her vision cleared to show Hillary and two young men, one of them the dark-haired man she had seen on the ship dock. He smiled at her warmly; the tall sandy-haired young man beside him did not. Hillary spread her hands dramatically. "There you are. Where have you been?"

"In captivity," Medoret answered sourly.

"That's what I thought," Hillary said, making a face. " 'Delicate nerves,' my ass. Isn't Sieyes a total creep-out? These hunks, by the way, are Samta Montes and Bjorn Svenson, our fellow peons. Samta's the brunette, Bjorn's the Swede—it's easiest to remember that way."

"Hi," Samta said. "You're prettier than your videos."

She blinked, then smiled back at him. "So I've been told."

"This is stupid," Bjorn said to Hillary, ignoring the interchange. "We can get in big trouble."

"So?" Hillary retorted, tossing her head. She gave Bjorn a look of disgust. "Excuse the child, Medoret, but we needed Bjorn—despite his adjustment problems. Bjorn's the tech who's playing a movie for the guard camera down the corridor a ways—you do know you have a camera?"

"I'm not surprised," Medoret said. Samta took a long step forward and bent to look at her computer screen, then smiled down at her. He seemed taller than his middle height, lean-limbed and brown in his shortsleeved jumpsuit, the clean planes of his face and high cheekbones reminding her again of Yucatan, the real Yucatan. His scents of dust, warm human flesh, and a faint cologne washed over her, and he stood so close she sensed the heat radiating from his skin. Quetzal feathers would become him well, she thought confusedly, like all Maya of those ancient glades. He raised an eyebrow. "Glyphs," she said awkwardly.

"That I can see."

"Why *are* you here?" Medoret asked, bewildered.

Hillary waved her hand airily. "We're collecting you. That's what archaeologists do, after all—and we don't have much time, either." She stepped forward and tugged at Medoret's sleeve peremptorily. "There's no help for it, Medoret—you're stashed."

"This is stupid," Bjorn repeated.

"Then go home," Hillary said impatiently. "Go the whole sixteen light-years, if you must!" Bjorn scowled ferociously, drawing his narrow face even narrower, his mouth pursed angrily. "Nobody forced you, Bjorn."

"Oh?" Bjorn said, his face sour.

Hillary shrugged disdainfully and tugged again at Medoret's sleeve. "Want to see a real Targethi city, Medoret? I thought so. Get your jacket and let's take a tour."

Medoret hesitated. She hadn't actually *promised* Ian to stay put.

"Is that a 'no'?" Hillary looked deflated, her voice rising in disappointment.

Medoret shook her head. "Are you joking?" she said. "Let's go."

"Great!"

"The going will be a little delicate," Samta warned. "Wait a sec." He eased open the door and looked in both directions, then waved them out into the corridor. "I'll leave you to dismantle your movie, Bjorn. We'll wait outside the airlock."

"I'm not coming any farther."

"Suit yourself, friend."

Medoret looked up at the contraption near the corridor ceiling as she slipped out of the room, marveling that they would take the risk. The hallway was empty in both directions, though she heard voices around the bend. Were they coming nearer?

"Come on," Hillary whispered. "This way."

She and Samta each took one of Medoret's arms and hurried her down the corridor and the bay-port, then down the ladder to the exterior hatch in a quick clatter. A few minutes later, they crowded into the outermost airlock and waited for it to cycle.

Doorways, she thought suddenly, her heart pounding. A moment later, the metal door slid open, admitting a wash of moist air from the darkness beyond, heavy with warmth and the scent of greenery. Medoret threw back her head in surprise as the scents washed over her, then stepped automatically after the others onto the ladder platform, looking to the right and left, her skin tingling. The airlock door swished shut behind her. Hillary clattered briskly down the ladder after Samta, and both turned at the base and looked up at Medoret, but she could not move, not yet.

On every side of the well-worn clearing grew a dark tangle of trees, vines, and underbrush. To the right, extending under the trees, were metal buildings of Earth manufacture, with the shadowed movements of people moving among them. She heard the whine of a ground car, the indistinct murmur of voices. Towering beyond the camp, just visible over the treetops, was the apex platform of the Targethi temple, its white stone glinting dully under starlight. She looked at the shadowed square of its Doorway and the stars it framed, its stone still radiating the heat of the day hours after the sun had set. All her life among the humans she had lived in the artificial environment of Ariadan's bubble-city, never knowing the reality of a truly living world beyond the small botanical garden at the city park and in her imagined Maya jungles. She stood still, drinking in the darkness.

It's beautiful. Oh, Serpent, can you see this? She lifted her arms, blessing the forest, as parrots again flew up the mountain in brilliant sunlight.

The warm air carried a dozen scents, a few sharp and bitter, some redolent with sap, others briefly sensed and gone. A warm breeze tickled her cheek, riffling her fine hair; she turned her face into it and breathed deeply, the touch tingling along her skin. She heard a murmur in the trees far to the left, the sharp cry of an animal, the sibilant movement of the forest on every side. *I remember this,* she thought, sorting the impressions. *But not here, in another place—places.* Yes, places: the memories stirred beneath her mind, like fish in a turbid stream, gracefully darting, sinuous, alive. She let her arms fall and filled her lungs with the warm air, every sense tingling.

Jaguar, she thought ecstatically, are you here?

Hillary gestured impatiently below her, her shadows warmly red in the pleasant darkness. "Quite a sight, huh? Let's go sightsee—out of sight, so to speak." She stamped her foot. "Medoret, will you come?"

"Come on, Medoret!" Samta called, and Hillary plunged away from the lighted buildings, heading for the trees. Medoret moved her feet reluctantly forward and descended the ladder. Samta tugged her off the last tread, his smile flashing in the darkness, then pulled her into a run. They ran into the trees and along the twistings of the path, following Hillary's sure guide. After a hundred meters, Hillary abruptly slid to a stop, nearly causing a collision, and pointed excitedly to a profusion of pale flowers just overhead. "Look: orchids!"

Samta snorted. "Collect later, you. Medoret wants to see the glyphs—don't you?"

"I want to see everything," Medoret said simply.

The three moved along the path, following Hillary's slower speed as the young woman scanned the branches overhead. The forest enveloped them with a warm darkness, subtle movement in every direction that teased. Medoret walked along the path, conscious of the slight jar of each footstep on the hard-packed dirt, of the measured rise and fall of her breathing. Life here: life everywhere. It's beautiful. She looked up at the darker pattern of branches against a moonless sky, remembering her dream of another path, where she had walked naked under the starlight as the Lady Rainbow.

"Beautiful," she breathed.

Ahead of them, Hillary crashed off the path, chasing another flower. Samta sighed. "She gets that way."

"It's all right." She half turned and smiled up at him. "This is wonderful."

"That I can see, and long overdue, I think," Samta said. "Hillary had a good idea in stealing you. Why does Sieyes have it in for you, anyway? You don't seem demented to me."

"Is that what he's been saying?"

"Oh, not exactly—but the upshot adds up to mental problems. Liftoff panic, general emotional collapse, a hothouse flower in need of her glass protections."

"Hmmmph."

"Tough being an alien pet," Samta said casually, making Medoret stop short and turn to him.

"How did you know?" she asked in sharp surprise.

"Sieyes has been on the videos almost as much as you, Medoret. Let's say I can recognize a certain kind of academic avarice. I grew up in an academic family and I know all the usual types—hell, half my relatives fit certain slots just fine. Dr. Sieyes is a particularly distinctive type. I'm surprised he let you loose onto Survey."

"Ian did that. That's my foster father." As Samta smiled and tipped his head at her, she sighed. "Well, of course, you know that. It's odd, everyone knowing me and I don't know them back."

"You'll get the chance."

"It's nice of you to be so confident." They walked slowly along the path, their footfalls muffled and lost among the murmurs of the forest.

"Do you like being a celebrity?" Samta asked.

"Not much."

"Well, there are lesser versions. Here I'm one of the token Maya—everybody thinks I should understand this place just because my ancestors built similar temples a thousand years ago."

"So you *are* Maya? I thought so." She turned and looked at him more closely, then remembered her manners. Samta might not like that kind of stare; she surely didn't. He shrugged, his white teeth flashing in the darkness.

"Not pure-blood, but I grew up in Yucatan." Samta took her sleeve and pulled her into a side path as they passed it, "Hillary, stop doing that stork dance and come this way."

"Who's a stork?" Hillary asked indignantly from somewhere up ahead, but she came back to them, anyway. "Samta," she said severely, "you have no sense of adventure."

"I'll differ with that: I'm just more focused." He smiled lazily, then laughed as Hillary stamped her foot. "Hell, Hillary, go stork-dance if you must. I'm easy."

"You think you know so much, Samta Montes," Hillary said airily. "Someday you'll get yours." And she flounced off again.

"Is she angry with you?" Medoret asked as Hillary vanished up the path. "Why?"

Samta shrugged. "Don't worry about it. Hillary just emotes for emoting sometimes, and she gets irritated when I don't react like she wants." He broke off a leaf and smelled it, then put it behind his ear. "Bjorn's a total stick, so I'm the expectable romance, I guess—affairs are traditional for pretty grad students on these jaunts, especially grad students from upper-class British backgrounds who think certain things come naturally with life." He shrugged again, but not unkindly. "She's Lady Hillary Dalton, by the way, but only call her that when you want to make her mad."

"I don't understand."

He grinned. "She thinks she's so unconventional, too. It'd help if Hillary was sure about what she wanted."

"Hm."

Samta laughed. "That's a nicely noncommittal sound."

She bit her lip, then decided she was out of her element. He laughed again, but a nice sound, not mocking. "Sorry, Medoret. I'm teasing."

"That's okay." As they walked down the path in the soft darkness, the forest's aliveness surrounding them, she looked at him surreptitiously. "So what do the temples really mean, O Token?" she asked.

"Beats me," he said lightly. "I suggested, just to get Mueller's goat—I'm on his Tikal Metals team—that we put on a Maya Serpent ritual to find out, but Dr. Mueller never did have a sense of humor. And I doubt he'd have gone much for the human-sacrifice part, even if we had the convenient war captives."

"I can think of a good choice for victim," Medoret said pointedly.

"Now that's neo-Freud, for sure—what would Dr. Sieyes say? But let's not forget Dr. Mueller—or Mrs. Temsor, that's a thought. Look ahead, Medoret. You'll like this."

The path widened into a sward of close-hugging ground plants and an open dark space dominated by the bulk of a stone arch. Medoret hurried ahead and touched the carved stone. "The Celestial Arch!" she cried, then heard Samta chuckle behind her. She turned, smiling as broadly as he. "Thank you. I've seen it in photographs, but. . . ." She turned back and ran her fingers over the smooth planes, then traced a curving groove of the alien bird's feathered tail.

The stone stood four meters tall, intricately carved in the distinctive Targethi iconography; she could recognize the design in the shadows and caressed it delightedly. Why the young grad students had absconded with her into this night-dark city, she couldn't say, but suspected a basic kindness, a perception that most of the humans she had met seemed to ignore. She paced around the arch, checking the panels, recognizing them all. The temple plaza must be very near, concealed behind the forest trees that ringed the small glade. Overhead, the night sky was strewn with stars, in a different pattern than she had seen at Ariadan.

Samta joined her at the stone and ran his hand over the glyphs, then glanced over her shoulder at Hillary, who had darted into the clearing to chase after something in the grass several meters away. "Monomania. All that energy suppressed for years, waiting for this. It may be a bit hectic around Hillary for a while, but she's okay, Medoret. You can trust her." He looked back at the shadowed stone. "It really does look Mayan, doesn't it? My father wrote dozens of papers comparing the iconography. You've probably read them all—Arturo Montes?"

"You're his son?" she asked in surprise.

"Yeah," Samta said, a little sourly. She looked at him more closely, wondering at the sourness. Arturo Montes had founded an entire school of glyph interpretation and had named all the primary Ophiuchi sites; his decades of scholarship had become the foundation of Glyphs at the Targethi sites. "Archaeology comes with the blood," Samta answered with a shrug. "We still have relatives back in Yucatan, living the ancient life in the jungle, as much as the Maya manage these days." His slender fingers caressed the stone a moment more before he withdrew them determinedly.

"You love the glyphs."

Samta looked around a moment, a faint smile on his lips. "I love this place, but not because it's Maya. It's not—it's Targethi. And that is something very special." He turned back to her, his dark eyes intent. "I've always wanted to meet you, Medoret, our one living alien. Not that I mean to make you feel odd at that," he said hastily. "I don't—and not that I just see you as a nonperson, you know . . ."

"I do tend to become an icon myself." Her fingers traced another curve.

"You can be both—just like me and the other token types on this project. I got into computers when I was a kid and spent the next couple of years talking microcircuits and databoards and nothing else—it just baffled my father, and we never did work that out. And out here, some academic types think Maya and computers are an odd fit—to his credit, Dr. Mueller isn't one of them. The others think I should still be wearing quetzal feathers and standing around looking picturesque." He grimaced, then shrugged away the irritation. "We get our own acclaim. They really *do* think we must know something they don't."

"How I know the feeling." She ducked her head shyly. "Thank you for bringing me out here, Samta."

"Sure. Of course. Listen, Hillary can bounce her way around, like she will—be sure to go along for the ride, it's great fun—but some of us understand more than you think. And a lot of us don't approve of the way that they've kept you hidden away like some kind of hothouse flower. You must have been very lonely."

She smiled up at him. "Sometimes."

"Well, not anymore—grad students don't have much pull, but Dr. McGill does, even with the captain. There have been big arguments among the Powers about Dr. Sieyes's decision, and I think she'll back us up. So perk up—this won't be your only escape."

"I like an optimist."

"Yeah, naive, I admit, but what the hell. Listen, we don't have much time out here—let's not press our luck and give Dr. McGill *too* much to defend—but before we go back, let's catch Hillary and go over to the plaza. The arch stone is famous, but the temple glyphs—well, you know all about that."

He called to Hillary and they tramped through the darkness down another path through the warm moist air. Medoret sniffed appreciatively, smelling the cool moist earth, the multiple scents of the vegetation, the occasional aroma of orchids overhead. Though she had visited the arboretums on Ariadan and knew the smells of such a profusion of living things, a cultured garden wasn't the same as a real forest. After the Targethi disappeared, the surrounding tropical forest had grown inward, covering stone, breaking pavement with their roots, remaking the land. She looked around at the tree branches overhead, looking for the movement of animals, then asked Hillary.

"Most of the animals here stay out in the hinterland," Hillary replied, sounding regretful. "Probably too much activity here; we've been too long making noise and bulldozing where we pleased. The site preservation here hasn't been very good." Hillary clucked her tongue in disapproval. "This strip of forest is the only jungle they left on site—everything else was cleared. They *could* have been more careful."

"You can't study a site without digging," Samta commented. "Nor land a spaceship on the tops of trees."

"I admit that, but preserving a site means just that—*preserving*," Hillary said passionately. "The ecosphere is the most fragile component of a site, and it's so easy to destroy it. We have the techniques and sensors now to be more careful; we don't have to dig pits all over. BioSurvey hasn't seen a jaguar here for years." She sighed and caressed a nearby leaf, then touched a cascade of tiny blossoms that gleamed dully in the darkness. "All of it's so beautiful—not just the stone and metal, but this, too. Why can't we respect it all?"

"It's better at Tikal, Hill," Samta said. "You'll see."

"I hope so."

Samta swatted suddenly at his face. "Ouch! Damn, it bit me." He inspected his hand, then wiped it gingerly on his tunic. "Sorry, Hillary," he added as his bug murder earned himself a reproving scowl from the young British woman. "Well, not all of the animals stay away—the bugs are still here."

"Bugs aren't easily dislodged," Hillary said, arching her eyebrow. Samta pretended to fend off her glare, and Hillary laughed, then looked over her shoulder at Medoret. "They've done some comparison studies between Targethi rain forest and the forest reserves on Earth: the proportions are about the same. If the bugs ever knew their business better, they'd take over in no time." She snapped her finger at a bush and set off a rustling as a minute shadowy form darted deeper into the bushes. "Stink bug. Watch out for them—they're an improvement over the Earth variety."

They emerged from the forest barrier into a wide space of paved stone fronting the site's temple pyramid. The Survey had burned and slashed the forest that had half concealed them, with new incursions by creepers and grass kept firmly under control. The square had a disheveled look of crumbling stone and occasional tufts of vegetation, but much of the original magnificence still remained: the Targethi had built massively in stair-stepped stone, decorating every vertical surface with their swirling glyphs of strange design. On the far edge of the square stood the row of tall columnar figures, mute Gods that watched the city decay by centimeters, oblivious to the human visitors.

"The Gods," Samta murmured, pointing. In the shadows the Vision Serpent seemed to stir under starlight, its eyes gleaming. Medoret looked away uncomfortably; her dreams came too close in this warm and humid night. She contented herself with just looking from the edge of the square, letting her eyes roam freely from pavement to temple to the geometric horizon of the small residential city, blocky shadows beyond the temple. A breeze blew steadily against her back, bringing its many scents of lush forest—and in the far distance, a faint chiming. She turned abruptly in that direction.

"What is it?" Hillary asked, noticing her swift movement.

"I hear a chiming."

"Chiming? From where?"

Medoret pointed beyond the south face of the temple.

"There's nothing down there that chimes," Hillary said, confused. Her companions looked at each other, and Medoret abruptly relaxed and turned to them with a smile. She did not want either to think her odd. She smiled more broadly at her own irony. Well, more odd than usual. She laughed aloud, confusing them all the more.

"I'm sorry. This is delightful." She waved her arm at the temple square. "I know all the glyphs so well—and I know it would take hours to look at them properly 'in the flesh,' so to speak. Maybe we can come out again tomorrow."

"No 'maybe' about it," Hillary said stoutly. "All we have to do is sneak you back again—assuming Bjorn didn't get caught."

Samta shrugged. "Sorry about Bjorn's attitude, Medoret, but he's a conservative type who worries about. . . ." he dropped his voice dramatically into a whisper, ". . . breaking the rules." He made a face of mock terror, and she giggled. "Come on."

They took another route back to *Narenjo*, skirting the north edge of the pyramid and plunging back into a brief fringe of forest. At the edge of the ship clearing, hidden by forest shadow, Samta calmly inspected the largely deserted scene.

"I don't see any outraged academics, do you, Hill?" he commented.

"I knew we'd pull this off." Hillary turned to grin at Medoret, then bounded forward to the airlock ladder and vanished inside the ship.

Medoret met Samta's eyes. "Thank you," she told him, then hesitated and plunged onward. "I saw you at the ship dock," she said hurriedly. "I wanted to talk to you then." She flushed. "I'm glad we had the chance after all."

"You're welcome, Medoret."

"I—well, I suppose we should go in."

As they walked to the ladder, she tried to think of something else to say, discarded a half-dozen possibilities, and so said nothing at all, like a stick. But Samta didn't seem to mind. With ceremony he conducted her back to her stateroom, waved blithefully at the corridor camera, then swept her hand to his lips for a brief kiss.

"Lady Rainbow," he murmured, and she gasped and yanked her hand away.

"What?" She stared at him, eyes wide. "What did you say?"

He looked startled in his own turn, and then flushed a deeper brown in obvious chagrin. "I'm sorry, really. I was trying to be too cute. I know that you like Maya myths and—oh, hell." He sighed. "I'm sorry. I didn't mean to startle you."

"It's just that—" She stopped, unable to continue. Should she explain how a Jaguar Sun danced with her in an imaginary glade? Show how alien she really was? She was suddenly aware of her different hands, her pale hair, her difference in nearly everything from him. She tried to smile, guessing it looked more pained than reassuring. "It's all right, Samta."

"I *am* sorry. Maybe later you can tell me what I did wrong, exactly." He glanced aside distractedly as they heard voices around the corridor turn. "I'll see you tomorrow, okay?"

"Okay. Good night." He hurried away.

Medoret turned and stepped into her room; as the door swished closed, she belatedly noticed that the ceiling light was off. She was sure she had left it on. She reached for the switch, and brushed against another hand, sensing him an instant later in the gloom. The light snapped on.

Sieyes looked at her with contempt. "Enjoy your little jaunt?"

Medoret stared back at him bleakly.

"I gave specific orders," Sieyes continued when she said nothing. "You are expected to obey."

Medoret turned away from him and walked to her bed and sat down, then studied her hands in her lap. She had learned many forms of denial over the years. Now the posture fitted the slow beat of despair that caught at her breath. I'll never get free, she thought.

"Do you hear me?"

She raised her head and looked at him, and felt a flush of defiance wash through her body. I am the Jaguar Sun, she thought. What would the Jaguar do? The dramatic, as befitting a Heroic Twin.

"What would happen, Dr. Sieyes," she said, "if I didn't keep to your regimen of sanity? What if I had shaking fits, gales of laughter, bloodied head-beating on the wall? I've often thought of turning autistic again; how long do you think you'd last before they replaced you? After all, I'm Earth's celebrated alien child—how long would your precious alienist career last if I went crazy?" She smiled at him, showing her teeth.

"You aren't crazy," he threatened.

"Nice to hear that, especially from you." She stood up and pulled herself to her full height, lifting her chin. "What if I killed myself? That's a thought." She saw the sudden flash of fear in his face and smiled grimly. "A few papers on cause and theory, and then you're just another Project psychiatrist, psychoanalyzing the other dead aliens like everybody else—if you even stay on Ariadan. What if I did kill myself? Personally, I think it a better choice more and more."

"This is nonsense." He turned angrily toward the door.

"Let me out!" she cried after him. "Let me out, or you will see what I can do."

He whirled and glared at her. "Stop it!"

"Among my people," she told him savagely, "all I need is to stop—and all the worlds stop with me." She raised her hands in ceremony, a gesture she had seen her mother use in her dreams; it strengthened her now. "I claim the True Dreaming; I lay the pattern of the future. This is no idle threat, Doctor. Believe it."

Dr. Sieyes snorted and crashed out of the doorway; the door hissed shut behind him, entombing her in the glare of the ceiling light. She lifted her head and faced the light squarely, then padded across the floor and snapped off the switch. The warm reds of the room enveloped her, scented by the tang of the ship's scents, the dust tickle of the air currents that slid slowly around her room from vent to vent. She moved around the room, slipping gracefully through her spider dance, and knew Sieyes believed her threat—and would not dare to tempt her into it. To risk all required a certain courage, and Sieyes did not have it.

Do I have the courage? she wondered, stretching her arms outward in the graceful pattern of a creature worlds away. Suicide is not a test I'd care to try, personally. She smiled and stopped her dance, letting her arms fall loosely to her sides.

It wouldn't have worked before, she realized; there wasn't enough of a crisis. But now, through Hillary and Samta, the crux gave the opportunity. She felt grateful to her new friends for their daring, knowing full well how academic punishments could descend on them both for defying the Powers. With a flutter of her hands, she included them within the scope of her threat to Sieyes, if he felt tempted to retaliate in another direction.

She danced across the room, her feet beating a gentle rhythm on the carpet. Perhaps she would tell Samta about the Jaguar Sun; perhaps he would understand even that. The hope swept her clean and she spun in place, dancing gracefully in the imagined shimmer of Lady Rainbow's robes. We rise, she thought; yes, it is much like that.

Chapter Five _____

The next morning, Medoret left her room and looked for
Ian in his cabin, but he had already left. She ambled down
the corridor, then went to breakfast unaccosted. Bjorn sat at
a corner table of the half-empty dining room, absently eating from a plate of food as he read the vid-pack propped in
front of him. She walked up to him and took a chair across
the table.

"Good morning."

Bjorn looked up, half choked on his mouthful of food,
and looked hastily around. "Uh ..."

"What are you reading?" She motioned at the vid-pack.
"Uh ..."

"Calm down, Bjorn. Nobody's in trouble."

"So you say." He glared at her. "I thought you were confined to your room."

"Not anymore," she said airily. "You object?"

He muttered something and glanced around the dining
room, seeing who might see them, then picked up his fork
and pointedly resumed his eating.

"Must be an interesting book," she said, not letting up on
him. Her choosing might not always be wise, but eventually
there ought to be an average.

He put down the fork again. "Is there a point to this?"

"Consider me an irritant." She grinned. "Which I am.
Where's Hillary and Samta?"

"They'll be along. Listen, I'm busy. Can you sit somewhere else?"

Medoret stared at him, knowing too well that humans rarely offered such rudeness to each other. *I'm always reminded,* she thought, *that I get different rules.*

"Afraid of the taint?" she asked.

She saw his flush of anger, a startling color in his blonde complexion, then the quick control as he carefully laid down his fork. As he opened his mouth, she got to her feet, not wanting to hear it. "See you around, Bjorn," she said, and stalked off, right out of the dining room and into the corridor. She wasn't hungry, anyway.

The corridor had its own smaller busyness as two and three people walked past, heading in opposite directions. Two gave her nods, one even a smile; she dragged together a smile in return, then chose to go left, away from her quarters, following the two who carried a box of data-faxes, their faces turned to each other as they talked about Bronson's theory of site analysis. They didn't notice her following, and at the next turning, she left them and headed toward the exterior port. *Narenjo*'s stop at 70 Oph would be short, Ian had said; this next hour might be her last chance to see the temple square again.

"Where are you going?" a watch officer asked as she walked toward the port.

She halted. "Outside?"

He hesitated. "Well, make it quick. We're lifting off in a couple of hours."

"Oh. Uh . . . thanks."

"Don't get lost," he called after her.

She tightened her lips. "I won't."

As she emerged onto the ship ladder, the orange light of 70 Ophiuchi enveloped her, striking at her eyes a moment and bathing her skin with the warmth of early morning. She stopped a moment on the ladder platform, listening to the forest's hum, then clattered down the steps, plunging back

onto the forest path at the edge of the ship glade. She
thought of going to the temple square to see the glyphs, but
her feet took her past the square and into the trees south of
the clearing. She found another path, less distinct than the
well-traveled path from ship to temple square, and followed
its windings contentedly. Her boots made a pleasant thud-
ding on the hard-packed dirt; fronds brushed her clothing in
the narrower spaces. She stopped to look at a vividly purple
orchid perched precariously at the end of a branch, then
walked onward, alert to every sound, her senses expanding.

In the distance she heard the chiming of the previous
night, and headed toward it. The delicate sound reverberated along her nerves, entrancing, calling. With a surge of
anticipation, she stepped into the frostflower glade.

There were fewer blooms than the garden she remembered from Cebalrai; only a few hundred that filled the narrow clearing, brushing up against the dark boles of the
surrounding trees. Through a gap in the trees, she saw another glade beyond, the frostflowers flowing through the
gap like a shimmering stream. They bobbed in the slight
breeze that eddied downward from the treetops, moving in
a mesmerizing pattern of white and palest gray, the reflected sun casting a greenish tinge on each bloom from the
dark forest on every side. She stepped forward tentatively,
brushing the first group of flowers with her leg, and they
responded instantly to her touch, their song a complexity of
delicate sound.

I am here among you, she thought, and closed her eyes
with a sudden longing, an ache that coursed through her
body, undefined but so familiar. I remember you, she told
them. I am here.

She stood transfixed, touched again and again by the
flowers at her feet as they bobbed in the breeze, hearing the
answering harmonics of sound that swept outward to other
flowers deeper in the glade, then sweeping back in response, an ebb and flow as entrancing as dancing light on

moving water. For hours she had watched the little stream in the rock garden back home, attracted by the cool mist of water, the delicate sound. Here lay the source of the entrancement, an older memory she never quite caught in her dreams.

I am here. She opened her eyes and watched the light move among the flowers, a rippling gleam as the muted sunlight caught the whiteness of a broad petal, the flash of moisture on a delicate blade or stem. How beautiful you are.

She stepped forward, evoking yet another ripple of response, then moved slowly into the midst of the glade, the frostflower sound rising to great crescendos all around her, soothing her senses, banishing all cares, removing the sting of human rejection. She bent and gently moved aside several blooms to make a narrow seat on the ground, then sank to her knees, surrounded by a living carpet of flowers. She swayed with their song, eyes closed, every sense tantalized and soothed. Minutes passed slowly, drawing her deeper and deeper into the flowers' dream-song. How beautiful, she thought vaguely. How beautiful.

"Medoret?"

She startled at the sound of the voice and turned sluggishly, still half-caught in the trance of the frostflowers. Hillary stood at the edge of the flowered glade, hands on her hips, her expression puzzled and disturbed. She looked at Medoret, then at the frostflowers. Medoret was suddenly aware of herself and how she looked, swaying among the flowers, and the spell broke in that mortified instant.

"What are you doing?" Hillary asked perplexedly, her voice jangling on the air.

Medoret sat back on her heels and opened her mouth to answer, then foolishly shut it. She covered her eyes with with her hand, sick with this sudden exposure, ashamed of her odd behavior. She heard Hillary move forward into the glade, the frostflower sound fractured and abrupt, cut short as Hillary trod several flowers into the ground, breaking their stems.

"Stop! You're hurting them!" Medoret cried, raising an urgent hand to ward her off. Hillary halted in alarm, her eyes fixed on Medoret's face.

"Hurting whom?" she asked slowly, then looked uneasily from side to side.

"The flowers."

Hillary's eyes widened.

"Oh, hell," Medoret muttered in embarrassment. She wrapped her arms around herself and stared at the delicate curls of grass by her knees, the bobbing stems of the frostflowers just within her peripheral vision, their chiming muted now—and wary. "Please back out of the glade, carefully."

"Only if you come with me, friend."

"Yes." Medoret rose awkwardly to her feet and walked toward her; the frostflowers brushed her legs with a delicate touch, but the spell was broken. She sensed a hush fall over the glade, a ripple of silence that spread across the carpet of blooms into the wider glade behind her. As she reached Hillary, she looked up and met the other's confused eyes, then looked away quickly.

"Are we about to leave?" Medoret asked.

"In an hour."

Medoret walked past Hillary, and the other woman turned to follow her gingerly. "I wondered where you were."

"Thank you."

As they reached the trees, Hillary caught at her sleeve. "What's wrong, Medoret? Did I say something wrong? You look so . . . defeated."

Medoret turned back to face her. "You aren't offended?"

"Offended? By what?"

"By my . . . strangeness."

Hillary smiled ruefully. "Well, communing with flowers

is something I understand, but you seemed rather far away—and with these?" Hillary toed one of the broken blooms. "They aren't even pretty."

"They're beautiful."

"They're oily and stinky," Hillary said, tossing her chin. "As much as I love any flower—"

"They are not!"

Hillary pulled back and stared at her a moment, then looked back at the glade with its thousand blooms. "They aren't?" she asked doubtfully.

Medoret sighed. "I'm so tired of being different. To me they are beautiful. Can't you see just a little of it?"

Hillary pursed her lips and studied the frostflowers. "Well . . ."

"You can't," Medoret finished for her.

Hillary looked at her askance, then broke into a laugh, "No, I can't—but I'll take your word for it. Actually, I'm glad: every flower should be beautiful and I've worried most seriously about these, the nasty oily things. There— now who's strange?"

Medoret hesitated, not following. "Strange?"

"Worrying about the which-all of Flower Truth. And there's nothing wrong with being different, friend. Take *my* word on that, just on faith. Okay?"

"You aren't . . ."

"Offended? I find that question very poignant about what it's like for you among us; I'll do my damnedest to avoid the rule." She held out her hand determinedly. "Shake on it."

"You *are* strange, Hillary," Medoret said with a smile and took the proffered hand. They shook ceremoniously.

"A nice strange—so are you. Come on, we'd better hurry, or the ship'll leave without us. Not that I'd mind *that* much—there's lots to see here—but it's not worth the long-winded trouble. How they *do* carry on." She flashed a grin and pulled Medoret into the forest path. "Race you back."

Medoret caught her sleeve, stopping Hillary before she bounced away. "You aren't in trouble about yesterday?"

"What're they going to do? Make us walk back to Ariadan?" The bright grin flashed again. "Besides, what was the harm? Right?"

"I hear a bit too much protest there." Medoret smiled at her friend.

Hillary sighed and posed dramatically, hand struck across her forehead as she pretended to swoon. "Actually, it was a beast, don't you know. All that talking and endless talking. Do you ever get the feeling they think we're still children?" She dropped her hand, grinned, then looked back at the frostflower glade. "There were thousands of those flowers here when we first came here—carpets of them. BioSurvey took samples but didn't bother to conserve them, there were so many. After that, the rest got lost in the site destruction when they cleared the jungle off the square. But, of course! Dr. Douglas found you in a garden—of these? These flowers are at Tikal, too?"

"Yes."

"A Targethi import! But I don't remember them on the lists." She stepped back and picked up one of the broken frostflowers, then looked at it more closely, her expression intent. She sighed and held it away gingerly. "I'm sorry, chum, but they still smell."

"And chime."

"Chime?" Hillary tossed the flower aside and wiped her hand on her trousers. Medoret made an aborted movement to catch it, then grimaced as its fall sent a fractured harmonic rippling through the glade. Hillary saw her gesture and the frown, and her full attention focused suddenly on Medoret, not the flowers or jungle or getting back soon. Medoret put her hands in her pockets and stared back. A slow smile spread across Hillary's pretty face.

"Thousands," Hillary murmured, and bent to retrieve the broken flower. "And they do chime?" With great ceremony, she tucked the flower behind Medoret's ear and stepped back to look. "A picture, indeed. You carry that—and don't lose it!"

"You *are* strange, Hillary," Medoret said.

"Comes from the alien company I keep—and relish the more we go on. And we *are* going to be late! Come on!"

As they reached the temple square, Samta nearly barreled into them. "Did you find—?" he started. "Well, obviously. Where'd you go, Medoret?"

"Exploring." She smiled at him.

"Good." He looked distractedly at the flower over her ear, then blinked. "The ship horn just blew a few minutes ago. We *will* be late if you don't pick up your feet." He set off at a trot, and the two women hurried after him. "When the Powers had their meeting," he called back over his shoulder, "they released the chains a little, but it's best not to push—not if you want to see Cebalrai."

"Which I do."

"So do we all." He slowed down to a walk and looked back at them. "Hillary's been there before, haven't you, Hill? Sucking up to site chiefs on Oxford sabbatical has its benefits."

"I do *not* suck up, sir," Hillary declared. "I charm. Be nice."

"As long as it gets you the grant, anything is practical. Old Mueller's too paranoid to be charmed."

Hillary tossed her head and gave him a smile. "And playing pranks last season on Mrs. Temsor really helped, Samta."

"I was young," Samta waved his hand airily.

"Mrs. Temsor remembers everything—and *never* forgives."

"Don't I know that." Samta swung around and walked backward to face them. "Hey, Medoret, now that you're loose, come to the liftoff dinner."

"I'll be there." Medoret set her jaw determinedly.

"That's the spirit," he said approvingly, and winked at her. He reached out and grabbed her hand. "There's the horn again. Come on!" He pulled her after him into a run and the three broke into the ship clearing, running fast for the ship ladder. They pounded up the treads and burst through the airlock, thoroughly startling the man at the watch podium. He scowled at Samta fiercely, then noticed Medoret behind him.

"*There* you are. Both Dr. Douglas and Dr. Sieyes are looking for you."

"I don't doubt that," Medoret said sourly.

"Come again?" the man asked.

She shrugged. "Never mind. See you later, Samta, Hillary."

She smiled at her two friends and ran up the stairs to the corridor above, then slipped into her stateroom. The ship siren hooted again over the loudspeaker, followed by the final announcement of imminent liftoff. Carefully she laid her frostflower on her desk, then arranged herself in her bunk and strapped down, her heart pounding with excitement.

Again the ship trembled and a giant's hand pressed her against the bunk mattress. *We rise!* She smiled with fierce pleasure, her blood coursing quickly, every sense coming alive. *Oh, we rise.* She closed her eyes and sighed, and felt a faint echo of the frostflowers' song in the roaring, alike and yet not alike, two natures bound into one.

Like Targethi glyphs with multiple meanings no one can define, she thought. I am a glyph, she thought, her good humor returning. Now what would Dr. Sieyes think of that delusion?

She was still lying comfortably on her bunk when her door-chime pinged ten minutes later.

"Come in."

The door swished open, revealing Ian's tall body in the doorframe. He stepped in, smiling, completely unaware of half that was happening to her now. "Hello, chick. How are things going?"

"Oh, up and down," she said.

"Very funny," he growled. "Ship goes down, then up—right?"

"About that."

He stomped over to her bunk and bent to kiss her cheek, then drew a lingering hand over her hair. She smiled up at him, drawing comfort from his presence, then caught his hand and laid it against her cheek.

"I'm sorry I shouted at you," Ian said. "You had every reason to be upset."

She shrugged, dismissing it all with a smile. "I shouted, too. It was a shouting moment."

"Which you solved by gallivanting off—" he began, then stopped as she raised an eyebrow. They eyed each other for a long moment.

"I'm sorry, Ian," she said, though she regretted only one or two recent things out of the many, and guessed he knew that. "Do I do make trouble for you?"

"Oh, nothing horrible. I just wish I had more authority, but I've been out of Survey too long—don't have the connections or the research papers to back up my weightiness with Captain Stein. He's a little too impressed by academic laurels."

"Meaning Sieyes is still working on him?"

"Conrad's limited, too—all his papers have related to you, not to Targethi research. But I expected Ruth to have more influence. After all, she's Glyphs director and Bigshot-to-Be. It was a narrow vote for a modified release—and can be taken away."

Medoret stood up and started to pace. "Then why bring me along at all? What do they want to do? Just keep me cooped up? I'm a scholar, too—of a sort. I've got my research, my studies under you, I've—"

Ian grimaced. "I tried, Medoret. . . ."

"Goddamn it! It's not your fault, Ian! Why make it your personal failure? I don't think that—I never have."

He turned away uncomfortably. "Still, I feel I ought to . . ."

"You don't fail me," she said earnestly. "You just don't. I wish you'd stop thinking that."

He looked at her unhappily, quite unconvinced. "I'll try to do what I can."

Her shoulders sagged; in his way, Ian was as stubborn as Sieyes. "I appreciate it," she said, defeated.

He gave her another quick kiss and smile. "Have to go now, back into the fray. I'll see you later."

"Yes, Ian."

She sat down on her bunk and shivered.

I don't understand; I don't understand anything.

She rubbed her hands slowly over her face, then let them drop into her lap. I wondered what kind of guards they would raise to keep me: why bring me along at all if they still insist on their gilded cage? Why *had* the Project Committee agreed to it? Somehow she mistrusted, as wild a thought as that might be, in the Committee's unalloyed benevolence.

Does Ian know? she wondered. She doubted it, if the Committee's reasons did sort into the declared and the real; Ian wasn't good at hiding things from her and knew it, and so rarely tried, a fact known to the Committee.

She lay back on her mattress and swung her feet idly, considering. So how do I play this game to win? For it is a game—always. Do I make more trouble? Do I seek my allies? Do I play passive-dependent to lull them into overconfidence, then burst for freedom when the time appears? Do we all pretend I fit in anywhere in their world?

Even so, she thought, I would like to fit somewhere.

At dinner that evening, Medoret tried to forget her confusions and, for a time, to be human. She sat with Samta and Hillary, a little too aware of the covert glances from nearby tables to be fully comfortable. Bjorn and an older man whose name she didn't catch sat at the grad table, too; both chose to talk to each other and ignore Medoret's presence. Hillary gave them a disgusted look, rolled her eyes at Medoret, and then plunged into an animated discussion with Samta, drawing Medoret deftly into the conversation whenever she wanted support. Hillary obviously did not like to lose an argument; listening to her and Samta, Medoret guessed she won about half with the young metallurgist. Tonight they returned to an apparently never-settled subject. Medoret listened, bemused, as the two discussed the pros and cons of biology versus metallurgy, both arguing their own discipline as the "real" key to the Targethi.

"Ah, hell," Samta concluded. "Everybody knows it's the glyphs." He pointed at Medoret accusingly. "But there she sits, shoveling food into her face and not claiming a word."

"Don't have to," Medoret mumbled as she chewed. "It's obvious." She waved her spoon. "All the answers are in the glyphs—trust me."

Hillary snorted. "Only *nobody* knows what the glyphs say."

"That *is* the rub," Medoret agreed placidly, and pointed at Samta's nearly empty plate. "Do you want that sweet roll?"

"Nope." Medoret transferred the roll to her own plate. "Do you think we'll ever decipher the glyphs?" Samta asked.

Medoret shrugged. "We deciphered the Maya glyphs—eventually. On Tikal we could really use some readable computer disks—and that's Metals, right?"

"Right." He turned to Hillary. "See? I told you all along."

"She said it was the glyphs."

"It sure ain't plants," Samta said smugly. Hillary tried to push him off his chair; he swayed, but kept his seat.

At the head table, Captain Stein rose and tapped his water glass with his fork, then waited impatiently as the murmured conversations in the room quieted. "Your attention, please," he said gruffly, then looked from face to face near him. Samta seated himself more firmly in his chair and grimaced at Hillary; as she opened her mouth, he shushed her, pointing urgently at Stein. Hillary rolled her eyes and resumed eating.

"As you know," Captain Stein said, "tomorrow we land at Tikal. Site Chief Layard has asked for an opportunity to tell the new members of the Tikal team about our objectives this season. Doctor Layard?"

An older man seated next to the captain, tanned and blonde and tall, rose to his feet and nodded benignly. Medoret had met the Tikal Site Chief once at one of the university parties; he seemed an intelligent man, less impressed than most academics by his own importance. She saw expressions change around the room like ripples in a pond, most of them approving.

Dr. Layard raised his hands, and the last murmur of table conversation stopped. "Welcome, people. I see a few from the 70 Oph team who now have joined the right army by defecting to us." He smiled wryly, inviting all into his small joke. "Dr. Freeman, your help with the Urban Map aerial surveys will be most appreciated." He nodded at a brown-haired man at the second table, then smiled more widely at the woman seated beside Freeman. "Ivana Tirova, your assistance with BioSurvey will be most welcome. I always enjoy seeing the reunion of old school colleagues, and I'm pleased that Olivia finally convinced you to leave your ivory tower at Pemsk." The Ukranian professor nodded sedately, and Medoret tried to crane her neck unobtrusively to see more of her face.

"Someday I'll be a bigshot, too," Samta grumbled, "and get my own perks of after-dinner accolades. Why doesn't he get on with it?" Hillary shushed him.

Dr. Layard turned to Ian at a nearby table. "And, Dr. Douglas, welcome. As you all know, the Committee has yielded to Dr. McGill's requests and sent Medoret with us, finally releasing Dr. Douglas from his exile. It's been too long, Ian, and I know you're eager to return to the field." Medoret looked down at her plate, feeling a slow wash of humiliation. As always, Dr. Layard was oblivious, meaning well; they always meant well. She looked up and Samta caught her glance, then gave her a wry smile.

"It never stops, does it?" he asked in a low voice.

"What?" Hillary asked. Bjorn gave them all a glare and motioned imperatively at the head of the room.

"But now, I'm sure," Dr. Layard continued, "you all want to hear about the progress made at Tikal last season. Urban Map has nearly completed their initial site-survey analysis, and we've identified all the main structures and much of the outlying support structures in four of the seven outlands. As you know, Tikal is several times larger than the outpost on Caracol, and we believe that it may have functioned as a provincial capital. The administrative complex is much larger and more complicated, suggesting additional governmental functions, and the glyph pattern seems to suggest more ceremonial functions, too. Urban Map's initial conclusions and data are available in the ship computers, and we'll supplement with the new work performed while *Narenjo* was on circuit. Dr. Beauchamp's team has made great strides in the last three years, and I know he'll welcome the four extra team personnel we're bringing on this trip."

Dr. Layard took a sip of water from his glass, then hooked his thumb in his belt, assured and confident. Medoret watched him closely, trying to gauge the reaction of the others, but all seemed attentive. He had a good presence, she decided judiciously, a good leadership—and felt ashamed when she immediately compared him to Ian. Ian's speeches were not polished and tended to drone. She craned her head and saw Ian at the table across the room, still eating as he listened, Dr. McGill smiling pleasantly at his side.

"The Project Committee has asked BioSurvey to begin a colony study—" Dr. Layard paused as a murmured protest swept the room. He raised his hands to still it. "Nothing has been decided about immigration, either at 70 Oph or Cebalrai. Even if both are opened to colonization by Tau Ceti, which needs the space most, I have received assurances from Earth itself that both Targethi sites will be preserved as a restricted site."

"Come on, Ed," Dr. Freeman protested. "We've heard that before. Tau Ceti's demands are just another version of the bulldozers. How can we police a site several kilometers square? We'll have colonists carving their initials in every rock."

"As I said," Layard continued, "nothing has been decided."

"And I don't believe their assurances, either," Freeman said angrily. "We got our 'special preserve' for Egypt, and it didn't stop the smog from eating away stone by stone. You simply can't bring industrialization next to a delicate archaeological site, even if we put up twenty-foot fences all around the city."

"I'm sure the debate will continue," Layard said, unperturbed. "And while we debate, immigration will be delayed. I'm sure that many here can contribute the useful words." He looked pointedly at Freeman, who quirked his mouth.

"Yeah, I'm great at waving my arms," the younger man said.

"Put some devotion into it, Bob, and we might get five more years. It'll count. In the meantime, the Tikal BioSurvey team has finished their initial survey of the surrounding ecosphere. They've discovered forty new species of insect, several small carnivores, and over a hundred new plant-forms."

"Now to sort out what's native and what's Targethi," Dr. Ruth called out.

"Keep that on the low burner, Ruth," Layard said amicably. "You'll have plenty of time to argue with Sten when you get to Tikal."

"I think it's obvious that not everything can be native," Dr. Ruth said. "Roger has mush for brains." Several in the gathering laughed, including Hillary.

"And, finally, Glyphs and Metals. Dr. Mueller continues to make progress on his analysis of the Targethi computers, and I think Dr. McGill may actually have the first key to the Xachilan Pyramid triumph sequence. At least our computer is satisfied with the logic; we'll see if the approach can decipher other sequences. Helping her, as I mentioned, will be Medoret Douglas, who has joined us on this survey." He looked straight at Medoret and nearly every eye in the room swiveled toward her. Medoret had a sudden urge to ooze out of her chair and hide under the table, but she managed a tight smile and nod, knowing that she probably looked arrogant as she did so. "Medoret will join the Glyphs team as Dr. McGill's second assistant, and I'm sure will be very helpful in advancing our understanding of the glyphs."

He meant to be kind, this time more deftly, but Medoret had grown too familiar with certain wary expressions on human faces. Across the room, Dr. Sieyes looked at her coldly, his displeasure written in every line of his face. She saw him jerk slightly, then don an engaging grin as he turned to the woman seated beside him and began talking to her animatedly. Medoret looked down at her slender hands and felt the old despair well up again. Layard moved smoothly on to another topic.

"Nothing quite like getting put on stage, right?" Samta asked in a low voice.

She smiled at him, surprised at his empathy. "You're so right."

"Well, *I* don't care if you're the greatest theoretical thing since sesame bread. Layard's okay, Medoret. Don't get upset."

"Do you always figure people out like this?"

"Comes from being Maya," he said obscurely, then grinned at her and saluted with his water glass. "We like mysteries, being still a mystery ourselves. And you're a mystery, too. Maybe at Tikal you can work on both puzzles."

"And how would you suggest I do that?"

"Oh, I don't know. But anything's possible."

She smiled at him again, liking him even more. "Thank you, Samta, for understanding."

"You're most graciously welcome."

"Understanding what?" Hillary asked, turning around.

"Gotta stay tuned in to get the news, Hill." Hillary gave him a disgusted look and pointedly turned back toward the front table. Samta chuckled. "Hillary's okay, Medoret. Someday, say fifty years from now, her springs might wear down, but until then what you've seen is what you get."

"I hope your diodes corrode," Hillary muttered, having heard every word.

"Never. I check into the repair shop too much just to polish my smile." He demonstrated, his white teeth brilliant against his copper-colored skin. Hillary snorted rudely, and Samta's smile widened. "See, Medoret? You just keep her off balance all the time; she keeps to her place just fine."

That time she did push Samta off his chair, and he caught himself hastily on the table. Eyes swiveled at the nearby tables, but neither seemed to mind. To not mind the eyes, Medoret mused: could I learn that?

"Trying to join my crowd of one?" she hazarded as Samta righted himself and sat down again, robed in his bronzed dignity.

"Why not?" Samta said. "I've tried my side of the universe; got some room on yours?"

"*Whatever* are you talking about?" Bjorn drawled unpleasantly.

"Nothing you'd understand," Samta shot at him. "You know, Bjorn, someday the universe might surprise you and mark you a null-digit on those maps of yours." Bjorn glared, then turned his shoulder to Samta.

Medoret looked from one face to the other, bewildered, knowing that somehow she had caused this. She always watched so carefully, but she tended to get behind in keeping up with the shifts the humans practiced. Samta winked at her. "Don't worry, Medoret. Once we get to Tikal, everybody'll have more than enough distractions, even you. After all, you're going to solve the glyphs, right?"

"Of course."

"And I'll solve metals, and Hillary will write the definitive text on Tikal vegetation, and Bjorn can watch our dust." He raised his glass. "To Tikal!"

"To Tikal!" Hillary echoed.

Medoret raised her own glass and copied the salute, then caught Dr. Sieyes's frozen stare, a twin to Mrs. Temsor's poisonous look at Samta from another table. Mrs. Temsor whispered to her cold-faced chief, and a few moments later Samta was summoned away to their table. Medoret sighed and looked down at her plate. *I wish I knew what the rules were,* she thought tiredly—or, rather, *which rules were mine. I don't seem to fit in, no matter how Hillary and Samta try.* Suddenly she wished she were safe in her cabin, hidden in the half darkness, a stupid wish after all the effort she'd taken to get out of it.

Stupid. I feel upways and downways and inside out. What did this academic self-congratulation have to do with her? Who cares if the humans drag in their colonists and destroy Tikal with fumes like their bulldozers destroyed the frostflowers at Caracol? Who cares, who cares? Across the room, she saw Ian nod and smile to somebody, then bend to listen attentively to Dr. Ruth, at ease in his element, the ebb and flow of the profession he fit so well. He looked ten years younger as he waved his fork enthusiastically, then pointed jocularly to make some point. Not once did he look at her, too intent on his professional comrades and the life he loved best. She watched him laugh, then scowl slightly, then tip his head roguishly, gestures that had been hers on Ariadan.

Jealousy doesn't become you, Medoret, she told herself. Grow up.

The murmur of conversation flowed around her, smothering her, would erase her if it could. She took her supplements vial from her pocket and swallowed the pills, completing her own meal, then waited for the right moment to excuse herself. Finally, she just nodded generally and got up and left, her feet dragging.

Probably it was a party, she thought. It looked like a dinner, but really it was a party. That explains it, I'm sure.

Chapter Six _____

She wandered the corridors a while, then stepped into the observation suite on an upper level. She sat down in one of the comfortable chairs before the wide view-window, watching *Narenjo*'s approach to Cebalrai and its Targethi world, a world the humans had named Yucatan. Like 70 Ophiuchi, Cebalrai was an orange star, smaller than Earth's own primary, older, with fewer planets and a narrower ecosphere. Yucatan orbited as second planet in Cebalrai's array of six worlds, a green, lush world much like Earth had once imagined a pristine Venus. The greens were subtly different than Earth-shade, shadowed into purple, with broad bluish sands near the long coastlines of a largely oceanic world. All her referents were Earth, of course—she did not remember any other homeworld.

Is this my home? she wondered, leaning closer to the view-glass. She knew it was not: the dreams of the Black Ship always implied a homeworld elsewhere. This was a Targethi world, and almost certainly not a first home to the Targethi. Tikal and its seven outlying homesteads occupied a broad peninsula on a northern continent; planetary survey had detected no other signs of colonization, though the Targethi sites had existed for centuries before their decline. They had come, chosen their territories on one small continent, then contented themselves with a thousand square miles of a single planet. Why?

The Project Team had completed its vegetation surveys

and identified certain plants—probably Targethi, by their proportion to the native life—that carried a different set of proteins. The random propagation of proteins during any biosphere's initial evolution was an established fact proven at Tau Ceti and Alpha Centauri; the Project had found the same truth here, only bifold, part native, part from elsewhere. When the Targethi had colonized this world, they had brought some plants and animals with them, foodstuffs against the chance that local life could not support them. Even if they had found compatibility, they would need dietary supplements, just as she had needed them among the humans at Ariadan. The Targethi glyphs had several friezes of their food hunts, sometimes hunting local animals, sometimes hunting the large feline predator the Targethi had imported and humans called "jaguars."

Much could be guessed about the Targethi, but little was truly certain. The humans little appreciated the alien reality that might lie unseen beneath their assumptions.

She stood up and walked to the window, then pressed her hand against the glass and spread her long taloned fingers. She examined her hand closely, seeing the faint tracing of muscles and the subtle pulse of her blood beneath the smooth skin, the grace of the long fingers, the smooth ovoid arc of her slender talons. An alien hand: nearly all her life she had been alien, one alone, set apart by a heredity she could not change. In only one place she knew, the Black Ship, would she not be alien and apart. Had they waited for her? Her logical mind told her they had not; only her dreams promised otherwise—and the humans did not believe in dreams. Should she believe?

Mother . . . she called in her mind, as if wishing could cross the gulf.

Had she been too long among humans, so that even the Black Ship would be alien? If so, she had no place her own, no people, a singleton among the many. The possibility frightened her; her kind sought the bindings, could not exist without them. She sensed this was so—yet she had survived alone, among the humans. How could this be?

In ancient Maya myth, none walked alone—even the Jaguar Night Sun had a twin brother who aided him in his battles against the Nine of Xibalba, a mysterious "God K" who bore flaking patches of death on his body and a smoking mirror on his forehead. In Maya understanding, together they were Venus, the morning and evening star, appearing separately in the sky at different seasons but bound together in myth and the essence of the heavens. In Targethi sculpture, only the Gods of the Avenue appeared alone, reminiscent of other glyphs but still distinct, as if the Targethi had enshrined them. She breathed on the glass, shading it into a smoky mirror of her own breath.

"Pretty, isn't it?" Samta's voice said behind her.

She gasped softly and drew back from the view-glass.

"I didn't mean to startle you, Medoret."

She turned and smiled. "It's all right."

He tipped his head to the left and looked at her, bemused. "And could I possibly guess what you were thinking? I doubt it." He hitched up one of the upholstered chairs and lounged on the chair arm, swinging his foot. "You didn't like the jokes at the dinner, did you?"

She turned back to the world drifting on the void. "It was all right."

"No, it wasn't all right if it made you uncomfortable. I'm sorry. We were trying to include you in having fun; all we did was make fools of ourselves, I guess. And Dr. Layard didn't help. *Will* you look at me?" She turned around obediently. "And not that way—only if you want to."

She sighed. "I don't understand what you want of me."

In the shadows of the observation room, she could see his face quite distinctly, though shadowed differently by the warmth of his skin in her infrared vision. She noted again the strong cast of the Yucatan highlands in the bone structure of his face, the clean high planes of his cheeks, the large dark eyes fringed by darker lashes, the strong mobile mouth of Earth's Amerindian peoples. He was a handsome man by Earth standards, she thought, though some human opinions of beauty sometimes tracked by bias, not by appearance. Did Hillary find him attractive? She seemed to.

His dark eyes regarded her soberly, though a quizzical smile tugged at his attractive mouth. "Is it that hard to understand us, Medoret?" he asked. "Is everything always disjointed?"

"How did you *know* that?" she asked with asperity.

His teeth flashed in a smile. "Hillary may enjoy the celebrity of being your friend; I hope you can forgive her that. It's not unkindly meant—it's just Hillary. I'm more interested in looking through your eyes, if it will help." He studied her face, sober again. "You seem very lonely."

"Is that so surprising?"

"No. Personally, I think the Project should have left you at Cebalrai. It would have been kinder." He looked beyond her at the greenish disk that grew visibly larger with every hour. "I've sometimes wondered what it would be like to be cut off from my own people, much less all humankind. I don't have a genuine analogue, of course, though we Maya endure our own ostracism. We're an insular people, even in this modern age—we're not really interested that others understand us, nor do we find much outside interest, the kind that counts. Either they confuse us with our bloodyminded ancestors, or they think we're quaint." He twisted his mouth and shrugged. "Imagine trying to explain to a gringo archaeologist that the Otherworld is only one step through a doorway, and that every day has its own god, for good or evil. I imagine the looks we get rather resemble some looks you've had, right?"

"I've tried to fit in. You wouldn't believe how I've tried."

"Why? Who says you have to fit in?"

"Ian. Dr. Sieyes. Every glance, every word." She turned

away from him to the view-window. "I still don't understand what you want of me, Samta." She paused. "I'd like to know, but I'm not understanding."

She heard the brush of fabric on fabric as he stood up, and then caught his distinctive scents as he joined her at the view-window. He looked out the view-window for a moment, the greenish glow illuminating his face, then turned to her.

"My father was a practicing Maya shaman," he said, "though that's not a fact widely published in his biographies, of course. But he believed in the Maya vision—the Twins and the Underworld and the Moon Goddess—not entirely, but enough to experiment with the old rituals. I believe in the binding, too—not enough to slash myself with flint knives like he and the others did, but enough to believe truly in the ecstasy of their Vision Serpent. The Otherworld is only a step away, if you have eyes to see it." He smiled at her. "I have considered very seriously, Medoret, that you aren't what you seem at all. You aren't an alien from out there—" He waved at the view of stars beyond the window. "Maybe you're Ix-chel, the Lady Rainbow." The comment was tentative, and she saw him watching her closely for her reaction.

She smiled and raised an eyebrow. "Am I?"

"Why not? Or perhaps the Celestial Bird, or even the First Mother, that dread Lady Beastie. I haven't quite decided which; I need more data. Am I confusing you even more?"

She shook her head vigorously. "Believe me, Samta, I'm an alien from out there." She waved at the stars beyond the view-window.

"Good: I'm glad you're certain, even if you're not quite certain what you're certain about."

"You catch the ambiguity quite well."

"Well, we share that. In one way, I'm my father's son, a shaman's apprentice and a descendant of Maya kings; in another, I'm your typical rational-minded archaeologist grad student, who knows such foolishness can't possibly be. Yet I'm both, without any paradox." He looked at her earnestly, willing her to understand.

"But why Metals?" she asked. "Why not glyphs like your father?"

He shrugged. "Father's shadow, I guess. I wanted at least a little proof that I got the posting on my own, not because my dad's who he is. Maybe the connection helped get me the Metals grant last season, but this second season I earned by myself and not, whatever Hillary says, by toadying to Dr. Mueller. I don't do that." His face flushed slightly with remembered irritation.

"If Hillary knows saying that annoys you," Medoret asked curiously, "why does she say it?"

"I'm not sure she knows. Hillary isn't always alert to things like that."

"But I know—it's obvious. Why doesn't she?"

He smiled. "Something human is 'obvious' to you?"

"Well, I can see that much—and the fact you know far too much about what I'm thinking for no rational reason."

"It's part of my personal fascination." His grin broadened.

"Hmmph." She leaned back against the window-ledge and crossed her arms comfortably, then scowled reprovingly. "What do you do for Mr. Mueller?"

"Help him with testing and analysis, sort of his right hand."

"And Mrs. Temsor?"

"Hates my guts. Until I showed up, Dr. Mueller ate grad students for breakfast and she was queen." He grimaced expressively. "But I'd rather be in Metals, really. Computers are computers, not artistic pretending 'it's really us' in glyphs. As you'll find out, I have a lot of private opinions, and one of them was the idiocy of pasting Maya labels all over Caracol. Uh, sorry." He looked to see if he'd offended her.

"I'm neutral."

"Well, good."

She felt amused when he actually looked relieved, guessing that Samta's easy charm hid a few uncertainties of his own. She felt flattered by his close attention, his surprising empathy; she'd never met anyone quite like him, and wondered if his understanding came in part from his own background, as it likely did. He'd said as much. "Do you ever dream of your Maya kings?" she asked tentatively.

"Often: I was raised in their constant memory. Do you dream of your Ship?"

"And of other things."

"Targethi gods?"

She stamped her foot. "How did you *know* that?" she demanded.

He grinned. "Just a good guess. After all, you and I grew up surrounded by their glyphs and temples, the holos, the studies, the single-minded fascination of every adult around us. Had I told you I grew up partly on Caracol?"

"I didn't know that."

"My father was one of the early pioneers on the Project. He was one of the Committee that made the decision to take you back to Ariadan. For our grace, there was a short debate about it—but Earth would not give up its only alien child. I'm sorry, Medoret—I'm sorry we did that to you. Another private opinion." He glanced at the view-window. "Do you think your ship will still be waiting for you?"

"I don't know," she whispered, allowing the yearning to show in her face, not minding if he saw it there.

"In the old times," Samta said quietly, "a person had a place in the world, one set there just for him by the gods. A king was a king, a farmer a farmer—but all understood that the Otherworld was open to all. The Maya never divided heaven like the Aztecs did, with only warriors given the blessing of their afterlife as a hummingbird or butterfly. All could share the Otherworld; all entered it, king and priest and commoner. Perhaps that's even true for a moon goddess and a Maya shaman. It's only one step." He gestured grandly at the view-window.

She smiled. "One step, literally, into another world?"

"If you like. I would like it very much, but only if Ixchel would deign." He linked his fingers at his waist and bowed gravely.

She looked again at the lush world before them. "All I've heard all my life is how I'm different. I have different dreams, different senses." She raised her hand and placed it on the view-glass. He quietly set his own hand beside it. "I can't eat your foods, not entirely. I can't catch all the subleties of what you say to each other. It's like I'm walled behind glass, the glass of this hand, these eyes and ears, catching some but not all."

"I've heard the Otherworld is like that, strange and familiar at the same time."

"I think most people would think this a very bizarre conversation, Samta."

"Do you?"

"No, not really." She smiled up at him, and he seemed to be pleased.

"Neither do I. At the least, the Otherworld will keep us from assuming our typical assumptions—yours about glass walls, mine in assuming you should be human."

She turned back to the window, where the ancient Targethi world hung suspended against a velvet blackness. "I appreciate that. Thank you."

"Any time."

He moved closer and stood just behind her, watching with her; she breathed in his scent and felt the faint warmth of his own body like a small glow against her skin. She knew the humans lacked such senses, not even knowing what they missed; she regretted that for Samta, then smiled to herself at the irony. All her life among the humans she had found herself called lesser than the humans—at least by their perception, confused and mixed as it was—unaware that there could be another point of view on certain things.

"Why the smile?" Samta asked, watching her reflection in the window. She saw his own vague image beside her in the glass and mentally added the Maya warrior's feathered headdress that would suit him so well.

"Nothing. Or maybe I'll tell you later."

"Ah, mysteries. Well, what else can I expect from a moon goddess?" She heard him sigh dramatically. Then he chuckled at himself, and it sounded a little like the Jaguar's laughter when he danced with Lady Rainbow.

That night, as the ship descended into its final orbit and slipped through the upper atmosphere, the air molecules screaming against its hull, she dreamt of the Hunt. Targethi voices chanted their cry as the aliens paced excitedly along a jungle trail in single file, each foot pounding a common rhythm. In a nearby glade, frostflowers sang to the night sky, calling to their brothers on another world far away in space, bending their fairy colonnades in a graceful dance that celebrated life and their Masters. Beneath a forest canopy on a high branch, a Targethi jaguar snarled its hatred at the hunters and leapt easily to another branch, its claws digging into the bark. With a flash of its short tail, it vanished into the screen of leaves.

We are the Masters, the Targethi chanted. *We are the Rulers of the Worlds.* At the front of their column, the priest raised his claws in ecstacy and slashed his knife across the folds of flesh at his throat, then whirled madly to begin the Dance, scattering his blood in an arced spray. *We are the Conquerors,* the others chanted behind him, beginning their own ecstatic dance as they followed, the rhythm building as clawed feet pounded on the jungle path. Faster and faster they drummed, filling the jungle with their fierce sound, then exploded forward.

The hunters leapt into the trees, running deftly from branch to branch with a flashing swiftness, outpacing their startled prey. The jaguar fled before them, snarling, then fought ferociously when the hunters caught him and slashed at him with a dozen sharp blades.

Medoret cried out as the knives plunged into her body. Furiously, she snapped and slashed as they fell on her, bearing her downward in a long fall to the ground. She struggled, stunned, as clawed hands seized her. With a cry of triumph, the Targethi priest plunged his knife into her eye, penetrating to the brain in the killing stroke. Medoret spun away into the darkness, plunging into a deep pool of pain and fear.

I begin Time, a voice echoed from the darkness, whirling into the feast. In the nearer distance, Targethi voices lifted in celebration as they lifted their burden and stamped along the forest path, the jaguar's body sagging loosely on its poles.

Mother. . . . Medoret mourned in her terror, her furry head flopping loosely as she swayed. *Where are you?*

An age later, the Targethi mounted the stone stairs of the Star Temple, clawed feet stamping a measured rhythm. Her limp body fell loosely upon the altar, her blood seeping onto rugged stone; her dead eyes stared sightlessly upward at the Targethi priest who towered over her. As his knife plunged, she screamed silently, then screamed again as the priest cracked her furred skull and fed her brain to the Gods.

No . . .

She awoke abruptly in her bed, her heart pounding raggedly. A breath of cool air sighed from the ventilator, joining the gentle currents of the enclosed space of her room. She blinked and turned her head, examining the dim shapes of desk and wall, the faint outline of the doorway, all suffused with the warm reddish glow of her night vision. Which was the reality, her dreams or this human place? Her heart beat its ragged rhythm, filling her ears with its sound. To escape such terrors, to forget all dreams, it would be so easy to succumb, to give up the hope, to abandon herself . . . to become human.

Once the Jaguar Sun had died as the Underworld's bloody sacrifice, torn apart with flint knives to please the Lords' lust. For a time, the Lords had triumphed, but the Jaguar and his twin had risen from death to confront them, taking their victory into new defeats, confounding the Lords, seizing ownership of the worlds. The Maya had believed that, celebrating the Twins as resplendent spirit, the source of all that they were given by life.

Would it be easy? She had fought it so very long, torn apart by her wishes to fit somewhere and the steady message of her dreams, tormented dreams that sang of apartness and loss and difference. Where is my victory if I give up dreams? Where is my victory if I surrender?

She turned on her side and closed her eyes, her head throbbing in a sharp ache from her ears to her nose that squeezed like the implements applied by the Targethi priest. She ran her fingertips over her face, rubbing slowly, reluctant to reenter any dreams, then threw off the bedcover and padded into the small bathroom. Frowning at her image in the mirror, she touched the thermometer plate and watched the reading climb upward.

Fever.

Not high, but enough to explain her throbbing head—and perhaps her dream. She grimaced, thinking of the grim self-immolation in its Hunt and sacrifice—she'd rather choose to be the victorious priest, not the jaguar victim. She'd had enough times of feeling the victim. Why such a dream now?

She opened the sink cabinet and took down the vial of her fever drug, then swallowed an extra tablet for the help.

The Ariadan biochemists had never found the virus that cycled in her fevers; their palliative had been devised by frantic trial-and-error based on the toxins in her body, with enough quick response to believe the chosen drug had effect. And, gradually, through the drug therapy, her cyclical fevers had waned in frequency and severity from nearly lethal illness to mild inconvenience, her version of the colds that plagued Ian from time to time. To Earth illnesses she seemed totally immune, protected by her alien origins.

She glared at the faint mottled flush on her face and skin, knowing Sieyes and Ian might see it, too—if, of course, she allowed them to notice. That was a thought. Crowds might have some use beyond bodies for a party. She grinned wolfishly at the mirror, practicing her totally excellent health, her blithefully good spirits, a determined mind over a willing body, then winced as pain lanced through her temples. She suppressed a groan.

Of all the times for her fever to show up again, this was the worst.

I won't have this, she thought and fluttered her fingers at herself in the mirror. I just won't. She padded back into the other room and stretched out on her bed, determined to be well by morning.

But why had she dreamed of the jaguar's death? She shivered from a wash of dread and her illness, unable to sort the feelings, then turned on her side and wished herself into more pleasant dreams.

Jaguar Sun, will you dance with me?

Lady Rainbow, I will, he answered, striding toward her across the verdant grass, all wounds healed, vibrantly alive, and swept her into his strong arms, to whirl her away into the brilliant sunlight that glanced everywhere into the glade.

I love you, my Jaguar, she told him.

Lady, we are legend. And they laughed together as they danced, delighting in each other's company.

* * *

By morning, her fever had partially subsided, but not enough to suit her. *Narenjo* had set down smoothly on Yucatan in the early morning, and the clankings and voices in the corridor outside her room grew steadily louder, signaling the crisis. She scrutinized her face in the mirror, frowning at the betraying flush, then paced her room for ideas. Her glance fell upon the wilting frostflower still on her desk and she impulsively tucked it behind her ear, copying Hillary's inspiration on Caracol. Given her friend's reaction to the frostflowers, a noxious flower as alien's decoration might attract much more attention than her flushed face—even being odd might have its utility.

She inspected the result in the mirror, then decided dodging would still be good backup. She had no intention of being stuck in a sickroom with Sieyes clucking I-told-you-so to Ian as Tikal lay all around her. She swallowed two more fever pills, willing them to have extra strength this day, then packed her carryall quickly, took a quick glance around for anything missed, and escaped out of the room before Ian or Dr. Sieyes thought to collect her.

She joined the thin stream of people in the corridor, exiting with them from the ship. *Narenjo* had landed in a broad clearing on the northern edge of Tikal, near a long sea bluff overlooking the flash of an alien sea. Medoret paused on the upper landing of the ship ladder, her face turned toward the beach where Cebalrai shone brightly in the morning sky, touching the wavetops with flashes of silver and brass. She sniffed delightedly at its scents, catching whiffs of salt and sun-warmed weed, a faint odor of rotting flesh, the metallic scent of hot sand, then descended the ladder hastily when someone jostled her impatiently from behind. At the ladder base, she stepped to the side and watched the flash of waves in the broad bay of Tikal's harbor for a few moments longer, then turned to study the tall towers of Tikal itself, a curving facade that stretched nearly five kilometers to the west and south.

She had seen panorama pictures of Tikal's seaward face many times, but the foreshortened view of a video could not catch the true dimensions of the alien city, stone after stone, building after building, until perspective reduced the long seaward wall to a final white rectangle far down the beach. With proper satellite lenses, Tikal was easily discernible from orbit, a unique squarish landform on the edge of a minor peninsula on the lesser continent. The strong breeze brought a scent of Tikal's stone dust and hot metal, dead smells among such blooming life of the jungle and sea, and the orange sun beat down upon her face, warming her skin, bathing all in a dazzling glow. She took a deep breath, entranced by the warmth and smells.

As the ship's personnel left the ship, others from the city came forward and met them. The humans gathered in groups and talked together in front of the ship ladder, many joking and waving their hands excitedly, though a few promptly stalked off toward Tikal, too impatient to wait for a ground car. Medoret edged backward into the ladder's shadow as Dr. Sieyes clomped down the stairs, then slipped beneath the ladder itself as he paused and looked around in every direction, obviously looking for her.

She watched Dr. Ruth come up and talk to Sieyes briefly, scarcely a few meters away from her pool of shadow, then pull him into another group to a tall man she vaguely recognized from a vid-tape bio picture, someone important in the Tikal excavations. Dr. Sieyes feigned a pained politeness, obviously distracted from his usual social charm, then excused himself and climbed hurriedly back into the ship. An instant later, Medoret slipped away from the ladder and trailed a party of scientists walking toward Tikal, insinuating herself into the back of the party, camouflaged by her similar ship-dress. Occasionally looking human had its advantages, she told herself, risking a glance back at the ship.

And flexibility is a mark of intelligence, she reminded

herself. She plucked her flower from behind her ear and put it in her pocket.

She looked around for Samta and Hillary, but didn't see either, though she did see Bjorn's tall form stalking along with a heavy case in his hand. Her own party ambled forward, busy talking in equal parts about themselves and ongoing projects, catching up the news—she was quite unnoticed as she followed them. Odd, she thought, how easily I become invisible. Or so she felt—and wondered how much her feelings touched on reality. I am the Vision Serpent, she thought defiantly, wiggling her fingers slightly; few saw the Serpent in their waking lives in these modern days of science and measurement.

As they walked onto a stone plaza between the first of the nearby Tikal buildings, Medoret detoured to look at a carved stone pillar, then hurried to catch up, only to fall behind again as she glimpsed the freize that soared up a tall building wall halfway down a cross-street. With a quick glance at the oblivious scientists, she veered off again. She tramped happily down the street awash in the mellow sunshine, surrounded by dust and sea smells and a faint whiff of vegetation. Impulsively, she skip-hopped on one foot, then spun in place, remembering a child's dance in such warmth and openness years before, so unlike the confines of the homeship and the limits of Ariadan.

I am here, she thought simply, here in Tikal at last, and felt the lingering dread of her dreams swept away by her excitement. Walking into Tikal can be perilous, she thought, smiling, and danced a few more steps. I feel well, she told herself, choosing to ignore her headache. I feel extraordinarily well. She stopped in front of the freize and planted her feet comfortably, then let her eyes move upward from panel to panel. There was Ix-chel, the Moon Goddess, and her row of dancers in contorted positions; there the Jaguar Sun, his face a ferocious mask. Human names—what had

the Targethi called their gods? She sighed with great satisfaction, celebrating this moment, this day.

On a high panel, Targethi sacrificed a jaguar to their
gods. I am the Jaguar reborn, she told the carved figures,
and all the worlds belong to me. She paced onward, looking up at the glyphs.

And there a Witz Monster with gaping mouth opened a
doorway into the Underworld, an array of star-shapes and
curving bird-forms on either side. Beyond his fearsome portal, the World Tree raised slender branches, sheltering jaguar and beetle-man alike. She touched the lowest carving,
tracing the line of the figure's brow. From their extensive
presence in the glyphs, the beetle-like figures were likely
the Targethi themselves, their actual size masked by lack of
perspective, sometimes small, sometimes overtowering the
other figures in the panel. Had the Targethi left this pretty
world, en masse in some great exodus, leaving all behind?
No one knew.

Row by row, the glyphs told a story no one could now
understand—yet the meaning was there, it was thought, if
only a key might be found. The humans had tried to understand these glyphs by naming their symbols from their own
Maya patterns, refusing to accept an alien gulf that might
defeat forever all attempts—and perhaps missing the key by
assuming aliens had anything in common at all with each
other.

Now, looking at the real stone, she saw differences, not
similarity. She frowned, staring at the glyphs. The Celestial
Tree did not look much like a tree, she decided, though it
bent its whorls vaguely upward; the glyph could be as easily interpreted as a geometric abstraction, or perhaps a styl-
ized river, or perhaps ... Even the Jaguar's face in this
frieze could be some other shape than feline, and, fairly
viewed, Ix-chel did not look very familiar at all. She
glanced back at the World Tree, thinking Ix-chel looked
more like the Tree than a moon goddess, then saw similar

blending in the Witz Monster, enough on a second look to doubt the glyph altogether.

The Targethi glyphs are mutable, she thought, startled, not fixed forms at all. The literature implied quite the otherwise, citing clear forms and patterns, not variants. She walked onward, looking upward at the carvings that marched steadily down the building face. In one panel she saw forms not identified anywhere in the literature she knew, one a curving five-lobed flower shape repeated a dozen times, elsewhere a flash of sea waves, a single staring eye. She pulled her frost-flower from her pocket and compared the shape to the flower in the glyph, but neither matched—the Targethi had chosen some other jungle flower for their message, whatever it was. In another panel, the familiar pyramid shape of a Targethi temple emitted broad rays to a pattern of stars: she had never seen that glyph published, either. Yet the literature implied, no, *stated* definite conventions and a limited array of glyphs, a repetition of pattern as extensive as the symbols in Maya Yucatan.

Maya glyphs did vary from artist to artist, but kept to roughly conventional forms, using the same symbols of kingship and identity from city to city. A Witz Monster always looked like a Witz Monster, not a blend of Jaguar and Underworld Lord. God K with his flaming mirror appeared again and again in the glyphs, always distinctive by his posture and conventions. The Maya kings had used their monumental temples to celebrate their victories and prove their right to kingship to a largely illiterate populace, based on a common set of myths familiar to all. Each temple complex told an elaborate story from those myths, every frieze linked by theme and symbol to others, showing the kingly authority in mythic symbol that linked the Maya to the Otherworld.

But with mutable symbols, the Targethi might have meant their glyphs for a completely different purpose. She scowled upward at yet another variant of Ix-chel. The glyphs might not be glyphs at all, not mythic language or symbol like that used by the Maya and certain others of Earth's ancient peoples, but something else altogether. But what? And nobody, it appeared, was even asking that question.

Samta's right, she thought. It *was* idiocy to see the Maya everywhere on Caracol, and she sensed past dispute between Samta and his father on that point. Arturo Montes had published much on the theory, she remembered, based on the limited glyphs at Caracol; Ruth McGill, his successor after he retired, had done even more at Tikal, drawing connections, proving the theory with glyph after glyph. But not with these glyphs, she thought, stopping at another panel. If the glyphs *were* the key to the Targethi puzzle, the Project had devised its own answers—most likely wrong answers—before even framing the questions. How could that be?

The sun beat down into the street, warming stone and metal. She sniffed appreciatively, recognizing the scent. At Caracol the jungle had overwhelmed the city, stretching its tendrils into every crevice, beginning the slow reclaiming and extinguishment of the Targethi buildings. Here the Targethi had built too widely for an easy conquest, even after centuries of abandonment. In some parts of the outskirts, where too many service robots had fallen into disrepair, the jungle might penetrate, but in the central city, the ceaseless vigilance of the robots and the strength of Targethi stone had preserved what was. She wandered onward down the frieze wall, letting her feet take her where they would, and found herself in a side avenue between other tall buildings, all intricately carved with glyphs, small and large from tiny detail to half a wall wide, all carrying a message no one could read. She watched a service robot roll single-mindedly across the street, then vanish into a shadowed doorway, remembering another time, a lost time she chose to find again, if she could.

Are you here, my Ship? she thought, looking around the deserted street. Somewhere hidden in the jungle, in the sea, in some hollowed building? How do I find you? She looked up at the bright sky, then turned around in place, seeing nothing but carved stone. Nothing. At a far corner up ahead, a service robot turned into the street and rolled toward her, single-mindedly following its worn track, tending deserted stone.

She looked back toward the plaza, tempted to explore further, but knew there would be questions if she dallied too long. Dr. Sieyes would be determined in seeking her— the last thing she wanted was a hue and cry for a "lost" Medoret, the Project's only living alien. For scientists fascinated by the Targethi, she wasn't the right kind of alien exactly, but Sieyes would raise the cry despite that.

You come seeking answers and only find more questions? Easy to choose what we will, easy to ignore the questions that come after. Perhaps the Tikal Project had caught itself in a similar ambiguity. Did humans, too, wonder who they were? They seemed so certain of many things, bent on their publications and theory, on academic politics and self-vaunting, as avid for the publicity she had usually hated. Did they wonder, too?

The robot rolled toward her, its faded lights blinking with certitude. She turned her back on it, irritated with its mechanical precision that never questioned, never needed more than the Targethi had given to it. Reluctantly, with several dilatory pauses to look at more glyphs, she retraced her steps and rejoined the last of *Narenjo*'s people walking into the city.

Chapter Seven _____

The Project had established its headquarters about a half kilometer from the seawall. In a small plaza, several ground vehicles burdened with equipment stood in a row; on the far side by a small squarish building, she recognized other bulky machinery, mostly sensors and calibrators used by Urban Map. The Project had appropriated a longish building on the adjoining side of the plaza, building an array of offices, meeting rooms, and a computer room on the first floor, with workrooms and dormitories above. She had seen this building in the Ariadan literature, too, though the articles were more self-celebration of the Project than discussion of the glyphs that covered headquarters inside and out. Medoret moved aside as a ground car whirled into the square, bringing the first of the supplies brought by *Narenjo* fo the Tikal Project's storerooms.

She followed the people entering the main Project building, then hesitated inside the door, looking around for Dr. Ruth. Instead, she found Dr. Sieyes, who gestured at her abruptly from across the room, then gestured again more impatiently. Her feet dragged as she walked toward him, hoping for rescue.

Targethi priest, indeed. Surely a ruler of worlds could switch a few roles now and then, just for fun, and give up the victim. Where was justice?

"Where have you been?" Dr. Sieyes barked, his voice loud enough to carry throughout the room. Several people stopped their talking and turned automatically toward the sound, an attention Medoret did not welcome. He intended to humiliate her, she saw, now at the beginning so no one would doubt, proving his control. She clenched her fists and stood in front of him, brave enough in her dread to glare at him. If she defied him, she only confirmed Sieyes's declarations; if she submitted, she set a precedent for all the days to come. The dilemma caught her into dumbness.

"I asked you a question, young woman," Dr. Sieyes said sarcastically, his voice still louder than necessary. Then he bent toward her solicitously, affecting concern. "Are you all right, Medoret? Is the strain too much for you? You look flushed."

I have the power, she thought, and calmly extracted her frostflower from her pocket and tucked it behind her ear. "Not at all, Dr. Sieyes," she said lightly. "Isn't this flower pretty?" Sieyes stared at the crumpled flower on her ear, disconcerted from any closer examination of her face. She lifted her chin and smiled easily, allowing her voice to carry too loudly, just like his. "I so enjoyed walking in the sunlight. How exciting this is, to finally see Tikal! I look forward to exploring the city even more."

"Hmmph. You still look ill to me." But his comment was tentative, lacking conviction. She saw those listening nearby lose interest and turn back to their own conversations; Dr. Sieyes saw it, too. He frowned. "Perhaps your fevers . . ."

"Nonsense," Medoret said cheerfully. "I feel wonderful." Still wearing her smile, she leaned forward and dropped her voice to a murmur. "And if I find a suitable flint in this city of knives, dear doctor, I'll summon the Hunt and give you as victim, you Underworld Lord. Don't think I won't."

Sieyes sputtered, for once lost for words. Fantasy is useful, she thought, and wiggled her fingers gleefully at him. I am the Vision Serpent.

With a pleasant nod, Medoret moved off toward a broad

map of Tikal on the far wall of the foyer. She stopped in front of the map and pretended to goggle in admiration, though she'd studied it on tape for years, then dodged leisurely behind a group of people and slipped up a bank of stairs to explore the upper levels. She strolled along the corridor, nodding at people who passed her and affecting intense interest in the carvings on the corridor walls.

Lady Rainbow, the Jaguar Sun whispered into her mind. *Will you come dance with me?*

Only if you eat Dr. Sieyes, Jaguar, she answered. *His flesh is tough and dry, but I'd consider it a favor.*

I may, if you wish it, Lady. He loped away gracefully, then vanished behind a stone-carved screen of leaves, quickly gone. She hoped the Jaguar would feel hungry soon. She looked behind her cautiously, making sure that Sieyes hadn't followed, then bounded up the stairs to the third floor.

On this floor, the Project had ripped out the interior walls and rebuilt the space into a large dormitory with a comfortable common room and a neat grid of bedrooms arranged along several halls, each with a bed, desk, a bureau, and small bathroom similar to *Narenjo*'s own appointments and no doubt from the same ship-stores source. She found her assigned room in the dormitory and peeked cautiously into Ian's room next door but found it still empty. He must be still hobnobbing downstairs, she thought, and she thankfully left him to the useful distraction. She tossed her carryall on her bed, then marched into the bathroom to check her temperature. Relieved to see it much reduced, she smiled at the bathroom mirror, noting only a slight remaining flush on her face, easily explainable as a touch of sunburn—if anyone even asked.

Willpower, she thought delightedly.

She pulled her frostflower off her ear and looked at it reflectively. With all the mashing in pockets and alien displays this morning, the wilted flower had crumpled badly.

Perhaps I can find others here, she thought, dropping it into the waste chute—though she wouldn't pick them, she promised, remembering the anguished sound when Hillary had broken the blooms on Caracol. Had the humans destroyed the frostflower glades here, too? She hoped not. She stared at herself in the mirror, concentrating on wellness.

"There you are!" Ian's voice boomed, and she jumped, badly startled. She turned and saw him standing in the bathroom doorway, a wide grin on his face. "How are you doing?" he asked.

"I'm great." She smiled. "And here *you* are on Tikal, too, Dr. Douglas."

He bowed gallantly, sweeping an arm to the side with a courtier's grace, then winked at her. "They needed me eventually, it's plain to see. A few weeks' work and everything will be known."

"I've no doubt of that, O Wise One."

She saluted him with the Cricket God's solemn greeting, palms together. He cheerfully returned it, his face alight, then winked at her again. She looked at him fondly, putting away her jealousy of his recent preoccupations and wishing Ian all the joys of Tikal and the life he had missed all these years.

"Meeting downstairs," he informed her briskly. "You can unpack later. Pick up your feet, chick." And he was off, moving fast.

"I'm coming." She hurried to catch up as he strode down the corridor, then fell in step with him, stretching her legs a little to match his strides.

Now it begins, she thought—though *what* might be beginning she'd have to discover as it unrolled.

As Ian and Medoret reached the ground floor, where people still stood around talking, a tall grizzled man raised his arms and shouted for attention, then all gravitated toward a

side hallway into a meeting room. Medoret followed obediently behind Ian, happily enthralled by the bustle and excited laughter. In the wide meeting room, nearly twenty meters long and now decorated with Earth chairs and front
tables, Dr. Ruth waved from a middle row and gestured to
the chair beside her. At the same time, Medoret saw Samta
waving from the back of the room. Ian veered off and
headed toward a colleague across the room, complicating
Medoret's sudden problem. She waved back at Samta and
hesitated as Ian connected with a short squat man several
chair-rows away, then went to join Dr. Ruth. The older
woman smiled up at Medoret, her dark hair neatly coiffed
on top of her head, her trim shipsuit freshly pressed. Dr.
Ruth looked crisply ready for friendly battle with her peers,
and her many successes in that area were never affected by
her small frame and lack of kilos. Dr. Ruth had polished
her determination to an art.

"There you are, my dear. Conrad's been looking all over
for you."

"Is that new?" Medoret asked sardonically. She looked
around the room apprehensively. "He won't be sitting here,
will he?"

"Not if I can help it." Dr. Ruth pulled on her arm to seat
her on the next chair. "You don't look emotionally bereft to
me."

"Oh, Dr. Ruth, you don't know the half of it."

"I'm more insightful than I look, child." She smiled benignly. "We're at Tikal now, Medoret—and I'm not the
likes of the captain." She pointed sternly at Medoret's self.
"You are *my* graduate student on *my* Glyphs team, and I
will expect hard work, self-sacrifice, and total slavery to
my demands. Is that understood?"

"Yes, Dr. Ruth."

"Good. That's a fine start. So you sneaked away to look
at a wall, did you? Which one?"

"The frieze two streets over from the sea avenue."

"Ah—with the birds and stars at the capital panel. I like that one myself, though there are so many, what with every available surface taken; in a city ten kilometers square, that's a lot of walls. The Glyph Team is still working on the initial catalog, with some time out for first analyses of the Great Plaza friezes."

"I saw your article in the *Cebalrai Review*."

"And what did you think of it?" Dr. Ruth dimpled as Medoret hesitated in her answer. Ian did not approve of comparative analyses to Earth patterns, which Dr. Ruth openly championed, and had debated vigorously every point in the article. "Medoret, I already know what school you belong to, being indoctrinated by one Ian Douglas throughout your education. But you now belong to me and I will see to the necessary correction."

"Targethi aren't Maya," Medoret said with spirit.

"Culture is culture."

"Not in an alien context."

"Archetypes are universal to a thinking mind, whatever its form of body and cultural aims." Dr. Ruth pretended to glower, a smile tugging at her lips.

"Archetypes are unique to each race," Medoret threw back.

"Oh? What's your proof?"

"Me." Medoret grinned at her. "My archetypes focus on the Star Mother and undocumented variants of Maya gods. What do *you* dream about?"

"Hmmmph. Personally, endless lines of little beetle aliens carved on a stone wall—after a while, the images do set themselves in the subconscious. And your Star is a leading Tarot symbol, easily adapted to Jungian classical theory. You'll have to argue better than that."

Medoret waved her hand, copying Dr. Ruth's blithe gesture. "Targethi are not Maya."

"And culture is culture. Come look at the friezes with me tomorrow and I'll convince you."

"Hmmmph."

"Little skeptic." Dr. Ruth's smile broadened. "You'll do quite well, my dear. I prefer stubborn minds—and I think your perspective is a fresh insight we badly need, so I had a hidden purpose, quite selfish, I'm afraid."

"Thank you for bringing me along, Dr. Ruth."

"You're welcome. And if Dr. Sieyes plagues you, Medoret, let me know. Out here I outrank him academically, whatever his official role as alien guardian."

"Sometimes he guards me too much."

"*You* aren't what he's guarding—and I think you know that quite well." She patted Medoret's hand. "Take comfort: Star Mothers come in many guises."

Dr. Layard took his place at the front of the room and raised his hands for attention, waiting patiently for the buzz of conversation to stop. Medoret settled herself in anticipation, conscious of Dr. Ruth's warm grasp on her hand.

"Welcome, all," Layard said. "We welcome the newly arrived team members, those new to Tikal and those who aren't." He nodded genially to several senior archaeologists. "Tomorrow you can scatter back to your individual projects, but for now we'd like to brag about all the work we got done while you wined and dined on Ariadan, wasting academic energy. Once you've settled in again, we'll continue our weekly cross-discipline meetings to keep everyone up to date, and I encourage you to occasionally read the computer-link reports from the other teams. We'll get along faster by sharing data, folks. As I have said a dozen times before, this is an archaeological *team*, not a university faculty with knives out. Is that understood?" He smiled, standing easily in front of the group. "Good—let's keep it that way. So here's the Team reports. Since Dr. Mueller was one of the departees this trip, I'd like his subchief to report for Metals. Mike?"

A sandy-haired man stood up two rows behind and blinked as he looked around the room uncertainly, then glanced nervously at a glowering Dr. Mueller and tight-lipped Mrs. Temsor seated on either side of him. Dr. Mueller cleared his throat and stared straight forward, his eyebrows moving randomly. Medoret leaned forward to whisper to Dr. Ruth.

"Eyebrows?" she asked playfully. "Is there a human meaning to that message?"

"In some contexts, I'll admit archetypes can be unique. Hush, you."

The sandy-haired man cleared his throat, then grimaced oddly. "We're still tracing the computer wiring in the main-frames discovered in the Jaguar Temple. The wiring pattern is quite similar to the other mainframes discovered at the Copan and Xachilan homesteads, but the hardware in the outlying sites is more badly corroded due to the greater environmental decay. Here in Tikal, the jungle acids haven't penetrated as thoroughly into the site. Once we determine the pattern, we can begin activation of the mainframe computer with the supply of crystal disks discovered in storage." He cleared his throat again and peeked at a clipboard in his hand. "Metallurgical analyses of the components used in Targethi construction is continuing: we've found a new alloy with electrical resistance nearly as potent as our best circuit breakers, but no sign yet of superconductors, not even in sealed circuits. The Targethi may not have used superconductors."

"How can you sustain a technic civilization without them?" a voice called out. "How can you build a spaceship without superconductors?"

"So where are the spaceships?" another voice argued. "Not even Caracol had a standing ship left behind, and I'm not so sure that landing field was *their* landing field."

"So they used the ocean."

"*Not* proven."

Layard raised his hands. "Quiet, please: we're just taking reports now. Bring your ideas to the cross-team meeting,

Joe—Urban Map wants some input on transportation patterns. Let's hear from BioSurvey." He looked around the assembly and focused on a woman near the front. "Olivia?"

The woman rose gracefully and half-turned to face the audience. Medoret leaned forward to see her better, guessing this must be Olivia Falk, Hillary's chief on BioSurvey. She was a pretty woman, neatly dressed and petite in her coveralls, with her blonde hair cut very short but attractively. She spoke in a light clear voice, her British accent quite noticeable.

"We have completed the targeted survey of fauna," she said, projecting her voice easily, "with enough distribution for amplified ratios. As with the plants, the proportion of native and Targethi life-forms is about one to ten, given the time for the species to radiate into the native environment. Our dissection of the jaguar we captured last month confirms its Targethi origin: it, too, has the L24 protein not found in other local bioforms. It is beyond question that the Targethi brought the jaguar with them, and we have confirmed two bird species that share the same protein. The sea-forms are ambiguous; although two of the pseudo-fishes have unique proteins, they are not L24, but something different. A dual line of protein evolution is possible, and so their origin may be native, not importation."

"Or the Targethi brought them from a second world, a world different than the jaguar's," Ivana Tirova suggested.

Dr. Falk nodded genially at her friend. "Also a possibility. As we've discussed several times with Urban Map, this Cebalrai colony—even with seven homesteads in the hinterland—is curiously incomplete. We've dated each of the homesteads as contemporaneous with Tikal itself, yet none of the sites increased in size for all the centuries of their occupation by the Targethi, nor were any other homesteads founded. Either the Targethi rigorously maintained their population size by ritual sacrifice, as some of the glyphs suggest, or the surplus in each generation migrated back to their home world or worlds. Even so, they would have needed to resupply several of their food animals: several of the Targethi animals became extinct shortly after the Targethi themselves disappeared."

"But not the jaguar," someone commented from behind Medoret.

"Nor the parrot or hummer. All three come from the same offworld source and found enough compatability with native proteins to survive without major dietary deficiencies. For this to happen twice with the jaguar and the pseudo-fishes is rather coincidental, so I favor dual evolution as the answer to those fishes."

"Coincidence happens."

"What spaceships?" a voice demanded again. "They didn't have a spaceport."

Dr. Falk smiled. "Doctor, they indubitably had a spacesport. We have three separate lines of protein evolution, a disrupted biosphere that still reverberates from the jaguar's elimination of all other major predators, a limited and isolated sentient community that never developed beyond its foundations, and no native source for several Targethi technological materials." She spread her hands expressively. "If there's any value in our multi-team approach, we've established conclusively that the Targethi came from elsewhere. Don't you agree?"

"No, I don't agree," the man said crossly. "Where's the proof?"

She scowled in return. "All around you," she said with sweet malice.

Dr. Layard tapped the table. "Urban Map?" he asked pointedly.

The effort earned him a few isolated chuckles as Dr. Falk nodded and sat down. Medoret did not envy Dr. Layard his job of juggling all the personalities on the team—and this problem of instant and acrimonious debate apparently characterized every joint meeting. She looked around curiously,

trying to catch the expressions on the faces near her: none
were bored, but many were upset or cross, others preoccupied. Aside from Ian's academic parties, which apparently
operated by their different rules, she had never attended
such a large group of scientists; there must have been sixty
humans in the room, all smart and determined and stubborn, with Dr. Layard having to manage them all. She spotted Dr. Sieyes near the back of the room and quickly
looked away before he caught her glance.

A short and squat man, his coverall heavily wrinkled and
quite dusty, stood up in the first row and turned to the
crowd. "Well, we've finished our aerial map analysis of
Copan, the last of the homesteads, and I'm awaiting the report from Remote Sensing about the subterranean structure.
As with the others, the grid map is set in the Jaguar Face
pattern, with the homestead temple sited at the left eye. Obviously, this pattern had religious significance, since it de-
fies normal community patterns—"

"*Human* patterns, Sieg," Dr. Ruth called out, surprising
Medoret. Apparently Dr. Ruth wasn't totally set on her theories, at least not when challenged by Urban Map.

"Ruth," the Urban Map chief countered, putting on a
strained patience, "tell me the utility of a wall blocking
your principal street."

"You don't know it's a principal street. The primary
glyphs appear on the other street axis."

"You *think* they're primary glyphs."

"Basic proportions, Sieg: the jaguar appears in every
frieze and the moon goddess in nearly half. Are you claiming that Jaguar Night Sun and Ix-chel are minor glyphs?"

"I'm not claiming anything—except that a wall across
your principal street is not rational."

"And so the reason has to be religious," Ruth finished
for him, obviously continuing a longstanding argument.
"Go ahead, say it again."

"Religion is the ultimate irrational force in any culture,"

the Urban Map chief responded, grinning at her, then sent around a defiant glance as several in the audience hooted at him—or at Dr. Ruth, Medoret couldn't tell which. "Well, it *is*!"

Dr. Ruth threw up her hands dramatically. "That's what happens," she commented to the open air. "The brain goes first."

Dr. Layard beetled his brows at her reprovingly. "This is not constructive, Ruth," he said. "You obviously want the floor, so you've got it. Thanks Sieg." Urban Map threw a gesture at Ruth as he sat down, and she promptly signed back just as rudely, both smiling widely. Dr. Ruth stood up.

"We're continuing to catalog the major friezes for our symbology analysis in the computer; we haven't completed the data base yet, but we're satisfied with the program's parameters. Even with partial data, we've confirmed a high correlation between four certain glyph patterns and specific points in the jaguar-face of the city design. Sieg's wall, for instance, carries an Ix-chel danzante procession; we found a variant of the same frieze at the same city-position at Caracol, and it appears that each homestead follows the pattern with Ix-chel and her dancers at the left corner of the jaguar's mouth. Similarly, the Jaguar Hunt appears on the left side of each temple facing west, or, if you orient it to the sea, the side facing away from the sea."

"Why would the sea orientation mean anything?" someone asked.

"Well, the spaceport was at the sea."

"*Not* proven!"

"That we'll settle another day, Roger," Dr. Ruth said briskly. "The Targethi were very precise in their arrangement of these major glyphs, and this encourages us to think the entire city may bear an overall message, with submessages placed within the larger pattern, and so forth downward to minor glyphs on the door-lintels. Some symbols are undoubtedly clan markings or names of rulers: the

Wiltz Monster dominates at Narenjo, the Celestial Bird at Palenque, for instance, and all seven of the homestead symbols repeat in a frieze on each of the five Tikal temples. Here in Tikal, we see the star-and-bird capitals, a pattern we don't see elsewhere. If we can identify definitive objects or city patterns associated with specific glyph-patterns— we've eliminated single glyphs as a useful key—perhaps we can decipher our first word. With one word, we'll have the key to all the others."

"Maybe," Roger said skeptically.

If they're words at all, Medoret added silently. Surely she's noticed the glyph variants—yet she talks about patterns? She fretted, wondering how she could ask such a question without offending the older woman. Dr. Ruth was well-known for her strong opinions, for all her affable charm. What a mess, she thought: Ian might chortle about "all will be known," but opening the debate could be tricky.

Dr. Ruth waved her hand at Roger. "I'll take that 'maybe,' Roger; it's better than 'you ain't got a chance.' " She pointed at him imperiously. "You concentrate on figuring out how the Targethi got here without a spaceship. Maybe they had astral travel and just *thought* themselves here."

"Well, maybe they did," Roger argued. "You can't impose human limitations on an alien culture. Maybe teleporting is possible, if you've got control of space-time, biologically or otherwise."

"If the Targethi could think themselves anywhere, they would have reached Earth."

"Not necessarily. Earth isn't an orange-star jungle planet."

Dr. Ruth flipped her hand dismissingly. "Two examples don't yield a statistical curve. We don't *know* that the Targethi preferred orange-star jungle planets. The robot probes found three other jungle worlds in Ophiuchus that weren't colonized."

"So we're on the fringe of the colonization sphere," Roger argued. "They hadn't reached there yet."

"The Targethi occupied Tikal for nine hundred years, and Kappa Ophiuchi is only eighteen light-years away—that's more than enough time. Why aren't they there, too?"

"Because ritual requires a *thousand* years of occupation before the ceremonies of New Launching of the Brood," Roger said, waving his hand airily.

"You're out to lunch, Roger."

Roger grinned. "Good luck with your glyphs, Ruth."

"Thanks." Dr. Ruth sat down and chuckled. "Roger is subhead of Survey Support," she murmured to Medoret. "He doesn't belong to any particular team, but he likes to stir things up with weird ideas."

"Maybe they *did* teleport," Medoret said impishly, and got herself a surprised stare. "It's possible."

"Hardly, my dear," Dr. Ruth said, looking displeased.

Medoret promptly backed off: obviously the senior woman accepted chaffing from Roger but drew a line elsewhere. I'm just her grad student, Medoret reminded herself, whatever pleasure that rank brought over token alien. "Or used the sea," she said placatingly. "An ocean landing would save on all the trouble of a ship cradle for your larger ships or building ship-to-ground shuttles—right?"

"*Your* ship landed on solid ground," Dr. Ruth said contrarily, still looking displeased. Medoret felt a brief flash of despair, knowing she was stumbling somehow and at a loss to repair the lapse. Was she allowed to disagree only when the topic suited her chief?

"We're not Targethi," she said.

"Hmmm." Dr. Ruth's attention slipped away pointedly, leaving Medoret in her awkwardness. Suddenly Medoret wished she could leave and wander alone through Tikal, unencumbered by human expectations and reproofs. What did I say? she wondered, feeling her face grow hot. I never know. I don't understand.

She listened dully to more talk from the front table as Dr. Layard gave general instructions for new team members, reminded returning scientists of other rules, and told jokes that amused some and left others looking puzzled. Meanings within meanings, she thought, seeing a pattern of her own in the human complications of such a group—with me as the glyph-decipher still looking for that first word. She turned and looked for Samta, then spotted him in intense conversation with Hillary and Bjorn in the last row of chairs. Did I hurt his feelings by sitting with Dr. Ruth? she wondered, worrying about that, too. Sometimes the social rules seemed quite odd to her, and shifted across the board for no reason she ever saw.

Or did this happen to humans, too? Dr. Ruth seemed invulnerable in her own way, taking charge and jousting with her academic adversaries; Dr. Sieyes had his own invulnerability of opinion, carefully guarded by deft manipulation. Did anyone ever feel awkward? Ian did, when it involved herself, and Samta had said a few things that suggested he did sometimes, too. Maybe she wasn't that different—but how could she sort out the parts that came from Medoret's oddness as token alien? Maybe that was the confusion. She frowned and studied her pale hands in her lap. Maybe. She'd never had enough of the nonalien reactions to tell.

"Medoret?" Dr. Ruth prompted, and Medoret looked up to see the meeting was breaking up. She jumped to her feet.

"What do we do now?" she blurted.

"Well, I can settle you into the dormitory and then show you how to access our Team's computer records. How about that?" Dr. Ruth smiled warmly, then took Medoret by the elbow and guided her toward the door. They stopped twice to talk to someone, first Roger, then the dark-haired Russian woman, Ivana Tirova, Dr. Falk's friend. Each gave Medoret a courteous nod, but their attention was on Dr. Ruth. Medoret watched them talk, half listening to the words said as she focused on the expressions. Aside from deciding that each liked and respected Dr. Ruth, she gathered little else. As she followed Dr. Ruth out of the meeting room, she wondered if she'd ever figure out the rules. If there were rules.

Now that's a thought, she told herself wryly. You can really run with that.

Dr. Ruth deposited her in her dormitory room, then bustled out for a few minutes, telling Medoret to wait until she returned. Medoret took the time to unpack her carryall, arranging the Targethi statues on a narrow shelf, then scouting for a hammer in the supply room down the hall to hang her Palenque bas-relief. As she emptied her carryall of the few clothes she had packed and opened her bureau drawers, she found a sheaf of Project forms inside the top drawer. She pulled out the papers, angered as she recognized them: more physiological and psych reports, the same intrusive daily forms she had endured on Ariadan and had decided to ignore. On the top was clipped a note from someone named Jan, informing her sweetly that although Dr. Sieyes had explained her recent mental difficulties, the Project would appreciate resumption of the daily reports as soon as possible.

She slapped the papers down hard on her desk, then swept them into the waste can alongside. *Mental difficulties?* What had Sieyes said about her? She could well imagine what he'd said, knowing him, and guessed Jan's phrase was a politeness compared to the written reality. She paced the room back and forth, then retrieved the forms from the waste can and ceremoniously shredded them into the bathroom toilet. She flushed them into the drainpipe with a flourish.

Forms? she thought. I didn't see any forms.

● She felt the insistent throb of a beginning headache and looked with alarm at her face in the mirror, muttering one of Ian's vivid curses when she saw the flush of renewing fever. Glowering at her face, she swallowed two more of her fever pills, then inspected the count in her vial. Not enough; she hadn't really needed them for four years. If she asked for pills, betraying her condition, Medical would sit up and run around excitedly and then bustle her into bed; if she didn't get pills, they'd notice just as easily when she ran out of pills and her fever started cycling into its more severe symptoms. At its worst, the fever disturbed her equilibrium, making her walk more a lurch than a glide, however she tried to control her feet—by that point, however, she was usually already in bed, her temperature too high for anything but half-delirious lying around.

They'll send me back if I get that sick, she realized. The Project would never risk her health if the fever soared past a certain point, not when Ariadan had an existing laboratory staff devoted entirely to her physical welfare and sophisticated hospital equipment to cover any crisis. The Tikal team had excellent medical support, as Ian had countered to Dr. Sieyes's mock worry, but neither man had expected her fevers to be a problem, not really. Neither had she.

But I was cured, she thought in despair, and kicked the unoffending washstand. I haven't had a fever in four years. Why now? Her headache throbbed, blurring her vision—the fever was rising fast this time. The best choice was to report to Medical and let them hover, with the hope her fever subsided before they shipped her back to Ariadan. She could hope for that.

What a comfort, she thought. She sat down on her bunk, depressed, then lay down to rest, her head throbbing in mocking syncopation with her heartbeat.

When Dr. Ruth hadn't returned an hour later, Medoret allowed herself a final path of freedom before Medical's clutches and wandered downstairs. She slipped outside to the end of the small plaza, peering down the intersecting streets to see the glyphs on the walls. It would be so easy to wander outward, from wall to wall, just for the looking, but she felt wary of pushing her luck, not entirely sure of Dr. Ruth's support for her curiosity, especially if indulged while swanning around with a temperature. She lingered a while longer, looking at the glyphs both she and Dr. Ruth loved, for differing reasons, perhaps.

This is an alien place, she thought, alien to both of us. There might be answers here, Dr. Ruth, if only we can hear them, what they are, not what we want to believe.

She leaned against the corner of the building and waited expectantly in the warm sunlight, listening to the echoing sound of human voices behind her, the occasional soft whirr of machinery as a service robot circled the plaza, and, before her, a sun-drenched silence. Once she lifted her head quickly, thinking she heard the metallic song of frostflowers, but it was only a trick of the echoes in the street. She waited, not knowing what she expected—and nothing happened.

Did I expect the Black Ship to swoop from the sky? she wondered wryly. How would my mother even know I was here, after ten years gone? If she even waited for me all these years—why should she? Why not assume I was lost to her and think of the ship's greater need?

We will continue, her mother had said in Medoret's dream. *Raise ship,* she had ordered, though Bael had disputed. And where had they gone when they left her behind? Stars away?

Where are you? she cried out silently, realizing she had waited all the years for this summoning—never thinking it might not be answered, not really, not beyond an inchoate fear she had avoided. And if it's not answered, she thought, her skin prickling, I have to spend all my life among humans. She looked back at the plaza, watching Urban Map at its ground cars, a BioSurvey group talking in the front doorway, a small trickle of Ship Support people going in and out of headquarters as *Narenjo* continued disgorging its supplies. Among humans for all her life—she thought about not belonging, being strange, different.

If I tried harder, she asked herself, could I touch them, be one of them? If I gave up hoping the Ship would come to take me away? I always assumed I would not be strange there on the Black Ship: easy assumption, likely delusion. Grow up, Medoret.

She looked slowly around the plaza one more time, then fixed her eyes on the glyph of a Witz Monster on the wall nearby. Stone, nothing more, she told herself, not a doorway to the Otherworld, not a way to find the True Home. Dreams aren't real, she insisted to herself, testing the conviction, then sighed. When you can believe that, Medoret, maybe you'll fit in. She turned her back on the glyphs and trudged across the plaza, returning to the humans who busied themselves there.

Chapter Eight _____

The next few days were a blur for Medoret as she lay in the Project's infirmary, recovering slowly from her bout of fever. She had a stream of visitors throughout the day, Ian and Dr. Sieyes, Dr. Ruth, Samta and Hillary, as well as others from the Project who took time from their work to drop by. The Site Chief, Ed Layard, sat almost an hour telling her improbable stories about Dr. This and Dr. That. She felt touched by the kindness, and the unexpected solicitude more than balanced Dr. Sieyes's snide remarks. On the third day, Medical asked in Ivana Tirova for a consultation—the Russian doctor had apparently studied Medoret's bio-systems some years earlier before moving to other Cebalrai analyses—and Tirova took the time to smile at Medoret and offer some encouragement. Medoret gathered that a debate had begun immediately among the Powers when she became ill, and was evenly split about transfer home to Ariadan—in the balance, the issue stalled into wait-and-see. Medoret obeyed Medical's strictures with meticulous attention, determined to do nothing that might tip that precarious balance against her.

By the third day, her fever had turned the corner and she was allowed to wobble around her infirmary room for a while, then sit in a chair. Her head still hurt, and she hid the physical effects as best she could: in the grip of fever, her muscles didn't always respond naturally, affecting her walk, adding a slight tremor to her hands, but that, too, had begun to subside. Neurasthenic fever, they called it, and had worried in the early years about permanent nerve damage, then argued among themselves about why and wherefores and Earth analogues. The source of contagion was unknown and seemed to cycle from deep within her cell chemistry, perhaps prompted by a recurrent virus that attacked several body systems, perhaps arising from a genetic disorder, perhaps both. Her medical knowledge about human DNA and rare Earth diseases went up every time she came down with her fever—and she was heartily bored by it all. But the drugs still seemed to work, and Medical's palliative care sustained her comparative health until the fever ran its course.

That afternoon, after Medical had stuffed her back in bed again and forbade her sternly to do anything whatsoever, Hillary brought her chief, Dr. Falk, for a visit. Medoret looked up from a bored examination of her blanketed toes to see her friend smiling in the doorway, her arms cradling several stalks of frostflowers. As Hillary moved forward, followed by Dr. Falk, the flowers seemed to chime faintly, their opalescence faded to near-nothingness. Medoret stared at the broken blooms, appalled.

"Hi, there!" Hillary said brightly. "Look what I brought you!"

"You killed them!" Medoret cried in dismay, too appalled to think better of it. "You killed them! I told you not to!"

Hillary's smile crumpled in an instant, and she instinctively turned toward Dr. Falk. The older woman shook her head and looked at Medoret severely.

"Of course we picked them," she said in her clipped voice. "How else do you sample vegetation? Put the blooms on the nightstand, Hillary. Surely Medical can find a vase."

Medoret watched Hillary lay the broken flowers on the stand. Her eyes met Hillary's, which were now shiny with tears. "It's all right, Hillary," Medoret said, trying belatedly to make amends. "It's all right, really. I'm sorry." Hillary turned away.

Dr. Falk settled herself comfortably on the end of Medoret's bed and smiled, then managed to make it worse. "Hillary told me about your ecstatic trance on Caracol with these flowers. I find that fascinating. What exactly attracted you to them?"

Medoret looked over at Hillary, appalled again that the young woman had so easily forgotten her word, so easily forgotten how an alien became odd. Hillary saw the look and abruptly fled the room.

"What in heaven's name . . ." Dr. Falk said, startled by Hillary's abrupt departure, then looked back at Medoret in obvious confusion. Then she scowled disapprovingly, making her judgments, and Medoret exploded in rage.

"Get out of here!" she shouted, not caring for courtesy or rank or prudence. Dr. Falk blinked in surprise, angering Medoret all the more. Who ever gave her the right to judge anything? "I didn't ask you to sit on my bed or bring me flowers or look at me like I'm another of your weird animals. Get out!"

"My dear girl!" Dr. Falk protested.

"I'm not your girl. I'm not anybody's girl! Get out!"

Dr. Falk lurched to her feet, her face white with humiliation, and swept out of the room, her chin held high. Medoret threw back the covers and stumbled to the nightstand, then thrust the frostflowers into the wall waste chute, wincing at the responding chime from the blooms as she touched them. "I'm sorry, I'm sorry," she whispered, weeping as they shattered further in her hands. When all the blooms were gone, she collapsed slowly down the wall and hid her face against her knees.

Fool, fool. She had been so careful, so correct, so stable. They'd send her back now, lock her up forever, helpless demented alien child, and watch her relentlessly.

Why had she reacted as she had, with such rage? Driven away Hillary, insulted Dr. Falk—for what? Flowers, stupid oily flowers. She trembled violently, swept by emotions she couldn't name, didn't know in herself.

Why? What kind of creature am I?

"Medoret?" And then Hillary was there, putting her arms around Medoret's shoulders and hugging her close. "What's the matter? Why are you crying?" Medoret shuddered and leaned against Hillary weakly, then felt Hillary shift on one heel to look at someone behind them. "Samta, go get the doctor—quickly!"

"No!" Medoret cried.

"All right, he won't," Hillary murmured quickly, and tightened her grasp. "Don't worry. We won't do anything you don't want to do, Medoret." Medoret heard the door shut quickly, then a murmur of voices outside.

Medoret looked into Hillary's face, bewildered. "You don't hate me?"

"Don't be ridiculous," Hillary said, then blinked shyly. "You don't hate me?"

"No. But you shouldn't have told, Hillary."

"Don't I know *that*! But what's wrong now? Why are you crying? Did I do that?" Hillary's face contorted with honest distress, fighting her own tears. "I'm such a sod! I'm such a rotten sod! Was it that bad, what I did? I'm so sorry, Medoret."

They heard the argument rise in volume outside her door, then a decided thump. Whatever Samta was doing might not last long. Hillary pulled Medoret to her feet and guided her back to the bed, then shoved her in without patience. "Tuck your feet in. Clear that face, right now! We're chatting so friendly and nice, aren't we?"

"Drag yourself together, too," Medoret retorted. Hillary wiped her face hastily with her sleeve and tried a ragged smile. A moment later, the door opened and a nurse barreled into the room, nearly knocking Samta off his feet. He staggered and caught himself on the doorframe, then stomped in, too.

"What's going on?" the nurse demanded.

"I lost my temper," Medoret said mildly. "I'll have to apologize to Dr. Falk. I haven't been myself." The nurse looked at Hillary, then at Medoret, then whirled to face Samta and took it out on him.

"Out!" she ordered, pointing at the door.

Hillary shook her head quickly at Samta, and he planted his feet. "No," he said haughtily, then dared the nurse with an imperious Maya stare.

"The doctor will hear about this!" the nurse swore, and stomped out of the room.

There was a brief silence. "We could steal her again," Samta said to Hillary. "Hide her somewhere until all this dies down."

"Oh, sure."

"Being a friend has its pinches," he retorted, and Hillary glared at him.

"I got the point the first time, Samta."

"Bouncing all over her, that's what you did." He scowled at her.

"Knock it off, Samta!"

Medoret closed her eyes and felt exhausted. She kept them closed as everyone showed up, Sieyes to argue with Ian, Dr. Ruth to argue with Layard, and the doctor and nurse to throw the lot of them out of her room. In the evening, after she had been patted and cajoled and tucked down, Dr. Falk came to apologize stiffly for whatever she had done, an offended apology that hardly seemed an apology at all, then left. Medoret stared at the closed door, wondering how much influence the BioSurvey chief had on Project politics, then tried to measure it against Dr. Ruth's charm and bustling aplomb, an equation that defeated her. Stupid, stupid, she told herself. But it deserved a shouting. She clucked her tongue chidingly, then took some time to flex her talons comfortably, in, out, in, out, before folding her hands neatly on her stomach.

I am the Witz Monster, she informed the room and all the humans beyond. And I wonder who made Dr. Falk apologize, I do, indeed. It certainly wasn't Dr. Falk's idea. She turned on her side and tried to sleep, half convinced that she'd be shipped back to Ariadan when *Narenjo* left in two days.

She dreamed again that night of the black plain beneath a jeweled array of stars. Again, she willed it otherwise, not liking the cold wind of that icy plain, for all it cooled her fevered body, and the sky descended into a forest glade. Again she walked the forest path, naked beneath the starlight, and entered the temple clearing. She lifted her arms and a brief mist surrounded her, enclosing her in shimmering linen, and the weight of her golden headdress settled heavily upon her head. She nodded, her jeweled earrings clicking as they bobbed by her ears, a familiar sound to Lady Rainbow. She paced the glade, waiting.

But the Serpent did not come, for all Medoret's willing. "Serpent," she called out, her voice echoing through the glade. "Where are you?"

She heard a thrashing in the underbrush on the far side of the clearing, then saw the Jaguar Sun pounce into view, black-furred and ferocious in his animal form. He lifted his broad muzzle and lashed his tail as he saw her, then arched backward, lifting his front paws. His body lengthened, taking on a human shape, though he kept his fearsome mask. He growled and stalked menacingly toward her, his white fangs glinting in the starlight.

She raised her hand in greeting. He paused, then flashed his black tail and returned her greeting with little grace.

"Lady Rainbow," he growled.

"Where is the Serpent? I called for her."

The Jaguar crouched and licked his fangs nervously with a red tongue.

"What's the matter?" She took a step toward him, bewildered when he retreated from her. "Jaguar?"

"The fever grows worse, captain," he told her in a gravelly voice. "Have we traced it to the right source?" He looked away and began to pace back and forth, his tail lashing the grass.

"What?" she asked, startled. "What did you say?"

The Jaguar looked at the Temple in wild distraction. "I can't stop the nerve damage. It's gone too far."

"Jaguar," she soothed, but again he retreated from her. "Where are you?"

He turned his face to her, his pupils dilated into black pools. "We landed on a minor asteroid, a Targethi mining station. Rojar got sick first. We thought it was nothing serious, a common virus that had mutated, easily identified. It happens sometimes on long voyages, new diseases from the old we carry with us. Then Rojar miscarried in her fever, and Taret's baby was born wrong." He threw back his head, baring his fangs at the sky overhead. "It's the spores, Captain! It's the spores! The plague is still here, after all this time, and we're enough like them to catch it. Goddess! Save us! We can't go home . . ." She reached for him, and he darted frantically out of her grasp. "Send the message to the Homeworlds," he cried aloud. "Send the message. Send the message."

He screamed as a bloody gash opened in his side and he fell thrashing to the ground, snapping at invisible knives. "Send the message! She's dead, Saryen! Oh, how will I live?"

"Jaguar!" Medoret cried, and ran to him, but he thrashed away from her frantically. With a low moan, he fled from her and crashed into the underbrush, vanishing into the jungle.

"Wait! What did you see?" Medoret stopped at the edge of the clearing, panting. "What did you see?"

The Serpent's mist swirled up and surrounded her with the crystal chiming of flint, then echoed with the silence of an empty black plain, air sighing through a ventilator, a scrape of a boot, a metallic clatter. Medoret's skin prickled, and the dream rose to encompass her, taking her to another place beyond dreams, to a real place.

But I want to get up, she said in her high child's voice. *Let me up.* She found herself on a comfortable mattress and pushed irritably at the coverlet. Her mother looked down at her sternly, waiting for a willingness to obey. *Please?*

No, her mother had said, adding no excuses, no inducements, no smiles. *You're too old to be wheedled, my daughter. When the fever comes, your life lies in lying still and obeying Rojar. Be glad that you survive the cycles. Do you understand?*

Yes, Mother, Medoret said sulkily.

Her mother smiled then, her lips quirking to the side. *I doubt that, child, but I appreciate the effort.* She brushed Medoret's hair back from her face and pressed her palm briefly against the skin, then turned to Rojar. *She is too hot,* she said. *Is there anything more you can do?*

I have tried all the palliatives. All we can do is wait.

Yes, her mother said bleakly, and caressed Medoret's face again. *I'll be back soon, Medoret.* She might have said more, but turned away quickly. Then she left the room.

I'm hot, Medoret complained fretfully to Rojar.

Yes, child, I know. Go to sleep now.

And in the disjointed dreams-within-dreams that followed, monsters came to pursue Medoret down endless corridors, their hot breath filling the air, adding to the steam of the overhead lights, the grates that issued hot air. She stumbled in her flight on her short legs, reeling from wall to wall, always inches ahead of the beasts that followed, never quite caught but knowing she could stumble at any time and be devoured.

Rojar! she cried out in her delirium, and Rojar came immediately to sooth her.

She felt a coolness on her face, smelled Rojar's warm scents as the woman bent over her bed. Rojar sang softly to her, comforting her as she slipped back into unconsciousness, escaping monsters and heat and fear into a vast darkness. She floated there, buoyed by the cold wind of the void. In the distance, a naked woman shimmered as she bent over a dark pool and cascaded stars from her hand into its whirling depths, her face illuminated by the glow of the fire she loosed.

I begin Time, the Goddess murmured, the sound resonating through the void. She smiled at what she had created, then straightened and looked directly at Medoret, her face shifting to her mother's face, her body clothing itself in the plain coverall worn by the people of the Ship.

Daughter. The severe lines of the face eased, and the eyes warmed. Saryen lifted her arms with a faint chiming sound.

"Mother!"

She woke suddenly, surrounded by the warm reds of her infirmary room, the blankets tangled around her feet. "Mother," she whispered in despair, and covered her face with her hands, feeling the fever's warmth.

The humans healed me of a fever, she remembered with horror, the fever that comes back even now. The fever that was killing the Black Ship. She remembered now other details that had made no sense to her as a child, how each cycle of fever damaged further, draining strength, distorting nerve function, especially in the adults. Even her mother had weakened, walking haltingly as she helped the others. Are they all dead now? Had she been lost during the last days of the Black Ship, when the adults hunted—for what?—so intently in the nearby buildings and she so carelessly left them? She groaned and lay still for several minutes, feeling the malaise of fever ripple through her body, rising to her head to throb relentlessly.

I feel so hot, she thought weakly. But I was getting better; I don't understand. She closed her eyes, not caring if they sent her back to Ariadan, not caring if this fever ended it all.

Jaguar, she called within her mind, grieving for him. *Rise from the death the Lords have sent you. Be with me.*

The Vision Serpent drifted into the room, her fronds chiming with the crystal sound of flint, then brought the Jaguar, alive again, and the Cricket God and all her friends, to gather around her bed.

Lady Rainbow, the Serpent said, her large eyes glowing, *we are here. We will never leave you.*

Medoret looked at her in despair. *But are you real, Serpent?*

The Serpent polished long teeth with a darting tongue and laughed, then looked roguishly at the Jaguar Sun. The Cricket God folded his hands and looked at her benignly. *Of course. How can you doubt that?* A graceful frond caressed Medoret's face, and Medoret felt herself lifted and borne away, into safety. *And in Xibalba we are one, forever. Who needs any other reality?*

"Easy answer," she murmured, protesting weakly, as the hospital room turned into shadowed leaves and the glancing sunlight of a temple glade.

Sometimes, child, the answers are easy, the Serpent said in Rojar's voice, and she sang Rojar's song for a time, as Medoret rested within her warm coils. *Rest now—all will be as it is.*

But did they die? she whispered, and the Serpent would not answer.

She awoke the next morning, in a human place, and lay listlessly in her bed, uninterested in questions she couldn't answer. To her surprise, no one mentioned her transfer to *Narenjo* in the morning as the ship made its final checks for Ariadan. The doctor breezed in and out, the nurse gave her smiles and patted her, frowning only slightly when she took Medoret's temperature. Medoret dutifully swallowed more fever pills, then lay passively as the nurse tucked in her blankets and brought her breakfast. On the next day, her temperature returned to normal and she was returned to her own bedroom and allowed to get up. To her disappointment, Ian and Dr. Ruth joined in Medical's insistence that she remain confined to Project headquarters. Medoret had tried to argue politely, anxious to explore the city, but found herself dismissed airily with a smile, then a pat on the arm about "patience."

All my life among humans I have been patient, she thought rebelliously as Dr. Ruth's aide, Nathalie, sat her down in the second-floor cubicle and showed her the Glyphs computer program, then disappeared outside. In truth, Medoret acknowledged grumpily, Dr. Ruth had more than enough computer work for her grad student and aide to catch up. Each glyph photo had to be entered, assimilated, and cross-indexed, a laborious task only little allayed by the initial interest of each new glyph—not that Nathalie seemed to help much.

Nathalie had made jokes as she loaded Medoret's computer desk with more graphics and tape, all to be carefully coded into Dr. Ruth's analysis program, then busied herself elsewhere. As Medoret noted the dates on some of the material, she realized she was doing work Nathalie had postponed during Dr. Ruth's absence on Ariadan. A few of the tapes were dated barely a week after *Narenjo* had left for Ariadan. As she watched the willowy brunette gravitate in marked patterns around Urban Map's George Seidel, one of Samta's several friends, she guessed at one preoccupation. One afternoon, bemused, she watched from the doorway as Seidel determinedly kept his head inside the innards of a balky Urban Map ground car, ignoring Nathalie as she chattered on from her seat on the fender. Perhaps Nathalie's obvious lack of progress, Medoret thought charitably, explained her extended time away from the glyphs.

Dr. Ruth seemed oblivious to Nathalie's mating rituals and had plunged back into her work, a cameraman and porter in tow, when she took Ian to a hinterland site to continue the progressive recording of the glyphs. Medoret's pleading to go along had earned her another pat on the arm and gracious smile, with Ian just as vague in his assurances. It was maddening: she felt fine, but nobody believed her.

I should adopt you as child and heir, she thought, glaring at her computer. We spend so much time together. But still Medical would not let her do more than enjoy the sunshine from the building doorway or stroll a few yards into the small plaza in front, and she knew she was watched when she did.

Dr. Falk had taken Hillary away to one of the outlying sites to continue BioSurvey's meticulous counting of lifeforms: Medoret missed her friend's bouncing enthusiasm. Sieyes hovered in and out, and Jan, a pleasant young woman with an officious air, renewed her daily forms and clucked when Medoret ignored them. But others watched, too, and it was a surveillance she didn't like at all, different somehow from the looks she had known on Ariadan—how it was different, she wasn't sure, but different. She thought of defying the stricture, but decided to wait a few more days, burying herself in Dr. Ruth's computer work as a counter to the Maya dreams that tempted her waking and asleep. Easier to escape to the Serpent's world, but stubbornly she remained in the humans' reality, adopting their preoccupations with Targethi data and Targethi reality as interpreted by human rules.

As Medoret explored the breadth of the Glyphs computer data base, she realized the initial photography must have consumed years of Dr. Ruth's meticulous efforts, a far more extensive project than Medoret had ever realized from the data published at Ariadan. Occasionally Dr. Ruth had dipped into the data to write a paper about a sector of wall here or a line of glyphs there, keeping up her academic credentials back home, but the data base included little real analysis beyond the broad generalization of a Maya analogue. Most of the academic work Medoret had studied on Ariadan had been generated by other glyphologists; Dr. Ruth herself had contributed little of substance. Medoret knew vaguely that other academics had requested direct access to Tikal, but Dr. Ruth had guarded the gates fiercely, with the Project connections to enforce it.

Curious, Medoret accessed the various correspondences over the years and found four requests by Ian himself, each genial complaint frustrated by the combination of Dr. Ruth's zealous guarding of her glyphs and Ian's conflicting responsibilities to Medoret. Others had requested, a few even pleaded, for direct access to Tikal, each time jogging loose a temporary spate of new photographs back to Ariadan. As Medoret encountered new glyphs she had never seen in the official Ariadan data, she noted a disturbing pattern in the data Dr. Ruth released to publication, including marked errors in location and context, nonrepresentative sampling that distorted the importance of the glyphs favored, or, in one frieze, suppressing several glyphs altogether, glyphs that appeared nowhere else and did not fit Dr. Ruth's theory of the city-wide pattern of a Jaguar Face. And she found few of the variant glyphs she had seen upon her entry into Tikal, though the photo plan was supposed to be systematic. Why would Dr. Ruth suppress glyphs? she wondered. She guessed Dr. Ruth found Nathalie's complaisance very useful indeed.

The computer had no access bar to Medoret's explorations, allowing her to range freely through the computer until Dr. Ruth thought to correct the oversight, if she did. Confined to the data-entry room for long hours, Medoret varied the drudgery by looking in other computer files. She found Dr. Ruth's notes for her definitive book on the Tikal glyphs, little more than snatches of ideas, but with an obvious slant to favor the scientist's key theory. With astonishment, Medoret found that Dr. Ruth thought the Mayan connection more than a chance parallelism in culture; she thought the Targethi had actually landed in Yucatan jungles a thousand years before, a direct First Contact that had sparked the Mesoamerican surge in culture. She looked again at the glyphs Dr. Ruth had omitted from Ariadan's tapes and noted that all had little analogue to Mayan inconography, strange shapes and alien creatures that never appeared in Earth friezes. If one looked at the *whole* of Targethi inconography, including the variant glyphs Dr. Ruth had chosen to not photograph, the percentage of matching points dropped by an asymptomatic curve: many, perhaps most, Targethi glyph-forms had little analogue to Earth.

Modern archaeology was based on a plan in advance, a series of questions to be answered by targeted excavations. Dr. Ruth had brought more than a plan to Tikal. She had brought a fixed preconception, far more mixed than Arturo Montes's philosophical speculations, and now used her strategic position to lay the groundwork for its proof, whether or not the evidence fit the theory. Or did Dr. Ruth even understand that much of her motivations? Ownership of a site was a common archaeological disease.

She hesitated to tell Samta, who was preoccupied with his own problems with his ascerbic and unpleasant chief in Metals. Something wasn't going well with the work on the Targethi computers, she gathered, something to do with a badly corroded alloy that the Metals Team had tried unsuccessfully to duplicate without contaminants. Samta's face grew unhappy and tired in the evenings, and so she let herself be drawn into his chaffing and wan jokes at meals, not stressing him with her own worries. Still she wanted to tell him—but what was the point?

I really needed this, she thought wryly. Why can't things be simple? Why can't things be as I want them to be? Why couldn't Dr. Sieyes walk into a hole and vanish from reality? Now that's a thought.

On the next day, she wandered outside the Project headquarters and idly watched Urban Map load a few hundred kilos of equipment on Seidel's ground car and somehow make it fit. She sat down on a low wall and stretched out her legs, and realized she was bored. She had asked Nathalie twice for permission to do some exploring, each time put off until Dr. Ruth returned, only to be no doubt put off again when Dr. Ruth *did* return. It didn't make sense.

She watched the Teams busy with their work, seeing the rush of activity, the excited conversations at meals, and felt strangely left out. Oh, they'd talk to her, even listen to her ideas, but still . . .

What did it matter, she thought, that Dr. Ruth had suppressed data that might solve the message of the Targethi's glyphs? Earth's solution of the Targethi mystery did not implicate Earth's basic interests: its colonies were flourishing, its science advancing without any major breakthrough found in Tikal. The Targethi had been spacefaring and obviously controlled a sophisticated technology different from Earth's, but they had chosen to stagnate their culture for millennia, obsessed with the hunts and ceremonies implicated by nearly every frieze in their decorated city. As a people with potential threat, the Targethi had probably ended long ago. The humans might wonder if the Targethi still existed on some further world, but she thought not. She remembered the series of dead worlds her own ship had explored—not enough a memory to satisfy her intellect but curiously true in her dreams. So what if Dr. Ruth thought her theory more important than the truth, her academic advancement more critical than science?

The humans had long enshrined the scientific method as the thought of the future, a brilliance of approach that had lifted them from the first combustion engine to the stars in a brace of centuries. Scientific bias was thought a casual thing, rarely occurring, easily discovered by the automatic workings of the method itself, though others disputed that fatuous assumption. After Earth's archaeologists had obsessed themselves with catalogs of artifacts through the early decades, archaeology had begun to borrow from the other sciences. Radar and other ground sensing replaced the destructive shovel, statistics disclosed wide-ranging settlement patterns, anthropology illuminated new patterns of cultural exchange, and environmental science revised old assumptions across the board. In the effort to understand their past, the archaeologists had built an entirely new science.

But was it enough to understand an alien race? They think they understand me, she thought. Make two new proteins, an antibiotic, socialize her to human patterns, tame her into polite complaisance. Label: The Alien We Understand.

As she sat, her shoulders slumped, Samta wandered out of Central and silently sat down beside her.

"You look like I feel," she commented.

"Tired." He pushed back his black hair, smudging his face with his dusty hand. "There's nothing like waiting around for an hour for Dr. Mueller to finish fidgeting his equipment."

"Did the experiment work?" she asked.

"No. No response. The console just sits there. Get this, Medoret: after two years of discussion and analytical papers and cross-comparison studies, Mueller decides to take the back panel off one of the consoles and see what's inside. I figured out last season he was meticulous—I didn't know he was frozen."

She leaned her elbow on her knee and looked up into his face. "Hasn't he made any progress at all?"

"Oh, we know what the components are made of—four

years to decide to take samples for metals analysis. God, you'd think I was working on the Dead Sea Scrolls all over again. If Mueller has his wish, he'd bequeath Tikal Metals to his children, if he had them—make it a family business for a couple hundred years."

"You are tired." Impulsively, she laid her hand over his and pressed his fingers. He turned up his palm and wrapped his fingers around hers, holding her hand in a warm grasp. They sat comfortably together, not speaking for several minutes. The sun slanted down into the narrow street, warming the stone with a reddish haze. She caught the scent of the trees, dank water, the distant crisp salt smell of the sea. All around her lay the ruins of Tikal, just beyond her grasp—but she could catch some of it through her senses.

Samta squeezed her hand and sighed. "It's not exactly what you expected."

"I could tear down a few walls," she admitted.

He turned and looked at her. "Sieyes been bothering you?"

"Just hovering, nothing serious. Mostly I just sit. I keep asking permission to go see the glyphs—I mean, something beyond this stupid plaza. There's a Star Goddess frieze I want to see, maybe a mile east, not to mention the Great Plaza itself. And I'd like to go back to where they found me, just to see. I had all kinds of ideas of what I could do here, hopes and fantasies and big plans." She shrugged expressively.

Samta looked over at the ground car. "Sounds familiar. George is going to help me trace some wiring patterns. Want to come along?"

"You do take risks."

"Just trying to balance why a little shouting always gets to be an issue for you. Dr. Falk just kept talking about it on and on until she mercifully left, oohing and clucking with the others about how weird you are." Medoret looked at her feet and flushed. "It never stops, does it? The watching."

"I can't understand why they didn't send me back to Ariadan. Sieyes had more than enough cause."

"But you got over your fever," he said, sounding confused. "There wasn't any reason."

"What does that have to do with it?" She looked at him and saw a quiet fury build in his face.

"That sucks, that really sucks. Excuse the grammar." He stood up and pulled on her hand. "Come on. You're getting a Tikal tour."

"It'd be better if I went off by myself. Sometime, you know, I have to do the acting, not just traipse along. And I *don't* want to get you in trouble."

"If you go off by yourself," he said reasonably, "they'll call you unstable and ship you off. If you go with me, you've just got bad judgment in letting yourself be carried along. So come carry along, Medoret, share the fault—it's called coping strategy." He pulled her to her feet.

"*Are* there rules?" she asked irritably.

"Sure. You just make 'em up as you go." She thumped his arm and glared, but he only laughed at her. "Ah, come on, Medoret. Get a life."

"So my feet are moving. So I'm carrying along."

"Good."

They strolled casually over to Seidel and watched him put the final touches on some sensing equipment. The Urban Map man looked up and gave Medoret a wintry smile, then climbed into the ground car. As he revved the motor, Samta pushed her back into the backseat and climbed into the front next to Seidel. "Let's go, George."

"She coming along?" Seidel asked, looking askance at Medoret.

"Not if you don't put your foot on the pedal." Samta looked back at the headquarters building warily, watching for spies. Seidel promptly hit the gas and they surged forward, gathering speed. Medoret gasped and grabbed at the side of the car.

"George is a horrible driver," Samta called back. "But he hasn't wrecked a car for quite a while now, right, George?"

"I am improving," George agreed equably, and whirled them around the corner out of the plaza. Medoret looked back at the plaza as they turned, watching for any pursuit. She tightened her fingers as Seidel swerved hard around another corner and accelerated loudly down the street. The buildings flashed past as they got to forty kicks before Seidel downshifted into another turn.

"The Plaza," Samta shouted over the roar of the engine. Seidel spun the wheel, squealing the tires in a wide U-turn. They bumped over a section of curb, bounced twice on the roadway, and the engine roared again as Seidel hit the gas, heading north. At the next turn, they reached the main north-south axis, a broad avenue nearly a kilometer long. The ground car accelerated to hair-whipping speed and Medoret laughed out loud.

"Fun?" Samta looked over his shoulder and grinned at her.

"Fun! Go faster, George!"

"No!" Samta said in alarm. "You're fast enough, George." Seidel glanced back at Medoret and pushed down on the accelerator. Medoret thumped him on the shoulder delightedly.

"Yes! Go, go, go!"

Chapter Nine _____

The ground car roared down the avenue, surrounding them with a deafening sound, whipping Medoret's hair into her eyes with the wind of their speed. The sunlight flickered as they passed each gap between the buildings, flashing visibly faster as Seidel hit the gas. Medoret beat a rhythm on the seat-back with her hands, drumming the machine to still greater speed, as the street flowed like a river beneath the car's wheels. "Yes!" At the end of the long avenue, the ground car shot into the Great Plaza and Medoret stood up to see.

"Damn it, Medoret," Samta cried, and grabbed to steady her. "Sit down!"

"Hell, no. Go over there, George." She pointed imperiously at the Jaguar's Temple, and George wheeled obediently to the left, though he did reduce speed to spare Samta's nerves.

The Great Plaza was four thousand meters square, each side dominated by a massive temple. She'd seen it so many times in the tapes, remembered it from an afternoon so long ago, an age ago. Directly across the square stood the massive five-sided pyramid of the Temple of the Sun, each side bearing a simple glyph in massive proportions repeated nowhere else in Targethi iconography. To the east stood the Temple of the Moon, built of paler rock with many terraces. On the west side of the plaza stood the Temple of the Jaguar Night Sun, its sunward face a complicated pattern of glyphs and friezes that formed the Jaguar Face; before it stood a row of massive figures she had seen a thousand times on tape.

They sped across the pavestones and slowed to a stop, and Medoret jumped out. "I was here! Right here!" She ran forward up to the wide steps to the Gods and touched the wide stone base of the Serpent. "Here," she whispered, looking up at the tall Gods that towered above her head.

Frozen in time, the Vision Serpent lifted its proud and beautiful head, its limbs poised delicately in an ecstatic dance; beside it, a horned Deer-Man crouched on bent knees, its many-fingered hands clutching a crystalline sphere. On a tall pillar, a salamander hung head-downward, its large eyes fixed on nothing, and beyond it the Celestial Bird stood solidly beneath its elaborate headdress, its wings tucked tightly to its sides as taloned feet gripped a carved pedestal. She looked right and saw the enigmatic blocky figure the humans had named Lord of the Underworld, its body hidden beneath a concealing shroud, and the Crocodile God beyond it, its long tongue flicking. Ian had told her stories about these Gods, wonderful stories she still half believed. What is reality? She looked up at the Serpent and spread her arms wide, greeting her friend ecstatically.

"I have missed you!" she cried. "Where have you been?"

She heard footsteps behind her and turned, to see Samta and Seidel watching her. Both wore very cautious expressions, but she didn't care. Today was a day to be alien. She grinned and fluttered her fingers at them. "I am the Vision Serpent," she declared.

"Indeed," Seidel said judiciously.

"Indeed." She looked up at the Serpent, then turned slowly in place, taking in all the Great Square. The brilliant sunlight bathed everything in warmth, glancing off white stone enough to glare. She sniffed at the scents of dust and metal, aware of the slight breeze that stirred the air and caressed her face, remembering an afternoon an age ago. She sat down on the uppermost step and held her knees, then sighed as the two men still hesitated.

"Sorry to be odd," she said reluctantly, wondering if she'd be apologizing for herself forever.

Seidel glanced at Samta, then shrugged. "Freedom is like that," he said, surprising her with a smile. Samta climbed up and sat down beside her, drawing up his knees. Seidel climbed the steps with his long legs and sat down on her other side. Together they looked out at the Plaza, warmed by the daytime sun.

"So you remember this place?" Samta asked.

"Yes. I found the Plaza the day I ran off." She grimaced. "I played here all afternoon, long enough to get back too late to the Ship."

"You remember the Ship?" Seidel asked, sounding surprised. "I didn't know that." She looked at him uncertainly, not knowing what an Urban Map man might believe about temples and fantasy dream-creatures.

"There's a lot that's *not* in the literature," Samta said. "And a lot that *is* there that's so much drivel."

"He's been bending my ear that way all week," Seidel commented dryly. "You definitely have a champion." He looked past her at Samta with a drolly tolerant expression.

"Do I need one with you, George?" she asked quietly, studying her knees closely.

"Well, waving hello at a statue isn't exactly normal."

She hunched her shoulders as if from a blow, and Samta saw it. As he started to protest, she stood up abruptly and walked away from them back to the ground car. She pointedly watched a service robot far to the left trundle across long acres of stone, not looking at her companions, as the two men followed and climbed into the front seat.

I'm tired of being polite, she thought, her exhilaration sighing to a dying breeze, gone and leaving her drained—and angry. I'm tired of apologizing for myself, and having Samta apologize for me. I'm tired of all of it.

Seidel started the engine and looked back at her, as if he wanted to say something. But he only shook his head and gunned the ground car forward.

"Medoret," Samta began.

"Thanks for bringing me along, Samta."

He opened his mouth, then shut it foolishly. "Sure," he said, and glared at Seidel.

"What'd I do?" the other man asked angrily.

Let's everybody be angry, Medoret thought tiredly. Let's stomp around and not understand anything. She watched the tall statue of the Serpent dwindle in size, then disappear as the car turned out of the Plaza. Will I ever stop being stupid?

Seidel drove them northward, and turned down a side avenue where the Metals Team had excavated into the street, hunting for power cables. He finally stopped and unloaded a sensor pack from the back, then directed Samta in retrieving other equipment. As the two men set up their machines, Medoret got out to look at glyphs, her feet scuffing heavily on stone. I simply do not understand my moods, she told herself, and tried to walk blithefully. Here I am with new glyphs, she thought, chiding herself further: get a life. She walked alone a ways down the narrow street, looking at the glyphs while the two men paced out a sensor track down the undisturbed pavement, then consulted again about the machines aboard Seidel's ground car. As Seidel made some final adjustments, Samta came over to her.

"If you have independent power," she asked curiously, "why can't Mueller get the computers to work? I mean, a computer's a computer, right? I hadn't heard that the Targethi technology was that different."

"Actually, it's not. But they just don't respond. We've hooked up a generator, picked our best guess at the entry leads, and turned on the juice. Nothing. We've tried building a duplicate machine to read some computer disks, but the corrosion is so bad that we don't know if it's our machine or the metal death this environment just adores. We think maybe the local system had an activation code, something that requires an original source." He shrugged. "It's a theory."

"Yours," she said.

He smiled. "Of course," he said, shrugging. "I just thought accepting the site for what it is might be a unique approach." He looked around the sunny street, then ran his eyes over the glyphs above them. "See any patterns, alien one?"

"Non-pattern. The glyphs are mutable." She toed at a roughness in the pavement. "Dr. Ruth's been suppressing glyphs."

He sighed. "No Jaguar Face city plan?"

"I don't know. Maybe there is, overall, but the smaller patterns Dr. Ruth says she's found in the iconography don't really exist—and I've only looked at two walls." She looked up at the Jaguar on the building wall beside them and pointed. "Look. Since when does a Jaguar carry a spear—if that is a spear? Maybe it's a rifle or a wand or just a stick. And look over there: Lady Rainbow has a Lizard God face. The Targethi weren't Maya. How do we know that their Vision Serpent was really a Vision Serpent? Maybe she's a word for Thursday. Dr. Ruth's been selecting data, repressing what doesn't fit her theory. Why would she do that?"

"Why does Dr. Mueller move at sludge pace? It's a matter of your priorities. Academic greed, I guess, protecting your grants, outproving your opponents, getting to be the grand old man in the field. God knows, I saw it enough with my father before he retired."

"But science doesn't mean that."

"The way they've checked and rechecked you and still see only what they want? We see what we choose to see— not Truth, but lesser goals, like keeping the colonists away from Tikal, like academic careers, like territory threatened by dastardly rivals. We've had a team here for nearly nine years, but it's never gotten much larger. There's room for several hundred people, but Project keeps it at less than a hundred. Why should you feel so surprised that it applies to you, too?"

"I'm a different issue."

"Oh?"

She shrugged and looked away.

"Listen, I'm sorry for Seidel's attitude. He's not the worst."

"Samta . . ." She hesitated.

"What?"

"When you talk about me to the others, it's just another version of their watching. I'm glad you understand, but defending me won't get you anywhere with certain minds. All they see is the difference. I mean, Hillary can bounce around and act extreme and everybody smiles indulgently; if I do it, they cluck and shake their heads and mark their charts." She looked down at her feet. "They see what they want to see—and you can't change it."

"I don't accept that."

"Now who's seeing what they want to see?" She smiled at him ruefully. "You are a true friend, but even the Jaguar Sun could never make the Underlords change their ways. Xibalba has its rules."

He studied her face. "You sound like you're giving up, Medoret."

She looked away from him. "It comes and goes. Let's just say I'm not looking forward to what happens to both of us when we go back to Central. It's not fair. I try and try and it stays the same. Well, that's not really true. I found you, and I think Hillary is still a friend, and there's Ian, and Dr. Ruth is still Dr. Ruth. . . ."

"Being caught between two worlds isn't easy, especially when you can't decide which one you want. If you had a choice, would you be Medoret Douglas, famous alien child, or Lady Rainbow?"

"Lady Rainbow—but only if you were the Jaguar." She smiled at him. "And Ian should be the Cricket God, and Hillary—well, I'm not quite sure which icon fits her. Maybe Lady Beastie: Hillary'd enjoy that. I want both worlds, I guess—that's the problem. I appreciate your sometimes forgetting I'm alien, Samta."

"I try." He looked away from her at the buildings around them. "We were so sure we could understand this place: all we needed was time, personnel, a plan! Only nobody knows it's really Xibalba, the unknowable, the unmeasurable. The Project rules don't apply and the Lords can do anything they want. And nobody notices when the Jaguar paces by, lashing his tail."

"I suspect that comment would mean nothing to anybody but me." He fluttered his fingers, invoking the Serpent at her. She chuckled.

"That's better," he said. "It worries me when you look so discouraged."

"Thank you for stealing me today."

"Any time." Samta went back to help Seidel, and she watched for a while, then wandered away to look at more glyphs. At the end of the street, she leaned against a building corner and studied a tall rendering of a Targethi Jaguar—not personified here, not a food animal forever in subjection, but with the same grace and ferocity, frozen in stone in perpetual grimace. Jaguar Sun, she thought, I need your crafty mind. The Nine Lords have hold of me—call up the Serpent, find the Cricket God, bring your guile. No easy answer this time, Serpent's shrug, Serpent's casual mystery: enter this world, too, and walk these streets. I need you here, too: oh, if only you could, my beloved!

She looked around at the curving lines and bas-relief of alien writing. Legend, the consciousness of endless time, the movement of a people's destiny, written in the sagas of each individual king, celebrating strength and cunning, the evanescent beauty of the unreal. Did the Targethi seek that knowledge, too? She strolled across the pavestones to a different viewing point, watching the faint film of dust covering her shoes.

This is a beautiful place, she thought, and looked up at Witz Monster towering over her head. Even you are beautiful, in all your terror. For years, the humans had thought the undeciphered Mayan glyphs spoke of ageless time and remote gods, not guessing at their real message of bloody war, ambitious kings, and ritualistic self-mutilation, choosing to see the beauty they preferred. She looked at the glyphs, admiring the curve of line, the sharp relief of the shapes, the play of shadow in the recesses. These are beautiful, too, she thought. Why must they be beautiful only in human terms?

As you must be, Medoret? she thought. Is that the only answer? Samta had asked if she'd given up. Had she?

She dug her toe against a tuft of grass between the pavestones. Can I only be beautiful if I put on my human self, in their eyes? Why can't they accept what I am, and value what I am? Fear of the alien? Lust to possess the alien? Or a refusal to share the universe with other than themselves? She doubted even the Project knew. In the end, it might boil down to nothing but petty academic avarice, no matter who was the sacrifice. At least the Maya had known the universe depended on their bloodletting, giving no quarter on ultimate meaning.

Was it merely academic ambition, possessiveness, and stubbornness that frustrated her connection? She doubted even Dr. Sieyes knew, if Medoret were to confront him again. He'd never admit anything so unbecoming. What if she refused across the board, forced the issue? She hesitated. That particular idiot mistake could get her sent right back to Ariadan—the same decision that had brought her to Tikal could be reversed, and would be. They should have sent her back when her fever cycled so high, but they had not—and she doubted the reasons were benevolent, for her sake.

And I'm not ready to leave.

She sniffed at the dust in the air and caught the faint touch of seawater and distant forest, even here in the northern district. *I like this place,* she realized, and puzzled at the why of that, too. Her principal memory of Tikal was unpleasant—the fear, confusion, and overwhelming sense of being bereft as she wandered for three days, then the cloying forgetfulness of the frostflowers, the terror of being seized by the alien, a man she feared for several weeks until she knew and chose him. She had blocked away much of that early memory, refusing it even in her dreams; now parts had reemerged, tamed by the passage of time into lesser fears. And by a stolidly gregarious academic who had spun magical tales of Xibalba, who cared for her. *No, I haven't given up.* She stretched her shoulders comfortably and smiled. *I want both worlds,* she had told Samta, and it was true.

After two hours, Samta and Seidel finished their tasks and reloaded the ground car. Medoret leaned back comfortably in her seat as Seidel whisked them back to Project headquarters, watching the bright sky framed by a flickering blur of rooftops. The car wheeled into the small plaza in front of headquarters, rolled to a stop without fanfare, and nobody noticed—overtly. No rushing up to protest, no shaking of fingers, nothing. Medoret scowled, sensing proliferation of mysteries on and on.

I need a memo, she thought, some announcement of rule changes, like the flimsies posted on the central board in the meeting room each morning, announcing this and that. She sat a few more minutes in the back of the ground car as the two men unloaded again, then decided to test the new rules. She was barely to the corner of the plaza when Nathalie came hastening after her, claiming some urgent project work upstairs before Dr. Ruth returned that evening. Medoret argued and found herself elbowed insistently back into the headquarters and up to the second floor.

"There," Nathalie declared, though she didn't elaborate on what "there" might be, and bustled out. Medoret looked at the blank computer screen, then at the pile of photographs and tapes Nathalie had helpfully left to fill her afternoon. Nathalie knew, obviously—or had talked to someone who knew, more likely. Apparently she could go off with company, but not alone.

Now why is that? Medoret thought. And who would know? Or, rather, who could be cajoled? She smiled and dutifully snapped on the computer, content to wait until Ian returned with Dr. Ruth. A Cricket God knew many mysteries.

Dr. Ruth and Ian breezed in around sunset, and Medoret hovered in the background as they chatted and joked with Dr. Layard, then followed Ian as he dodged and padded off to the Project sleeping quarters on the third floor. She followed him into his room, not caring if she irritated him with her persistence. Ian was sometimes a hard person to pin when he didn't want to be pinned, for the same reasons he prospered so well in academic warfare. "Ian, I want to talk to you."

"God, I'm tired." Ian smiled at her and swung his arms briskly. "This is the life. There's nothing quite like being on site."

She bit her lip in chagrin, knowing he had totally missed the implied comment on her—like a snake shedding a skin, Ian had plunged back into the archaeological life of a working dig. Don't be a child about a parent's inattention, she chided herself. Give him this time. He deserves it. On the other hand, she had her own agenda, too. She perched a hip on a cabinet of drawers and jiggled her foot idly, watching as he turned down his bed neatly.

"I'm glad you're having a good time," she said pleasantly. "Any progress on finding a word?"

"Umm, moving along. This Layard is a smart man. I can't find a thing to criticize in his project plan. And Dr. Ruth has some very interesting theories about the symbology—seeing the glyphs on site makes her very convincing." He grinned at her, looking ten years younger. He snapped open a cabinet and pulled out a pajama top. Body language, she thought sourly.

"That's great. I wish I could get out, too. Like you, I've been looking at pictures for years—though I did get out today with Seidel. Can't you ask for me so I can go exploring on my own?"

Ian looked embarrassed and quickly turned away to hide his expression. She knew it. Medoret dropped her foot to the floor, making a decided thump.

"All right, what aren't you telling me?" she accused. "It's a plan, isn't it? Not just 'we'll get around to it' and 'maybe in a few days.' Sieyes has no intention of letting me out into the city alone. Why?"

"It's not that way at all," Ian huffed—but still he wouldn't look at her. "Dr. Sieyes hasn't given any such order," he said then, using a tone she had never liked. It classed her about age six.

"Bullshit," she said forcefully. "Will you *look* at me, please? Thank you. If Dr. Sieyes hasn't given the order, who did? Come on, Ian: I'm not stupid. You bring me here across two dozen light-years as this great alienist expert, then sit me down to do computer work I could have done back at Ariadan. I want to *see* the glyphs, contribute something to Dr. Ruth's research. And you may think she's convincing, but I'd like to show you some things I've seen where you weren't looking. I want to see the city as it is, not on tour. What's the problem?"

"You'll have to be patient." Ian set his jaw and looked at her stubbornly.

She stared at him in disappointment, and saw a slow flush spread up his neck from his collar. "You've gone over, then. You're on their side." He opened his mouth to protest but she cut him off abruptly with an angry chopping of her hand. "So Sieyes was right all along. You did resent being away from site, all those years with me just a blank spot in your life. Well, here's your environment, Ian. Get on with your life. I'm glad you're happy."

She pushed off and started for the door.

"Now wait a minute, young woman. Medoret!"

She whirled in the doorway to face him. "What?"

He sighed and ran his fingers through his graying hair. "Sit down. I'll tell you."

"The Committee had another reason for letting me out of jail."

"Basically," he acknowledged, looking unhappy. "We've never known why we found you here. We found traces of the ship—and you. But nothing else, nothing. At first we thought maybe the local fauna might be intelligent, maybe the jaguars, but they're all nonthinking animals. Whatever people lived here aren't here anymore. So where are they?"

"I'm not Targethi, Ian. The predominant figures in the glyphs are those beetle-men, and I don't look anything like them."

"But you come from somewhere. If there's another race around here, maybe they have facts we need, quite aside from First Contact with them."

"If they're around here. Maybe they've gone home, think I'm dead."

"We've found more traces . . ."

She stiffened, her eyes widening in shock. "What *kind* of traces?"

Ian grimaced. "Another ship landing, out at Copan, the homestead by the northern coast. Three, maybe four years ago, as best we can tell. Copan was the last outpost we found, you'll remember—they landed a year before we got there, then left again."

She stared at him in shock. She had provoked him to get a reaction, but hadn't expected he knew something like this. "Why wasn't I *told*?" she asked, tears springing to her eyes.

"It was thought it would upset you." Ian had the grace to look ashamed.

"Upset? *Upset?*" she shouted at him. "God give me strength! They were *here* and you didn't tell? How could you?" She turned away helplessly.

"They're obviously looking for you, so the Project agreed—for other reasons, too, including your unhappiness, Medoret, you must believe that—to bring you to Cebalrai."

"To make Contact?"

"Well, bluntly, yes. So the Project wants you kept under observation so we can be there when they reach you. We've sent radio messages, probes, pictograms at sites we then overtly abandon—nothing's worked."

"And what if they don't want Contact with you? Is there some universal law that they have to?"

"No, but if that's so, also bluntly, they don't get you back. Don't you think I've hated this? It's not fair to you, but what can I do? What *could* I do? If I didn't cooperate, you would never have gotten away from Ariadan. At least you're here." He spread his hands expressively, visibly distressed. "You are a daughter to me, Medoret, a genuine daughter I've tried to care for as best I can. I haven't been the best father for you, but I've tried. At least give me the nod for that."

She turned away from him, hunching her shoulders. She heard his cluck of irritation, and it flicked across her. "Medoret, this is bigger than you or I: this is an event of a century, two alien races coming into Contact. It *must* happen. I'm sorry that you're becoming the victim—"

"*That* is nothing new." She turned back to face him.

"Don't be paranoid," he said irritably.

"Don't say that! I'm not crazy!" she shot at him, and stamped out.

"Medoret!"

She walked quickly down the corridor, then stepped into an empty room to compose her face, taking deep breaths, then shaking herself vigorously. Calm down. Let it go, calm down, she chanted to herself. It doesn't matter. *Oh, but it does.* . . . It doesn't matter. Calm down.

As she stepped off the staircase onto the ground floor, she heard Dr. Ruth's voice in a nearby room. Would Dr. Ruth turn on her now, too? What was her fault? She clenched her teeth, guessing how it could go when she disputed, and took a step toward the voice, then flinched as Dr. Sieyes appeared at her side.

"Where have you been?" he demanded.

"I went for a ride with Samta." She moved away from him warily.

"You're to ask permission. Why can't you understand a simple order?"

"Permission? Why?" She glared at him. "I'm a member of the Project team, and I can go where I will, Dr. Sieyes."

He seized her arm, his fingers painfully tight. "You think so? We'll see about that." He half dragged her off her feet toward the room where Dr. Ruth was talking.

Everyone in the room turned as Dr. Sieyes marched her quickly across the foyer, Samta hurrying after them. She writhed with embarrassment and plucked vainly at his fingers. "Let go of me!" As he pulled on her, she suddenly panicked, sensing bars descending again, the ending of hopes, the seizing against her will. They would use her as bait, bringing in the Black Ship, using their love for Medoret to catch them, to *own*, as they sought to own everything. "No!"

"Come along!" Sieyes blatted at her, yanking at her arm. His eyes narrowed angrily, surprised by her resistance and determined to overcome it. She stretched her talons and raked wildly at his face, and heard his gasp of pain as she scored his cheek.

With the strength born from her panic, she tore violently loose from Sieyes's grasp and ran across the room, bursting through the outer door into the dusk outside. She heard a shout behind her and dodged left, then ran down the plaza, her feet pounding on the pavestones. She heard more shouts behind her and ran faster across the square, then fled into the shadows of the street beyond.

She ran down that street, then down another, then a third, then had to slow to ease her aching lungs. She stumbled onward, the evening filling with a warm reddish glow as the sun set. Finally she chose an open doorway ahead and slipped inside, sneezing at the dust in the air disturbed by her steps. She sat down on a stairstep of stairs leading upward and concentrated on her breathing, trying to still it and stop the frantic pounding of her heart.

They would search for her, and she thought of the means they might use to look. An archaeological team had a number of devices that could suit. Now was the time to move before they brought out the infrared detectors and put one of the aerial reconnaisance copters into the air—in the cooling evening the warmth of her body would be all too apparent.

This is madness, another internal voice told her. Then let me be mad. She stood up, determined to put as much ground between her and the Team headquarters before she found a sanctuary, for as long as it lasted. It may be predictable, she decided, but I want to see my frostflower garden again. Northwest. She emerged into the street and oriented herself to the pale violet shadows of Cebalrai's setting, then hurried onward down the streets. It wasn't that far—no more than two miles—and she'd have to watch out for the Urban Map team that might be working late. But she would see her garden before her rebellion caused the inevitable countermeasures. She knew human stubbornness—but she could be as stubborn, for as long as she had the opportunity.

She kept an eye on the sky behind her, wary of any approaching flyer, and hoped they'd wait for her to return before deciding on more drastic measures. She walked close to the buildings, enough to stretch out an arm and touch a carved Bird, a row of danzantes, a spray of stars, as if a river of stone flowed by her, telling its story. So beautiful, she thought, feeling reckless with her freedom. Maybe I won't go back. Maybe I can live here forever. I'll starve in short order, but maybe it might be worth it, to be free, to own myself. And maybe, if the Goddess sends her blessing, the Black Ship will find me. She ducked down an alleyway to the next thoroughfare beyond and jogged along the street, every sense alive to the night.

The scent of the city filled her lungs, dust and sea scent and distant jungle; the city glowed in endless shadings of red, blazing from the stone-warm buildings, darkened in the occasional vegetation that clung to the crevices like gaping wounds. The air sighed against her skin, tingling as subtle variations of temperature coursed over her nerve endings. This is Xibalba, she thought, her spirits exalted, and ran easily down another street, feet moving smoothly in perfect rhythm. She raised her arms high and moved them gracefully against the air of her own speed, then spun in a spider turn, perfectly balanced on her toes. Once she had run like this, in a street like this, before the Otherworld fractured into a doorway and took her away to bind her. Once, like this. She laughed, the sound of her voice echoing off tall stone, surrounding her with the echoes.

I am the Jaguar, she thought exultantly, and ran into another street, skipping around a robot tender, flipping her fingers at it in disdain, then hearing in the distance the first chiming of the frostflowers, faintly in the distance, barely perceptible. She turned up another street and ran hard, pounding her feet on the pavement, exulting in the movement that none fettered.

I am coming, she thought: I am coming back to you—*now*. She waved her arms wildly, leaping along like a madwoman, as surely she was. Here I am! Find me!

The wild activity soon exhausted her and she slowed to a more moderate pace, then tramped along happily, one foot in front of the other, moving at a ground-eating pace north. The ship had landed in the north: it was one place to start, even if the humans might guess her destination. She would simply get there first.

Chapter Ten _____

As the chiming grew louder, she slowed cautiously, knowing that Urban Map was working somewhere in this sector. She wished she had checked more closely. She slowed to a walk and moved quietly from shadow to shadow, all senses alert. Then, in the distance, in a different direction from the frostflower chiming, she heard noise, a dim murmuring, then a clang on stone. She drifted across the street into opposite shadows and carefully made her way around the Urban Map team. She caught the glow of their lamps off the stone ahead and moved another street away, circling the block of shadowed buildings to approach the garden from another direction.

The faint sound of the frostflowers reverberated in her senses, soothing nerves, dulling her caution. She resisted it, not wishing another oblivion like that which Hillary had surprised at Caracol. Later, perhaps, she told herself; after I am sure I am alone. She sensed a different coolness in the air, a coolness of living things different than the sun-baked stone, and followed it, then turned a corner and saw the glimmer ahead.

She stopped on the edge of the frostflower glade, her body swaying with the pull to plunge into the swath of dancing, glowing blooms. For a moment, she let the music bathe her body, healing its rhythms, soothing away all hurt, all care. She spread her arms: I have returned. I remember.

The frostflowers sang onward, oblivious to her presence. Slowly she lowered her arms and felt their spell lessen.

They do not remember me, she realized. It has been too long. She saw the dark blotch where Dr. Falk had taken her sample, four times as large as the small armful of blooms Hillary had brought her. A discordant chiming still spread from the broken stalks, disturbing the song of the others. It spread outward in ripples, like sound heard as light, then merged into a different pattern, richer in its harmonics but more cautious. She shook her head slightly, confused by her alien impressions.

To the humans, the frostflowers had little attraction, and they had trampled them carelessly wherever they walked over them. But to her they sang, strangely beautiful music that called to her strongly even now. Because this was her last memory free of the humans? Or because of a deeper reason? What were they? Targethi? Or something other?

I am here, she called to them again, spreading her hands. I have returned.

The flowers bobbed faintly in the breeze, their opalescent shimmer sweeping back and forth in mesmerizing pattern. But they truly do not hear me, not this time. Because I don't surrender to their call? She frowned, surprised at her own reluctance to touch them again.

Like a warning rattle in the distance, she heard a faint stutter of copter blades and turned to look at the sky behind her. The sound moved toward the Urban Map installation, not here—but they would come to this garden. Better to take the chance of an obvious destination than a sector-by-sector search for a moving target. If nothing else, Dr. Sieyes was determined, as were they all. She looked back at the frostflowers. I will come back. Like a flickering shadow, she withdrew to the surrounding trees and plunged into the darkness of the forest barrier.

The evening breeze sighed through the upper canopy, surrounding her with a sibilant noise. She heard things moving, small bodies pushing hastily away, swishing tails, crabbing talons, soft hisses of surprise. She pushed hastily through the underbrush, its coolness a pool of blackness lit from the warmth of the branches above. After several dozen meters, the forest thinned and gave way again to a narrow plaza and another sector of buildings dominated by a facade of carved stone dominated by a single vague shape, little more than sweeping lines that sketched a head and a body and a single hand that poured stars into a pool. Some years before, Medoret had stumbled across this facade in the many panoramic tapes of Tikal, and had returned to the obscure tape again and again, seeing her own Star Goddess in a limited glyph Dr. Ruth and her team chose to ignore. She skipped quickly across a barrier of cracked earth and twisted vines, then ran across the street into the building, choosing her safety in the impulse of that memory.

The interior was as cool as the forest and nearly black to her vision, illuminated only by muted red shadows cast through the open door. She turned and looked back at the rectangle of heated air that entered through the door, a neatly defined shape that blurred a few feet into the room at all its edges as it met the cooler air; she sensed the air current on her face, still faintly warm from the evening outside. She moved farther into the wide room, conscious of great space within, as if the entire lower floor were a single room. As she moved deeper into the shadow, her vision adapted, picking out the faint outline of the farther wall and three rectangular doorways. Careful of any obstacle on the floor, she headed for the doorways, trusting the air current that blew most strongly into the central doorway. The copter would have infrared sensing devices, some capable of sensing through a single thin ceiling of stone—she needed more stone above her to hide herself.

Beyond the center door, a stairway curved downward, lit faintly from below with a pale reddish light shaded into yellow. She kept by the curving wall as she descended the stairs, touching the stone lightly for balance. At a lower landing, she paused by an open railing that looked out into a hollow darkness, the air cooler still. She sniffed at the air, smelling dust and corroded metal, a wisp of moisture. She padded down the next curving segment of stairs and felt the wall change from fabricated stone to the knobby feel of limestone. A limestone well, she thought, with the building built over the pit in the foundation stone. The Maya had thought such wells a sacred place: perhaps the Targethi built in a similar pattern, constructing downward to enclose the well rather than up into multiple stories. How deep did it go? Another segment of stair curved, taking her downward. She stepped out on the next landing into a warm radiance, faintly scented by the oil of machines.

A sudden noise startled her and she shrank against the protecting wall, then recognized the slow clanking of a service robot. She turned her head one way, then the next, identifying its location by the echoes, then stepped forward tentatively. As she stepped off the final stair, the room abruptly flared into light, striking at her eyes. She sprang backward in surprise, then gasped as the light abruptly disappeared, plunging her back into darkness.

She clucked at her own startled reaction, then bent forward and swung her arm across the last tread of the staircase. The light flared and she blinked quickly against its flash, then swung her arm again. Some kind of sensor beam, she decided, though she could feel no particular mechanism in the pylons that bracketed the last tread. She stepped off the stair again, activating the light, trying to remember if any of the Project reports mentioned active lighting in the city. Most of the city utilities had apparently run by computer, with all computers now corroded into uselessness, but a simple light beam could survive. Had Urban Map found this place? Tikal had many buildings. She walked forward several paces and stopped as her vision adjusted, deciding abruptly they had not. This place would have been noted.

She saw a low-ceilinged room a hundred meters long and nearly half as wide, with every wall covered with serpentine shapes, a bewildering twining and interleaved pattern that resembled nothing she had ever seen in the Targethi glyphs. The wall did not tell a story, nor divide itself into horizontal friezes: all she could see was the random twining of vines, each several centimeters in diameter, all a cherry red in the ceiling lamps. She turned and saw that the pattern continued up the wall to the staircase; she moved closer, then touched. Not stone. This looked like fired pottery. Why would the Targethi in this one place use ceramics? She turned in place to see all the room again, her heart pounding in excitement. Something new here, completely new. Dr. Ruth might impose her patterns on what she chose to notice, but Urban Map had fewer preconceptions.

Slowly she made a circuit of the walls, examining the vine pattern, touching here and there, then reached a narrow doorway, barely a meter tall, in the far distant corner. She bent and looked into a small room beyond and saw box-shaped canisters that looked even to her Glyph-trained mind like machine consoles. She crouched and stepped forward awkwardly over the doorway threshhold, then walked over to the nearest console. It had readouts, a few levers, a definable keyboard; above was a blank screen that seemed almost glass but looked to be a fine blue porcelain. She touched it tentatively, then firmly put her hands in her pockets. Exploring this place was a job for Metals and Urban Map, not a glyphologist.

She turned in place, looking at the consoles, thinking delightedly of Samta's face when he saw this place. These machines were in far better condition than the damaged hulks on the surface, where the harsh tropical environment dug holes in metal and corroded wiring and circuit boards into so much junk. And here the Targethi had built in ceramics, in a well deep into the ground where weather could not intrude. It was possible the machines still worked.

She wondered if Dr. Mueller had also selected his data for Ariadan's journals—certainly nothing like this had been reported. Had Urban Map missed it by the luck of a random survey? A city a hundred kilometers square took a while to explore.

She circled the smaller room, examined each console more carefully, then found yet another small doorway in the far corner, narrower than the first and concealed from easy view by a tall console. She could see nothing beyond except blackness. Rooms within rooms, she thought, studying that small accessway that led deeper into the well. How far down did it go? Feeling reckless, she bent double and felt with her hand through the doorway, touching nothing but cool air, then stepped through and straightened cautiously until her hair brushed a lower ceiling overhead. She reached up and traced more ceramic vines, looping and twined around each other, then followed the pattern forward, moving carefully in the blackness down a winding slope. The light from the room behind her shed a pale shadow and she waited for her eyes to adjust, seeing less this time in the deeper and colder gloom.

As she moved forward, the light steadily lessened. She guided herself by a hand on the ceiling, slightly bent over by the enclosed space, and sensed the air becoming more and more confined as the walls bent in upon her. After a hundred steps, she tentatively reached out to the left and found a wall, then switched hands and waved it vainly to the right. She moved to the wall she had found and walked forward, orienting herself by ceiling and wall. After another several minutes, her questing hand found the opposite wall as the room became a curving tunnel, winding downward in a tight spiral. She moved forward more slowly, comfortable in the darkness as her senses accommodated to the lack of vision, becoming keener. She heard the sigh of the air current, felt its gentle touch on her exposed skin. The fresh coolness of the air tickled her nose, less dusty and growing moister, adding a faint sheen of water on the wall beneath her fingers, palpable to her sensitive fingers. Gradually the floor began to slant downward, subtly at first, then more pronounced, preparing her for the first tread of another stair.

Time seemed to stand still as she moved through the darkness, descending in a curve round and round, the wall vines twining beneath her fingers. She counted the turns as she descended, then saw a vague change in the darkness on the fourth turn, a light that steadily brightened into reddish-gray. How deep had she come into this subterranean mystery? She smiled and nearly laughed aloud, relishing her discoveries. Never in her life had she been alone in this way, and she liked it, reckless about any aftermath. I am Medoret, frostflower's child, she thought defiantly, and slowed her descent, savoring the novelty.

On the next turn, the light had changed to pale gray, barely tinged by a faint pink of infrared; her skin noted the slight rise in temperature suggesting a heat source ahead. She descended another turn of the stairway and abruptly stepped out on even floor into the light. She gasped.

All around the walls she saw the Targethi's Ix-chel, the Lady Rainbow, a tall slender figure depicted in exquisite detail of curving ceramic, not human as the rougher stone representations suggested, but clearly alien, more akin to the beetle-like Targethi. Medoret could see the definite trace of a carapace, the claws that tipped each slender finger and toe, the heavy skull that squared brow and jaw. In one panel, Lady Ix-chel bent over a Targethi priest, her claws extended in blessing; in another panel, the Lady raised her knife high, ready to slash at the Jaguar that snarled at her feet; in yet another, lines of danzante curved around her in an endless march, contorted in their dance.

Before each panel stood a low table littered with objects, small statues carved in the round of the Targethi icons, jaguar and priest and monster, ovoid spheres that glittered dully in the light, pyramids and cubes, still odder abstract shapes she recognized from other glyphs. She drifted around the tables, touching a few objects lightly, then stopped short as she glimpsed a slim shape among the others. In polished white ceramic, the Star Goddess bent gracefully over a pool, a glittering stream of tiny stars on hair-thin wires streaming downward from her outstretched hand: not the Targethi's dread queen, bent on death and sacrifice, but the unbreasted pale Goddess with Medoret's own physical form, the luminous Star Goddess of her dreams. She bent forward, hardly breathing, to look at it more closely.

Not Targethi, she thought, her breath hardly coming at all, and knew who had placed it here, in this building marked with the Targethi's own Star Goddess, for her to find. She sank to her knees and leaned against the edge of the table, trembling, staring at the small carved figure. How long ago? When were you here? Oh, when?

Along the side of the figure's narrow base, she saw a faint line of carved marks, dots and lines and curving shapes; below it a second line of two symbols in a binary pattern. Writing? A binary code? But how could she read it? She remembered nothing of the Black Ship's writing, not even its language. A key to this place? A key to another?

She reached over several flasks and boxes for the carving. As her fingers brushed the ceramic, she felt a flash along her nerve endings and hastily jerked back her hand. She moved back hastily as the carving began to vibrate, a shuddering sound palpable against her skin. She retreated still more as the object warmed, growing reddish in the grays of the room's light. She waited warily, watching the statue, but its vibration did not wax further, nor did it increase its glow. Then, greatly daring, she stood up and stepped forward to pick it up.

The statue pulsed against her fingers in a steady rhythm, warm in her grasp. She turned it over in her hands, caressing it, letting herself be drawn to its steady hum. Here was not the intoxication of the frostflowers that erased mind, but a comforting rhythm, a sense of half-glimpsed memories, of home and security, of dreams that came true. Left for her to find. To comfort? To prove her people had existed, more than tortured memory beyond the void she had survived? What comfort to know and not have? She put the statue back on the table, rejecting its message, then retreated to the far wall and sat down, covering her eyes with her arms.

What good to me to know that? she thought in despair. How do I find you? She hid her face in her arms.

What do I do? The humans would send her back to Ariadan, most likely, back to psychiatrists who clucked and reproved, back to a prison of a comfortable room, back to the disappointment in Ian's eyes, an endless round of years. Is it better to just stay here in this room and end it? She hadn't brought her dietary supplements, and that omission placed a time limit on her explorations. She couldn't digest Targethi foods any more than she could the human. Even if she hunted for food in the jungle, the difference in proteins would kill her eventually. Stay here? She did not like that answer: her mother had never accepted defeat, for all the foolishness of continuing onward—she remembered that best, though what defeat had struck the Black Ship she had not understood at the time and still lacked full understanding. What do I do?

She sat for an uncountable time, growing cold and cramped in her uncomfortable seat against carved stone that dug into flesh, hard stone that chilled her buttocks. Finally she arranged her legs more comfortably and leaned back against the wall, uncaring about the sharp points that dug into her flesh. I am lost and I don't know how to find my way home. I thought the frostflowers might tell me, but they don't remember me. And this place is Targethi, not my own. With a sinking heart, she knew she would have to return to the humans eventually, but she put that choice off, taking what measure of time she had here for herself. She looked around at the Ix-chel panels, studying each in turn, each one a face of the Targethi goddess: life, death, struggle, triumph, a symbol of mere chance that bridged the light years between, crossed cultures that had never met. Random.

She sat for an hour, occasionally shifting her seat as her muscles protested, tempted to dream a waking dream, but thinking little to avoid the endless loop of what awaited her when she returned. She tensed as she heard a clanking noise from the stairwell, then relaxed again, waiting for the service robot to roll into view. The room was well-tended, safe from the dust of the streets, but no doubt the robots kept their patrol here, too. She studied her hands, remembering another robot that had ignored her, as all the robots ignored anyone who moved and breathed in a single-mindedness that had survived the centuries. The clanking came closer, a thump-whine measured by each step descending into the vault. She sighed and rested her head against the wall, still lost in her questions.

She heard the clanking begin the last descent of stairs and lazily turned her head to watch the robot come into view. A narrow boxlike shape with extendible legs hitched downward the last step and rolled forward into the room, its lights blinking. She felt a faint rise of interest, stirring her from her lethargy. Her interest suddenly flashed into alarm as the robot veered and rolled straight at her. She jumped to her feet and dodged, then gasped as it turned to follow.

"Stop!" she shouted automatically as it wheeled fast toward her, then retreated to the opposite wall, stopped by the panel table. As she jogged the table, a figure tipped and smashed against another in a clatter. The robot slowed its advance, then wheeled backward quickly, and stopped.

"Melatani asip Medoret-achain," the machine intoned in

a high metallic voice, then shifted downward a register, becoming recognizable in a sense that prickled her skin. She stared at it. *"Melatani asip Medoret-achain,"* the machine repeated patiently, its lights winking slowly.

"Melatani . . ." she murmured, then ground her teeth in frustration. It was just like her dreams—almost there, tantalizing, confusing. She knew those words—yet did not. "Melatani," she said in a louder voice, demanding knowledge from her memory. "Melatani!" She groaned and covered her eyes as nothing answered. "I don't remember. Oh, God!"

"My stock of human speech is limited," the machine intoned, "but this necessity is within my instructions. I have listened to the humans for many years. You are Medoret?" it inquired flatly, giving her name the rolling lilt she had nearly forgotten in all the years of not hearing it from human lips.

"I am. Are you from the Black Ship?" She held her breath to hear the answer.

"Yes. I am a Varen machine, constructed inside this service robot by Bael. I have waited for you. Will you allow examination?"

Varen. The name reverberated, then fit suddenly into her memory. Varen. She eyed the machine warily. "What kind of examination?"

"The Varen have learned the price of biological contamination. Before I send the signal for the Ship, I must guard against further plague."

"Signal?" Her head reeled, and she felt the room grow tight and stretch in an odd direction. Her blood pounded in her temples, and she swayed against the table. "Signal? They're still here?"

"Not in this star system." For a moment, the machine hesitated. "But my data is many years old. I am instructed to send the signal, if contamination is avoided."

"I have lived among humans and ingested their drugs. Is that contamination? What plague do you fear?"

"The Melasoi flowers, of course. The plague that destroyed the Targethi in the midst of their triumph."

"Tikal has many flowers," she said, guessing all too well which flowers he meant. Her preoccupations had a certain unmistakable pattern. Had the Targethi, too, heard the frost-flowers' music and doomed themselves by breaking the stems? I knew it, but didn't know what I knew. Involuntarily, she glanced at the Star Mother statue and the panel above. Archetypes. Part of the waking dream-world. But what did the dream-world really mean to the Varen?

"The flowers that chime," the machine said, sounding irritated—if a machine could feel irritation. It rolled backward several centimeters, increasing the distance between them.

"What are Melasoi?"

"I do not have that data in my programming. Nor do I understand why you ask these questions."

Medoret spread her hands in a conciliatory gesture. "I underwent a psychic shock when the humans took me. I do not remember many things—and what I remember comes only in hints and tantalizing dreams I cannot understand."

The machine thought about that. "Acceptable. Ask your questions."

"Is my mother still alive?"

"I do not know. It has been several years."

"So you don't know if they'll return."

"I am to summon them."

"But you don't *know*." She curled her fingers into her palms, digging her nails into flesh.

"I am to summon them—once contamination procedures are completed."

She could see this was an argument she might not win. A machine had an unassailable logic that always prevailed—

she'd had enough experience with Ariadan computers to know that much.

"Describe the contamination procedures."

"Evidence of plague, progressive neurological damage, altered biochemistry with the plague profile—"

"Wait a minute. How could we catch a plague designed for Targethi? Are we Targethi?"

"Identify Targethi."

She waved a hand at the room. "The people who built this place and other worlds like it."

"They are dead."

"Were they Varen? Are the Varen the same as the people who built this? Where are the Homeworlds?"

"I do not understand your questions. I have no data beyond the ship and what I have accessed from the city vaults."

She scowled at the machine. Bael's prudence, she decided: if the Black Ship could carry contagion back to the Homeworlds, so could the humans if they captured Bael's machine and followed unwise astronomical directives.

"Vaults?"

"This place and the levels above."

"This is a data repository?"

"Will you allow examination?" the machine persisted.

She thought a moment, cautious of allowing this "contamination" study by the machine. The humans had crafted drugs that simulated proteins they said she needed for nutrition, had done other things for her fevers and her mental depression. For twelve years she had breathed Earth air, eaten most Earth foods, built substance from another world's substance, in a literal sense. She doubted if her biosystem still matched what this machine expected, not to the identity it would demand.

"Describe the contamination procedure. What are you looking for?"

"Evidence of plague, neurological damage that has progressed, altered biochemistry with the plague profile," the machine repeated patiently.

"And what will you do if you find such confirmation?" This was madness, debating such things with the machine that held her future within it—and could guard it against her.

"The ship must be preserved from further contamination," it answered flatly, confirming her suspicions. She might get only one slender chance, a fortune ruled by this machine's imperatives.

"I will think about it," she hedged, and sidled to the right around the machine. It turned to face her as she circled the room, its lights blinking quickly. As she passed the back table, she reached for the Star Goddess statuette, feeling the tingle again as it touched her skin. "This is a signaling device?"

"To summon me to you. It tentatively identifies your biocarbons as Varen."

"I *am* Varen, you damn machine."

"You may be contaminated," the machine repeated stubbornly. "My function is to prevent further contamination and—"

"I heard you the fifth time. Continue your patrols for a while. I'll think about your offer."

She slipped quickly past the machine and ran up the circling stairway, outdistancing any pursuit, then slowed to cradle the statue close to her middle. It hummed against her, a comforting vibration that might mock later, but she would take it with her. She moved quickly through the upper console room, then the larger room with the serpentine ceramic walls, then climbed to street-level. In the distance, she saw lights moving in the sky, a faint echo as someone shouted some order. Her statue cradled against her, she set out to meet her human pursuers.

She walked quickly down the street, heading for the Urban Map outpost that had obviously become a center of the search. As she turned the corner and saw the lights and moving shadows ahead, she walked calmly down the middle of the street, not hurrying, not dawdling, showing in her walk a sober spirit, a collected mind, an alien free of its temporary mania. One corner of her mouth quirked upward, half amused by her own defiance. Well, defiance had worked before, if reason had not. She ignored the fact of her other madness of eluding the Varen machine as she had. For the moment, she still had the illusion of a hope, as long as it was untested.

She walked into the circle of light of the project lamps and approached two Urban Map men standing by a motorized cart. One looked around casually and saw her, then straightened in surprise.

"Hi, George," she said casually, knowing it was no doubt the understatement of the day. She held out the statuette. "Look what I found. And I found a vault with ceramic walls, something you should really see." She turned and pointed backward up the dark street. "I think it's a data vault."

"*Where* have you been?" Seidel demanded.

She turned back and affected confusion, hoping the light was good enough for the expression to have its uses. "Exploring. Didn't Dr. Sieyes tell you?" She looked around, as if she just now noticed all the bustle, then goggled openly as a copter chattered into view a half-kilometer off, its searchlights arcing down into the streets. "What's going on?"

"They're looking for you, that's what's going on."

"Me? Why?"

The question lay on the air a moment, then Seidel exchanged a quick glance with his companion. "I'll let Central know," the other man muttered, and headed off toward another truck.

"You stay here," Seidel commanded.

"Sure. Don't you want to see the statue?"

"Just keep it, Medoret, okay? And stay put."

"Sure." Medoret ambled away and sat down on a low bench, then stretched out her legs and turned her statue from side to side, examining it anew in the strong light, for all that the lamps dazzled her eyes. When black spots started swimming across her vision, she half turned on her seat and looked out at the more comfortable darkness, smelling the air, and feeling the cool touch of the breeze on her exposed skin. The night was alive—she could sense it.

In a farther shadow, she saw the blurred form of a boxy robot stop and watch her. Wait a while longer, my friend, she told it silently, you of the rigid imperatives—at least until I figure a way around them. Then we shall see.

Chapter Eleven _____

Seidel returned and gestured sharply to her, then led the way to another ground vehicle. "I'm to take you back to headquarters."

"Okay." Medoret cradled the statue like a talisman and took a deep breath, then climbed into the passenger seat of the ground car. They zipped off down the street, jouncing over the paving-stones, with the rush of the cooling evening air brisk enough to snap Medoret's hair around her face. Seidel drove furiously, roaring down each street and turning sharply enough to make her sway hard against her seat belts.

"I found an underground computer," she said casually, loud enough for him to hear over the roaring of the engine. "Ceramic wiring conduit, with control machines in a subbasement." She hefted the statuette. "This symbol might be a key to the language." What language she didn't say, but the ambiguity didn't bother her.

The Urban Map man glanced at her, then looked back more sharply as what she said sank in.

"An underground—what?"

"Computer. Well, a data repository, to be precise. You might tell Metals."

It got his attention. He slowed the furious pace of the ground car, then pulled over to the side of the avenue. "Let me see that," he said gruffly. She handed him the statuette. "Maybe the key to the programming is the first line of

181

symbols," she suggested. "Then the math." He turned the statue over in his hands, squinting at it in the dim light reflected back from the headlights, then grunted and got out of the ground car. She crossed her arms and watched him bend down into the headlight beam, peering at the markings along the statuette base.

"Binary code?" he muttered.

"Two symbols, off, on, on, on, off."

"I can see it myself, Medoret, thanks."

"Eyes are useful," she commented.

He straightened and looked at her. "You seem remarkably calm for a crazy lady."

"I can show you the building."

Seidel hefted the statuette in his hand, considering, making the tiny metallic stars shimmer in the headlights. He scowled. "I have orders to take you back to Central pronto."

"I doubt anybody could find the place, actually," she said casually. "Lots of buildings around here, and lots of them look alike." She draped her arm over the side of the ground car and lounged, smiling at him. "And after Dr. Sieyes gets done sedating me, puts me in isolation, and ships me back to Ariadan, you could take months finding it—*if* Dr. Mueller believes you, which he won't, and if Urban Map will lend the effort, which I doubt." She glanced around at the buildings in every direction. "Lots of city still to map, and seven outposts, too. It'll take years." She clucked her tongue, then shrugged. "That *is* too bad."

He stared at her for a long moment, then gave a bark of laughter and stamped back to the driver's side of the ground car.

"I am the Vision Serpent," she informed him severely.

"Name your direction, Serpent. You've got a deal." He handed the statuette to her, then climbed in and shifted gears.

"Left, next intersection, then back up the main avenue."

"I want to collect Johnny first. He's second to me on the project."

"They'll take me away from you if you go back to Urban Map right now. I'll show you the place first."

"And they'll still take you away after."

"Yes," she said quietly. She bent her head over the statuette and caressed its sleek base. "Yes, they might."

He looked at her several times as he drove, but said nothing for a few streets. "They said you had a hysterical fit and ran off."

"Don't humans have a saying about 'eye of the beholder'? Could be something like that."

"The story's been embroidered since, too," Seidel said. "Violence, irrationality, typical alien stuff." He sounded almost carefree. She refused to look at him, not wanting to see his expression. She suspected it might be kind, and she'd been fooled before, and by him. She tightened her fingers on the statuette.

"I'm not surprised," she muttered noncommittally.

He turned a corner expertly and gunned the motor again. "I think you need a friend or two, Serpent. Like a volunteer?"

"Snap judgments can get you in trouble, George."

"You should know, I'd hazard. However calm you look now, I don't think your running off was exactly planned. What set you off? Sieyes?"

She shrugged.

"He's your basic toad personality, I think, not that I've seen him much. He just sits in the back and watches people." Seidel spat over the side of the ground car. "Shrinks," he said disgustedly.

"Slow down around here." Medoret peered into the gloom ahead. The street had lost much of its warmth in the cool forest evening, concealing much in the deepest of red shadows. "There." She pointed at the building with the

Goddess frieze. "You'll need a handlamp: no lights on the first level."

"But lights later?" he asked, his voice hoarse with suppressed excitement. He brought the ground car to a stop with a squeal of tires, snapping her head forward as she was caught unawares. He climbed out and rummaged in the backseat. "Aren't you coming?"

"Oh." She laid the statuette in the driver's seat and unbuckled her belts. He snapped on a flashlight and joined her.

"Lead the way."

She looked up then into his face and saw the smile. She shook her head and turned away from him. I will never understand humans, she thought. He caught her arm and pressed it gently, checking her. "Medoret," he said in a gruff voice.

"What?"

"I could say you got away again, if you can't go back and have what you want. This isn't a bad city to live in, if you're careful. Not everybody on the Project agrees with the bigshots—and not everybody's blind. There was no reason to keep you restricted—you're part of the team here."

"I can't eat the food. I've got two proteins that don't fit, not even here."

"Hmmm." Seidel dropped his hand. "Supplements? I seem to remember that."

"Yes."

"What do they look like? Pills? Injectants?"

She turned back to him then, her eyes widening. He smiled again, obviously amused. "God, what you must think of humans by now. Where would I find them?"

"In my room at headquarters. Samta knows what they look like, I think."

"He's a good friend." He studied her face in the handlamp's cone of light.

"I have a few. He's one."

"Well, I'm one, too."

"Can I ask a question?"

"Why I'm a friend?"

"That's the one."

He grinned, his teeth flashing in the lamplight. "Maybe I don't like people being pushed around, and hadn't noticed what I should have. Maybe Samta's a friend of mine whom I disappointed badly, just by being flip. Sometime I'll tell you more, when we've got the time and you're looking less white-faced and desperate. Come, show me your vault."

She reentered the building, Seidel following close behind. She pointed across the wide floor at the doors. "The middle door."

"Any guards?" Seidel asked, looking quickly around the dark room. A few remote sites in the hinterland had remains of old light-wards and warning systems, probably to guard against the native wildlife. Near Tikal the jaguars kept their distance, but the smaller outposts had fewer intimidations.

"Not that I met," she hedged. The Black Ship's robot wasn't exactly a guardian, not in the way Seidel asked.

The Urban Map chief snapped on his handlamp and hurried ahead toward the far doors, his bootheels echoing on the floor, stirring up a faint haze of dust that swirled up into her nostrils. She sneezed, then looked around hastily for her robot, seeing nothing in the shadows. Seidel disappeared through the central door, and she ran lightly to catch up with him.

Together they descended the long flights of stairs. In the room with the ceramic walls, Seidel exclaimed and seemed tempted immediately to pry up some of the circuitry for closer examination. She tugged at his sleeve, drawing him toward the corner and the further stairs. "This way."

She took him down to the machine room, showing the accessways, then led him downward to the last room and watched him walk, amazed, from panel to panel, then carefully touch each of the icon statuettes and other objects, bending to peer closer at the carved writing on the bases.

"I think you're right about their connection," he muttered. "Christ. For years we've been taking pictures of the surface, trying to match everything in the computers. We've even had sonograms of subterranean structures, excavated several. We never found anything like this."

"Eventually you would have found it."

"When? Three decades from now? This sector isn't exactly an urgent area of exploration, and Ariadan's always kept the Tikal team small for logistical reasons. The city's a hundred miles square, and that doesn't even count the vertical dimensions." He turned toward her. "Even so, Tikal's not that hard to search, not with copter infrared and sniffers—and a determined bigshot who wants to find something."

"Aboveground."

"Oh, he'll look aboveground first—then they start the sound beams. We have full remote sensing equipment, Medoret, the latest technology. Comparative sonar, magnetics, even geochemical sniffers looking for the phosphates in your bones—let's say it might step up the systematic mapping of Tikal real quick."

"But earlier you said . . ."

"I've had time to think about it."

She shook her head violently. "I won't go back—not to that kind of captivity, not again. Not now. I'd rather take my chances in Tikal. All I need is my supplements."

"I believe you." He looked her up and down, frowning. "Ever heard of the purloined letter?"

"Another of your human maxims?"

"A very old story—with good literature's tendency to include universal truths. How would you like to work for Urban Map?"

"Come again?"

"Will you trust me, Medoret?"

She hesitated.

"Or has the evidence against us been that one-sided?"

"No, not at all." She smiled ironically. "That's part of my problem. It would be easier if you were all certified minions of the Nine Lords."

Seidel chuckled. "With all Xibalba to lose? Hell, the Twins win, every time. Read the glyphs." He bowed mockingly, making Medoret wonder exactly what Samta had told him. "I prefer the winning side." He took one last glance around the room, then sighed in deep satisfaction. "Wonderful, simply wonderful. What a gift you've given us, Medoret. Maybe now we can finally make some real progress in understanding this place. I've always thought we've been spinning our wheels, us and our great theories. Come on."

"Where are we going?" She didn't move.

"I have a team mapping the interior tunnels of the Moon Temple. The Plaza's not that far from Central, and all that crew are good people. We might even sneak you in and hide you in a room in Central itself, suitably bundled up. The easiest way to hide something is right in plain sight— that's what 'The Purloined Letter' was about."

She gave him a dubious look. "George, half my problem is not looking exactly human. How can *I* hide in plain sight?"

"That's solvable with the right clothes—and some suitable conspirators, plus some fast footwork, nimble hands, and outright lies. It'll be fun." He bent to look at her face. "Sorry, bad joke. Seriously, they'll look for you up here in this sector; you can't stay here. The best place you can be is where they won't look."

She looked away and bit her lip, doubting him.

"Please?"

She looked at his open face, seeing the gruffness, the awkwardness. It was a face to trust, she thought, mad as the idea might be. Oddly, he reminded her of Bael.

"When I am crossed," she said, "I turn into a Vision Serpent and devour everything in sight."

"I like the Crocodile God myself: more teeth."

"Less mobility," she sniffed.

"All you got to do is catch them once. What's the difference?" He reached out his hand. She hesitated a moment longer and put her hand in his, feeling his fingers enclose hers tightly. "Sometimes when a trust is given, Medoret, it binds even more closely than the promise itself." He raised his other hand solemnly. "I promise on the Vision Serpent to keep the trust," he intoned, making her smile. "That's better. Let's go now. We don't have much time."

Seidel drove even more madly on the trip back, making a long circuit around the outskirts of the city to the ocean road, then cutting back to approach Central from the south. Once past Central, he cut the ground car's headlights and crept through the empty streets, keeping to the middle and driving by starlight. "Good for the nerves," he muttered, peering ahead into the shadows and veering quickly around an obstacle. "God, why couldn't they leave the stone columns in the parks?"

"Let me drive. I've got infrared."

"We're almost there, anyway. You do?"

"Yep."

"Next time mention it sooner. Okay, kiddo, I'll let you out here. Do you know where you are?"

"Not exactly."

He stopped the ground car and pointed over the rooftops. "See the top of the temple at one o'clock? That's the Moon Temple. The team goes back to headquarters at night, so just the equipment's down there. The entrance is on the west side. Go down the first tunnel, take a right at the second side-tunnel, then a right again at the third side-tunnel. I'll find you. Got it?"

"What's down there?"

"Glyphs. You can read while you wait."

"That's humor, right?"

"Ah, sarcasm—you're improving. Here's the handlamp."

"How're you going to explain not delivering me to Central, George? Layard could take your hide."

"Don't worry about that, Medoret—I'm a great talker. The key is constant distraction. Just stay put until dawn. Promise me?"

"No, I won't promise."

Seidel shrugged. "Fair enough. But give it a try, okay?"

"Maybe. Thanks, George."

"Anytime, kiddo."

She climbed out of the ground car, concealing the Goddess statuette against her side, then prudently shifted it behind her as Seidel put the ground car in gear. He hadn't specifically asked for it, and she wasn't yet ready for the humans to tamper with a Varen artifact. Let Seidel play with the others. She nodded back genially as he flipped her a salute.

The ground car turned in a neat circle and roared back down the avenue. Medoret slipped the handlamp into her pocket; then, cradling the Goddess figure in her hands, she took her direction from the Moon Temple and set off in a wide circle through the nearby streets. Twice she ducked into buildings as a copter passed nearby; as she neared the Temple Square, she heard voices in the distance, the roar of another ground car, and the blatting sound of a copter's blades as it idled. Lights flashed dimly off high stone: Seidel wasn't kidding about the fervency of the search. She circled even more widely and approached the Moon Temple from the west, watching the Plaza for activity, wary of the splash of light from the avenue ahead that led to Project Central. Another copter roared by high overhead, heading north.

If I weren't so sure Sieyes would use my running away,

she thought. If there weren't so many times they didn't listen.

She ran quickly across the last stretch of stone and slipped into the Moon Temple, descending quickly into her hiding place. She found the small side-tunnel Seidel had named and walked forward to a small room at its terminus, then flashed her handlamp into every corner. One corner gaped blackly into another tunnel—a way out, perhaps. She explored into the passageway, returning after several turns to the upper tunnel. The Temple was a honeycomb of these tunnels, only a few showing any markers by Urban Map. She stopped and leaned tiredly against a wall. Seidel was right: this was a good hiding place. Maybe trusting Seidel wasn't crazy after all.

She returned to the small room and set her Goddess icon carefully against the wall, then sat down inside the passageway door, drawing up her knees. When she switched off the lamp, the darkness was profound, eased only by the faint reddish glow of her own body. She relaxed back against the wall and listened, hearing nothing but the subtle whisper of the air currents that moved over her arms and face—she would hear them long before they came this deep.

She waited patiently for a long time, amusing herself with visits by the Serpent and a pacing Jaguar, magnificent kings marching to battle, the Star Goddess pouring stars into the void, filling the darkness with Her light. The stone grew hard and she shifted position uncomfortably, then lay down and curled up her knees into her chest, yawning. Don't fall asleep, she warned herself, and kept herself on the edge of awareness, drowsing as she escaped into her fantasies, the Varen icon warm against her hands.

She roused as she heard a footfall above, then silently got to her feet, ready to slip down the passageway.

"Medoret?" a voice whispered, and she saw light glance dimly down into her sanctuary. The light strengthened and she stepped into the side passageway, watching.

"Medoret? It's Samta."

"Samta?" she whispered back. The footsteps quickened in response, slapping hastily down the last corridor. She pressed herself against the passage wall as a figure moved into sight, then stopped in confusion, its flashlight flicking into the far corners of the small room. "Show your face in the light," she whispered. Samta promptly complied, squinting as he dazzled himself.

"Are you satisfied?" he asked, sounding faintly irritated.

"I'm over here." She put her hand out into the room and moved it up and down, catching his eye. He turned and sighed in relief.

"Are you all right?"

"Hungry. Is that food in that pack?"

"You betcha—and two weeks' supply of your supplements, too, and a vial of your fever drug. Those problems you're not going to have." He moved over to the passageway door and motioned her to move onward, deeper into the passageway. "Let's dine in the dark. I wouldn't put it past Sieyes to put a watcher on me." She stiffened, and he gestured reassurance. "I was very careful. How Seidel loves a mystery!"

"He's a good man," she said tentatively.

"Don't worry about that at all, Medoret. You should have seen his embarrassment act about losing you—I swear that man can blush and sweat at will. Layard chewed him out royally in front of everybody, bought the whole thing. They're searching the northern quarter inch by inch." He reached into his pack and pulled out a sandwich. "You must be starved."

"I found a computer vault up there," she said, and unwrapped the sandwich hungrily.

"So did the search party—by accident, of course, while looking for you. Seidel said, 'God, I saw something move over there!' and pointed frantically and everybody trooped in. What a ham."

Medoret threw up her hands in mock alarm. "And then he said, 'God, there's a shadow by the central doorway!' Point, point. Right?"

"You're so right. I'd swear you were there to watch. It was a treat." Samta handed her a flask, then held up a thin tube of pills. As she took a big bite of the sandwich, he leaned forward and peered at her. "How are you, really?"

"I'm okay. But I sure needed these." She popped one of the supplement pills in her mouth and washed it down with a swig of the cool water in Samta's flask. "I get shaky knees without them, and they always warned me brain damage comes pretty soon after."

"Pits. Speaking of brain lack, Dr. Sieyes is having apoplexy. What did he say to you, anyway? Not that he didn't deserve the scratches."

"More of the usual. It never changes much." She shrugged. "Samta—" she began, wanting to tell him about the robot but suddenly hesitant. She stopped, puzzled at her own reluctance.

"What?" he asked when she fell silent.

"Uh . . ."

"So tell me later," he said easily. "Want another sandwich?"

"Thanks. How long are we safe here?"

"I don't know, but this temple is a warren. As long as we're quiet, we can even elude the Urban Map team that works here."

"Dr. Mueller will miss you."

"Not that much. He's too busy arguing with Urban Map that a computer isn't a computer. I'll just put in an appearance in Central sometime today, maybe—or maybe I'll just hang out with you." His voice was tentative.

"And get sent back in disgrace to Ariadan if we're caught, just like me. You know, we keep discussing that point. What about your grad grant?"

"So we don't get caught." Samta shrugged.

"Hmmph."

"We all make choices sometime—and you can't have Heroic Twins with just one warrior." He bent his arms into near contortion, then curved his fingers at his forehead in imitation of a flaming mirror. "Don't I look like God K? Look at that divine jaw."

"You're such an idiot." She laughed.

"No, just a little enchanted by you, but we can talk about that later, too, maybe. What did Seidel suggest we do next?"

"Sneak into Central and hide somewhere."

"Oh, sure. That'd really work."

Medoret looked at him in confusion. "You think not?"

"Let's put it this way. Would the Jaguar walk into a Nine Lords banquet? With him on the menu?"

"No." She grinned. "Well, what do you think we should do?"

"Hell, I don't know."

She leaned forward and touched his arm. "Before I ran away, Samta, Ian told me that the Committee let me come because they want to attract my people into Contact. That's why they didn't want to let me out at Caracol; there's been no sign of any alien ship around there—it's too close to Earth and too busy. And they kept me close here, too, so they could notice when I got contacted."

"After ten years? I know you're hoping, Medoret, but the odds might be against you. They don't even know you're alive."

"The Black Ship landed in the north only a few years ago. They left traces. And I've always been in the news, even here—and radio is radio. It's not hard to guess the Ship knows lots of things." She swallowed. "And I've had my own proof."

He sat up straighter, his eyes widening. "What?"

"A service robot followed me down into the vault and talked to me. It found me through this." She reached inside the passageway and brought out the Goddess. "It's sensitive to my touch—and it's a symbol I would recognize. The Black Ship left it for me." She offered it to Samta and he took it carefully.

"It's beautiful, Medoret."

"It's the Star Goddess I dream about, maybe the one symbol I *know* isn't human-derived. When I touched it, it sent some kind of signal to the robot and it came to me in the Vault. It wants to test my biosystems to make sure I'm who I am—only I don't think I'm what my people expect, and I didn't want to blow my one chance at finding them. I didn't let it touch me, but I think it'll still prowl around, waiting until I'm alone again."

"A service robot?"

"The Black Ship used a Targethi robot as a shell."

"That was smart. We ignore those things completely now. Oh, we caught one and took it apart in the first year, but the analysis didn't help us much with the bigger mainframes. Idiot memories don't help when components are so much mush." He frowned, then handed her the icon back. She set it carefully on the floor beside her.

"I didn't have much time to talk to it, but I think it will try to find me again. Mechanicals get persistent."

"But only if you're alone, you said. You've been here a week and it didn't come near you. If I'm there, too . . ."

She shrugged. "I don't know."

"Okay," he said reluctantly. "I'm not going to let you miss the chance." He started to get to his feet. She yanked on his sleeve, overbalancing him.

"Have I asked that?"

"You don't have to."

"Why do you assume my choosing is that obvious? It wanted to test me for plague, Samta, something Targethi that my people caught. They can't go home because of it."

"A plague ship?" His eyes widened again.

"Something they caught on some other Targethi world,

something to do with the frostflowers. That's why I got the fever again, tramping around in the Caracol glade—and Hillary reinfected me when Dr. Falk collected the flowers here. The Black Ship's been searching for some kind of answers, maybe the cure, maybe the reasons for what happened here. That's why they were here at Tikal when Ian found me."

"But you were cured on Ariadan."

"Mostly. For the past several years I'd get a slight fever, nothing more than flu—but I remember the plague *killing* people on the Black Ship, crippling them, deforming babies and causing miscarriages. I remember the despair, Samta—and they had no one to help them."

"Frostflowers?"

She shook her head, losing the elusive thought. "Something in my dreams . . ." She looked away from him, her eyes unfocused. "Damn. I wish I could understand them better, but I just don't have the control. The Jaguar mentioned spores, then ran away from me. If we're not Targethi, how could we catch a Targethi disease? But that's what the dreams seem to say."

"You can't control dreams." He look confused.

"I think my people could. They used the Dream-Knowledge, and I think it was something like I use the Maya myths, as if I substituted something human for what is natural when the pattern got disrupted by my capture. I was catatonic for almost a year, and it was a narrow chance for many months afterward—until Ian started telling me Maya stories. Does any of this make sense?"

"I'm listening."

"Samta, what if the Otherworld is real? Not as a genuine universe, but a function of mind, a conscious patterning of thought that makes dreams real, too. To the Maya, Xibalba had more reality than the physical world. Maybe dreams are the same for my people—somehow." She twisted her fingers together. "I've been trying so hard to understand my dreams. They're important somehow, and the more I focus on them, the more I remember of the Black Ship. Don't you think that's reason to continue?"

He shrugged and gave her an encouraging smile. "I'm a shaman: I believe in dreams. Of course you should."

"Thanks for the support. A psychiatrist would warn against courting fantasy as the doorstep into madness. That was why Sieyes made Ian stop the Maya stories, I think."

"That was stupid. Science doesn't believe what we can't see or measure; magic believes only in what isn't there. Maybe dreams are somewhere in between."

"Maybe."

"So what have you got to lose?"

"More than you'll admit." She fingered the vial of pills. "I have to take the fever drug to my people, give them that chance. But the robot won't summon them until it satisfies itself of whatever rules it has." She slumped against the wall and scowled. "I keep looking for answers, and all I find are more questions. It's frustrating."

"If they listen to radio, maybe you can send them a message in the Ship language."

"I don't remember the Ship language: it was all replaced. Even in my dreams, the Ship people talk Anglic. The robot started talking to me in some other language, and the words sounded familiar but didn't mean anything."

"So send a message in Anglic. If the robot talks Anglic, maybe the Ship does, too. Maybe they've monitored our radio transmissions."

"Maybe. I suppose it's worth a try. But once we send it, every hunter will swoop down on our triangulation, then follow me right to the Ship. Tikal is wired with every detecting machine Ariadan can provide."

"Unless the robot sent it. When everybody rushes to the scene, they won't see anything but Targethi cleaner robots. Right?"

"Hmmm. Listen, you understand computers better than I

do, how they think within their restrictions. I'm afraid I might screw up the logic and chase the robot away permanently. I don't like being a goat staked out on a jungle trail—I don't want my people to find me that way. So maybe if you could talk to the robot, you could figure out what it wants and how we could get it to contact the Black Ship. See? You should come along after all."

"It's worth a try."

She smiled in genuine relief. "Thank you, Samta."

He tried to smile back. "I'll miss you," he said quietly, so quietly she almost couldn't hear him. She watched him look away and twist his fingers in his lap. He was such a good friend, risking trouble for himself in being her champion, even if his efforts sometimes went a little astray. Well, so did hers.

"Remember what I said about obvious choices," she said. "Honestly speaking, Samta, how can I know I even belong to them anymore? Maybe they won't want me, the way I am."

"I like the way you are," he said stoutly.

"So don't assume Lady Rainbow dies. Right?"

"Okay." He looked around them at the enclosing walls. "I doubt if your robot will come down here—the service robots stick to the streets, and it would attract too much attention wandering into temples in daylight. If it contacted you in the north, it'll take a while to get back down here. Robots don't go at Seidel speeds. We need to get out in the open."

"Is it dawn yet?"

"Not quite. We have an hour or two to lose ourselves somewhere and hide, somewhere where the service robots are still functioning. Then we can wait for it to come to us."

"If it does," she said gloomily.

"Oh, it will. Machines don't have lots of choices, and the

usual reaction to nonstandard behavior is getting stubborn about rules. Sounds familiar to you, I'm sure."

She grinned at him.

"So finish your sandwich and maybe some of the fruit," "while I think of some possible places." Samta said, "I've done most of my exploring to the east and along the sea-wall. That's probably best."

"You're the shaman guide."

"Thanks so much. Eat."

Chapter Twelve _____

A quarter-mile south, Medoret and Samta had to duck into a building as another copter thundered by overhead in the predawn darkness, its searchlight stabbing down into the street. As the copter moved off, the sound merged into the quieter rhythm of the surf, only a few hundred paces distant beyond a seawall, then vanished. Medoret listened to the sound of the water a moment, then heard the copter swing back in their direction. She frowned.

"They're really determined," she muttered, a little awed by the determination. The search had been going on for six hours, with no particular sign of letting up.

"You're Earth's alien child," Samta said dryly. "The key to the Targethi."

"The bait, you mean. Remember what Ian said?"

"I can't believe it was just for that," Samta protested. "Dr. Ruth really wanted you here for your insight."

She slumped down and dangled her hands on her knees. "A lot of insight I have. I've been waiting for you to seem more real than Lady Rainbow and the Jaguar."

Samta made a rude noise. "I wish you wouldn't put yourself down. I think you have insights that are valuable, just like me. After all, we're the only two people on this planet who believe in the Otherworld, the residents being dead, after all, and already *in* the Otherworld. And who says the Jaguar isn't more real?"

She turned her head and peered at his face in the shadows. "You are something else—what, I don't know. Are all Maya like this?"

"Well, this one is." He reached out and took her hand, then tugged her gently backward, insisting. With a sigh, she stretched out her legs, then scooted back to sit by him against the inner wall. She felt his fingers take her hand in a warm grasp. They sat in silence for several minutes, listening to the rumble of the surf and the skitter of sand against stone as the freshening dawn breeze slipped neatly into alleyways and coursed through wide streets. The copter made another pass over the seawall, but still came no closer to their hiding place.

"I suppose we'd be seen if we tried to move now," she said at last.

"It'll change search pattern soon," Samta said, and shrugged. The night outside the doorway had turned to warm red-grays as the sun began its rising, touching his face with muted highlights. She saw his dark eyes watching her—for a man who'd had precious little sleep the night before, he seemed amazingly alert.

"Maybe you shouldn't come along, Samta," she said, worrying about him again. "If they find you with me, your career is shot."

"You keep mentioning that. Do you think I care?"

"You *should* care, Samta. You've spent years preparing for this, wanting this like your father wanted it." He shrugged again, little more than a shadow against the cool darkness. "Well, I appreciate it," she said awkwardly.

"Any time."

Outside the small building, the sky had begun its changes to reds as Cebalrai dawned. The light heightened the planes of Samta's face with clean shadows, bronzing the skin. He looked strangely peaceful, and she watched the light change on his face, content to sit with him as he thought about his secret things, whatever they were. A shaman took the time to look at the world, she remembered. Samta, too, lived in two worlds—and seemed to balance them better than she balanced hers. She saw him looking at her Goddess icon where it sat gleaming by his carryall bag. He frowned slightly and shifted his position, then sighed softly.

"Do you remember the story," he said in a low voice, looking down at his brown hands, "about Lady Xoc, the Yaxchilan queen? King Shield-Jaguar had ruled so long, over sixty years, that he outlived all his sons by Lady Xoc, and then he married a young foreign princess from Calakmul, Lady Eveningstar. When Eveningstar bore him a son, Shield-Jaguar named him heir, passing over Lady Xoc's grandsons. To placate Lady Xoc, the king ordered new carvings that showed Lady Xoc in a bloodletting ceremony."

She drew up her knees. "I remember. I always liked that bas-relief."

"I know—I saw it on the wall in your room. It's one of the best glyphs of the Vision Serpent. But the Lady Xoc carving was the first time the Maya nobles, the ahauob, appeared in the glyphs; it was the first sign of the eventual collapse of the Maya state in central Yucatan. By the time the Itza Maya invaded from the coast two centuries later, all the interior kingdoms had disappeared. You don't share what the gods have given you, not when you're a Maya king: it tempts the Underworld." He looked at her soberly. "Xibalba has its rules."

Medoret shook her head. "The Twins never accepted that. Nor did the Maya. When the male line failed at Palenque, they rewrote the Xibalba myths to draw the king's divine authority through the feminine line—and carved the most beautiful glyphs of Classic Maya culture to do it."

"Some things you can't rewrite." He looked away.

"So?" she prompted. "Where is this leading? I'm guessing you're talking about us, not Xachilan or Lady Beastie.

I think you're looping around to argue again you should leave me."

He looked exasperated. "Don't fiddle with me, Medoret. I know you better than you think. I've read everything I could about you for years and—" He broke off and looked away, the heat rising to his face.

"Samta," she said quietly, "I think the Otherworld survives change. Sometimes you can't adapt enough to save the whole, but a portion remains. That's like me: what is alien survives in my Otherworld of my dreams, greatly changed in all aspects except that. Do I lose that essential by becoming human in the waking world? I've wondered, perhaps more than you think."

He frowned. "I'm not tracking this, but I'm listening."

She smiled at him. "You *do* listen. You understand the essentials. I don't always. I'm patterned to human ways, but sometimes there isn't the proper connection. Lady Xoc could not accept her dynastic misfortune and so she forced a change in Maya politics that ultimately contributed to the end of all she coveted. In Palenque, the change preserved the dynasty for four hundred years, making Palenque one of the powerful and beautiful cities of the Classic Maya. One choice ended, one choice preserved. When you choose to change what is, the results may not be what was intended, and you may close doors to what could have been—or not. And you can't always tell which is which."

She thought a moment, trying to choose her next words carefully, for his sake. "I sense you're trying to give me up, Samta. Are you so sure that's what I would choose?" She looked out the doorway as Cebalrai spread its reds across the city. "Do I choose the human which I know, or the alien which I have nearly forgotten? Do I close doors or create a new reality? I see you as friend, and I know intellectually how friendship can deepen between human men and women into something new—yet I don't feel that response, not in the way it's described."

He abruptly flushed and looked away again.

"Now stop that, please. All I know about sexual relationships is what I've read in novels—and that was none too clear. I've told you I have trouble tracking on how humans relate to each other, and I was never given explicit data about sex outside of fiction. I mean, how could sex education be relevant to me?"

"I hear Dr. Sieyes's opining in that. Did he actually say that to you?"

"And other things. He can be very pointed when he wants to."

"I can believe it." He looked down at his hands again. "I can't help how I feel about you."

"Neither can I about you and maybe it's not the same, but it's not rejection in human terms. I may not even be sexual yet. If you've read everything, I'm sure you've read that speculation, too." She blushed and felt irritated at herself for doing so.

"Tri-sex drones?" His mouth quirked.

"Oh, God, you read that, too."

"I told you I read everything. The literature is pretty relentless, but I did skip over the one with the explicit pictures."

"I hated that article. I've always hated being their lab animal, always. I don't know anything about my people's sexuality except what humans have speculated, and they don't know, either. I'm not even sure how old I am. Perhaps my being raised by humans has permanently blocked my sexuality. Even if it's not and if we choose to be together, if that happens, I may never be able to give what you would naturally expect from a human woman—just because I am alien. I can't change that as easily as Palenque reordered the Maya Otherworld; my otherworld may not be as changeable. Do you understand?"

"Yes, I do." He looked away again, his face still flaring with its heat.

She slumped against the wall, feeling discouraged. "Maybe we could have talked about the Twins, not Maya history. Half my dream world is Mayan, anyway. I'm sorry."

"What for?"

"For being so strange." She twined her fingers together and bent forward over them in despair.

"Love is like that, Medoret," Samta said quietly. "And not all of love is sexual love. Have you ever had a real friend?"

She turned her head to look at him. "Well, Ian is . . ."

"I meant your own age."

"Not really. They had to take me out of school, and Jimmy had pretty much poisoned any chance with the others. I had tutors afterwards, so I mostly played with the Jaguar and the Serpent."

"Come again?"

She shrugged, embarrassed. "The Jaguar Sun and the Vision Serpent. We had, uh, fantasy adventures."

"Now *that* isn't in the literature." He was smiling now. "Is that how you survived? By creating a whole other world?"

"You sound like a psychiatrist, Samta."

"Be nice now. Don't you understand yet? Don't you know that you can say anything to me and I won't scowl and shrink away, say golly you're odd, and generally treat you like a bug under glass? I *like* you, Medoret, I like you for what you are. Hell, I'm probably in love with you. I don't want you to be anything else, and the more I see of you, the more I like. I've been a little nutty about you for years, as I blurted, and now, meeting you, it's gotten much worse." He flushed slightly again, but did not look away.

She smiled tentatively. "So, speaking from the Otherworld, what do humans do when friendship starts to change?"

"Surely you've seen enough of that, the way Nathalie's

been behaving about George—and I'm not so sure about Ian and Dr. Ruth."

"Dr. Ruth?" Medoret stared at him. "And *Ian*?"

He was grinning at her now. "Why not?" She scowled, thinking about it. His black eyes danced with amusement at her reaction. "They've been friends for years, and Ian isn't bad-looking for an old man."

"He's not old," she said firmly.

"Conceded."

"But does one have to act so much like a fool?" He leaned back his head and laughed outright. "I am funny?" she asked irritably.

"No—no, Medoret. I'm sorry. I just now realized how *little* you understand. . . . Well, when a beautiful woman grows to your . . . Oh, hell, what a mess. I guess they kiss each other. That's where it starts."

"So kiss me and let's see what happens."

His smile vanished into uncertainty, and she wondered if she'd made an irretrievable mistake, whatever he said about saying anything she chose. He shrugged, trying to make it nonchalant. "Likely it wouldn't be much more than Ian kissing you."

"Ian kissing me?" Now she felt totally confused. "Why would he do that?"

"Well, not on the mouth, I suppose." He looked at her curiously. "Hasn't he ever kissed you in any way? Or hugged you?"

"Not much. Was he supposed to?"

"Well, he's your father—supposed to act like a father, I mean."

"Did your father kiss you?"

"Sometimes. He loved me, despite our quarrels. It's a gesture of affection."

"So you and I could kiss even if it's only affection."

"Sure—but you tend to want something more after that if you're inclined."

"Like sex, you mean."

"Goddamn it, Medoret. You don't just say 'oh, like sex,' like you'd ask 'what's for lunch?' It's supposed to be magic."

"Oh." She thought of dancing with the Jaguar Sun, but the dance had never led to explicit sexual fantasies. Maybe she was unsexed. She frowned.

"What's the frown for?" he asked.

"I wish I knew all things." She sighed.

Samta leaned forward and gently took her face in his hands. Startled, she raised her hands to his as he brought his face closer to hers, their eyes only inches apart. Her heart thumped strangely in an odd rhythm, then seemed to stop completely as he kissed her slowly, drawing it out. Then he released her and sat back.

"How about that?" he asked.

"That's a kiss of change?" she asked doubtfully.

"No, that's mostly a kiss of affection. A lot depends on the intent, and what I intended was where we are now, not what I want it to be. Let's table the kiss of change for a while." He studied her face, a slight smile on his lips. "Are you afraid I'm going to get hurt?"

She shrugged. "I'm ignorant about too many things. Maybe that's why Ian never kissed me."

"Absolutely not," Samta said forcefully. "God, they've brainwashed you royally, haven't they? Don't you get tired of the litany of how everything's your fault?"

"Why are you angry?"

"Not at you, Medoret—at them. Personally, I think your Ian is a stuffed shirt who properly belongs in a tape library all alone, academically and sexually—and, apparently, in other relationships, too. Now don't defend him," he added, raising a hand. "I know he's been good to you in some ways. But he doesn't like women, and that blunts what he should have given you."

"He doesn't like women?"

"Take it from me. I can tell."

"How?" she demanded.

"Oh, go on, you. How can you understand Lady Xoc and not Ian?"

"Lady Xoc?" She stared at him. "What does Lady Xoc have to do with Ian?"

"About as much as Palenque does with me."

She hissed in exasperation and thumped him hard on the arm. He pretended alarm and warded her off, then grinned at her.

"I think I'll feed you to the Jaguar Sun," she informed him disgustedly. "He ought to be hungry about now."

"You're something else, alien."

Impulsively, she leaned forward and kissed him back, off balance and missing half his mouth as she did, then felt his hands close on her arms tightly. The second time was much more satisfactory. He turned his mouth into her kiss and pulled her against him, slipping one arm about her waist and raising his other hand to her hair, burying his fingers in its silky mass. She threw her arms around his neck and pressed close to him, then felt him shift position as he lowered them both to the stone floor. Then, abruptly, he broke off the kiss, then raised himself to one elbow to look down at her.

"This is getting out of hand very fast," he said huskily.

"Magic," she said, smiling up at him.

"Oh, really," he said skeptically. "What happened to 'I don't feel the response you want'? Remember? Lady Xoc and the parable of the inalterable alien?"

She grimaced. "I told you I was ignorant."

"God, this is complicated." He rolled onto his back and she laid her head on his chest comfortably. "Let's just lie here a moment until I've got my brains back where they belong."

"Excuse me?"

"Never mind." She felt his chuckle against her ear and

breathed in deeply the scent of him, then relaxed languorously against his body. "That isn't helping, Medoret," he said, squirming slightly.

"What?"

He pulled his arm from underneath her body and sat up, then rubbed his face slowly, his hand trembling.

"I'm sorry," she said awkwardly, and sat up, too, sorry she had acted impulsively, sorry she had somehow finally made the mistake she had dreaded. She edged away from him slightly, giving him the room he apparently wanted.

"The literature says it's physically possible," he said in a low voice.

"I've read that literature," she said archly, struggling to find some balance between them. "I wasn't impressed."

He dropped his hand and looked at her. "I don't want to hurt you, either," he said in anguish. "Would I? What are the rules?"

"I don't know." She felt tears come into her eyes. "I don't know at all. I'm sorry, Samta, I. . . ."

"Sorry? What do you have to be sorry about? For *what*?"

"Please don't be angry."

"I'm not, really I'm not. I started this by showing too much. I should have known better."

They looked at each other a long moment. "Does this mean," she asked finally, "that I don't get any more kisses?" He blinked in startlement, then started laughing. She grinned as she watched him, hoping she had chosen the right question. She couldn't tell quite yet, he was laughing so hard. "Well?"

"God, what a woman!" he said, and laughed again, then seized her and kissed her emphatically. "Definitely. Always."

"Good. But I agree on the other—for a while." She looked at him sideways, checking his reaction. "*Are* there rules to all this?"

"Not at all. In fact—"

She raised her hand abruptly, silencing him, then turned her face to the doorway. Had she heard a slight sound?

"What is it?"

"Shhhsh. I heard something." She listened again, catching a faint scrabble on stone, more than sand sifting into the streets, then the distinctive faint whine of a machine. The sound came closer, then stopped. "This is my friend, Samta," she said calmly, raising her voice. "We are waiting for you. I wish to speak to you again, robot."

The robot rolled into view a meter beyond the doorway and stopped, its hood lights blinking slowly. It hesitated, rolled half out of view, then divided the difference, showing its conflict in its actions.

"This is a human," it intoned flatly. "Contact is not within my parameters. Remove him."

"I will not—and you will remain. Aren't you programmed to accept my orders?"

"Within parameters," the robot said loftily.

"Your voice is familiar, almost like Bael's."

"Bael This-sa programmed me. It is logical he would use his own voice." Samta watched both of them in fascination, his head turning from one to the other, but he wisely kept silent. She didn't know how limited the robot's programming might be, and a second voice, especially a human voice, might stress its "parameters" too much. She wrapped her fingers around Samta's arm and pressed tightly.

"Where is Bael This-sa?" she asked.

"Aboard the Ship."

"And where is the Ship?"

The robot stood silent.

"Answer me," she commanded.

"You will bring this human to the Black Ship?"

"That is my decision and not within your parameters to say," she countered, hoping her conviction had some accuracy. "Where is the Black Ship?"

"I do not know."

"Send the signal."

"You have not accepted examination."

"Ask it for alternative options," Samta whispered. "Jog it off that track."

"Consult your data for alternative options," Medoret ordered. "What are you to do if I refuse examination?"

"You are demented?" the machine asked uncertainly, and Medoret felt Samta's amused chuckle. She elbowed him hard in the ribs.

"I am of unknown status—and I refuse examination. Send the signal and let Bael decide."

The robot flipped its lights. "That is not within my parameters."

Medoret bit her lip and looked at Samta. Jog it off track, he had said. "Could the Black Ship land down the coast, in the sea, and not be detected?"

"You will bring this human?"

"That is my decision and not within your parameters," she repeated stubbornly. Could she bypass the machine's stubbornness? "Can they land without detection?"

"Unknown. The humans' detectors are sophisticated, especially the mapping devices in orbit."

"There is only one satellite in orbit," she argued.

Samta nudged her. "Two," he whispered. "Urban Map put up another last year."

"There are two in orbit," she amended. "Can the Black Ship elude?"

"I would have to query," the machine said uncertainly.

"Do so." She held her breath.

"Sending signal."

She let her breath out with a great gust. They waited, watching the machine.

"Do you have contact?" she asked when the waiting had become unbearable.

"No."

"Will they meet me?"

The robot said nothing.

"This human is my friend," she said, trying again. "He can be trusted."

"Hell, Medoret," Samta whispered urgently. "Let that go if you must—this could be your only chance to see them."

She turned to him angrily. "And what if I just disappear? And what happens to the Black Ship if my fever drug doesn't help? What about Ian? Do I just disappear and forget you?"

He set his face. "Sometimes you can't change the Otherworld."

"I don't accept that, not without trying. Don't be so noble."

"If that machine won't cooperate, you'll miss your chance."

"Maybe I never had that much of a chance. Will you come with me?"

"My parameters—" the robot began.

"Blast your parameters!" she shouted at it. "If you must, ask the Black Ship!"

"Agreed. I have received a contact signal."

She stared at it. "You have direct radio communication?"

"Telemetric data signal. I am asking your first request now. Transmission time will be six minutes."

"Can you send an additional message?"

"What message?"

She closed her eyes and clasped her hands tight in front of her, squeezing painfully on her fingers. She paused a moment to organize her thoughts. "Send this. 'Mother, like you, I have chosen to continue, but I have lost myself between dreams and the waking day. Please come to me. One human I will bring, but the others will not know. Please come.' " She hesitated. "End transmission."

"Sending."

She let out her breath in a gasp, then bowed forward,

wrapping her arms around herself, fearing she would be too human, fearing her dreams had wandered too far.

Samta touched her shoulder. "Why didn't you tell them about the fever drug?"

"That wouldn't be enough to bring them in, not in risk of contact. Bael wouldn't believe it, I don't think, and I'm not sure if my mother has that much control of the Ship by now. She pushed too far in insisting once—and obviously she's continued to insist."

They waited, watching the robot.

"Acknowledged," it said finally. "The Ship agrees to contact. I will guide you to the place."

"And Samta comes with me?" she said sharply.

"He may come." Did the robot hesitate a fraction too long before that answer? She studied its blank face carefully, all her suspicions of this literal machine on new alert. The Jaguar Sun would never permit such idiocy, she thought: one never trusts a Lord of the Underworld. She looked at Samta, knowing he was Underlord to the Black Ship and wondered what treachery the machine intended, if it intended anything. What did she really know of her people?

"Where is the meeting place?" she asked.

"Twelve kilometers east on the shoreline," the machine answered dutifully, for once its parameters helping instead of hindering. "The Ship will make an ocean landing and travel to that place."

"We will be there." She pointed at the machine. "*You* will remain here."

"I am your guide."

"Not anymore. You will stay here." Who knew what nasty little devices Bael had put in this machine? And she distrusted that slight hesitation. She looked over at her Star Goddess statue by Samta's haversack and realized with a pang she dare not take it any farther, not when the robot could track her by its transmissions. The Goddess glimmered in the half light, caught motionless in an instant of time by whatever hand had fashioned Her likeness.

"That is not within my parameters," the machine said stubbornly.

"That is my direct order. You are programmed to obey me. Do so."

"Acknowledged."

Medoret scowled at the machine and thought that "acknowledged" did not always mean agreement, not to this machine. They would have to stay alert—and hope that a sandy beach might hinder other 'parameters' enough to outdistance it if it followed. "Come on. We can keep under the shelter of the trees until we're farther away."

"Why not take the robot?" Samta asked.

She shook her head violently at him and signed him to silence. Though his eyes questioned, he nodded.

"Okay."

She got to her feet and walked toward the robot, which retreated slowly from the doorway.

She put her head out the doorway warily and looked up for any sign of the Project copters, then listened for several moments, using her sensitive ears. She could hear the faint hum of the robot's inner machinery, the squeak of a wheel as it moved backward; she tuned those out. She heard the sigh of air through confined streets, then a faint throbbing in the distance—copter, she identified—and a distant faint murmur of what might be voices. The humans were near, but no nearer than Project Central a quarter mile away. They still looked in other directions.

She touched Samta's sleeve and he bent to pick up the carryall and icon; she signed him to leave the icon behind, another decision that made him look puzzled. Together they slipped into the street, then ran lightly along the building wall and darted into the first alley. Keeping an eye on the sky overhead, they dodged and weaved through the maze of streets leading to the seawall, the last city barrier southeast to the shoreline beyond.

Chapter
Thirteen _____

A kilometer beyond the city, the beach narrowed to a stretch of blue-white sand bordered by impenetrable jungle and the surf. In the trees that towered overhead, rustles and soft complaints marked the busy life of the local animals. Medoret saw a flash of white fur among the branches, then the quick heat trail of the small predator's body as it hunted smaller creatures in the canopy. A dozen kinds of strange insects hovered over the beach, basking in the warm air, then darting into the branches out of sight. She pointed out a large birdlike creature sitting on an upper frond, preening its feathers and fixing them with a baleful yellow eye.

Samta stopped and looked up and down the tall leafy barrier, a slight smile on his face. "I hadn't realized the forest had this kind of activity; I guess we scare the animals away from Tikal."

She shrugged. "Oh, maybe not. You can't hunt very well among Tikal's stones; here all is good living, I think. Look at that dragonfly!" A large insect swooped down upon them, its wings a full handspread across and shimmering in the morning light. It hovered in front of them for several seconds, its head turning curiously on a segmented stalk; then it flung itself away over the sand, its wings beating furiously. "So fast—look how it moves!"

"They're not afraid of us at all," Samta said wonderingly. He reached out his hand toward a tiny birdlike animal, bright crimson and yellow and green, that fluttered on a nearby branch. The animal moved prudently away from Samta's hand, clucking to itself in mild irritation, but didn't move far. It watched Samta with bright dark eyes, its head turning to give each eye a long look. "Hello there!"

"Maybe you should have joined Biologicals instead of Mueller's computer hunt."

Samta ambled onward to join her again, clucking back at the bird as he passed its branch. "Hmmmph. Not hardly. Biologists have to catch things and then cut them up to understand what they are; I just like to look." He slipped his hand into hers as they walked onward, his grasp warm. "At least computers don't mind getting dismantled."

"Are you sure?" she asked, teasing him.

"No whichness of the why today, Medoret." He waved his other hand at the lush jungle. "This is Xibalba. All is peaceful, and there is no fear anywhere—except when the Nine Lords stir things up, of course, but there are still lots of days like this one. Do you think they'll be waiting for you?" His eyes were on the treetops.

"The robot implied as much. They've been waiting for me for a long time. My mother is a determined woman."

"You remember her?"

"A little—mostly in dreams. She's captain of the Black Ship."

His head swiveled around to her. "Now *that* isn't in the literature. Really?"

"It doesn't get into the literature if I don't tell anybody, right?" She scuffed her boots in the sand, making long shallow grooves. "But I remembered her only recently, in my dreams. I've been wondering about my dreams, especially now. Dreams mean something important to my people, Samta—I don't know exactly what, but I think our dreams are different than yours, a part of choosing and thought that is valued. I remember my mother saying clearly 'I choose the Dream-Knowledge,' as if that settled some important issue." She shrugged. "I wonder what Dream-Knowledge could be. I think I've experienced some of it recently, but it's all mixed up with the Twins and Lady Rainbow." She shook her head, confused. "Have I told you about Ian's stories when I was little? I think the stories got into some kind of mental index, substituting human terms for whatever images my people dream, but I'm not even sure of that. Maybe I'm just crazy."

"I don't think you're crazy—but who am I to say? After all, I think I'm a Maya shaman, and if that isn't delusion, what is? The Maya culture ended a millennium ago, and their Otherworld with them."

"Do you really think so?" She smiled at him. "Do gods extinguish merely because their temples fall into decay?"

"Or perhaps they move elsewhere, like this place," he said. He smiled at another brightly colored bird on a high branch. "The Aztecs believed that warriors became hummingbirds and butterflies in the afterlife—this after their priests butchered thousands of victims and terrorized central Mexico with their ferocity, but the sun could not rise, in their view, unless they fed him daily with human blood. At least my delusions are milder and harmless."

"And I play with the Vision Serpent and dream of faces I long to see."

Samta took a long shuddering breath and tightened his fingers on her hand. "I'll miss you."

"I told you not to assume that. They may not want me, the way I am."

"Now who's assuming?"

The sun rose higher in the sky, beating down upon the beach with a shimmering heat. They moved higher up the strip of beach into partial shade, but found the looser sand harder walking. A fine sheen of sweat covered Samta's face, and Medoret felt sticky under her clothes, too. By noon they had walked three or four kilometers and Medoret suggested a rest.

"The robot said it was a day's walk," Samta demurred. "We ought to push on."

"I'm tired and the sun is too hot. Is that fruit edible?" She pointed to some luscious yellow globes on a branch.

"I still have some food in the haversack. We ought to eat that, don't you think?"

Medoret sighed and looked at him squarely, raising an eyebrow. "Prudence is boring, Samta."

"But smart." He dropped his pack on the leaf litter beneath a tree.

"True." She sat down beside him and hugged her knees, staring at the waves as they crashed and rolled up the beach. A fish splashed twenty meters out, chasing something in the waves. "Life everywhere. Not confined to a park, not hiding under a bubble-dome. Even if you travel years in a ship, I think it's important to have a world somewhere like this, a place to go home to." She looked around, hearing the movement of small bodies, the breeze slipping through fertile branches. "My people saw only death on Targethi worlds," she said musingly. "I wonder why. How could worlds so full of life bring such despair?"

Samta rummaged in his pack. "Did they know who the Targethi were?"

"I think so—and they knew something that worried them." She covered her eyes with her hands and rubbed her temples. "I wish I could remember. I lost so much in those first few years—and I didn't understand that much as a child."

"Well, you'll get your answers." He handed her an apple.

"Our answers," she corrected gently. She dropped her hands and looked at him. "I'm not that alert when it comes to the human subtleties: I keep missing clues that humans seem to catch."

"And maybe we miss clues of yours."

"Probably. But perhaps we share an awareness of false

cheer, masked dread, unhappy expectations when the issue is really in doubt—"

"All right, already. So I'm not that great of an actor."

"Why would you want to be?" she asked curiously.

He tipped his mouth wryly. "Oh, I don't know. Acting helps avoid problems, I guess."

"Or creates them."

He scowled fiercely, beetling his eyebrows at her. "You're relentless. I'd rather not talk about this, Medoret."

"We could always discuss another Maya parable, maybe about Narenjo this time. That was a good story."

"Please. . . ." He dropped his voice in anguish and would not look at her.

"Hell and damnation!" She glared at him, then raised her arms and fluttered her fingers over her head. "I am the Vision Serpent. I cannot be denied—and I won't go off with them, if I do, with this left unresolved between us."

He set his jaw stubbornly. "We should have left you in the garden. You belong with your people—and I'm not going to set up anything that might change that."

"You think it hasn't already?"

"God, I hope not." He looked down at his hands and twisted his fingers together, a muscle working in his jaw. "I really hope not, Medoret. Then I'm just like them, the scientists who put you in prison."

"And which is worse, Samta? To be in prison and have no hope except abandonment of what is important—or to see a promise that could be there? You're the first real friend I've had among humans, the first time the real world ever rivaled what I share with Jaguar Sun and the Serpent. Why is permanent separation the only right answer? Why must there be division?" She spread her hands. "Why can't reality and the Otherworld have a connection? The Maya thought they did; so do I."

"I will *not* deprive you of what you should have had." He set his jaw stubbornly.

"I think you're wrong. So let's vote."

"What?"

"We'll vote. On your side is you. On my side is me and the Vision Serpent and Lady Beastie and *both* of the Twins."

"You can't have both the Twins—I get God K."

"No way! Whose fantasies are these, anyway?"

"And Lady Rainbow votes with me, too. It's even."

"No, it's not." She shook a finger at him. "Don't mess with the Otherworld, Samta: only the Twins get away with trickery—and you're not one of the Twins."

"Are you so sure, Serpent?"

"Absolutely." She smiled at him. "When do I get to do some choosing? I could worry, too—about starting something that we don't finish, leaving you alone. Would you really rather not have had anything at all?"

Samta sighed and ran his fingers through his hair. "I said it was complicated. Maybe we just ran out of time, Medoret."

"Time? Time is ageless. All we hear are her whispers—in monuments of stone, in the suns the Goddess created in her shimmering pool, the life all around us. She whispers many things, and not all make sense to us." She looked out over the ocean, an expanse green and gray and cool, moving in its own rhythms. "Like dreams sometimes don't make sense." She listened to the sea and heard the jungle answer in its own rustles and movements and swaying green, becoming one patterned sound together. One could find metaphors everywhere, she thought, then smiled. Archetypes.

"What do you see out there?" Samta asked quietly.

"Coolness. Sound, movement, things I can't quite glimpse. It's an essential, somehow. Maybe my people came from an ocean world like Earth; maybe the sea means something special to us." She raised her hand and turned her palm to the sea, feeling the cool moistness of the wind that blew across it. "Time—time is there in its cycles. Time for everything: Targethi to build their monuments, my people to wander across their emptied worlds, humans to dig and study and speculate. And time beyond—to what, I wonder?"

She turned to look at him. "If only the Vision Serpent answered specific questions, every time, not just what interests her. She can be maddening in what she won't tell."

"Maybe part of the fascination is because you're alien, not Medoret."

"Medoret *is* alien. What's the difference?"

He lay back and put his hands behind his head, studying the branches overhead. "Maybe I want fame and fortune— Samta Montes, the brave explorer who *solved* Medoret Douglas, Earth's alien child."

She shrugged. "Well, if you solve me, why shouldn't you have fame and fortune?"

"Pat answer, Medoret."

"Best I got." She looked out at the ocean again.

"Are you suggesting we have sex?" he asked in a low voice.

"No, not if you don't want to."

He made a restless movement.

"Now, wait a moment," she said, raising a hand to forestall him. "You've been debating wisdom, not wanting—am I right? Even if you decided to try, you'd still wonder later. I think matters need to be surer than that."

"It's a rather typical problem for men and women." He twisted his mouth.

"Maybe for both our peoples. I don't know. But I debate, too, only I'm not wanting the way you are wanting, and I'm not as concerned about wisdom. And so the sea speaks to the land." She smiled at the ocean and watched a seabird plunge through the high air, riding the wind. It flew over them and vanished behind the screen of trees.

"What?" He sounded totally confused.

She grinned at him and took his hand in hers, tightening her fingers when he reflexively started to pull it away. "I like to touch you. And I liked kissing you—though the reasons why were out in the dream world, unclear and pointing in several directions. Mostly I like the way we talk, and the way you get bent out of shape about things, and the way I worry about what to say. And I like you being here with me and worrying about the future, when you should be just enjoying this day. Can't some days just be enough, just for that day?"

"Maybe they can." He smiled and pulled gently on her hand, bringing her closer. "Let's table that and just listen to the day for a while." She moved nearer to him, then lay down against him, then resettled as he slid his arm under her neck. She laid her head on his chest and listened to the slow thumping of his heart, then closed her eyes. His fingers entwined into hers and they rested together, not moving.

"This is nice," he murmured some time later. "Did you sleep?"

"Not really." She gently disentangled her fingers and sat up, then looked down at him. He reached up and brushed her hair back from her face.

"You are very beautiful, Medoret."

She bent down and kissed him. He tensed at first, then relaxed into the kiss, pulling her mouth tightly against his. After a long moment, she broke it off and smiled down into his face.

"That was nice, too," she said.

"Yes."

"I rather think—" she began, then lifted her head suddenly and looked back down the beach. In the distance, in the direction of the city, she heard a faint beating rhythm, barely more than a vibration on the air.

"What is it?" Samta asked, pushing himself up. He

looked in the same direction distractedly, then back at her face.

"Copter, I think. The Underlords are having fun, I think. Just when we're getting somewhere interesting, we get interrupted."

"Medoret. . . ."

She waved him to silence, watching the beach behind them. They had walked near the trees and avoided the sand and its revealing footsteps, but she knew they were still exposed. "Seidel said the Project has infrared scans."

"Of course. And a bunch of other sensors." He grunted irritably. "I hadn't appreciated their uses. Do you think they're tracking us down the beach? Could we leave infrared traces?"

"I don't know. I can't see anything, but maybe their machines are better than my eyes. Well, if they are tracking us, it won't work. I'm not leading the Project to the Black Ship, not until I have a chance to talk to my people first. Why do humans think they should always get what they want?" She scowled, then looked quickly at him in apology. "I'll take back the 'always.' You've been an exception to the rule."

"Thank you." Samta got to his feet and put out a hand. "Though I will admit there tends to be a rule." He pulled her up and then examined the leafy barricade behind them. "Call it impenetrable, I'd say."

"Think Jaguar, God K."

"That jungle has real jaguars in it, Medoret," he warned. "And snake-things who don't bother to prophesy, just chew."

"Good thing both our ancestors could climb trees."

"So can jaguars—and snakes."

"True." She looked around quickly at the beach and sea. The sound of the copter grew palpably louder, tracking them—or just searching on the chance? If the Project kept on in this direction and overflew them, would it discover the Black Ship's landing place? If they had landed. She looked at the sea and remembered Dr. Ruth's insistence on seaports. She only hoped the Ship had sensors, too, and could slip away. "Damn!" she exclaimed, as she realized the implications.

"What?"

"What if they drive away the Black Ship?"

Samta seized her hand and pulled her to her feet. "Listen, we can move faster running on the beach, and the surf'll hide our tracks. If they're scanning the jungle, they won't come too fast. They'd expect us to hide in the brush." He turned and looked at the sea, then looked on down the beach. "It gets rocky down at the next point. See?" He pointed down the beach. "Reef formation. Rocks."

"And water to hide infrared."

"Let's go."

He pulled at her hand and they ran down to the edge of the surf, then raced up the beach, the water lapping at their feet. Samta released her hand as they fell into single-file, running easily with a long loping stride. She matched her steps to his, falling into his loose-limbed rhythm. The sea air freshened against her face, whipping her hair into her eyes. It was exhilarating to run, to breathe the mist-cool air into her lungs. She pulled even with him and laughed, then raced ahead, daring him to catch up.

"You think so?" he called, and pounded after her. As he nearly caught up, she increased her speed, keeping just ahead of him to tantalize him with the race. As they reached the first rocky outcroppings of the point, the race became a nimble sidestepping around and over the rocks embedded in the sand, then slowed as each risked a pratfall on the rocks at a higher pace. Medoret slowed to a jog, then stopped and looked back up the beach. Panting hard, Samta padded even with her. She waved at him to try to silence his heavy breathing, her attention behind them and the long stretch of beach hidden behind the curve of the bay. Samta bent over and breathed more deeply, his hands on his hips, then walked around in a circle, smiling.

"I beat you," he said.

"You did not!"

"Are they any closer?"

"I can't tell."

"Let's walk on a bit and get our panting under control, then you can listen with those ears of yours. I can't hear a thing yet—they must be a couple of miles away."

"Maybe." She raised her chin as she caught the distant whuffing of the copter again, coming toward them. But Samta was right: they weren't coming fast. She looked at the jungle and decided he was right about that, too. Their body heat would show up like neon signs to infrared scanners.

"Come on. Let's keep going and find a place to be when they turn the corner of the bay."

"Right."

He reached out his hand and she slipped her fingers into his, then let herself be pulled against him. He kissed her quickly and smiled, his face still flushed from his recent exertion. His eyes sparkled as he looked down at her. "I'd forgotten how much fun it is to run."

She hugged him and felt his lips press warmly on her forehead. They stood close for a long moment, the sea breeze whipping at their clothes. Then she stepped back a step and blew out a breath, puffing her lips, and fluffed her tunic away from her neck. "I should do more of it. This doesn't say much about my physical conditioning."

"Mine either." He looked back up the beach and then shook his head ruefully. "I still can't hear the copter. Those must be some ears. According to the literature, your auditory frequencies range from—" He grinned as she pretended to hit at him. "Come on, alien. Let's move our feet."

They walked quickly into the rock formation of the

point, trying to stay out of sand pockets and its betraying footprints. The ancient rocks stretched out far into the water, creating a triangular massif of half-submerged rock rising to several monoliths several dozen meters beyond the surf. The water crashed into spray against the dark rock, splashing upwards into a thin fan of sparkling drops. Beyond the point, the beach again subsided to a long stretch of white sand, turning inward into another small bay. As they clambered over a wide stretch of rock decorated with small pools, each shadowed with small tentacular forms and sea grass, Samta turned his head back and forth, scanning the formation. He pointed at one of the monoliths just beyond the white water of the surf, then raised an eyebrow.

"Could be a bad current," Medoret said judiciously. "Those waves have a lot of power."

"They'll see us in the jungle, Medoret. We'd never have time to hack in far enough to get out of range, assuming we had something to hack with, which we don't."

"Oh, I'm not arguing. Just looking."

He laughed. "We may have to get wet, but if we can get on the other side of that rock. . . ."

"Right."

Rock by rock, they picked their way out into the surf toward the monoliths. Alongside the dark rocks, the water surged back and forth, carrying a patterning of foam and bits of sea-wrack. At one point, they had to jump a meter's span of water that rushed through a gap in the rocks. As they worked outward, the gaps increased. The sound of water surrounded her, blotting out any sounds beyond them; she kept a wary eye on the bay point toward the city, expecting the distant black shape of the copter to wing into view any moment. How far away was it? She hadn't enough experience with discerning the distance of sounds.

They reached the last gap to their chosen monolith, a four-meter span of surging water through a channel. For the first time, Samta looked nervous as he eyed the water, then looked at the nearly sheer rocky face beyond. "We can't climb that easily—and it may have an undertow." He pointed at the hollowed base intermittently revealed by the waves.

"Swim around?"

"I'm thinking there could be jaguars in the water, too. I wish I'd read that BioSurvey paper more closely about the sea life." He took a deep breath. "Well, here's to the Twins." He bent and stuffed their haversack under a ledge facing the sea, pushing it deep into the hollow, then straightened and saluted her jauntily. He made an awkward dive into the water, then bobbed up several meters outward and started swimming a wide circle around the monolith. Medoret hesitated a moment longer. All her swimming had been in an artificial pool at Ariadan, both sport and therapy carefully monitored by adults—and without waves and rocks and maybe sea jaguars. She looked back at the bay point and smiled slightly. I am a sea creature, finned and graceful, she thought determinedly, and wondered if the Vision Serpent ever went swimming. Well, she'd find out. She plunged into the water.

The cool water absorbed her, sweeping her deep into its embrace. She struck out with her hands and legs, trying to get back to the surface, but caught a side current that pulled her deeper. She broke free of the restraint and struggled hard, then broke into the air for a breath, then paddled farther outward to get around the currents that swirled near the rocks. Ahead of her she could see Samta's dark head and the flash of his arms as he swam prudently outward, then began angling in to the other side of the tall rock. She followed, wary of the tug of the sea at her body, but floating easily. The water divided at her hands, supported her as she swam, her spirit exulting in its delicious coolness and its power. I am a sea creature, she thought ecstatically, and turned onto her back, pushing easily with her hands and legs. The water bore her upward in a great surge, then descended with her, sweeping her alongside the monolith and outward.

As she turned inward on her circle, she saw Samta clambering upward onto the easier slope of the seaward side of the rock, then get splashed by a big wave, almost losing his grip. He turned his face toward her and she saw a big grin. She paddled inward, watching the surge of the water onto the rock-face, then rode a milder wave to its edge and caught hold of a projecting point with her talons. With a heave of her arms, she lifted herself from the water, found a ledge for her knee, then scrambled upward before another wave might pluck her off. Samta caught her arm and pulled her upward. Several meters above, the rock-face leveled out into a mossy ledge before climbing more steeply to a blocky point. She settled down beside Samta and drew up her knees, the wind sharp against her wet skin.

"Can you hear the copter?" Samta asked anxiously.

"Are you kidding?" She waved her hand at the waves breaking beneath them. "In this noise?"

"Ah, well." He looked upward at the rock-face, then shivered involuntarily. "God, I'm cold."

"In a tropical climate?" she teased, and slipped her arm around his waist, then felt him respond with a tighter grip on her shoulder. "We'll dry out."

He relaxed backward and she turned on her side, wrapping her other arm around him and laying her head on his chest. She heard the distant thumping of his heart through his tunic and felt him shiver again, then slowly lose his remaining tension as the sun-warmed rock gave its heat to their bodies. They lay unmoving on the ledge for a long time, bathed by the sunlight and the cool moving of the air, the surf only meters beneath them.

"Nice," he murmured drowsily.

"Lovely," she said. "It feels like I could lie here forever, just with you."

"Thank you." He caressed her hair slowly as they listened to the water and the cry of a bird flying over the beach. Beneath the sounds, so faint as to be almost missed, Medoret heard a flat rhythm beating toward them. A moment later, Samta raised his head. "I can hear the copter. They've come around the point."

"Don't move," she said languourously. He lifted her chin with his hand and kissed her. She responded easily, wrapping her arms more tightly around him. All of this was so new to her, bound in and around her liking for this man. She caressed him slowly, then eased off when she realized how he was responding to her touch. A moment later, he broke off the kiss and took a shaky breath.

"God, what you can do to me," he whispered.

"You are the Jaguar Sun."

"No, I'm not. And this is an utterly stupid argument."

"So stop arguing," she said, trying to sound braver than she felt at the moment. She didn't quite understand Samta's hesitation, not knowing why he felt torn in two directions, not knowing if it was rejection of her or himself, and not knowing if her contrary persistence had more to do with an alien child lost among humans or the woman she might now be. She sighed unhappily, not knowing what to think, and he abruptly turned and pulled her still closer to him, his lips seeking hers. He kissed her urgently, then slipped his hand to her chest, seeking a breast that wasn't there. Startled, he looked down at his hand and started to laugh, his mouth distorted.

"Stop that," she commanded, then shook him hard. He quieted and looked away, a dull flush in his face. "That's part of loving me," she said, trying to sound light. "But there might be other compensations." He looked at her, startled again. "I read that in a romance novel. They never did explain what the 'other compensations' might be, but perhaps we could experiment." She smiled at him, their faces close together. "I don't want to hurt you, Samta. Yes or no, perhaps I'll hurt you, anyway. I don't know, either."

He closed his eyes, then kissed her palm. "Complicated."

"Or very simple."

Samta grimaced. "And as the copter takes a wider swing around the beach, the infrared scanner picks up a shot of . . . us. That would be truly ducky, being found literally in the act."

"So?" The copter's blatting rhythm was quite distinct now as the search copter came slowly down the beach. "Can you think of a better way to wait?"

"That line from another novel?" he asked skeptically.

"Same one, actually." She grinned up at him and felt her heart quicken with joy and relief as the tension finally eased from his face.

"Hell," he muttered helplessly.

"Xibalba," she corrected, and pulled his head down to hers.

Chapter Fourteen _____

Some time later Medoret lay drowsily against Samta's body, listening to the copter in the far distance as it rounded the next point of rock into another bay. Samta made a rattling snore into her ear, startling her. She edged backward, careful to not disturb him, then raised herself to an elbow, cradling her head in her palm, and watched his face as he slept, studying the curves, the straight dark hair that fell across his forehead, the faint sheen of sweat that dried quickly in the breeze. She reached out and gently slipped the wisp of hair upward, then tickled his ear. His eyes opened halfway.

"Stop that," he said.

"Stop what?"

"That." He reached up suddenly and seized her hand, then firmly placed it back in her own space. As he released her wrist, she promptly returned to tickling his ear again. "You're a pest," he declared, a smile tugging at his mouth.

She stretched out her bent arm and laid her head down by his. "Do you really think so?"

"Definitely." He smiled and closed his eyes, her fingers again caught warmly in his. She watched his face, happier than she had felt in most of the times she could remember.

She had felt awkward during the lovemaking, not knowing quite what to do or expect: the novels had usually focused on intense interest in the preparation, without many specifics about the goal, but enough of a clue to go along with what Samta had proposed midway. But she had liked the closeness and her awareness of Samta's intensity; after several minutes, he seemed to forget completely the copter making its slow way down the beach toward them. And, after more time, so did she, rising with him in her awareness of the pleasure she gave to him.

Perhaps the experience should have been more in some incomprehensible way, she thought judiciously, looking at him now: she puzzled about the ways, not minding at all that the supposed ecstasy had eluded her. How she liked this man—it was an intimacy between persons she treasured.

His eyes opened again. "What are you thinking?"

"I've never done this before."

His mouth twisted slightly. "That I know."

"Was I that awkward?" she asked, worrying. He promptly pulled her against him and held her close, then kissed her in apology.

"I'm awkward, not you," he said. "Forgive me. You were wonderful."

"Thank you." She caressed his face. "Was it everything you wanted?" she persisted. It seemed it had been—he was extraordinarily relaxed—but she felt impelled to ask, anyway. Samta had all the wisdom on his side in arguing against this, but she had felt too aware of time shortening, of a need for the bond, of the need for him. He smiled at her lazily.

"The way this works, Medoret, is a vagueness of exact goals, leveraged by a need for practice. Not exactly a scientific experiment, but with certain similarities in some respects, with perhaps a wider range of possible hypotheses." His smile broadened to a grin as she showed her puzzlement. "I love you. Always remember that."

She smiled and laid down her head again on her arm; he turned his face to her. The breeze stirred his dark hair as he watched her expression.

"What are you thinking?" he asked again. Did he sound anxious? she wondered, feeling herself on the edge of a precipice, so easily wrong if she misjudged—wrong for him, and now that choosing seemed very important. She guessed the rules were even more insubstantial in such things as this, but perhaps rules were less important, too.

"I feel so ignorant. It's complicated." She traced the curve of his jaw with a finger, then pretended to tickle his ear again to provoke him. "Does it always feel like this, like you're tiptoeing around rocks in a garden?"

"I don't know—probably. I've never been in love before."

"You haven't? Why not?"

He shrugged. "Too hooked on you, maybe. Missed running into the right woman. Too busy with academics, probably. Waiting for you."

"Hmmmm."

"I won't ask for what you can't give me, Medoret." He was serious now, his dark eyes intense.

"But you still want it?"

"Not necessarily. Like I said, this needs practice—and maybe part of the practice is learning some new expectations. Does that make sense?"

"Absolutely," she said. "I treasure you. Is that the same as love?"

His face filled with sudden joy and she marveled at the power of a few simple words, true as they were. "I don't know. I'm not an expert." He raised her hand to his mouth and pressed his lips against it, looking at her over their joined hands. "It's all new to me, too." Then she saw the sadness, just as sudden, and knew the reason. He assumed she would leave him behind, might even insist on that, in his stubborn way that was all too human, choosing for her against himself. She had her own stubbornness, though the ways of keeping both worlds might not be obvious as yet. Was it wise?

She smiled at him. "Wouldn't it be great to live in the jungle forever, or just right here, like this?"

"Lack of food supply, unless you have a hook and line. Shelter could be better, too."

"Don't be practical."

"There's nothing else to be."

"Really? Well, you can be as practical as you want, but I don't have to. I don't have to do anything I don't want to do. I'm the Vision Serpent. Nobody pushes me around." He opened his mouth to speak again, and she quickly laid her fingers on his lips. "Reality later, Samta. Don't worry until you have to. Does *that* make sense?"

"Easy to say, not so easy to do, my love."

"There are lots of easy things." She moved closer to him and caressed him provocatively, lightly moving her hand from shoulder to hip to thigh, then, bravely daring, slipping her fingers inside his loosened trousers. His eyebrows rose in surprise. "Experimenting," she said, then watched him laugh in delight. "Should I stop?" she asked.

"No—please no." He reached down to press her hand deeper, then guided her fingers in the caress he wanted as he bent to kiss her again.

An hour later they watched cautiously from behind the top of the monolith as the copter beat its way back up the beach. As the machine rounded the far point of the bay, Samta crawled backward and tugged her after him, cautious of being sighted. They slid down farther to their ledge and sat together, listening to the sound as the search team, still moving slowly as it scanned the jungle a second time, crossed the beach behind them and headed north for Tikal.

Samta squeezed her hand. "Parameters are useful. They went as far as they thought we could walk. If they'd found the Black Ship, they wouldn't be returning like this."

"The robot said it was a day's walk."

"Maybe farther, too. But they'll be there, when you look for them."

"When *we* look for them," she amended, heading off one possible option he might be thinking. He shrugged humorously, catching her in the thought.

"We," he conceded.

The copter faded into the distance, its sound vanishing into the nearer sounds of water and air. Samta took her hand and got them to their feet, then picked his way gingerly down the steep slope to the surging water. He watched the waves, waiting for a good time to plunge; she watched with him and they chose the same moment, splashing back into the water together. She followed him in the swim around the rock; then, streaming water from their clothes, they retrieved Samta's haversack and skipped across the chain of rocks back to the empty beach. "South," he declared, and took her hand. "To whatever's waiting there."

Nightfall found them several kilometers south, and Medoret's leg muscles ached from the unaccustomed exercise. Samta looked as tired as she felt, and they comfortably agreed on a resting spot beside a huge tree a few meters into the jungle brush. The tree had rotted from within, strangled by a flowered vine similar to Earth's lianas, and its hollow core made a comfortable dark closeness around them. A small stream tumbled nearby, spilling into the sea, and they rinsed their clothing free of salt in its warm cleanness.

The coolness of the dusk made the constant breeze cold, too cold to put on newly wet clothing, and so they hung their clothes from makeshift knobs inside the hollow tree as the sunlight faded and lay down together near the back of the hollow trunk, shivering with chill. Medoret held him contentedly, happy to just lie together as they warmed themselves with each other's body heat, then felt his hands begin to move tentatively. In the faint light, his body glowed with infrared, showing her a shadowed ruddy curve of shoulder and hip, the length of his legs, the movement of his arm muscles as he explored her body with his hands, taking time. She caressed him slowly, responding to his intent concentration on her body, aware of his scents and warmth and the subtleties of his movements. When he entered her for the third time, she wrapped her legs high around his waist and pulled him closer than ever before, riding his passion with him until he shuddered and cried out with his release. He lay heavily upon her afterward, his breath slowly quietening; she caressed his back slowly, running her hands over his skin, reveling in its softness, the definition of the muscles underneath, the heat against her palms.

"Medoret. . . ." he whispered against her hair, but said nothing more.

The murmur of the forest canopy surrounded them, alive with soft cries of nearby animals, the muted hum of insect wings, a subdued crash through brush some way off, all underlaid by the constant sound of the surf. The air, moving softly inside the hollowed space of the tree, was silken on her body, awakening every nerve almost to the point of ecstasy. And throughout it all, she was intensely conscious of Samta's nearness, of the aliveness of him, of his heartbeat and breath, his warmth, his scents, his measured drowsy caresses.

Love. . . . It might be this, she thought. Not the ecstatic dance with the Jaguar Sun, nor the wild out-of-self emotions her novels described, but this in the aliveness of their bodies lying so close together as the warm air whispered over them.

If one could only hold such a moment forever, she thought, knowing that time was not that merciful. And she knew her dilemma would be harsher for it, as Samta well knew and had tried to warn her, had tried to sacrifice his own longings for her sake. Was I wise to make this happen? she wondered sadly. Was I wise? She suspected an answer she didn't want, not now, not like this.

She drowsed and chose to dream of him, clothing him in the Jaguar's fierceness as they battled the Underlords in a jungle glade. Her dream drifted away and fragmented, then regathered into a dream of Targethi sacrifice. She watched, horrified, as the Targethi led their victims up the steps of the temple, the Vision Serpent fluttering overhead. A flint knife slashed downward, ripping through carapace and muscle, severing blood vessels and nerves and organs, contorting the dying body into spasm and jerkings. Scream after scream poured out of the victim's open mouth, high-pitched, shrieking, ending suddenly in a spasm of silence. The conquerors danced ecstatically, surging into the silence with their maddening chanting, their segmented arms uplifted to the Serpent, praising her. Then all stopped to watch the next victim die, their jaws slack with anticipation, ovoid eyes bright with stimulation.

She looked down at her worshipers, coiling her bright-scaled body, her teeth sharp, her muscles deft and smooth. They advanced on her and she hissed at them in warning, but still they advanced. "Nooo!" she cried as their claws seized her and dragged her up the temple steps. She fought them, whipping her powerful tail into their faces, tearing away whole fronds from her neck and slim body as she struggled in their grip. She snapped her jaws viciously at them, killing, maiming, overpowering them with her anger, then broke free and circled above them, screaming her curses. They cowered, raising their clawed hands in fear, then ran in all directions as she pounced on one of the priests and ripped him apart, then, laughing, threw his dismembered body at the others as they fled. She alighted on the uppermost step, her neck bent in a double-looped curve, delighting in their terror.

"I am the Vision Serpent!" she shouted at them. "I take,

not give!" She gestured her defiance, then froze as they brought a struggling human figure toward her, one she knew, one who had bonded flesh with her in a long-ago time she barely remembered. As she wavered, the Targethi laughed maliciously, a silvery sound that shattered the daytime. Take him, they called up to her mockingly. Take him, She Who Takes! A chiming sound filled the air, overwhelming her, and she fled from the Targethi, abandoning the Jaguar to their cruelty.

"No!" she cried, and struck out, denying the dream, dimly aware her hand had connected hard with flesh. "No!"

Samta caught her hand and forced it away as she struck at him again, lost in the terror of her dream. He seized her and they struggled until she abruptly saw him, a shadow in the warm darkness. He pulled her close with a desperation that caught at her throat. "Medoret! What's the matter?"

She sobbed, a deep racking sob that rose from her belly, then began to weep helplessly, torn by emotions she didn't understand. He enfolded her in his arms and began to rock her slowly back and forth, offering comfort, his heartbeat a measured quick rhythm against her ear. He held her until her weeping ended, not asking the cause, and she clung to him desperately. After a time he arranged them both more comfortably and lay down with her, keeping her close.

"Do you know why?" he asked, his voice muffled by her hair.

"No."

"Then it's okay. Just let it go for now." He caressed her hair and kissed her, then lay quietly beside her, encouraging her to relax as his own body eased back into a drowse, his hand moving slowly over her hair. Though she resisted, she felt herself slipping back into sleep, fearful of new dreams.

I do not wish to dream, she cried silently. I do not wish to know these things.

* * *

The Vision Serpent waited for her in the temple glade, her deep-set eyes glowing, the sun shimmering on her bright scales.

"Lady Rainbow," the Serpent greeted her.

Medoret bowed gracefully. "Serpent, I see you."

"It is the fourth day of the seventh cycle: today the God of the Razored Flint reigns and holds all within himself. Hear his scents; touch his voice." The Serpent turned toward the jungle that surrounded the glade. "Look there."

"No."

"You will obey!" the Serpent cried in her voice of slivered flint.

"No." Medoret crossed her arms across her chest and glared at the Serpent. "You betray me with your dreams of blood and death. I will not give him up."

"Betrayal? Never!"

"You betray me. This is not truth. I do not accept it."

The Serpent drifted closer, her fronds moving lazily, and she gnashed her polished teeth in anger. "I am Death," the Serpent announced, fluttering her fins. "I am Life."

"I could hate you," Medoret whispered. "And I do not accept."

She awoke to cool air moving over her body, a pale light glancing in from the forest beyond. Samta lay deep in sleep beside her, his arms still holding her. She relaxed against him, comforted by his warmth as she watched the pale light quicken, touching the dew on the leaves into silver and rubies. The morning breeze stirred, beginning the hushed whispers of the forest; in the distance, birds called a greeting to the dawn. All around them life was stirring.

Death? For whom? She closed her eyes in pain, understanding all too much now. The plague explained her fevers, the Black Ship's desperation, the harshness to her mother's face that eased less and less. She slipped her fingers to her pocket and found the vial with the drugs the humans had made for her and brought it out, turning it in her hand until its plastic sides caught a reflection of the dawn light. In my hand, she thought, I have the key—maybe. The fever drug only eased, not cured, and the Black Ship had its own palliatives; but if the humans knew the cause, had not assumed it a natural function, could they find the real cure? Could the Black Ship go home, as she knew all aboard her desperately wanted? But where was home?

She turned her head and looked at Samta's face in the shadows. Her dreams had a truth she still valued, whatever her defiance to the Serpent, but she lacked the skills in knowing their full meaning: what would her mother say of Samta? What could Medoret say to her? Had she crossed a line not to be permitted? Her fingers tightened painfully on the vial.

I don't care, she told herself. He is too much to me to care about that. Even if it's death to me, I don't care.

But she doubted her own resolution, even for his sake. She let her arm fall to her side, the vial clutched in her hand, and closed her eyes wearily. Let me be free of dreams, she wished. This was a knowledge I didn't want.

She knew nothing of how her own people loved one another, how a man chose a woman, a woman a man. Likely the physical act was much the same, but what of the emotions, the expectations of each other, the manner of the joining of two lives? She remembered her mother as alone, without husband; she frowned, knowing vaguely that her father was dead, but how and why she couldn't remember—nor even why she knew her father had died. Had he died of the plague? Had her mother taken ship to find a purpose in her aloneness?

There's so much I don't know, she thought, so much I don't understand. How can I ever bind with them again, when the knowledge might be no more than a tale told of strangers? Her Maya dream world was as real as her memories of the Black Ship, and neither truly real. At this moment, only Samta seemed real.

I've waited ten years, yearning for them, and now I'm afraid of what I'll find. Easier to imagine anything I wished and not have to face the truth, easier to escape into a fantasy world, keeping everything and not having choices. For there would be a choice. Samta knew that, whatever her own protests.

She lay quietly beside Samta, watching him sleep, until he stirred sleepily, the dawn well-advanced. He raised his head and looked at her face, saw her watching him, and smiled. She lifted her hand and laid the palm against his cheek. "Good morning," she said.

"Yes, it is." His eyes were shadowed, though he tried to keep an air of good cheer. "Today's the day, isn't it?"

"Yes." He kissed her quickly and then got up, snagging his clothes as he slipped out the doorway. Medoret moved more slowly, her thoughts heavy on her mind. When he returned, she was rummaging through the carryall for the rest of their food; he dropped an armful of fruit on the ground by the carryall, and they ate quickly.

"Are you going to tell me about your dream?" he asked.

"I don't know what my dreams mean, Samta," she said, not looking at him.

"You said your dreams have significance. A different kind of knowledge." He stopped awkwardly, then bent forward to look into her face. "Medoret?"

"I don't want this knowledge."

"About me?"

She bit her lip, wishing Samta was less quick in his shaman's guessing. "It's complicated."

He took her hand and raised it to his lips. "Thank you for giving yourself to me. Thank you for having the courage. It may end up a total mistake, but thank you. I'll always treasure the memory—and hope I haven't hurt you.

That was the last thing I wanted, ever. Please don't regret anything."

"I don't regret it."

"Oh?" He smiled at her, but his eyes were troubled. He, too, felt a shadow on the bright morning.

"I'm not my dreams, Samta—and I'm not really Lady Rainbow, whatever the Serpent says." She shook her head, then raised her eyes to his. "You are my friend. It was an honor—I choose to believe that, even though I don't understand anything else at all."

She got to her feet and pulled him upward. He picked up the carryall and slung it across his shoulders, then followed her through the narrow screen of brush back to the beach. They paused a moment and watched the surf tumble onto the beach, then set off again southward to whatever waited for them.

Medoret fingered the vial of drugs in her pocket as they walked, troubled by her uncertainties. All her life on Ariadan she had wished for the Black Ship, anxious that she not change too much to lose that bond forever. She suspected she had changed, knew she had changed. How could she not?

The humans had demanded she conform to their ways, following their rules, fitting their purpose. Would the Black Ship demand she be something she had never been, choosing *their* purpose for her life?

What do I answer? She listened to the sea tumble up the beach and watched a fish jump from the waves far out into the surf. For I suspect I could deny them, too, if they asked too much.

They walked along the beach at an easy pace all the morning, talking occasionally, with Samta determined to be cheerful—for her sake, she knew. She allowed him to cajole her, smiling at his jokes, setting aside her dread and uncertainty for the brightness of the morning and his company. The beach swept around another curve of a new bay, then another, the whispering forest on one side, the crashing surf on the other, a bath of sound that lulled and finally eased her fractured mind. This was a beautiful world: had the Targethi chosen it for its beauty? Had they seen what lay here—or had their dark dreams of the Hunt and sacrifice overborne every other knowing? Had they grieved to lose it when disaster ended all they possessed?

"Look at the bird," she said, pointing at a flash of bright color. "Parrots."

"Pretty."

"Maybe we could homestead, like the Targethi did here, and live like this all our lives in this Xibalba."

"Would you like that?" Samta asked, and shifted his haversack to his other shoulder. She slipped her fingers into the curve of his free hand, comfortable with his touch.

"Would you?"

"I asked first."

"Ah, you dodge." He chuckled and contrarily let it sit, though he had indeed asked first. She thought about it, looking at the trees and the small creatures that made their home there. "Well, we both have problems with local proteins. Eating is a basic reality."

"A practical thought," he said, teasing her. "You'd have to be a study project, with me as archaeologist scrutinizing and writing my reports—only I'm in Metals. Team conflict there. Have to be Hillary, I guess, to get it back with BioSurvey, you being bio and all."

"I don't want to live with Hillary. I want to live with you."

His smile flashed. "Oh, Hillary's not that bad. Better than Dr. Falk."

"True. Maybe you could switch specialties."

"Or reacquire an earlier one, one that better fits the blood? Shaman better fits life with a Maya goddess."

"True. We could both be a study project. How'd you like to be studied?"

"Not much," he said lightly. "I left all that to my Maya ancestors."

"You'd look good in parrot feathers, shaman."

"You look good in anything, Ix-chel." He looked at her curiously. "Second thoughts? Why that particular daydream?"

"Nerves, I guess. Imagine what it'd be like if you had to walk into Narenjo or Copan—the real ones back on Earth centuries ago—and fit in. No archaeology grants, no spaceships, nothing of all that's happened since, no life you've had in any respect. It's all irrelevant."

"Is that what your dream told you last night?"

"I didn't listen to what it said. I didn't want to hear." She tightened her fingers on his and watched her feet scuff over the wet sand, conscious of the light breeze, the sounds that bathed the air, the life all around them. "I think my choices don't fit together, and I don't want to hear that. I don't want to lose you." She looked at him quickly. "Now *don't* start blaming yourself. I made the choice first, not you. Right?"

"What will they think about it?"

She grimaced. "That's the problem, Samta. I don't know. I don't remember enough. How do I even know if I belong to them anymore? And that's a possible answer I don't want, either. You said Xibalba could be a bridge—but what if the Black Ship doesn't know Xibalba, anymore than Dr. Falk or Dr. Mueller or the others who choose to not see? Where is the bridge then?" She stopped and pulled him around to face her. "But you are here, on the bridge. I think that's why I chose what I did—some one person to be there with me, after so many years of feeling disconnected from everyone, even myself, to be there if it doesn't go well, if all dreams crash into oblivion. Do you understand?"

"Yes." He bent to kiss her, then caressed her hair slowly, as if nothing else counted at that moment. "We're only mortal, after all. Only the gods can hope for infallibility—and who among them always wins? Even the Twins had to face death and the ultimate defeat."

"You do understand." She caught his hand and brought it to her lips.

"I try to. All that counts to me is that you find what you most wish for, that all things are righted, that the balance is made. If I fit into that, it would be wonderful." His eyes focused on her face, gravely serious. "And if I don't, all that counts is you."

"And if I'm saying all that counts is you. . . ."

"We could get in trouble." He glanced around at the beach and jungle, then drew in a deep breath of the scented air. "You keep telling me I'm throwing away my grant by helping you. You're probably right. But I get tired of chasing the wrong things, as if today's data run is a crisis of life, that Dr. Mueller's moods rule the day, that all this measuring and theorizing and academic self-congratulation should consume everything. I get tired of how it dents people. I get tired of blindness like my father's. He interested himself in the Otherworld, but even his shaman's rituals were calculated studies of cause and effect. The others are just as blind. Ian lets his love for you get blunted by his ambitions, Dr. Ruth sees only what she wants to see—when all that counts is the vision that sees the truth."

"I should like to see what's real, but I pick and choose, too."

"We all do. I'd rather be a Maya shaman, Medoret, but that life has been passed by. The temples are crumbled ruins and the Maya kings are long dead."

"I asked the Serpent once if I could live in her world forever. I suppose I could: if I can choose my dreams, perhaps I can choose my own madness." She stepped closer to him and wound her arms around his waist, then felt his hands tighten on her back, bringing her still closer. They stood together for a long moment, listening to the sea and forest.

"But you have to go see how it is with the Black Ship," he said. "You would always wonder."

"Yes. But come with me, Samta. Don't believe that I am better off without you."

"I can't help my believing, my love. But I'll come with you."

They continued onward, splashing comfortably in the surf hand in hand, surrounded by the warm breeze and the ever-moving sounds of Tikal's verdant world. By early afternoon they had walked several kilometers and Medoret began to watch the sea and beach far ahead, her heartbeat quickening. She pulled ahead of Samta for a time, though she was tired as he was with the two days of walking—but the next bay was as empty as the several they had passed. Disappointed, she glanced back at Samta and tripped over a tree root half-concealed in the sand.

Samta lunged to catch her as she stumbled; at that same instant, a hollow explosion sounded from deep in the jungle underbrush and Samta was hurled away from her. She staggered around to her feet and saw the jagged wound in Samta's shoulder as the world froze into an instant of diamond clarity. She threw herself between Samta and the jungle, shielding him, then pivoted on her knee to face the attacker.

"Bar-asin matu!" a voice called behind a screen of bushes. She turned slowly on one knee to face in the exact direction, careful to keep her body between the voice and Samta. Her eyes narrowed, searching the underbrush for a revealing shadow, conscious of the rapid pulse in her ears, the alertness to every change around her.

"I don't understand your words!" she shouted. "Show yourself!"

A tall figure stepped into view, a weapon in his hand. He was dressed in a simple ship suit, dull gray in color, his hair whitened and as fine as her own—and older in the face than his apparent youth, with a face already faintly lined with strain and illness. She examined him carefully, but did not recognize him, had never seen him in her dreams. It disconcerted her, and she realized belatedly he was near her own age. One of the Ship's children—but which one? She had rarely dreamed of the children, and she did not know him. She watched him, using the Jaguar's fierce alertness.

Enemy, she thought, caught half into her Maya dream world by the surprise attack on Samta. Were her people the kind who killed from ambush, without mercy or inquiry? Were they Underlords, the enemy of all that breathed and thought and differed from themselves? She did not remember the Varen as such, but what were dreams if untrue?

"Move aside, Medoret," the other said in Anglic. She stared at him challengingly, her chin lifted. "Move aside," he repeated, gesturing with his weapon.

"No."

"I said move aside," the young man insisted. "He is one of *them*, the child-stealers. I intend to remove the taint. Move aside!"

"No. Where is my mother?"

"She is very ill. It is her time in the fever cycle."

Medoret reached into her pocket and pulled out the vial of her drugs, then tossed it forward onto the sand. "Among those capsules is the drug the humans used to heal my fevers. It might be better than your palliatives. Take it to her."

The young man stared down at the vial and made no move toward it.

"Take it!" she repeated.

She turned her back on him to bend over Samta. "Can you walk?" she whispered.

"Why did he shoot me?" Samta asked, dazed, and dared to look at his shoulder. "Oh, God."

"The laser cauterized the artery or you'd be bleeding worse—that's a blessing. Here, let me help you up—keep behind me. He'll kill you the instant he has a clear shot again."

"But *why?*"

"Medoret," the stranger called peremptorily, his voice tinged with alarm as he guessed at her intention. "Move aside."

"No! Take the vial to my mother." She half lifted Samta to his feet, keeping herself carefully between him and the stranger, then began walking him away. "Kill something else if the blood pleases you."

It hit close, she could tell, though his expression promptly settled back into determination. "Where are you going?" he asked.

She shook her head violently, denying him an answer. She wished him confusion, her rage growing over his unprovoked attack on Samta, and his pursuit after to the kill.

I am kin to the Lords of the Underworld, she thought in anguish, no better than the Targethi and their Hunt. The Vision Serpent told me last night, warned me.

She looked back and saw the man hesitate, then hurried Samta over the sand, supporting him as he stumbled, achingly conscious of his soft gasp of pain as he stumbled again. Never, she vowed. I won't give Samta up to sacrifice. Not to the Serpent, not to my own people. Never.

Chapter Fifteen _____

Past the screen of trees beyond the bend, she tried to hurry Samta to a better sanctuary, guessing the Varen would follow. She needed a place to tend him, guard him. Desperately, she guided him into the jungle and found a rotting log several meters into the screen of trees, a forest giant that had fallen decades before. She lowered him to rest against it and tried to arrange him comfortably, all too conscious of time running out, time that slipped through her fingers and could not be retrieved. Removing the carryall from his shoulder was agony to him as she pulled the strap over the wound. He gasped and his eyes rolled upward into a faint, his brown skin visibly paler. He was injured badly; even though the laser had stopped any blood loss, the shock might kill him. She knew nothing of tending wounds: this was not a fantasy where a Heroic Twin could blithefully return to life by his own willing.

I am Death, the Serpent had told her. She crouched in front of Samta, cursing her own helplessness, her not knowing, her believing in too much.

To see the truth, he had wished. Can I be that strong?

She heard the underbrush crackling behind them and looked around quickly for a weapon, anything at hand. She seized a fallen branch and broke off the end, making a jagged pike, and then turned to stand over Samta's body, facing the sea.

"This time I'll kill you, Underlord!" she shouted in defiance as a shadow moved under the trees. "I am the Hunt! Show yourself!"

She fixed on that position, waiting for the charge—then gawked as a different man stepped out into the dusklight, not a human man, but . . .

"Bael," she whispered in recognition.

He had aged cruelly from her memory, no longer vibrant but bent and hesitant in his movements from too many courses of the plague. He limped toward her, his expression implacable. As she raised her stick in warning, he stopped and spoke to her in the Ship's language, like the other had.

She shook her head. "I don't understand," she said. "I don't remember our speech." Behind Bael the younger man stepped out, his stance as arrogant as before, his weapon still in his hand. Bael took another step and she brandished her rough spear. "Stop!" she warned Bael. "Stop where you are!"

Bael stopped and inspected her, then inspected Samta's limp body at her feet, his distaste for the human milder than the younger man's but just as apparent.

Medoret lifted her chin. "I have defied human intolerance all my remembered life: I can survive yours. Go back to your Ship with your scorn. I don't want it."

Bael cleared his throat and gestured at Samta. "He is injured," he said in understandable but accented Anglic. Her breath caught as she heard the lilt of their own language behind the alien speech. The sound tantalized, as if she had only to touch to regain it all, a sound that cajoled, wishing at her, drawing her in. She shook her head slightly, keeping her focus on Bael.

"Yes. I have no remedy—he survives the wound or he doesn't." From the corner of her eye she saw that the younger man had stopped under the shadow of the trees and was watching them both.

"What is he to you?" Bael asked curiously.

"A friend."

"A human?" Bael's voice sounded shocked. Medoret laughed without humor.

"And who else shall be my friends, Uncle, in my exile? Only fantasies? Or should I have stayed in nothingness, refusing life and all dreams? Yes, he is my friend."

"Your mother has waited for you," Bael said more gently. "For many years."

"I honor my mother." Medoret's eyes filled with sudden tears and she clenched her teeth, wishing to show no such weakness, not here, not now. The Underlords could be crafty, she remembered, pretending themselves something other than they were.

"Medoret," Bael said, "put down the spear. How can I examine his wound with you swaying above him like a jas-serpent?" He spread his hands. "I am not armed. There is no Hunt today to sacrifice, only to find."

Medoret hesitated, her glance flicking to the younger man in the shadows of the trees.

"Jaleel was hasty, and thinks much of his own judgment. He will follow mine now, as is fitting," Bael said.

Medoret studied Bael's calm face and hesitated. In her dreams, she had loved this man, a man who had often taken the place of the father she had never known, who knew her mother as kinswoman and captain, who led as she led when there was need. All my years I have believed in the dreams, clung to them. Do I abandon them now? She hesitated a moment longer while Bael waited patiently, then tossed the branch on the sand.

"Good." Bael walked forward calmly and knelt on one knee beside Samta, touching his injured shoulder, then turning it gently toward the setting sun. Then he felt Samta's face, leaning forward to look more closely. "Jaleel, bring the pack." Jaleel half made a gesture of protest, then turned and vanished obediently back into the jungle. "You must excuse Jaleel," Bael said to her. "The young are often fierce in their emotions."

"As I have proved." It was a half-apology—but only half.

"The young are rash," Bael said contentedly. It calmed her further, as no doubt he had intended. Bael had stood second to her mother for years, for good reasons. He looked up at her, his eyes questioning.

"I have dreamed of you, Uncle."

"I am pleased of that; I would hate to be forgotten." Bael bent forward and fingered the fabric of Samta's shirt, then began ripping the sleeve downward. "Sit down before you fall down, child."

"I'm not a child."

He looked up again and scowled. "I am a logical man, yet I forget the years; I expected the child we had lost. You look like your mother did at the same age—and just as angry. Are you determined to be hostile?"

She grimaced, then reluctantly crouched down on her heels and hugged her knees. "I'm confused."

"Jaleel has reasons to be angry."

"That doesn't excuse him."

"Not even when you haven't even asked his reasons?"

"Did he ask mine? No, not even then."

"Hmmph. You are your mother's daughter, Medoret." His hands moved competently on Samta, square and slender, his talons pricking delicately at the fused cloth surrounding the laser wound. Even in his faint, Samta moved in response to the pain, then sagged more limply. She bit her lip in worry, then looked at Bael, seeing pain there, too, a pain of years that never ended, never eased, a heart pain he would carry to the grave. Yet he continued patiently. In that moment, the uncle of her dreams and the waking day merged, becoming one man, this man. She touched his sleeve gently.

"The humans have a partial cure for the plague, Uncle."

Bael's hands stopped abruptly in his caring for Samta, then resumed more slowly. "We have our own palliatives."

"The humans are clever. They had to make two proteins for me that we don't share and then a fever drug, though they aren't quite sure why this drug stops the fevers. Mine still recur at intervals."

Bael looked at her intently. "How short of intervals?"

"Every few years."

Bael closed his eyes and sank back on his heels, then looked at her in naked pain. "Years," he breathed. "Our fevers cycle in months."

"And usually a mild affliction."

"Mild," Bael muttered, closing his eyes again.

"It's the frostflowers, isn't it? The frostflower spores. With that link and what you know of the Targethi, they might cure all the fever, end it. They want to meet you. They brought me to Tikal to be the bait."

Bael scowled and set his face. "Why did you bring this human with you? Does he assure the bait?"

"Because he would not leave me, and I needed his balance to remember what I am—what is a dream world and what is human, my uncle."

Jaleel emerged from the trees, carrying a heavy pack. As he walked up to them, he raised his eyes and looked at her, his arrogance written in every line of his tall body, then dropped the pack beside Bael. "I am Jaleel," he said.

"You are nothing," she retorted.

Bael promptly reached over and jerked hard on her pants leg. She sat down hard on the leafy dirt, hard enough to make her squawk in surprise. She glared at Bael, infuriated with him.

"That's enough," Bael said reprovingly. "Now you sit there and Jaleel will sit there." He pointed at a spot three meters away. "When either of you children can be civil, you may speak again."

Medoret crossed her arms and looked toward the sea, seething, then gave up her irritation to watch as Bael tended Samta's shoulder. Jaleel sat down as obediently and ignored

Medoret as determinedly as she ignored him. Their stubborn attitude focused great attention on Bael, which he ignored in turn. His fingers moved quickly, packing a lotion into the wound from a flask in his pack, then gently binding the wound with soft greenish gauze. "A bad flesh wound," he muttered, "but treatable. This is an antiseptic we developed years ago on another world for jaguar poison; the gauze will give cleansing heat."

"The jaguars come from another world?" Medoret asked. "The humans had thought so."

"Of course they do," Bael said. "They're native to the Targethi motherworld, and are taken to every world to be hunted—and worshipped. Haven't you seen how they dominate the city's glyphs?"

She touched Bael's sleeve again. "Bael, who were the Targethi?"

Bael's lean face grew even more severe. "A people who Hunted—until they Hunted once too often. Then the Hunts ended, thank the Goddess, for all time." He turned to her, his eyes cold. "The Targethi did not tolerate rivals in their chosen view of the universe. You've seen their monuments of these greater Hunts in Tikal's plaza. The humans call them gods. Had we Varen or the humans emerged into space earlier than we did, we would stand among them." He shrugged. "But the Melasoi killed the Targethi with their frostflowers, even as the Destructor ships rained death down into their skies." Bael spoke calmly, without passion, only that great coldness. Perhaps, after a time, she thought, one grew used to great tragedy—or tired of living too much to care as keenly as the young.

"Which of the avenue gods were the Melasoi?" she asked, guessing the answer.

"The Serpent, fourth from the left." His eyes showed interest. "You have dreamed of this?"

"The Vision Serpent has been a companion and protector since my earliest memory: she is the doorway to remembering my mother." She looked down at Samta and reached to brush his hair back from his face. "I do not understand my dreams. How can I know what I can't know?"

"The Dream-Knowledge is an ancient gift, much prized by the Varen."

"Varen? Is that our name? The robot named us that."

"What do you think your name is?"

"Lady Rainbow." She smiled tiredly. She spread her arms then, wishing him a peace beyond what he had found, wishing all the years away to when a little girl had played under the table. Bael pulled her tightly against his lean body, pressing almost too hard. "Uncle."

"My own," he murmured. He set her back, his hands on her shoulders, and looked her up and down. "How you've grown!"

"It's been ten years."

His mouth turned down at that reminder, and he glanced involuntarily at Samta, his eyes glinting.

"So that's Samta's personal fault?" she challenged. "He was a child, like I was, when it was done."

"What is he to you?" Bael said resistantly, and released her.

"My friend, precious to me. Is this what the Varen are? To deny bonding? I remember the bonding. Are we so mean that we don't share it with outsiders?" She turned her shoulder to him and heard him expel an exasperated breath.

"Your mother will want to see you as soon as possible. Jaleel will watch the human."

Medoret shot a quick glance at Jaleel, and decided Jaleel would not do any such thing. "I won't leave him."

"Your mother is ill, Medoret. She can't make the trip, much less stomp through this rampant greenery."

Medoret set her jaw. "I won't leave him."

"He is more important than your mother? Than us?" The question was an accusation and she saw Bael draw back, his face remote.

"Why must there be such a stark choice, Uncle?" Medoret asked sadly. "Him or you, denying one or the other? Is that what we are, we Varen?"

Bael tapped his fingers on his thigh, obviously perplexed, then shook his head in dismay. Medoret's eyes slowly filled with tears as she watched him. She saw the judgment move into him, a judgment she had seen a hundred times in Sieyes's eyes. His next words confirmed her reading of him.

"What have they done to you?"

She turned away, her breath suddenly gone. She got to her feet convulsively and walked several steps, stopping to stare at the shadowed trees, aware of the rustling of the living forest. For a moment she wished the Vision Serpent truly existed, could beckon her to a temple glade—now, at this time, this unjoining—where she might dance with the Jaguar Sun forever.

Bael cleared his throat uncomfortably. "We will take your . . . friend," he said reluctantly. "Your mother must decide this. I cannot."

Medoret turned and stared at him, not conceding anything.

"The biopack works quickly with a minimum of drugs; I'd hate to poison him." He waited for her response, then scowled. "Jaleel, help me get him to his feet."

Jaleel came forward, his face an expressionless mask. He looked at her squarely, giving nothing, as she gave nothing to him. She did not remember him, though she caught for a moment an image of the small boy who had played with her in the Ship glade, the tall metal walls of the ship hull towering over them. "I don't remember you," she told him.

"You don't remember many things," he said disdainfully, and she could have struck him. He took a startled step sideways as he somehow caught her thought and their eyes locked.

"I am who I am," she declared, as if he were an enemy.

"If you cannot accept that, I still choose what I am." He hesitated, then turned away, dismissing her. She laughed harshly. "I welcome me home."

Bael shot her a quick glance, his face openly alarmed. She crossed her arms and turned her back on him, her emotions a tumult. This wasn't what I expected, she cried silently.

She heard Samta's voice murmur behind her, then turned to see Bael and Jaleel pulling him to his feet, balancing him as he weaved. He blinked groggily and sagged loosely against Bael, then focused on her. "Medoret?"

She crossed the distance dividing them in a quick stride and laid her palm on his cheek. "Be easy. This is the day, remember?"

As Bael drew Samta forward, Jaleel moved too quickly and tugged hard on Samta's injured shoulder—deliberately or not, she didn't care. As Samta cried out in pain, Medoret moved with the Serpent's own grace and hit Jaleel hard on the chin with her open hand, lifting him up and sideways away from Samta. He grunted in shock and struck back instinctively, missing her widely as he lost balance and fell with a crash.

"He is mine!" she shouted at him. "I defend the right!" She dared Jaleel contemptuously with a gesture, aware of a fierceness that coursed through her veins, as time compressed and dreams become reality, the Serpent's or her own, she didn't care. "He is mine," she repeated, her voice a hiss, and raised her hands to flutter her fronds. Now they all looked at her, Bael and Samta and Jaleel, universally dumbfounded. She dropped her hands to her sides and sighed. "Oh, hell."

"Xibalba," Samta said firmly, his eyes alight with amusement. "He didn't hurt me that much, Medoret. Not enough to flip the Vision Serpent at him." He gently detached Bael's fingers on his arms and stepped gracefully aside. "Thank you, sir. I think I can walk unassisted." He moved toward Medoret the few paces that separated them. When he reached her, he laid his palm on Medoret's face and traced its curve with a slow finger. "Today is the day, alien. Let's temper the Serpent a little."

"They want to end you," she warned.

"Perfectly reasonable, I'd say. Can't think of a better way to spend the afternoon."

She scowled at him. "I think you're as crazy as I am."

"Of course. And you've thoroughly disconcerted your uncle and whomever this younger idiot might be." He turned to Bael. "Ten years, wishing for you, putting all her hopes in you, and you end up acting like an Underlord."

"I don't understand," Bael said tightly, his eyes flicking from Samta to Medoret.

Samta smiled. "Personally, sir, I see the glimmer of the Jaguar." He looked at Medoret, his face tender. "And she, of course, is indeed Lady Rainbow, who knows all mystery and would dance with the Jaguar in a hidden glade." He raised her hand to his lips. "Honor, Lady."

She smiled at his foolishness. "Maybe we're all crazy."

"Of course." He waved his good arm at the forest surrounding them. "This is Xibalba." Then he shrugged and looked straight at Bael. "All her life among us, sir, she has lived more in our legends than among us, making playmates of gods and fearsome beasts—anything to escape a human reality. She pretends it wasn't that hard, but has always yearned for you. I would give anything I own to make amends. Will it ease matters if I stay behind?"

"You aren't staying behind," Medoret declared.

"Attacking me on sight has implications I can't ignore, love. Xenophobia is a possible racial trait, one that hasn't been exactly unnoted in you. You spent your first year with us in nearly complete catatonia. Catatonia isn't a normal response in a child, however stressed—and you nearly defeated us by willing us away. Will it help, sir?"

"Yes," Bael admitted.

"No," Medoret riposted. "I told you, Samta, we'd have a problem like this."

"Let's not have a stupid argument," he said, frowning. "I told you. . . ."

"I'll knock you out myself and drag you if I have to, don't think I won't."

He eyed her suspiciously.

"I am the Vision Serpent." She crooked her fingers at him. "And I will remain the Serpent until all is heard. And I will not leave you behind."

"Will you fight us all?" he asked with a scowl. He waved at Bael and Jaleel. "They want to leave me behind; so do I."

"I am the Vision Serpent." She lifted her chin defiantly. "Let's go," she said.

Samta sighed. Bael walked toward her and looked at her quizzically as he passed her, then led the way onto the beach. Medoret slipped an arm around Samta's waist, offering support whether he claimed it or not, and followed her uncle, a scowling Jaleel bringing up the rear. On the sand, Bael waited for them and walked apace of Samta's halting steps. They walked on in silence by the point and along the curving beach. Medoret looked out across the restless water, where the wind was turning the waves into whitecaps far out into the bay. "Where is the ship?" she asked Bael.

"Hidden."

"Uncle," she said with some asperity, "since we are going there now, is there any reason to keep a secret?"

Bael grunted and said nothing.

"Maybe I was right, Samta," she said. "Only one chance, just like it so often is among humans: be odd, different, and they cut you off as—"

"I'm not cutting you off," Bael said angrily. "And don't compare me to humans."

"Xenophobia," she said to Samta. "Definitely."

"If you think I'm getting in the middle of this," Samta

said equably, "you *are* crazy. He's your uncle, not mine." She glanced at the sheen of sweat on his forehead, the tightness to his mouth as each footstep jarred his shoulder, and regretted her childish baiting. She tightened her fingers on his ribs and concentrated on helping him walk. He smiled at her, watching her face as if he could not fill his eyes enough with the looking. Seeing what in me? she wondered, wary of his shaman ways, and felt a stab of fear.

How much do I know? she thought. Half the time I think I live in a Mayan forest. I don't understand humans; how can I understand a people I've seen only in dreams most of my life? She looked beyond him at Bael's upright figure as her uncle strode along the sand, memories sifting at the edges of her mind, tantalizing her with their vagueness. Why did he feel, all too convinced, as he must be, that his niece was mad?

She had loved him—she remembered that. But was he not the man she remembered, as she was not the child she had been? But she had loved him.

"I've remembered you most, Uncle," she said softly, "you and Mother. I didn't dream for years, except through my waking dreams as Lady Rainbow—but then I remembered a black plain, a garden, laughter around a table." Bael did not look at her, but she thought he was listening. "I ached so much for the Black Ship, thinking it the end of pain, the ending of lostness and misunderstanding and all questions. You were a hero, a model for the Heroic Twins of Samta's Mayan legends. And my mother—" She paused and closed her eyes. "She was the Star Goddess who poured stars into the void, close sister to the Vision Serpent who protected, I thought. When are dreams real?"

Bael turned his head and looked at her dubiously.

"The humans were kind to me—tried to be. But I am alien and they could never forget that; neither could I. But with Samta sometimes I forget; sometimes the emptiness for the Black Ship leaves for a time. And there were a few others who saw past the difference, not perfectly, but enough to distract me from Xibalba. I do not know who I am now, but Samta and the others are part of that."

"How could any people who would steal a child from her people have any gift?" Bael asked, his face stern. "This is deluded thinking."

"And leave me to starve?"

"Better than to die from a tormented mind."

"How could they know that? And whose fault that I was left behind?" she asked quietly. "How did that happen, my uncle?"

His face spasmed and became old. "We were too preoccupied in the Vault," he said. "For the first time we found a biochemical description of the spores, a preliminary report the Targethi completed before the spores took them into oblivion. If we'd had time . . . We tried to take the time and waited until the last minute before the human ship came into orbit—you had wandered off. We have waited ten years to find you again, to erase that fault."

"Then be forgiving and trust my dreams."

He shot a startled look at her. She shrugged uncomfortably. "Perhaps I am a little crazy, but much has been mad in my life."

He shrugged, not conceding but not refusing. They walked on in silence to the midpoint of the bay. Bael stopped and extracted a device from his pocket, then aimed it at the sea and depressed a button on the device. He turned to look at her, then at Samta, his jaw tightening. "You are not responsible, Medoret. None is your fault."

"I don't concede any wrong—where is the fault?" She looked at him squarely, but he would not concede. She wondered idly if stubbornness ran in her family. Likely so. Bael waited, his eyes on the sea; she was conscious of Jaleel taking station behind them. Silently, they watched the Black Ship emerge far out in the bay, shedding chasms of water as it rose from the waves.

The shape was as she remembered, tall and sleek and beautiful, more rounded in form than the human ships, more a squarish shape than the needle shape favored by Earth, but large and magnified still more by the growing darkness. Its black hull glinted in the dying light of the day, lit from within by a pallid gleam from many portholes. Medoret caught her breath, rooted to the place where she stood, as the Ship moved slowly toward the beach. Her grip on Samta tightened involuntarily, and he quietly slipped his arm around her waist, enfolding her.

The Black Ship sailed smoothly into the shallows, rising on plumes of water still higher as the water shoaled, then lifted from the water and glided onto the sand, extruding a ramp as it descended with a hissing of jets. A doorway opened at the top of the ramp, revealing shadowy figures within. Bael gestured for Medoret and Samta to precede them.

Will they kill him? Medoret thought suddenly, and wavered. Should she run away to save him? In her dreams, her mother's strength suddenly seemed implacable, and this decision would be hers alone. Would she love a child enough she hadn't seen for years, one she could think mad?

"Medoret," Bael prompted.

Closing her eyes, Medoret took a short step forward, convinced that it was horrible error. In the distance, the jungle seemed to thunder with Targethi drums, demanding sacrifice. What is the answer? Will I ever know? I *am* mad, she thought. Slowly, supporting Samta, they climbed the ladder and entered its dark interior through a wide doorway. Several shadowy figures awaited in the small entryhold beyond the hatch; as her eyes quickly adjusted to the low illumination, she saw their many faces, all shocked into silence by the human at her side. But too few faces, she realized, not the many she had remembered, so desperately had the fever struck the ship. She saw Rojar, the ship's healer, the plain-faced woman in a simple ship suit who had tended her in her illness, her face even older than Bael's, then saw other faces in the warmth of the Ship, one or two vaguely familiar. She should know them all. She had forgotten so much. Samta stumbled on the coaming, and she realized the room must be near blackness to him.

"Careful," she murmured, and backed him up against one wall of the entryway. "Stand there a minute."

"I hear breathing," he said shakily, and peered around himself, blinking. "So this is infrared?"

"You're too smart," she said. He chuckled.

Behind them, Bael and Jaleel entered the ship and the hatch slid closed, entombing them with the Varen. "This way," Bael said, and gestured down the corridor that led from the small hold. The people standing there immediately moved aside, making clearance. Medoret slid her arm around Samta and guided him into the reddish gloom.

The corridor led past several shadowed rooms and ended at a large room where others awaited. Equipment banks circled the walls, rippling with instrument displays and patterned rows of lights. Padded chairs stood at measured intervals around the room, circling a smaller group of chairs and side tables in room center. Two Varen watched the displays at their stations, others stood in the far shadows of the room, immobile. Medoret halted in the doorway and stared at the woman sitting weakly in one of the center chairs, her face pale as death. For a long moment, her mother stared back at her, her chin lifted as if struck by a blow.

"I honor you," Medoret said directly to her, all her heart in her voice. She leaned Samta against the wall just inside the doorway and made sure he had his balance, then turned. "Jaleel, the vial."

"It should be tested," Bael argued.

"For once, don't resist me—please." Reluctantly, Jaleel brought her vial out of his pocket. Medoret's fingers closed around it and she turned again, then walked the few meters toward her mother. She stopped, then sank to her knees, blinded by tears. "All the years of wanting you so desperately, escaping into desperate dreams, aching—it was worth the price, my mother." She raised the vial and held it out. "The small brown tablet—it cures my fever, not permanently but enough to give you strength. Please."

Her mother reached out a trembling hand and took the vial, shaking her head at two Varen who moved forward in protest. "And who are you, Daughter?" she asked in a whispery voice.

"I am Lady Rainbow, daughter of the Star Goddess, who spills stars from her hand and knows all things—your daughter, my mother." She smiled.

"And sometimes the Vision Serpent, who threatens her elders with mayhem. Bael wore a monitor button."

"Sometimes I am the Serpent," Medoret conceded. "And my uncle deserved it."

"And are you mad, my daughter?"

"Sometimes, I think. It is hard to know."

"Reality can be hard." Saryen studied the top of the vial and opened it with a quick twist. She spilled the contents into her palm and studied the pills. "The brown tablet?" Medoret pressed her hands hard together and nodded. "Water, please, Toreen. I see at least two left we could analyze. And these other pills?"

"Dietary supplements. Two proteins the humans do not share."

"A clever people." One of the others brought her a cup of water, and her mother quickly swallowed one of the fever pills. She shuddered with a sudden chill, then focused her attention on Medoret's face, her lips tightening. "Explain to me this human with whom you claim kinship. Explain to me, Daughter, why you are sometimes mad."

"I claim the Dream-Knowledge. I will not permit him to be harmed."

Her mother stared at her. "Where did you hear that phrase?" she demanded.

"In my dreams, which are sometimes true. You claimed it, when all disputed; you chose to go forward, when all sought despair." She spread her hands. "I claim my dreams, and in those dreams I am the Moon Goddess, the Lady Rainbow; I bring the light into the darkness, dim and cool in my warmth. I am shadow and pearl, the gleam of metal and white foam upon the night sea. I am the Bridge between Worlds, belonging to neither and finding myself in both. I am Xibalba, the Otherworld, where humans and Varen meet. And I am the Way to an end of death and exile."

No one moved in the room. She kept her eyes fixed on her mother's face, scarcely breathing. Her mother frowned, troubled. "And," Medoret conceded sadly, answering that frown, "perhaps I am mad. I have missed you desperately, Mother."

"I, too." Saryen touched Medoret's hair in a quick caress wonderingly, then ran her taloned fingers over her face, touching chin and mouth and eyes. "I, too. I shall consider this, Daughter." She unbent still further, giving her a slight smile. "I feel I have half a mind now, with this fever and such a long-awaited day. Which is worse, I wonder, with you talking such nonsense?"

She smiled genuinely then, then looked past Medoret to Bael. "We should take the ship back into the bay waters for a time. Treat the human gently, as befits a friend of a Moon Goddess." She stood, weaving off balance but catching herself on the chair arm. "Then we shall see."

Chapter Sixteen _____

They led Medoret and Samta to a small room, where a low mattress beckoned instantly to Samta. He hobbled forward and lowered himself to the bed with a deep sigh. She sat on the mattress edge beside him, then watched as Rojar lit a wall lamp, sketchedly demonstrated a water tap, opened a door to a bathroom, then exited the room, her expression unreadable. As the door closed, Medoret heard the lock snap, Rojar's comment on the whole matter, with the universe between and above. A Vision Serpent comes from Serpent stock, she told herself; no reason for particular surprise.

"May I ask?" Samta asked wryly.

"Likely they have monitors in this room."

"I'd still like to ask." He eased his shoulder to a more comfortable position, wincing, then turned his head to look at her. "I'm not criticizing, mind you, but Maya myths?"

"It seemed right. Haven't you figured it out by now? I haven't the faintest idea what I'm doing most of the time."

"Some of the literature speculated . . ."

"The fabled literature."

"Deservedly fascinated by you, love. Anyway, this rather insightful writer—not all the literature is fatuous condescension, you know—speculated that the most alien part of an alien might be the mentality. Maybe living half in a dream world is normal for you. His theory didn't get much credence—no confirmation in Sieyes's observations. Sieyes shot him down contemptuously with a few pithy papers."

"Dr. Sieyes is one of the Nine Underlords," she said dismissingly, flipping her hand. "No self-respecting Twin would trust him an instant."

"There you go again. How real is the Vision Serpent to you, Medoret?" he asked more quietly, his dark eyes more sober than made her feel comfortable.

"This from a Maya shaman?"

"Well, that's fair." He relaxed into the mattress and closed his eyes. "And dodge if you want. I can accept dodging." She curled her fingers around his hand and felt him press back. "Lady Rainbow," he muttered indistinctly, his face slack with exhaustion. She watched his face ease as he fell asleep, treasuring the slow rise and fall of his chest, his shadowed face in the ruddy light of the room.

"Jaguar Sun," she whispered.

She looked around the sparsely furnished compartment, and thought her confinement here wasn't that different from the isolation imposed by Dr. Sieyes. While adults discussed her elsewhere, she awaited their decision. Couldn't there be another pattern? Would a Serpent so tamely accept such a truth? She doubted it. She got up from the bed, careful not to jar Samta from his sleep, and walked to the door and tried the latch. Locked, as she had heard.

Ten years I have waited to see your faces, she thought sadly, and my measure is restricted by you, too soon, too soon. She stood in front of the door, staring at the area of metal directly in front of her eyes, and settled herself stubbornly to wait. No pounding on the door, no calling out: just a locked door four inches from her face.

She waited ten minutes, her breath slow and easy, when suddenly the door opened before her and she faced Rojar's impassive face.

"I remember you," Medoret said, "when I had fever."

"I am a healer, that is true."

They stared at each other for several seconds, then, reluctantly, Rojar moved aside. Medoret stepped gracefully into the corridor and turned to watch Rojar key it closed. Then, every sense alert, Medoret walked the corridor of the Black Ship, bathed in the ruddy gloom and warmth of the air, her footfalls muffled on the floor. She was aware of Rojar following cautiously, but ignored her as she looked at everything. Her hand caressed a wall carving of the Star Goddess as she slowed beside it, then continued onward over the bare metal wall, fingering the row of metal studs at a seam, touching the metal strips that bound a doorway. As she walked her Ship, Medoret felt a deep satisfaction begin to glow, spreading throughout her body, as she found herself home, at last.

Is it home? Do I want to see that truth, however it falls?

At the next doorway, she looked into a small side room, where two Varen raised their heads and looked at her, startled by her sudden appearance. She nodded courteously and passed onward, descending a ladder to the lower level. She sniffed greenery and passed a small garden, then walked by a wide room with many comfortable chairs, then sensed vibration down another stairwell, a slow steady beat that pulsed against her skin. To each Varen she passed she nodded courtesy but said nothing, and padded onward, reclaiming the ship. At another ladder she ascended and took a right turning, Rojar still following her without interference. She walked calmly back into the captain's section of the ship she had seen before, command deck and private quarters. Her mother still sat in her wide chair and watched as she entered the room, Bael standing stiffly at her side.

Medoret circled the room, looking at the control panels one by one, reaching suddenly to caress a sculpture of the Vision Serpent in an open cabinet, then continued her circuit. No one moved to stop her, though most looked at her as warily as Bael. How must I look to them? she wondered. Do they wonder now how they look to me? At the end, she stepped down the single riser into the center of the room and took one of the empty chairs facing her mother. Rojar, her shadow, sat down, too, though cautiously. It would take Rojar a while to trust her madness, Medoret thought: she had lost much, grieving for all, as a healer would do. Medoret saw with pleasure that her mother's fever had visibly waned, giving her greater alertness and movement. Saryen lifted a glass of water from the table at her side and swallowed, then calmly set down the glass.

"The humans' fever drug causes some dryness of the mouth," she commented, as if nothing were untoward or out of place. "Toreen is analyzing its composition now."

"I am glad you trusted enough to take it, Mother."

"Did you have frequent fevers?"

"Less in recent years."

"And who has inflicted you, Daughter, that you chose to pressure a closed door?"

"Dr. Sieyes built a career on my existence—he had reasons to ensure its object." She shrugged. "Like you chose today, he denied intimacy and confined me while decisions were made elsewhere." It was a challenge, and she saw her mother's displeasure.

"Suitable for a child," Saryen said firmly.

"I am not a child anymore. Is logic pointing in two directions a Varen trait?"

"Quite so," her mother conceded. "I have received much counsel, my own, counsel of caution and waiting, of treatment and despair."

"Of fear."

Her mother looked severe as Medoret's comment flicked again against her anger. "The Black Ship does not fear."

"Not even death? Or worse than death, permanent exile. You couldn't go back, could you? Not with a plague aboard ship."

"We warned the Homeworlds—and, yes, we couldn't go back. Half the ship's personnel died in the first few months—but there is a graduated sensitivity to the spore. The frostflowers were designed for the Targethi and could not stretch quite far enough to kill all of our Ship. And your humans are apparently immune, for all their years of trampling the frostflower glades." Saryen shrugged fatalistically. "We other Varen survived, in varying debility, with even those less touched subject to the cyclic fevers. Our terror truly began when the first children were born after our infection." Her face spasmed. "None were spared, and you were among the last we dared to conceive, my daughter. Of the sixty of that crew that went out, only fourteen still live, none of them children now."

"It would have been easier to stop," Medoret said softly. "Or easier to go on and forget me."

"I am as stubborn as you are—and dreams can enter the waking world."

"That I remember." Medoret smiled. "And perhaps, my mother, you entered an unknowing dream, forgetting me when you would always remember—to seek hope. How could I be left behind?"

Her mother's face spasmed again. "I have asked myself that," she whispered. "Again and again. But I did forget—I don't know how I could have . . ." For a moment, her mother looked old, aged by a long-held torment. "Forgive me, Medoret."

"Did you think I would not forgive, my mother? As I feared I would never find you again—and when I did, would find all bonds severed, all hope gone?" Medoret spread her hands. "But I am here, with you at last, and still I honor you—and love you. Mother, I sing you a song, of new hope among strangers—and, if the humans are very clever in their searches, the hope of Home. Will you not listen?"

"Easier to forget these humans," her mother chided. "With your fever drug, we might have the key we sought vainly among rusting data plates and the dust of centuries.

Why won't you try to forget them?" But the protest was halfhearted, Medoret could see. Her heart expanded, sensing that the bond between them still lived, though tattered by their mutual loss, in a hope as unlikely as a Twin returning to life against all accounting.

"The drug might be the key—I told you that it doesn't cure. I was reinfected by the frostflowers the first time I encountered them again. Is bare living enough to satisfy you?"

"For fifteen years bare living is all I've desired—and saw its surety slip beyond my grasp again and again." Saryen studied Medoret for several moments, then laughed softly. "I expected a child. I forgot the years passing, in my stubbornness. But I am not disappointed, Medoret."

"I am pleased, my mother." She fluttered her fingers gently at her mother, and saw that she amused Saryen greatly with that gesture, that her mother knew exactly how and why she used it.

"This human you brought with you to the ship . . . I have questions."

"How much do you know?"

"Enough to guess at certain things. Why would you choose both worlds, when it means having less of your own, perhaps risking its loss forever?" Medoret saw her mother's perplexity.

"How much of your world would I have, my mother," she answered gently, "after all my years among the humans?"

"Have you mated with him?"

Medoret hesitated and saw severity settle into all the faces, especially Bael's. "As humans do," she acknowledged, knowing she had answered already with her hesitation. "On the way here, when all we could see was our parting forever, the time that had grown too short. He still thinks the parting must be forever; perhaps he is right."

"But how could this be?" Bael exclaimed. "How could

you bond when you humans are immune to the plague? If they have the biochemicals for one, they must have the other."

"I don't understand. I don't know how Varen find one another." Her mother and Bael looked at each other in perplexity. "After all, I *was* a child."

"Hmmmph," Bael said. "Usually this information comes a little earlier, but I admit the opportunity was lacking. Varen sexual response is keyed by sexual chemicals, with the affinity beginning in early childhood. By the time the two reach maturity, the affinity awakens their sexuality and they bond. Does this make sense?"

"Indeed."

Bael scowled at her. "No chemicals?"

"Not that I'm aware of." She saw Bael's struggle against his prejudice. "Have we met any other alien peoples, Uncle?" she asked.

"Only in stone. The Targethi destroyed them all."

"Then why assume all aliens follow Varen physiology?" Bael scowled.

Her mother and Bael exchanged a glance. "We will discuss this issue further at a later time," Saryen said firmly. "We still have the question of your 'hope' you would wish on us." She frowned. "We Varen are a reclusive race, but still searchers; the Targethi tolerated no one, not even at a distance. All races that encountered them died. We may regret trusting humans to be different."

"That is a risk," Medoret acknowledged. "But I have found kindness among them—much else, but that I can claim. And they fascinate themselves with the ruins the Targethi left—and seek you, though their motives aren't unalloyed."

"And what is the taint?" Bael asked sharply.

"Preoccupation with their rank and studies, little more. Perhaps every people has its own kind of blindness." She stared at Bael until he shifted his weight uncomfortably, though he conceded nothing quite yet. "Mostly they control access to answers. The Vision Serpent is not easily defeated, Mother. Perhaps some Melasoi still survive, and could tell the secret of their spores."

"Don't you think we've thought that?" Saryen asked with asperity. "Why do you think we've searched through the worlds?"

"And the humans possess the vaults where you finally found some mention, out here on the edge of Targethi space where the Targethi had just enough time to realize their doom—and its source?" Medoret spread her hands. "Isn't it obvious what you must do? Is this not what the Dream-Knowledge provoked years ago when the humans entered Cebalrai system and I was lost?"

Her mother scowled. "I don't like that answer. I do *not* like that I would abandon my own daughter, whatever the reason."

"Come talk to Samta. See him as he is, and then decide."

"If I see him, I will see him through your eyes too easily," Saryen said resistantly. "I know my weaknesses too well."

"Then that, too, is part of the dream, is it not?"

Her mother gestured noncommittally. "Let him rest awhile, for he is injured. Then I will talk to him." Saryen rose and crossed the space between them, then lifted Medoret from her own chair. Medoret embraced her and pressed close, all time stopping for a moment in that contact so long awaited; they stood together for a long moment. Finally her mother moved her away gently, then smiled. "Come: see our ship through *my* eyes for a time, Daughter, and meet all the people who loved you."

"Yes," Medoret said shyly as her mother embraced her again.

"Then we shall."

Two hours later Medoret watched anxiously as Rojar tended Samta, whose condition had worsened. Samta's face was flushed and beaded with sweat; he tossed his head feverishly, only partly conscious. "I cannot give him too much of our painkillers," the older woman said. "I don't know the biochemistry—he should not have been poisoned like this by the antiseptic."

"Bael didn't give him much," Medoret said.

"Perhaps it had no effect, not enough to heal the incipient infection. Our microbes follow our proteins, not his." She looked at Medoret in distress, her healer's sympathy overbalancing her distaste for the alien. Medoret turned to her mother and Bael, who watched from the doorway.

"I am worried for him," Rojar told them. Her mother frowned.

"If there is no contact with the humans, he may die, Mother." Medoret glared at her uncle as he shrugged his indifference—only slightly, but enough to see. "And if you shrug once more, Uncle," she said angrily, "I will carry him out of this ship and back to Tikal and forget you all!"

"Medoret, he is not of your kind," Bael remonstrated, obviously distressed by her anger.

"Such sentiments killed seven races, did it not?"

That angered Bael greatly. "We are not Targethi—we are not that kind of evil."

"I suggest you tempt that evil by risking just one injured alien."

"Enough," her mother said quietly. She turned to Bael. "My brother, we have often disputed, and since Salal's death, you have wished too often to feel nothing; we have all been tempted to that, in the face of pain and ending." She swept her hand toward Samta. "Here is life for Medoret; don't deny her what you no longer wish."

Bael crossed his arms and frowned at her. "Your judgment is affected."

To Medoret's surprise, her mother smiled in amusement. She glanced at Medoret. "I sense my daughter has often heard similar comments, have you not? I have read this Sieyes's papers on you with great attention. So have you, Bael. She has a point about repeating patterns she has no reason to like."

"Samta thought you might have intercepted information about me all these years. How much do you know?" Medoret asked curiously.

"Some, but not as much as I wanted. We intercepted ship-to-ground radio traffic whenever we could, especially their routine data transfer. Many of the reports about you were sent to Cebalrai. We got more by tapping directly into their computer when we landed on Tikal again a few years ago. Bael himself crossed the jungle and lurked through the city, then left the Goddess icon for you—that was why you insisted on entering Tikal, was it not, my brother, not for needs you claimed? And you pretend you no longer care."

"He is human," Bael said resistantly, conceding nothing. "And you're changing the subject."

"Uncomfortably for you, I admit. And he is indeed human." Saryen walked forward and bent over Samta; she touched his face curiously, then fingered this thick black hair. "I have wondered, my daughter, if my obsession about retrieving you was a disease of the mind as rigorous as that which has afflicted my body. All on the Ship have wondered, as I have wondered. Even the Dream-Knowledge can become distorted, if the mind itself is mad." She straightened and turned to Medoret. "Perhaps we are both mad."

"Dr. Sieyes would love to tend you, Mother."

"Yes: we must discuss what to do about Dr. Sieyes. How much influence does he have with the Project? His articles imply a great deal."

"You sound like you intend—" Bael protested, then scowled as Saryen fluttered Serpent fingers at him.

"What is the icon for such an opponent as Sieyes in your Maya dream world, Medoret?"

"An Underlord."

"Ah. Need I comment further, Bael? And how much longer will you pose? It may be that Samta's body can fight its own infection, for he likely battles only his own microorganisms, but I will not take the risk if his condition worsens further. Contact must be made, if only to return him to his own physicians."

"I can go back," Medoret said. "I know them."

"With some proof, I think." Saryen's gaze centered on Bael and she waited patiently.

"You will do what you choose," he growled.

"In this case, I will not—unless you agree. We have Medoret with us, and so my goal is accomplished—but the plague still exists on our Ship. Eventually Rojar will exhaust her attempts at new palliatives; eventually, too many will weaken to care for the others. We have seen this ending since it began, have we not? Are we not on the edge already? I would choose another ending, if we can. And if the human dies," she added, her glance shifting to Medoret, "she will never forgive. I would not, and she is my blood." She spread her hands. "Once I chose against your firm will, saying your objection was no more than the wish for nothingness in your grief. Now I rue that choosing and return the honor to you. Choose for us, Bael."

Bael looked at Samta as he lay feverishly on the small bed, then quickly at Medoret. "You mean this, Saryen?" he asked slowly.

"Yes."

"With the hope that once I have the choosing, I will consider different options. I know you, Saryen."

Her mother smiled. "On every Ship, there must be an Underlord to check the Serpent's mad impulses. Is that not so, my daughter?" Now her smile was for Medoret alone. "Though we Varen have our own icons who fill such roles from our myth that continually evolves; I have read about some of your Maya symbols, Medoret—the humans seemed obsessed with finding themselves in the truly alien, but I look forward to hearing how you processed them through the inner mind. Truth lies in that changing; we believe that—and find it so too often to think otherwise."

"I believe in it."

"I am pleased it survived your captivity; I had worried about it, for without the dreams, the essence of what we are is lost." She faced her brother again. "Well, Bael?"

"Am I a jaguar to be caught neatly in your Hunt?" He thought a moment, scowling at them both. "All right. But allow me to choose our emissary—Jaleel."

"Ah, Bael," her mother exclaimed, "you set too hard a task."

"I didn't hear any conditions on your offer, Saryen."

Her mother gestured wryly. "True. My daughter, when you make a noble gesture, be sure that you don't leave an escape door in the corridor you want the other to walk. It's called prudence."

"I don't understand what you mean," Medoret said in perplexity, looking from one to the other. Among the humans, certain subtleties always escaped her, to her frustration; she suspected others had just zinged by here. Her mother looked more amused than dismayed, as she seemed to pretend.

"You'll see in time. Inform Jaleel, then. We'll move farther up the coast before we surface. In the meantime, Rojar, do what you can to make Samta more comfortable."

"Yes, Captain."

Bael retreated backward a few steps as Saryen stepped out of the room, his face inscrutable. "You *are* an Underlord," Saryen told him as she passed, but Medoret heard the affectionate amusement in her voice, as if Bael had made a deft move. Somehow Bael's choice had pleased her mother, as if it had mended something long divided between them—not that anyone bothered to explain how. She followed her mother and Bael, wondering if she'd ever feel un-alien in either of her worlds.

"Jaleel doesn't like me," she warned her mother.

"Mutuality is ever a bond," her mother said complacently.

"He doesn't like the humans, either," Medoret persisted. "What help will he be if he just sneers and walks away?" Bael smiled grimly, no doubt wishing exactly that—though her mother smiled strangely again and waved him to silence.

"I don't understand." But neither would say another word, leaving her in her frustration. Did I expect *everything* to change? she asked herself irritably. And she frowned at her mother dauntingly as Saryen gave orders to the Ship and the others moved quietly to do what their captain bade them to do.

Chapter
Seventeen _____

Shortly after dawn, the Black Ship surfaced a mile south of the city, within distant sight of Tikal's towers. Medoret and Jaleel waded ashore and walked into the shelter of the trees, then watched the Ship submerge again into the bay.

"I'm doing this only because Bael asks," he informed her.

"Not because my mother asked?"

"Saryen's dream is distorted," he said dismissingly, waving his hand.

His young-old face settled into a hard severity that did not become him, and Medoret wondered how much the other Varen had contended with Saryen in recent years about her choices, as Bael had once contended at a crux-point. But Bael knew limits to his own will, enough to concede for the sake of other things; looking at the set lines of Jaleel's face, she realized others might not. She sat down and crossed her legs comfortably.

"Then let us sit where we are." She picked up a twig and toyed with it idly, then began drawing circles in the sand with it. Once God K had tried such a gambit in a close place with an Underlord, and the ploy disconcerted Jaleel just as much.

"Sit?" he asked, bewildered.

"Samta will die and the Black Ship will die, and we can all blow to dust just like the Targethi. Is that what you want?"

Her sarcasm angered him all over again, feeding an anger that had simmered for years, she thought, though the why and how she didn't understand. I want to understand, she realized. I want to know how it has been with them all these years.

"You're as distorted as your mother," he said harshly, his displeasure in her drawing down his mouth into ugliness. He glared at her in contempt and condemnation, as if she should know her own fault and grovel. She set her own jaw and tried to temper her own stare into reasonableness, not entirely successful at it. He was maddening, and she couldn't forgot how easily he had tried to kill Samta, without question before, without regret after. What *was* this man?

"Have I had a choice in that?" she said calmly. "Is that how it is on the Black Ship, choosing a closed mind because it pleases you?"

"You don't know how it's been with us. You weren't there." His tone seemed to imply a fault in that, as if she had dallied elsewhere in luxury while her own suffered. Maybe he saw it that way. She squinted up at him, remembering that Jaleel *was* her own—and presently a very angry young man. Did anger rob Varen of all sense and fairness? She frowned.

"Then tell me, Jaleel," she said.

"No."

"Then sit."

"No."

"Then tell me why my uncle's sending you pleased my mother. Bael is an honorable man; it can't be only the unfairness of a biased emissary."

Jaleel hesitated, obviously wishing a fight and not getting much satisfaction from his object. What had he expected her to do, if anything? More retorts and harsh words, like she had given him before? I was wrong to do that, she told herself candidly, wrong to cut him away so easily—as easily as he aimed his laser gun at Samta. Perhaps we are alike, she thought.

"Tell me," she said gently. "I want to hear."

Jaleel sat down on the sand heavily and stared at the empty waves. "I don't want to tell you. What's the point?"

She drew in a sharp breath, feeling the pain he meant to inflict. "That I can see—but I want to listen, Jaleel. It seems right that I do." She hugged her knees and looked at the sea. "Sometimes it's so hard to know what is right. But I would like to hear."

There was a long silence, broken only by the splash of the waves and the living sounds of the forest behind them. "The worlds stopped when we caught the plague," he said at last. "Everything stopped. Even the children sensed it, though the real understanding didn't come until we grew up. You and I were among the last-born, the last children born whole. Destined for each other."

"Destined?"

He studied the woven fabric stretched taut on his knees, plucking at a loose thread. "The beginnings of sexual affinity can be obvious between certain children—and it is the years of association, as we grow up together, that makes the bond mature, physically and mentally. Divide the children the Goddess wills to be one and neither is ever truly whole, even if they manage to bond to others. The bond attenuates, ends." He turned his face to her, his expression cold. "They forget," he said, and again his tone was an accusation.

"Except in dreams." She looked away, unable to meet the bleakness of his gaze.

"*Even* in dreams," he corrected. "You dream like a human—that's what they did to you. That's what you allowed to happen."

"Humans don't dream," she responded softly. "Not as we do. And who's to say where knowledge comes, whatever the form?"

"Vision Serpents? Jaguars?"

"Or Melasoi—and a child remembered. You are jealous of Samta?"

"I'm jealous of everything." He gestured angrily at the bay. "What kind of life have we had since you were lost? We could have gone to another Targethi world, where other Targethi like these had time to realize who had destroyed them, knew the source. We could have found the answers there—and find life as it should be, a doorway to home. But your mother stayed here, dooming us all, waiting for you, the celebrity child." He glowered at her, his mouth drawn down in his displeasure. "How could you let him—" He broke off abruptly and surged to his feet, then began to walk away blindly.

Medoret jumped up and caught at his arm, then dodged as he suddenly swung his fist at her, exploding into the violence he had barely controlled. I've felt that same violence, she remembered, when I wanted to kill Dr. Sieyes. She dodged the blow and retreated as he moved toward her, then caught his hands as he struck out again. They struggled, strength against strength, until he pulled her off balance and she yielded instantly, falling on top of him as he crashed backward onto the sand. He cursed roughly in the Ship language, but she caught his hands again and forced them down on either side of his head, then sat on his chest. He squirmed, trying to undo his disadvantage, but plague and despair had drained his strength.

"Get off," he ordered finally.

"It wasn't my fault, Jaleel. We were children."

"You ran away."

"Into the sunlight. What did I know of shadows?"

"You ran away." He turned his head and refused to look at her.

"Jaleel."

His jaw muscles moved, but still he would not look at her. She smiled down at him. So much alike, so very alike. She bent forward until her hair nearly brushed his face.

"Jaguar Sun," she said softly, "come run with me."

"I'm not a Jaguar."

"Of course you are—and so is Samta, in my human self. But I am two selves, and I wish to choose both worlds, Jaleel, not one over the other—and I have wished for Xibalba all these years, more than you can know, our Xibalba, the one lost to me and remembered only in dreams. I did not forget you, not completely—I think I remembered you as the Jaguar. He was my beloved in my dreams, fierce and tender, who danced with me in jungle glades." He turned his face back to her, still unwilling. "Have you ever walked a jungle trail? I have. Have you danced in a temple glade? I have, many times, with you, in my dreams. And who says bonds are broken forever?"

"They are. It is well known."

"And so the Underlords win, just like that? And so you choose to forget me? Who now has the fault?"

"You love a human."

"Yes—but I have two worlds." She released one hand and touched his face, feeling the smoothness of his skin with her sensitive fingers, then touched the fine strands of his hair and brought her hand to her nose, smelling his scents, strange and familiar at the same time, forgotten and remembered. He stared up at her, then tentatively lifted his hand toward her own face; she caught it fiercely, bringing its palm against her mouth. His fingers explored her face and she shivered at his touch, then yielded backward as he sat up. He confined her from moving farther and continued his explorations, then let his hand drop helplessly.

"Medoret . . ."

She touched his face. "I don't know what the rules are," she said softly, "but then that's nothing new for me." She smiled. "Are there rules?"

"There have to be," he said firmly. "Otherwise the universe lacks order and meaning."

"You sound like Bael," she retorted.

"That's an epithet?" But a smile tugged at his mouth.

"Come walk with me on a jungle trail, Jaleel."

"What about the humans?"

"They've had ten years—they can wait a few days. And we won't go to them unless you are willing." She caught her breath in pain and looked involuntarily toward the bay. "Samta would understand." Her mouth quivered and she covered it with her hand.

"Your mother won't let him die, Medoret," Jaleel said softly. "And Rojar is clever in her tending. If there is a crisis, they'll let us know." He tapped at the small device on his collar.

"Hmmph, I forgot about that. Is Bael listening to us now?"

"No. And he's probably ranting because I haven't turned it on yet." He fingered the collar device until it gave a slight click. "Sir, Medoret and I are going to explore the jungle a little before we go on, but she is worried about the human."

Bael's voice sounded thin through the receptor, but his irritation was unmistakable. "Where are you?" he demanded.

"Still on the beach. I forgot to turn on the monitor." Jaleel smiled tightly at Medoret, a wintry smile but still a smile that pleased her. "And I'll be forgetting again, to let you know. Signal us, please, if his condition worsens."

"Yes."

"I can trust you on that?" Medoret asked Bael anxiously.

"You doubt my word?" Bael sounded outraged.

"Is he always so fierce?" Medoret asked Jaleel.

"Usually. Comes with the bloodline. He'll tell you. Turning you off, sir." He clicked the button, cutting Bael off in midword, then looked at Medoret, his expression both bemused and resistant. "Broken bonds cannot be restored. You could have accepted, as I have."

"Have you?"

"I have dreamed of you," he said quietly.

She leaned forward, bringing their faces close. "I am Lady Rainbow, and always I have helped the Jaguar in his game with the Underlords. He is my beloved, my warrior, the demigod who cannot be defeated when I am there with him. My dreams told me this." She tugged hard at his hair, rebuking him. "And you doubted."

He smiled, his expression easing. "But what is the Immortal without the Jeweled Goddess? How can he help doubting when she isn't there with him?"

"I am here now. Tell me where you have been, Jaleel, all these years."

"That would take a while. And there is still the human."

"His name is Samta Montes, not 'the human.' And he's not going to disappear. He is a part of me, and a part I will not give up."

"I could make him disappear," Jaleel warned, his eyes glinting.

"No doubt you could. The Jaguar is a fierce god, no doubt much like your Immortal. But would that win you the Goddess?"

He scowled, thinking about it. "But what good will it do, to pretend the years didn't happen?" he asked, unable to hide the anguish in his voice. He looked away, flushing slightly. "What good?"

"I don't know." She got to her feet and stretched out her hand. "Samta told me once it is enough to just know the day, as it is. You're not the only one who can grieve over endings, Jaleel." He did not like the comparison to anything human, she could see that, but he accepted her hand and stood up. It was a beginning.

They found a path into the jungle several hundred yards down the beach and walked in silence for some minutes, then began to talk. She told him about her life among the humans, trying to make him understand the confusion, the bonds, the distresses. He told her about the years aboard the Black Ship, of her mother's obsession in finding her daughter, of the anger and disputes and dangerous fevers. She told him about Ian and Hillary and Dr. Ruth, about her adventures with the Vision Serpent and the Jaguar; he told her his dream-adventures with a Glittering Scorpion and an Immortal. They watched the birds flying overhead for a time, then moved prudently away from a loud crashing in the underbrush, then, as the sun set, lay together through the night in the shelter of a hollow tree. She told him then about Samta and he was silent.

At the dawn, she awoke to find him gone and searched for him worriedly, then met him on the path, his arms laden with fruit and several tubers.

"We can eat these," he said, putting them down on the grass beside the path. "The green one is really good."

"And what was I to think when I woke up and you were gone, Jaleel?" she asked with some asperity.

He had the grace to look abashed. "Well . . ."

"We haven't actually settled anything yet," she said, still irritated at his thoughtlessness. "What are you waiting for?"

He scowled. "I want it all."

"What if you can't have it all? Will you have nothing?"

He sat down and took a folding blade from his pocket, then silently peeled one of the fruit. She thought of walking away from him, thought of sitting down, and did neither. "Will you have patience with me, Medoret?" he asked quietly, bent over his fruit. "It takes time to undo the single thought of years." It was the first time he had spoken mildly, without resistance, through all the hours they had talked.

"I'm not even sure I like you that much."

"I'm not sure I like you, either." He looked up again and she saw the amusement in his face, another change. Well, she thought, Lady Rainbow always was rather irresistible. He offered her the fruit, then motioned at her to sit down. "Surely somebody has to be blamed for this."

"You choose to blame the humans," she accused as she arranged herself comfortably beside him.

"Or your mother."

"Or me."

"Or myself." He began to peel another fruit. "Had I been as fascinating as I should, you wouldn't have left."

"That's not fair, Jaleel. We were only children."

"The Immortal was fascinating as a child. Even the fish paused to listen when he talked." He looked up at a parrot that examined them closely from a high branch. "And birds, too."

"What did he say that was so fascinating?"

"No one knows."

She clucked her tongue, exasperated at being so deftly led, and he chuckled, then stretched his shoulders in an easy movement. "Thank you for doing this. It would have been easier for you to drag me off to the humans."

"I told you I'm giving you that choice."

"What if I chose you to come away with the Ship and leave the humans behind?"

"Including Samta?"

"Especially him."

"You want complete ownership, no friends, no loves but you? You want me to be a fish fascinated by your wonders?"

"Yes. All that gazing in adoration would be quite satisfying—but even an Immortal eventually thinks of the fish." He concentrated on peeling the fruit, his pale hair glinting in the morning sun. "But will you walk with me for another day or so?" he asked in a low voice, occupied again with his fruit-peeling. "In case this might be all we'll have."

"I don't choose that this be all. A Moon Goddess is not so easily constrained."

"The humans constrained you for years, Goddess."

"Nor does a Moon Goddess remember inconvenient reality. You risk that, you know: that they might capture you and put you in their box, too." He gestured his indifference, and she suddenly wished that indifference away, that Jaleel might have hope again, real hope instead of his brave pretending. Did the fever affect the spirit? Or had he seen despair too much of his life to know its absence? What was this man, so strangely part of herself, yet divided from her? She had felt that division with Ian, so many times. "Without your help, Jaguar, the Underlords will win. Will you help?"

"You really believe all this? That Varen and humans can come together to something new? That blending worlds is a good thing? And don't wave at Tikal like that. The Targethi never even saw a choice—they just destroyed, probably instinctually, certainly blindly."

"Maybe a few saw a choice. Maybe somewhere among the glyphs a Targethi protested the choice. How can we tell until we have read all of the walls?"

"Let the humans read the walls. I'd rather find the Melasoi, if they're still alive."

"And blend three worlds? Now who's odd?"

He pushed fruit peels off his legs and grimaced. "All the worlds are odd. Truth is lost in the Goddess's pool and tall empires sway to their destruction. Time stops." He smiled at her. "What else to do but to walk as Lady Rainbow and the Immortal—for a time?" He reached out his hand and tugged her closer, then kissed her briefly. "I have missed you, Lady Rainbow."

She blinked, not entirely sure if she should have encouraged matters to a kiss, but he returned to his peeling, asking nothing more. *I feel so confused,* she thought irritably, *but since when haven't I felt confused by nearly everything? What are the answers?* She looked up at the canopy overhead, filled with shifting leaf-shadows and constant sound. *Even in Xibalba, they elude me.*

"I told Samta," she said, "that I didn't know if I could

give him what he wanted. I don't know if I can give you what you want, Jaleel. Maybe I can only give to one of you, and that being caught between worlds ends certain things. But maybe it also creates new opportunity."

"I'm not interested in becoming friends with Samta, if that's your drift."

"Not even because I am friends with him, to see what I see, to please me? To turn your back on that part of me? Do I then ignore parts of you as my revenge?"

He glowered at her. "Hmmph. It was easier to be angry, and know matters were set forever." His expression softened, making him look younger, less fierce. "Would you give him up, if I asked? You offered that earlier."

"Would you want me when half my spirit is lost into emptiness? Do you want me to be where you have been all these years?"

He sighed and idly tossed a fruit peel at a nearby treetrunk, then sat with his hands dangling loosely in his lap. "I don't know," he said slowly. "It shames me that I don't."

"It's not easy to stand on a bridge," she said unhappily.

She watched the birds above their heads for a time, listening to the forest. The soft wind brought her a dozen scents she couldn't name, and bathed her with its silky caresses on her skin. She listened to the distant crash of the surf, blending air and light and living things into their silence. Do I attempt too much? she wondered. Should I choose one over the other, as Jaleel and Samta both wished at her, each in their own way? But by choosing, she would lose part of the Jaguar that blended them both. She was conscious that Jaleel watched her surreptitiously, perhaps as caught in his own dilemma as she was.

"You love Ian?" he asked suddenly, surprising her.

"Yes, I do."

"And Hillary and Dr. Ruth?"

"Yes, each in their own way."

"Dr. Sieyes?" he asked impishly, looking very young when he teased.

"No. Are you insane?"

"Well, then he certainly can't come along."

"Come where?"

"When we go to find the Melasoi, of course. I'm a stubborn man, Medoret—you'll find that out, if you don't know already—but I would follow you into your two worlds. That was the jousting between Bael and Saryen on the ship, that I might choose such. In his choice of me as emissary, Bael finally risked a new future instead of a past of torment; it has been many years since Bael hoped for anything. He loved Salal very much." He handed her another peeled fruit, making a small ceremony of it. "There may be pain: you may be partially lost to us—and me. But I can choose to believe in your dreaming, mad as it is."

"What we find may be something different than either of our wishes."

"Maybe, but perhaps our dream together could be what is real, answers for both of us. Does this make sense to you?"

She smiled. "To half of me."

"I doubt if that problem will ever change very much."

"You're probably right," she agreed equably.

"Then why do I think I'm a fool? I don't want to be a brother to you; I want to be your lover and husband. I want to undo the years we lost. I want Bael to have hope again; I want the Homeworlds. I want everything that's happened to be erased, gone. And I haven't entirely given up the idea of putting your Samta into the Hunt."

"Would that make all the other things happen?" she asked lightly.

"One can hope." He stared at her levelly with a Jaguar's stare, stubborn in his wishes—as she had been stubborn in so many things. She flipped her fingers at him and saw him smile in response. But wishes can come true, she reminded herself, and death can be defeated, when you are a god.

They wandered north around the outskirts of the city during the next day, wary of possible detection by the humans, then entered the city from the northern periphery and slept in an empty building during the long night, surrounded by warm shadows. On the third day, Medoret headed cautiously for the Star Goddess vault, knowing Urban Map would be there. She preferred to find Seidel first: he had a crafty mind about arranging good events. She circled wide to the east of the vault, hoping to hear the roar of Seidel's ground car. Jaleel accompanied her comfortably, looking curiously at the glyphs on the walls, though likely he liked the delay.

In the evening they risked a call to the ship, and Rojar said Samta was doing well, though still feverish and confined to his sickbed. To her pleasure, Jaleel did not scowl and pull his face into comments at the news, giving her that courtesy. Finally, impatient with their profitless lurking around for Seidel, Medoret asked Bael to send his robot to her for new instructions, then sent off the robot to find Seidel.

They waited on the edge of the frostflower garden in the cool concealment of the trees, watching the evening. A purr in the distance grew closer, then echoed in a nearby street before the hurtling ground car turned the corner. Seidel stopped with a squeal of rubber and leaned an arm on the steering wheel. He took a long moment to inspect Jaleel from top to bottom, then gave Medoret a wide grin. "They chased you everywhere," he commented.

"What's the official academic opinion, George?"

"Likely you fell into the sea."

"In a way I did," Medoret said impishly. "This is Jaleel." The two men nodded cautiously at each other.

"Where's Samta?" Seidel asked. "He went with you, didn't he? I figured he did."

"He's on the Black Ship."

Seidel scowled at that. "As a hostage?"

"No. He was wounded and couldn't travel, but the Ship says he is recovering well. I'd like to see Ian. Could you bring him here, George?"

"He's being watched, something that's familiar to you, right? So is Dr. Ruth. It'd be hard to get them away." He shrugged and made a face.

"But not you?"

"Me? I'm no particular friend of yours, alien." He grinned lazily.

She got to her feet and walked over to his ground car. "Whose orders that they be watched?"

"Layard, though the orders came directly from Ariadan. The Project isn't pleased, Medoret. Here they had you all wrapped up, docile and obedient, and you run off, messing up the plan. Tsk."

"Suits." She glanced back at Jaleel. "I won't risk two captive aliens—much less a ship of them." She thought a moment, considering her options. Layard had always been fair, a gifted academic politician but not as obsessed in it as some of the others. And he had the authority to make certain orders she needed that Ian and Dr. Ruth didn't. After all her years among Ariadan's academics, she could divine a few rules that probably applied. "Can you bring Layard here, George?"

"The Ship is agreeing to Contact?" Seidel asked eagerly.

"Not yet. Sorry." Seidel's face fell in disappointment, and she curled her fingers over his hand, a touch that surprised him. "Let's say it depends on a bunch of things. Can you do it?" Seidel looked down at her hand, then smiled and gunned his engine.

"You got it, kiddo. Back in half an hour." She stepped back and Seidel roared away down the street, his hair snapping in the wind he so easily created. Maybe Varen dreams had an icon for Seidel, someone they would easily recognize. He deserved an icon. She smiled.

"Another friend of yours?" Jaleel asked, sounding disapproving. It is amazing, she thought as she turned back to Jaleel, how he could make an opinion out of anything so brief. She glared at him reprovingly.

"A friend of many. This Layard is the chief of Tikal Project, the leader of the scientists. He'll have authority to impose the rules we want."

"But you said you don't know what the rules are."

"So we'll improvise. Are you changing your mind?"

"No. Just standing my ground." He got to his feet and walked over to her, then stood close, inhaling deeply of her scents. "Hmmm. Nice." He turned to look at the frostflowers as they shimmered under the trees. "They *are* beautiful," he said with an admiring wonder. Jaleel seemed determined to stay within the boundaries of the day, she could see that.

"And deadly when you disturb them."

"True. What type of mind would choose to kill with beauty?"

"That which defends all that is loved, I think. I'd like to meet a Vision Serpent in the waking world."

"If the Melasoi survived."

"If. We should go see."

"Yes. We should go see." He turned and smiled at her. "Stop frowning at me, Medoret. What rules did you have in mind?"

Hours later, Medoret waited on the beach before Tikal's seawall with Hillary, watching the waves lift and fall in the city's broad harbor. Ian and Dr. Ruth stood a few paces off, trying to carry on a conversation with Jaleel; Medoret sighed to herself as she heard Jaleel not cooperating, apparently proof even to Dr. Ruth's charms. One step at a time, she thought, though still she sighed. Who is the Jaguar? she wondered, watching him. Perhaps we define ourselves.

Three hundred yards behind them along the seawall, the Project had arrayed every camera and detector it had, each tended by a crew and hangers-on. Everyone on the Tikal Project, excepting only a few compulsive types who would not leave their experiments, had turned out to watch—but at a suitable distance. Layard had conceded that distance, as Bael had conceded some smaller things—and so they turned out to watch. She saw Dr. Sieyes standing alone at the edge of a group by the wall, his expression sour, and repressed the impulse to wave at him.

She looked around at Ian and Dr. Ruth and Hillary with a quiet joy: she had chosen the rules here, choosing the humans who would meet the Varen. Jaleel had persuaded Bael of their plan, and once her uncle accepted the first step, she and Jaleel had yielded to the details Bael insisted. It would never be easy for the Varen to meet humans full-faced; in her choice of the Contact team, she could ease that meeting as much as possible. And, if all went well, there might be more later—if all went well. She saw the apprehension in Hillary's face and linked an arm companionably with hers, then smiled at her sober-faced friend.

"So what do you think of looking for people who know everything about plants, Hill?"

"A preoccupation I could like, I think." Hillary smiled at her, a pained smile. "This is scary, Medoret, I don't mind telling you. What if I screw it up, bouncing around like I do? I just can't believe you chose me for this."

"What's not to believe?"

"Medoret . . ." Hillary waved her hand helplessly.

"I am the Vision Serpent," Medoret said complacently. "Serpents know things like that."

"Oh, sure," Hillary retorted, though the smile came more easily. "And I'm Lady Beastie."

Far out in the bay, the Black Ship surfaced, shedding

cascades of water off its sleek metal. It hovered above the water for a long moment, then moved forward gracefully on baffled jets to the shallows. She heard the murmur of excitement from the humans by the seawall, the click of cameras and the whirr of machines. Now it begins, she thought, her heart lifting. Now it begins.

"As a matter of fact, Hill, you're more right than you know." She chuckled as Hillary tossed her head impatiently.

As they waited, watching the Ship move steadily toward the shore, Medoret heard quite distinctly, chiming faint and distant on the air above the city, the voices of the frostflowers. Dream of us, child . . . they sang, as they had sung to her years ago.

I do, she thought. For dreaming's sake.

Also by

PAULA
DOWNING

**Available at bookstores everywhere.
Published by Del Rey Books.**